Praise for

Virch

"An intricate race for redemption and love, *Virch* had me questioning my own reality in the most entertaining way. Get comfy, you won't want to put this book down!"

—Leigh Statham, **author of the Daughter 4254 trilogy**

"Nothing is what it seems in Laura Resau's beautifully written new science fiction novel. As always, Resau deals with social issues just as deftly as she handles provocative ideas that keep the reader guessing. Highly recommend this new foray from a masterful writer."

—Amy Kathleen Ryan, **author of the Sky Chasers trilogy**

"A whirlwind novel that combines everything I love—characters you want to root for, fiery relationships, and mind-bending concepts—into a fast-paced, lyrically written sci-fi adventure. This is a book people will be talking about."

—Todd Mitchell, **American Fiction Awards winning author of *The Namer of Spirits***

"What a cool, twisty, mind-bending novel *Virch* is! Laura Resau has built an immersive future world that will keep readers guessing about what's real with every page turn—and asking big questions about where our own high-tech society may be heading. High stakes, layered characters, and sweet romance round out a story readers will find impossible to put down."

—Tara Dairman, **author of *The Girl From Earth's End***

"Brimming with lyrical prose and the sweetness of first love, this sci-fi will leave you breathless and asking yourself: real or not real?"

—Emily Layne, **author of *Of Starlight and Bone***

"*Virch* offers a masterful blend of fast-paced adventure, epic world-building, complex relationships, and ideas that might just blow your mind—or at least your perceptions of reality! Written in beautiful yet snappy prose, Resau's novel is refreshingly engaged with the damage that greed, inequality, overabundant technology, and environmental abuse can wreak on a planet. Inhabitants of *Virch's* futuristic world must come to see the beauty and fleetingness of all things—and reading this book is a reminder that we must too."

—Joanne Rendell, **co-author of the System Divine trilogy**

VIRCH

Laura Resau

OWL HOLLOW PRESS

Owl Hollow Press, LLC, Springville, UT 84663

VIRCH

Library of Congress Cataloging-in-Publication Data
VIRCH / L. Resau. — First edition.

Summary:
In the year 2154, virtual reality is an enticing escape… but just for the privileged. For others, like sixteen-year-old Liv, reality means living by a contaminated bay that's sickened her little sister to the brink of death.
Liv is determined to find a cure. But as she infiltrates a tech empire owned by the world's most powerful man, she must confront a danger beyond anything she could have imagined.

ISBN 978-1-958109-50-2 (paperback)
ISBN 978-1-958109-51-9 (e-book)

To Dad, my favorite scientist in any world

Stars, darkness, a lantern, a phantom, a tiny drop of dew,

a bubble

A dream, a flash of lightning, and a cloud:

Thus we should look upon all that was made.

~Buddha quoted in the Diamond Sutra

A Dream

Day One on the Island
Year 2154

CHAPTER ONE
The Island

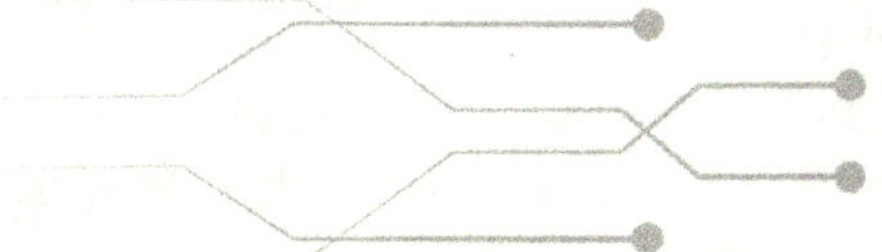

Forehead pressed to the heliplane window, I took in the tiny island below. White sand and turquoise shallows surrounded the oval of deep green rainforest.

We were heading to a *real* tropical paradise?

The internship acceptance notice had mentioned a theme of "tropical paradise" but kept the location classified—not even our families would know where we'd be for these next two months. I'd expected a nondescript building full of labs, the only beaches created by computer programs. A lush virch setting for meetings and classes.

But this was *real*.

As the heliplane approached the airstrip by the beach, sunlight flashed from a silvery building across a patch of grasses. Maybe the labs were in there?

I tore my gaze from the window and glanced around the dim cabin. The other interns weren't bothering to look out the window, lost in the worlds of their virchlenses. I wore mine, too, but had turned it off so that I could observe my strange surroundings.

The virchlenses—thin, transparent discs worn over the eyeball—contained chips that triggered the nervous system to produce phantom smells and sounds and visions and tastes and sensations, creating immersive realities.

I tried to mimic the relaxed posture of the other interns, who probably flew on heliplanes all the time. Reclined in their sparkling clothes and peacocked hair, glittered eyelids half closed, they seemed oblivious to the island we were approaching.

Except for one boy, sitting diagonal from me across the aisle.

He was staring out the window, eyes covered by dark sunglasses, cap pulled low. Copper-tipped curls sprang from beneath the rim to rest on bronze cheeks. He wore orange swim trunks, a cotton T-shirt riddled with holes, and vintage flip-flops. His feet were propped on the unoccupied headrest in front of him.

When we'd boarded, he'd carried a duffel smaller and more beat-up than mine, while the other interns had 'bots toting their shimmery suitcases. He'd kept his distance, letting his hair fall over his sunglasses, blocking us out.

He must be a retro—the style I was going for, although I didn't have to work at projecting the image that I came from last century. Until ten months ago, I might as well have been living back then. My home in the Cove had none of the virch and holographic tech that the other interns had grown up with. It didn't even have electricity and running water. I came from the poorest of poor communities—a contaminated, off-limits zone by the Chesapeake Bay.

Posing as a retro was my cover, my attempt to blend in and stay under the radar until I found the treatment my sister needed.

If anyone exposed me during this internship, I'd be sent to a so-called refugee camp.

Which would mean I'd have no chance of saving her.

Shell would be forever dead if I didn't get her cure.

Within two months.

Across the aisle, the boy swept hair from his face to observe a hologram of a morpho flit past. He pushed up his sunglasses and watched as the blue butterfly flew toward me.

Our gazes followed its flight as it landed on my finger. His eyes met mine.

He gave me a nod, maybe to acknowledge we were the only ones present here, now.

"There was this guy, Zhuangzi," he said, as if we were already in mid-conversation.

I glanced around to make sure he was talking to me. But no one else's eyes were open.

"Excuse me?" I hoped I wasn't being rude. Who knew how these rich sharks interacted with each other in real life?

The boy continued in a low, lilting voice. "He lived, like, a thousand years ago."

I nodded, trying to follow.

"One night he dreamed he was a butterfly. When he woke up, he wondered if he was a man dreaming he was a butterfly or a butterfly dreaming he was a man."

Whatever I'd expected from my fellow interns, philosophical conversation wasn't it.

"Hmm," I said. Although he piqued my curiosity, he was just a distraction.

The morpho flew off and I shifted my gaze back outside, releasing thoughts of dreams and butterflies.

As the plane descended toward the airstrip, the silver building passed beneath us. Solar panels covered the sides of the structure, and in the forest surrounding it, white windmills rose above the canopy.

The plane landed smoothly and glided to a stop. Around me, interns shifted in their seats, zigzagging their eyes back to this world.

We shuffled down the steps into the bright sunshine, everyone looking groggy except for me and the sunglasses boy. I squinted at the gleaming tarmac with its neat line of shiny autocars. A surprisingly strong little 'bot started moving our bags from the storage compartment in the belly of the plane onto the tarmac, zipping back and forth.

The brisk sound of clapping accompanied a woman's shrill voice. "Over here, everyone, over here, let's go!" She oozed enthusiasm from her spot by the bottom of the stairs.

I shielded my eyes to better see the woman—and then I dropped my hand and forced my face to remain impassive.

A three-foot-long horse tail hung from the seat of her pants and grazed her ankles. A mane of sparkling auburn hair sprouted from the center of her waxed-smooth scalp. She tossed it over her shoulder as we stopped before her.

I'd noticed this wild horse style on teachers in my virch classes but had assumed it was a trendy avatar for their generation. Seeing it now, in the flesh, made it hard not to smile. Especially when I pictured how my sister would be rolling on the ground, giggling with abandon. Shell found humor or beauty in everything.

"I'm Soraya, the Virchuous Teen facilitator," the woman shouted over the wind. "Hold out your hands!"

She walked among our group, spritzing our hands with sanitizer. Then she pulled a small storage case from a bag and instructed, "Now remove your virchlenses."

Gasps and murmurs rippled through the group.

As I removed my virchlens, Soraya held out the case for me. After I placed it inside, she snapped on the top with gusto. When she turned to the intern beside me, he shied away.

Flipping her tail impatiently, she approached others, but they looked like they'd rather re-board the heliplane than part with their virchlenses.

I could understand their distress. I'd first started using a virchlens ten months ago, but these interns had probably existed in illusions since they were babies. The disorientation I felt now would be much worse for people who'd worn virchlenses for their entire lives. Not to mention, they wouldn't be able to communicate with anyone off-island.

No big deal for me—none of my other friends and family had virchlenses. Only Delfina, my teacher who felt more like a mother.

"Let's go!" Soraya commanded in a strident voice. "Hand over your virchlenses!"

An intern girl spoke up. "But that's like a violation of our human rights."

Soraya gave a loud sigh. "Research at this facility is *highly classified.* Remember what a rare privilege it is to be here. We can't risk anyone sending information out. You can use the public airscreens for on-island communication or anything else you need."

"But that's not fair," a boy muttered.

Soraya shot him a stern look. "If you violate this rule, our security guards will happily toss you in a holding cell while I arrange for your swift departure." A sticky-sweet smile spread over her face. "You'll adapt to virchlenslessness in a few days."

Ironic. Virchlens*less* in the very birthplace of the virchlens.

One by one, the interns removed their virchlenses and placed them in the cases that Soraya held. When she got to the retro boy, he let his hair fall over his shades.

"Come on," she said when he made no other motion. "Out with it!"

"I don't have one."

She furrowed her brows. "Take it out."

"Don't have one." His voice was soft and raspy, unhurried. He raised his head to meet her eyes.

Of course, Soraya could probably only see her reflection in his sunglasses. She looked about to tear them off and inspect his eyeballs. Instead, she skimmed her gaze over his flip-flops and ripped clothes. "You'd better not be deceiving us."

He matched her stare.

With a snort, Soraya tossed her mane over her shoulder and snapped the virchlens case shut. She trotted to the front of the group and, at top volume, began to drone on about rules and amenities—but mostly rules.

I tried to listen, but the sun glinting off the body mods of the other interns distracted me. Reminded me how out of place I was. How did the hues of their skin shimmer and shift with the light, like bird wings? How did the fabric of their clothes ripple like fish scales under water?

By every comparison, I was rough and dull. My irises weren't dyed glistening purple or blue but remained the muddy hue of brackish marsh. My hair was a lusterless brown, falling in frizzy waves over my shoulders. I ran my hand over it, wishing I'd tamed it into a braid. My fingertips grazed my cheeks, tawny and mottled and roughened from Chesapeake Bay wind and sun. I lowered my hands, clutching them together, feeling the raised ridges of scars left by oyster knives and scrap metal.

Even my neutral clothes—which had seemed so luxurious when Delfina had bought them for me—now struck me as a backfired attempt to fit into a foreign world. How had I let her convince me to come here? But even as I questioned it, my spine straightened. Her voice joined my own in my head, reminding me of my purpose.

Save Shell.

I didn't need virch communication to hear my teacher's voice. It was part of me now.

I glanced at the retro boy. Despite Soraya's threats, his posture was relaxed and confident. In faded swim trunks, he looked like an old-fashioned surfer dude, as if he'd be right at home with a surfboard tucked under one arm.

Soraya clapped her hands, startling me. "Now that we've gone over the rules, you have a couple of hours to settle in before the orientation starts. Don't be late. The legendary Casper Palacios Lim Moiret will be saying a few words. In the flesh."

The interns widened their eyes and a wave of excited chatter swept through the group. Soraya gave a vigorous nod of satisfaction.

Casper's aloofness from the public was well known, even in the Cove. The hundred-and-fifty-year-old founder of the Virch Empire—a giant corporation that was world-dominating enough to count as an empire—didn't need live appearances to help his public relations. Not only was he one of the richest people on Earth, he also had dozens of celebrity children known as the Progeny, whose dramas served as "news" for the sharks.

Both he and his Progeny repulsed me.

Soraya continued with zeal. "We've assigned you each two intern partners. One is for research support, who you'll connect with later. The other is for emotional support, who we'll announce now. Consider this person your built-in buddy." She smiled again, too large to be natural.

I wasn't the only intern whose face fell. The guy next to me groaned as if he *really* didn't want a buddy, just wanted his fratching virchlens back.

"You'll go to the facility together in an autocar and start bonding with each other." She observed the groups' discomfort and sighed. "As I said, there's plenty of public virch world access at the facility. You'll be able to view your schedule, room assignments, dining options, infirmary location, and anything else you need."

As she ticked off pairs of names, my insides lurched. I'd planned to keep my distance from other interns until I could emulate their interactions and blend in. Delfina had prepped me on how to talk like a shark, especially which slang to avoid—like *zuggers,* a curse word we used a hundred times a day in the Cove.

What if I accidentally let my guard down? How would I hide my true self from a *buddy*? A buddy who might get suspicious and expose me.

My apprehension grew as the paired-off interns walked to their autocars, with the 'bots carrying their luggage. There were eleven interns total here, which meant there was one group of three instead of a pair—Soraya looked distressed when she explained that one of the interns had arrived by private jet and was already in the facility. Clearly, she liked order and control.

Soon there were only two of us left: me and the retro boy.

"All right, you two," Soraya said. "Liv and—"

"Call me Wolf."

Frowning, she motioned toward the last autocar. "Go ahead, then."

He stayed put. "I vote we do our *emotional bonding* on the beach."

"Of course, whichever virchrelax setting you'd like." Exasperation edged her voice. "As I said, there's access at the facility. Now off you go!"

"I mean the real beach," he said, motioning with his chin to the shoreline.

After a stunned moment, Soraya spoke as if managing a young child. "It would be better to access a beach through virchrelax."

He turned to me. "Hey, buddy, you okay with a real beach?"

"Um." I wanted to go straight to the research labs. And I didn't want to get on Soraya's bad side, not when she controlled so much of the intern experience. At the same time, I couldn't afford to start off on the wrong foot with my partner—someone who could ruin my plans. "Maybe?" I said.

"Great," said Wolf. "We'll see you at the orientation, Soraya."

She narrowed her eyes. "Don't be late."

With a salute, he turned and cut through a patch of wild grasses, forging his own path toward the beach.

I gave Soraya an apologetic wave and jogged after him.

CHAPTER TWO
Strange Boy

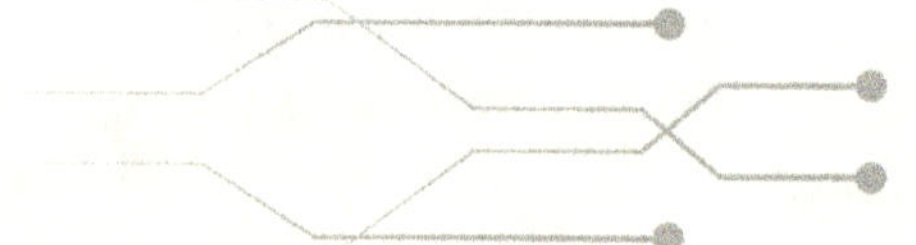

As I followed Wolf, I squinted at the ocean before us, a labyrinth of glitter. When the soil transitioned to sand, I took off my sandals and let my feet free.

This island is real.

I couldn't help marveling over it. The shock. The irony.

Above, white-feathered terns dipped and rose in unpolluted blue. Smooth jade hills rolled toward me, waves swelling and breaking into a million bubbles. White sand stretched like silk from sea to forest.

Too perfect.

It could have been a virchrelax setting: Tropical Island Paradise. I'd had an anatomy class with that backdrop a few times.

Wolf plopped down in the sand near the surf's edge.

I sat down next to him, keeping a careful meter between us. Knees tucked against my chest, I rested my cheek on my hand, feeling the familiar ridges of scars across my knuckles. I breathed in the sweat-tinged scent of my skin, the trace of wood smoke lingering in my hair from last night's tea by the hearth with Dad and Delfina.

I scooped a handful of damp sand. Squeezed. A tiny shell jabbed my fingertip.

Evidence of reality. It hid in the twinges of pain, the unsavory details, the subtle flaws. With the prick from the shell came awareness of the slimy seaweed in the surf. The dead frond dangling from a nearby palm. The faint odor of rotting fish.

And the kelp stuck to the leg of the strange boy beside me.

Strange as in I couldn't figure him out.

His hair was at the mercy of the wind, long and flying wild as fall leaves. He'd taken off his cap and shades, and I got my first good look at his eyes. The irises reflected water like silver rockfish scales. His forearms were a landscape of muscle outlined below the skin's surface. The skin there seemed to sparkle—body mods, I guessed with a stab of disappointment.

Then he shifted, and I realized that crystals of sand had caught in the fine hairs of his arm, glinting light. No mods after all. At least, none that I could see.

I closed my eyes, annoyed. I was supposed to be in a lab. I was supposed to be saving Shell.

For most of the past year, my sister had been in hibernation. The state of suspended animation meant she was technically dead with the potential for revival. One year was the upper limit for hibernation, and she was nearing that mark. In two months, she'd die, forever—unless I brought her the cure in time.

With a sigh, I reminded myself that no matter how fast I got her treatment, I'd still need to wait out the two-month internship for the heliplane to take me home. I was cutting it close but had no choice—I'd have to play out this ruse until the end.

The boy's presence intruded: a trace of sweat and honeyed soap, disturbingly real.

Not what I'd expected, but very little of this internship had been so far.

With a reluctant sigh, I turned to him. Hopefully I wouldn't blow my cover in my first real-world conversation with a shark. "So, why'd you want to meet out here?"

He shrugged, twirled his sunglasses. "Reality."

"Reality?" I echoed, feeling puzzled.

"Won't be much of it in the facility."

He leaned forward on his knees, digging his hands into the sand. The sun reflected off something on his wrist. From the corner of my eye, I studied it—a watch, the ancient kind with hands, at least a century old. I'd bet he used an actual keyboard and solid-screen monitor, too—the kind my sister and I had disassembled thousands of times at the junk heaps. It was like he'd time-traveled a hundred and fifty years, all the way from the turn of the millennium.

He'd begun shaping a sandcastle and moat. What would a slacker retro boy be doing at the most cutting-edge lab in the world? How had he been selected? Connections and money, no doubt.

Again, I made an awkward attempt at conversation. "They weren't kidding about Tropical Island Paradise."

He glanced up, rocked back on his heels. "Illusion versus reality. Ever wonder if one day you won't be able to tell the difference?"

It was a strange question, made all the stranger since I'd asked Delfina something similar last fall, back when I was just getting used to a virchlens.

I'd returned from a virch class in ancient Rome to see her making mint tea in her kitchen nook, long black hair illuminated by hearth light. And I'd had a fleeting sensation of not knowing which was real.

"Delfina," I'd whispered. "Does real life ever feel like a dream? And the virch world like reality?"

Our eyes met, hers full of kindness. "That's one reason I came to your community, Liv. To be in the real world. In a place where no one had virchlenses. Of course, I couldn't stop using mine completely because of my teaching resources—but now I'm more in touch with reality than ever before."

She put her hand to my face. "*Mija*, listen."

I did. I always soaked it up when she called me "daughter".

"Make sure you always know which is the dream and which is reality."

Now, on the beach, I stared at a damp glob of kelp on Wolf's sandcastle turret with gnats buzzing around it. Reality. I thought of his comment earlier, about butterflies dreaming. "You mean do I wonder if I won't be able to tell the difference between real and virch worlds?"

"Right."

I refrained from saying that until recently, I'd lived in reality for sixteen years straight. "Nope."

"Really." He sounded unconvinced.

"For one thing," I said, "illusions are perfect. Reality's flawed." I grabbed a fish-scented glob of kelp and tossed it in the air to make my point.

He reached out and caught it, then draped it over his sand moat, looking satisfied—as if that was just what he'd needed.

I continued. "And even when I get über-immersed, I always remember to zigzag my eyes back to the real world. I can feel my real body in the background anyway, can't you? And haven't you noticed how fuzzy virch worlds are if you look at something up close?"

"That's how things are now," he admitted, tucking a strand of hair behind his ear. The curls were perfect corkscrews, spiraling in silhouettes against the bright sky. I wondered how it would feel to give one of those curls a good, hard yank.

"But the way tech's headed," he said, "and the research they're doing in the Virch Empire… it just makes you think."

I gave a little shrug. My mission here was about reality. Stark, unjust reality. Illusions—and philosophical prattle about illusions—were distractions. "Well, let's get this over with."

He smoothed out the curves of the castle moat. "Our bonding?"

On instinct, I flicked my eyes to make my virchlens to re-play Soraya's instructions. Then I remembered it was in a box for the next couple months. With my bare eye and naked brain, I struggled to remember the details. But all I came up with was *emotional bonding.*

"This isn't exactly the best use of time," I said. "I mean, bumming around on a beach."

"Tragic," he said flatly, sculpting a bridge. "Is the real breeze getting real sand in your real eyes?"

He didn't speak with scorn, not exactly, just smug superiority. A retro trait?

I stared at the scars on my hands. Maybe Wolf had gone on old-fashioned adventures in virch worlds, but had he weathered a real, deadly hurricane? Had he felt the sting of chemical spills or scrap metal gashes? Had he gotten scars from real blades instead of 3D tattoos? Watched someone he loved be put into a coffin?

My voice turned to iron. "You have no idea what reality is."

He closed his eyes. "And you have no idea…" His voice was so quiet I could barely hear it over the waves and wind. "*No idea* what reality I've lived through."

He stood, stamped out his castle.

I'd gone too far. I was supposed to be staying under the radar, not scaring people off. And his words had sounded genuine, as if they'd come from an underground place, like a hidden well I'd accidentally tapped.

I opened my mouth to apologize. But in a flurry, he pulled off his T-shirt, dropped his sunglasses, stepped out of his flip-flops, and ran into the ocean. Straight into the surf, until he held his nose and ducked under a crashing wave. He splashed around like a little kid learning to swim.

I wanted to be in the water, too, but I couldn't be dripping wet and late for the orientation meeting. I'd already felt embarrassed by my damp clothes when I'd boarded the heliplane this morning. They hadn't dried after my pre-dawn swim from the junk freighter to shore.

Wolf swam farther and farther out, a haphazard mix of doggy paddle and crawl, until he was just a tiny head bobbing among the waves. Against my will, my gut knotted. Even though he was a mawmsey rich kid, he was human. A vastly different human than me, but still of my same species.

Keeping an eye on him, I imagined Shell here, twirling and flipping in the sea like a mermaid, beckoning to me. *Come play, Livvy!* It was easy to feel her presence, right down to the bits of plastic stuck in her cedar-brown hair, gleaming with sweat and sun. Her skin, a shade lighter, always made me think of smooth driftwood. And her eyes, bits of green sea glass. To me, her features looked designed by an invisible artist's hand.

Like everyone in the Cove, our genes were a chance mix from ancestors who'd found themselves in our pocket of the Chesapeake Bay over the centuries. They'd come from nearly every continent on earth, forming a DNA mosaic for their descendants.

I moved my attention back to Wolf, who was floundering farther into the ocean. I bit my lip. I couldn't have my buddy dying on me. That would *really* attract unwanted attention.

Annoyed, I plucked seaweed from between my toes. If I replaced the turquoise sea with brackish murk, and the palms with heaps of e-waste, and the bird calls with crashing machinery, then I could be sitting on our beach back home.

The Cove's beach was a familiar hillscape of ancient wires, circuit boards, broken screens, dissected phones. There in the junk heaps, we picked through metal shards, dragged speaker magnets on strings, carried buckets of chemicals to separate minerals. In the smoke of burning plastic, kids with cloths tied around their mouths pulled out copper strands with tiny fingers. Our sweat-laced skin shone in all shades of pink and brown, burnt and freckled, scarred and leathered.

With thoughts of the junk heaps came more memories of Shell—and the moment everything had changed.

Last year, on a summer's evening after work, I'd gone diving for oysters—some to sell on the black market and some for ourselves. As I waded to shore with my full bag, I spotted Shell running toward me. With every stride, her hair rippled and her seashell necklaces bounced. She leapt over debris on her bird legs, as graceful as a heron.

Then she stumbled.

She regained her balance swiftly, so swiftly I didn't see it as a sign something was wrong. It wouldn't be until later that evening that she'd collapse.

We sat together on the beach between a rusted sign reading NULL ZONE and another reading UNFIT FOR HUMAN OCCUPATION. Just part of the scenery in our Cove.

With a knife, I pried open an oyster shell. "Voilà, sis."

She slid the oyster meat into her mouth. "Exquisite. How lucky am I? My own sister—best oyster hunter ever."

I drew her in, felt her warm, small body against my still-goosebumped skin. She was only a few years younger than me—eleven to my sixteen—but tiny and bouncy enough to pass for nine. Since our mother died after her birth, I was the closest thing to a mother Shell had.

And now I was the only one who could save her.

I shook myself, bringing my mind back to the here and now.

With a start, I scanned the waves for Wolf.

My stomach torqued. He'd *vanished*.

But wait, was that him at the distant breakers?

I sat up straight, keeping my eyes trained on his pinpoint of a head. Tiny fins cut through the water around him. Dolphins? Or sharks? Impossible to tell from here. I stood up, waving my arms. "Wolf!"

No response.

"Hey! Come back!"

After a moment, he seemed to be trying to return to shore. But his flailing only grew weaker, and he looked even farther out than before. A sorry piece of driftwood. He was caught in a riptide with no clue how to get out.

So much for me keeping a low profile.

I kicked off my sandals and, eyes glued to his head, I ran into the surf.

CHAPTER THREE
Riptide

This ocean was warmer than my Chesapeake Bay, bluer, clearer, cleaner. I gulped a deep breath, zeroed in on Wolf, and dove beneath the waves. Tasting salt, I torpedoed along, arms and legs and torso moving automatically, lungs doing what they did best—conserving oxygen. I'd learned to hold my breath for five minutes over the decade I'd been diving for oysters.

When I surfaced, I was just a couple meters from him. He was sputtering and coughing, barely able to keep his head above water. Yet his face showed no panic. Determination shone beneath his exhaustion. And something else flashed in his eyes… *pain.*

I scanned the water for blood—or shark fins. Nothing. Without wasting breath on questions, I wrapped my arm around his chest, and with the other arm, swam deeper into the ocean.

"Wrong way," he coughed.

"Keep fighting the current, you're dead."

Holding him tight, I stroked more or less parallel to the shore, not fighting the ocean as it pulled us out deeper.

"You sure?" he sputtered.

"Save your breath."

A hundred meters down, the riptide let up, and I swam back to shallow water, keeping our path diagonal.

When my feet touched the sandy bottom, I released him.

He stood there, shaking, his goose-bumped arms crossed over his broad chest. "Thanks."

I shrugged. "You okay?"

"Yeah." Looking humbled, he limped through the foamy surf. As his legs emerged from the water, I noticed his left calf, swollen and red.

"Wolf, your leg. What happened?"

"Don't know. But it hurts." He peered at it. "Didn't see any-thing."

"There are sharks out there, I think, but your skin's not bro-ken. Maybe a jellyfish?"

He winced. "Maybe."

I couldn't help feeling sorry for him. This might have been his first encounter with a jellyfish. Definitely not a creature you'd find in virch territory.

Sure enough, when we reached the surf's edge, I noticed a couple of transparent blobs in the wet sand. "Box jellies," I guessed. "They can be pretty venomous. Painful stings. A hid-den danger in the tropics. Real tropics, at least."

My naturalist impulse was to stop and examine the crea-tures. I'd studied them in biology class—some subspecies could be fatal to humans. They had a bunch of real eyes, which made them clever predators to boot. I tamped down my curiosity and looked back at Wolf, seeing his face clenched in pain.

"Maybe you should go to the infirmary." Soraya had mentioned one, and Delfina had told me she had an aunt who worked there. "Want me to take you?"

"Nah, I'm okay. Just need to rest a bit."

I helped him stagger up to the dry sand, dripping seawater. My palm rested on the bare curve of his back, just above the waist of his swim trunks. It felt much more intimate now that I wasn't saving his life.

Breathing hard, he said, "So you've swum in real tropics before?"

Great. He'd noticed my swimming skills. "No." It was true—my bay was a far cry from the tropics.

"Where'd you learn?"

"Here and there."

Maybe he was in too much pain to push further. His face, just a few centimeters from mine, was scrunched in concentration—I couldn't tell if he was suspicious.

My gaze fell to his torso, a perfect upside-down triangle with wide shoulders and a narrow waist. And I was touching it.

I let go. *No distractions.*

He sat down, rubbed his neck, grimaced at his inflamed calf.

I sat beside him, hugging my knees and staring straight at the ocean. "So are you suicidal or just stupid?" As soon as the words left my mouth, I wanted to snatch them back. *Way to get on his good side, Liv.*

He coughed a laugh. "Just want to push my limits. Go face-to-face with whatever's real. Even if it's death."

"Hmm," I murmured, resting my hand at the hollow of my neck, just above the necklace Shell had made me for my birthday last year—hundreds of tiny shells strung in a cream-purple-gray pattern. I refrained from pointing out that it was a luxury to go looking for death. For the minnows—and especially the so-called Nulls—death found us pretty easily. Nothing philosophical about it.

Gracelessly, I peeled the wet shirt material from my torso and squeezed out the hem. I tugged at the shorts clinging to my thighs, the unfamiliar fabric too thin. I felt naked with just these scant bits of wispy cloth protecting me. I missed my practical, frayed-but-sturdy clothes from home.

"Hey," Wolf whispered.

I turned toward him, and he stared at me without speaking.

"What?" I asked, defensive.

"Your scars," he said after a beat, gaze dropping to my hands. "They're not tattoos. And that way you walk, and talk—it's not an act. I had you pegged as a retro. But you're not. You're the real deal, aren't you?"

Heat rose to my head, panic engulfing me. An hour on this island and I'd already been discovered?

I hid my hands in the crook of my knees and tried to calm down. So he'd realized I was no shark, but he'd have no reason to think I came from a Null Zone. That my home—my entire life—was a violation of the law.

"I'm a minnow," I admitted. Some version of the truth was the only option now, so I might as well lighten it up. "From a pure bred, noble line," I added with a wry smile. "You could say I'm minnow Progeny."

He stared at me some more. Droplets of sea laced his eyelashes. "Not a minnow. Not Progeny." He tilted his head. "Angelfish," he settled on.

"What?"

"Angel. You saved me. And your swimming—pure bellitude. Skills rivaling a fish's."

I made a face but went along with the banter. At least he wasn't trying to dig deeper into my background now. "Angelfish are a little too… *flashy* for me."

"There are all kinds. I used to keep aquariums of them. Chocolate Angelfish—like the color of your wet hair. Veil Angelfish—hard to figure out at first glance. Ghost Angelfish—elusive, mysterious."

What if he knew who he was actually flirting with? Against my will, hot blood rose to my cheeks. At the same time, part of my mind recoiled at *aquariums of fish* simply for one's pleasure. And then there was my compliment-cringing reflex. And the need to stamp out any thoughts of romance—or even friendship—he might have.

I let out a garbled *hmph*.

"There are even Blushing Angelfish."

My face burned. Fratch him, fratching aquarium-hobbyist.

"I'm sorry," he said. "We got off on the wrong foot." He held out a hand. "Hey, I'm Wolf. Nice to meet you, Angelfish."

I eyed him. "You don't remember my real name, do you?"

"I just think Angelfish suits you. Angel for short."

"What's my real name?"

His smile turned sheepish. "Um."

"It's Liv." I reached out my hand. The saltwater residue made our palms stick together. It felt strange to meet someone from outside the Cove who wasn't a teacher or a health worker. And except for Delfina, every shark I'd met there wore a hazmat suit, as if we ourselves were contaminants. No handshakes had ever been offered.

I unstuck our hands and feigned fascination with the sandpipers dancing along the surf. They searched for tiny treats in the wet sand, advancing and retreating, somehow staying just a step ahead of the waves. That's how it felt talking with this shark boy, skirting the edges of something vast and unknown.

I turned to him to suggest we head to the facility when he whispered, "Who are you, Liv?"

"Just another intern."

"Where are you from?"

"Just another beach."

"Why are you here?"

I looked away. His gaze was too intense—earnest or suspicious or both.

"Let's get to that orientation meeting." My focus flickered to my peripheral vision to check on the time. But of course, my virchlens was gone. When would I get used to this? "Know how much time we have?"

He glanced at his watch, the hands slowly ticking around. Somehow the thing was still working after a century—and a saltwater bath. And he actually knew how to read it. "A half hour."

I leapt up, cursing. Really? I'd be late to the first official activity? *Way to make a good impression, Liv.* I slipped on my sandals and slung my duffel bag over my shoulder, considering whether to change into dry clothes. But that would make me even later, and anyway, there was nowhere to change. "Let's go."

He didn't move.

"Your leg feel okay to walk on?" I asked.

He sat for a moment longer, winding the watch, moving the tiny knob between his fingertips, then putting his ear to it. After one last look at the ocean, he stood, testing out his leg. "Just dreading what comes next."

Curiosity overtook me. The pieces of this boy didn't fit together. His question about illusions, his comment about whatever reality he'd lived through, his recklessness in hurling himself into the sea, and now his unexplained dread—none of it made sense. I gave him a measured look. "Why are you here?"

No hesitation. "To change the world."

I held back a scoff. How deluded. Some of us didn't have the luxury of changing the world when we had to save a single life that mattered more than anything. I didn't give him the satisfaction of asking a follow-up.

He grabbed his T-shirt and shades, slid on his flip-flops, slung his bag over his shoulder, and started limping toward a patch of palm trees at the top of the beach.

"Here, Wolf, let me take your bag."

"No thanks, I got it."

I shrugged. We headed toward a path in the direction of the facility I'd seen from the heliplane.

"I told you," he said, "now you tell me. Why are you here?"

I twisted the necklace my sister had made for me. I knew every tiny shell by shape and texture as well as I knew the birthmarks and angles of my sister's body. I thought of Dad's last words to me this morning.

"To do my best," I said. A partial truth.

Wolf and I continued along the path edging the forest, and then cut through a grassy field, leaving the beach and trees behind. The call of gulls faded, replaced by cricket chirps and bird songs. The salty breeze calmed, and now the smell of green and the warmth of the sunshine settled over me.

After about fifteen minutes, the trail widened, and the crashing of waves grew more distant. Now we were on a narrow dirt road, the enormous metallic building filling half the horizon ahead.

I glanced at Wolf's calf, now a darker red. Even with his T-shirt back on, his silhouette was distinct: lean hips, wide shoulders, damp hair hanging like spiraling ropes at the sides of his face.

As we walked, I rooted through my bag, searching for a comb to tame my tangled mop. My hand rested on something wooden, something I didn't remember packing.

For an irrational moment, I lit up inside, thinking it was a going-away present from Shell. She was always giving gifts—

jewelry or sculptures or mobiles made from bits of beauty salvaged from the sea. Then I remembered she was in a coffin.

Slowing my pace, I pulled out the item—a twisted piece of driftwood. Burned into it were roughly formed letters: LIV, MY HERO, DO YOUR BEST, THATS ENUF.

Tears sprung to my eyes. Dad must have made this and snuck it into my bag. I imagined him covered in sawdust and woodchips, carving in deep concentration. A carpenter by trade, he was self-conscious about writing—he'd stopped school at age seven to work. It must have taken him forever to make this.

I ran my fingers over the letters, heard him saying the words in his gruff yet tender voice. *Liv. My hero. Do your best. That's enough.*

"What's that?" asked Wolf. He'd paused and was looking back at me with curiosity.

Shoving it back into my bag, I said, "It's nothing."

His face registered hurt as I brushed past. I tried not to think about how vulnerable he looked as he limped beside me under the weight of his duffel. I had to nip any hint of friendship in the bud and keep my distance. I grabbed his bag from his shoulder, slung it onto mine.

"Let's pick up the pace," I said and hurried ahead toward the silver palace.

CHAPTER FOUR
Virchuous

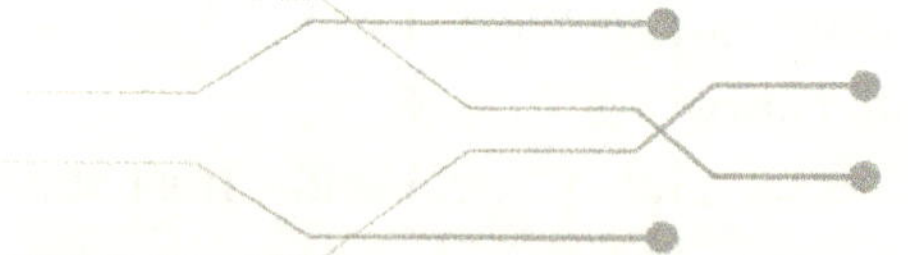

By the time I reached the facility, my heart was drumming—either from the sweltering walk or nervous anticipation or both. Head back, I gazed up at the enormous cluster of mirrored silver domes. I felt like a mud crab beside it.

"I liked my castle better," Wolf said, just catching up to me.

"Right, this one's missing the rotting kelp décor."

Still, his nonchalance couldn't put a dent in my awe. This was the birthplace of most of the world-transforming technology of the twenty-second century.

We walked toward the entrance, where a sign read VIRCHUOUS TEEN SCIENTISTS: ORIENTATION and pointed inside.

Virchuous was the humanitarian arm of the Virch Empire, the one that sent health workers and teachers to communities of minnows and even to Null Zones. The branch that offered educational opportunities like this teen internship program.

Delfina had come to the Cove as part of Virchuous after being inspired by her favorite aunt, Zinnia, who had worked in another Null Zone a couple of decades earlier. This was the aunt who now worked as a doctor in the Virchuous infirmary. They'd had limited contact because of Virchuous's tight communication security, which I'd now experienced firsthand. Delfina had said she'd tried to let Zinnia know I was coming, but that we couldn't count on her help.

My teacher's connection to Virchuous was what had gotten the internship program on my radar. And thanks to her tireless guidance and her gift of a virchlens, I'd managed to get accepted. Without her, I never would have known that this place was the epicenter of a cutting-edge treatment for severe cases of heavy metal toxicity.

Exactly what we needed to save Shell.

After a quick retinal scan, a pair of doors slid open. Inside a vast lobby, I noted that the high ceiling was a glass dome, letting in the apparently real blue sky above us, flecked with clouds.

I glanced at Wolf, who wore his sunglasses again, expression unreadable.

If Shell were here, she'd be so wonderstruck, a poem would already be spilling from her mouth. "Aren't you the tiniest bit impressed?" I asked him.

"A moat," he said. "If there was a moat with deadly jellyfish, I'd be impressed."

"Right." Maybe the sharks saw this kind of grandeur every day.

We followed signs past the infirmary and dining hall and security department, down a corridor lined with palm trees. I reached out to touch one, but my fingers brushed through the trunk.

Startled, I looked closer. These were the most high-quality holographic projections I'd ever seen, nearly indistinguishable from reality. I examined the walls and ceilings for any sign of the hidden micro-projectors used to create the illusion.

And that's when I realized I was the only person in the lobby gaping at the faux palm trees. Dozens of others—presumably scientists—were bustling around without giving the holoscape a second thought. Wolf, too, had probably lived much of his life in this realm.

He pushed the shades onto the top of his head and stared at me, as if wondering about my wonder.

I made my expression blank and stepped away from the palms. My fingers flew to Shell's necklace, the reminder of my mission.

"Let's go," I said and hurried through another set of sliding doors into a giant meeting room.

Around the perimeter were palms and sand and ocean—all holoscapes. The real shore was in the other direction, the island wasn't that narrow, and you couldn't see any of the windmills scattered over the landscape. The inside air smelled salty but sweeter than outside, and there was the lightest breeze. Yet there were no actual windows to open, and the smell was a touch too pleasant, manufactured to evoke coconut oil and tropical flowers.

I gave myself a little shake. This place was disorienting, like being in a virch world in my head, only this was real life... sort of. Was this the sharks' existence, one illusion after another?

I focused on what was real in front of me—ten teens seated in a colorful, sparkling semi-circle around a low, rounded stage with a red velvet curtain.

"Zuggers," I cursed under my breath, realizing Wolf and I were the last ones here. Then I froze.

All eyes moved to us, followed by a flurry of whispers and gasps. But they couldn't have heard my incriminating whisper. So what was this about? My dud hair? Or my clothes? They were sandy and damp—could anyone tell?

I flushed, wishing I could flee back to the beach. I slipped into one of two empty seats at the end of the half-circle, tucking my duffel beneath the chair. Back and forth, I wound Shell's necklace around my fingers, the sharp edges piercing my skin.

Wolf sat beside me, looking uncomfortable, too, and studying the fake-sand floor. The other interns were all about our age—sixteen to eighteen—most of them excited, sneaking glances at us.

Actually, I realized, at *Wolf*.

The only intern not looking at him was a boy with a chiseled, square jaw and spiked hair glimmering like the inside of a mussel shell. The way his green-glitter eyes flickered was mesmerizing. His skin mod evoked fish scales, luminescence shifting from silver to blue to copper. And his T-shirt fabric subtly moved like a glowing jellyfish. He was all rippling rainbows.

He must have been the intern who came on his private jet. I definitely would have noticed him.

Distracting.

I shook myself again. How much had that guy's shirt cost? Twenty or thirty mil? He probably had no idea what that kind of money would mean to people in the Cove. It could have paid for a decent chunk of my sister's treatment.

The light dimmed as if a tropical dusk were falling. The curtains parted. A man stepped forward onstage, ghostlike in a blue-tinged spotlight. Casper Palacios Lim Moiret himself glided to the front of the stage. A mythical king materializing before us.

As all eyes fixed on him, I had to remind myself to breathe. One of the most powerful humans in the world was right here, in this room. He evoked a god, descended from the heavens to consort with mere mortals.

Even under the gentle stage lighting, he appeared odd, a pale patchwork of pieces that individually looked young, but all together created something vaguely unnatural. Something not quite human. A side effect of living a hundred and fifty years.

I vaguely recognized the three Progeny who walked onstage behind him, although they didn't get as much screen time since they were in their thirties or forties. Of course, it was hard to tell, considering their anti-aging treatments.

The chatter and gasps around me had me restraining an eye roll. My only exposure to Casper and his Progeny children had been in the clinic where Dad and I had taken Shell when she'd been dying. The clinic airscreens had shown Progeny "news" nearly the whole week we'd been there, mostly about two half brothers fighting over their father's favor and then one going missing. As I'd held my sister's limp hand, the Progeny's endless drama and obscene wealth had driven me to despise them.

Casper had nearly a hundred children and drew from his personal stash of genetic material to create more Progeny with each latest wife. Each child had been genetically designed—illegal for most everyone else, but he'd found loopholes. All his children were brilliant and beautiful, bodies varying in color and shape and size, minds with a range of talents and interests. Or so the news script went...

The teen Progeny were the ones most often in the limelight—Casper believed that late adolescence was the time the human brain was at its prime for making earth-shaking discoveries. The world waited with bated breath to see what the latest Progeny teen genius would unleash.

The girl beside me was actually squealing as she gazed up at the stage.

Despite myself, I felt a tiny thrill in their presence. Modern-day kings and queens, princes and princesses. Right here, breathing the same real air as me. *Oh, Shell, if you could see this.*

A hush fell over the room as one of the Progeny walked to the front of the stage. Her gossamer turquoise dress and cascading black curls gave her the air of a mermaid. Fake moonbeams shone onto her dark skin.

She positioned herself beside her father and raised her two perfectly muscled arms in a welcoming gesture. "Hello, Virchuous teens! Years ago, my brother and sister and I were sitting in your spots, excited to begin the most meaningful two months of our lives. And we owe it to our father for having a vision over a century ago and creating the Virch Empire. Virchlenses and virchips and virchgames and virchrelax—we have him to thank. Even everyone's favorite… virchdates," she added with a wink.

After the audience tittered, she continued. "Great man that he is, he funnels his profits into Virchuous, the most monumental charitable institution in the history of our planet. Not only does Virchuous give teen scientists from all walks of life the chance to develop their talents in a state-of-the-art setting, it also changes everyone's lives for the better. Of the fifteen billion humans on the planet, 99.8 percent of us now have virchips implanted in our heads. This means we can receive top-quality health care through lightning-speed genetic, neural, and metabolic pathway analysis."

A bitter taste filled my mouth as she continued.

"Indeed, Virchuous is committed to tracking down every last human on the planet, no matter how Null, and giving them this equal opportunity for health care. And their pets, too! Thanks to our father, we—and maybe one day, Fido—may all live to be one hundred and fifty years old!"

Pearly teeth glinting, she paused for a round of applause.

My hands clenched into fists. *Equal opportunity health care?* The virchip program was a load of rotten seaweed. The Virchuous workers came to the Cove yearly in hazmat suits to implant a chip into every baby, even though none of us could pay for diagnostic scans, much less cures. When my mother had fallen sick with a postpartum infection, we didn't have to scan her virchip to know she needed non-resistant antibiotics—which we couldn't afford.

Shell's diagnostic scan had cost all that my Cove community could scrape together, along with a huge contribution from Delfina. Virchips did nothing for us. What was the point?

The Progeny woman's half siblings, also dressed in jade-sea-themed clothing, came forward and gave equally glowing—and deluded—speeches, lauding their father and the Virch Empire, until finally, Casper himself spoke.

"My brilliant dears! You have been handpicked as a think tank on this year's topic: Creating Our Future. With your mentors, you'll explore projects from nanobiology to virch entertainment."

His hair, thick and gelled into stand-up points, glowed as white as his teeth. "You've already met your first partner today. Soon you'll meet your second—your research partner. But for now, let's get to know each other as a group."

Light illuminated our circle of seats. Now the surf of the fake ocean was visible, the lapping of waves audible once again. Faux pelicans flew across the simulated sky.

"I'd like you each to stand up, introduce yourself, and ask the what-if question you plan to explore here. All great ideas and inventions begin with questions."

We went around the half circle, thankfully starting on the other end. More time to compose my what-if question, and myself. I tried smoothing my hair, frizzed up after my dip in the ocean. Most of the interns' questions were academic, reflecting school research projects. I mentally rehearsed a short summary of my own.

When the boy in the jellyfish shirt stood up, a round of whispers broke out. Everything about him shimmered, from his abalone hair to his disco-ball irises.

"Hey," he said. "I'm Spiro."

Spiro. Right. He was Progeny. I'd heard his name and seen him on the news. I was trying to recall the details when he leaned over to a large bag beneath his chair and pulled out a fuzzy black-and-white bundle of fur. With a smile, he held it up.

A baby panda?

Beyond all belief, it was a giant panda cub, the size of a medium dog, not counting its explosion of fur. It looked around the room, blinking, docile in his arms.

A collective sigh of "Awww!" filled the room. Big, black, droopy spots marked its eyes, with more dollops of black on its little ears. The sad smile on its face said: *Hi. I love you. I hope you love me, too.*

"This here's my sidekick, Sugarpie." He tucked the fur ball against his chest, let its large head rest on his shoulder.

Details flooded back to me. *Spiro*. The Progeny heartthrob always seen with a baby animal—baby tiger, baby pig, baby weasel. They changed week to week, from what I remembered.

He was a popular Progeny, one I'd heard my classmates talk about often. Most had spent virch nights with a virch Spiro and his virch baby animals.

Out of curiosity, I'd tried a couple virch dates over the past year—just un-famous guys, free with ads. I couldn't afford someone well-known, not that I'd want to. It made my blood simmer, knowing that the celebrities got commissions on each date, which made them even richer by doing nothing but selling rights to their image.

I'd never been able to fully relax into the virchrelax scenarios with my guys. One had taken me to a Japanese tea garden café and the other to a brasserie by the Eiffel tower. They'd been programmed to gush compliments, not artificially intelligent enough to figure out that flattery roused only vomit inside me. Both times, I'd left before dessert.

I glanced at the other interns. Most were blushing just looking at Spiro. And yes, he was stunning… but my guess? They were responding to the *intimate* virch moments they'd spent with him—or at least, with his carefully programmed avatar.

In an oddly tender voice, Spiro said, "You all can guess why I'm here. My love of animals. Sugarpie here is suffering from a rare virus. The vets say it's incurable. But what if it's not? What if, with the help of Virchuous, I can give her a second chance at life?"

As the room dissolved into sighs, I pressed my lips together. Of course saving endangered creatures was a good thing. But part of me cringed at the resources used to cure an exotic pet instead of a human child. Instead of my sister.

At my side, Wolf shifted in his seat, jaw clenched. Leaning toward me, he whispered, "Rather be caught in a riptide than listen to this drivel."

So he didn't worship the Progeny. Surprising. A kindred spirit? I stared at him, trying to figure him out. This close, I was acutely aware of his smell of sunshine on dried sweat-and-salt-coated skin. The realness of it cut through the synthetic sea breeze.

With a grimace, he added, "I'd even take more box jelly stings."

I let a smile slip out, then leaned away, focusing on the next intern to start her speech. After two more, it was my turn.

I stood up, my sea-dampened shorts sticking to my thighs. I hoped my tank had dried enough not to be see-through. *Okay, Liv, keep it simple. You can do this. Go.*

My pulse raced and blood thumped in my ears as I began. "I'm Liv. My question is: What if we can provide affordable treatment for victims of heavy metal poisoning?" So far, so good, except for my shaky voice. I gave statistics on cases of illness and death in populations vulnerable to pollution, skirting around the only case I cared about.

My gaze swept across the interns, who looked bored, to Casper, who looked half-asleep. I came to the end of what I'd rehearsed when I heard my voice rise, firm and loud. "This is urgent. There are children dying. Dying because their families can't afford treatment."

The energy in the room shifted, growing charged. I kept going. "What's the point of implanting virchips if most people can't afford the cures? Listen to me. All of you."

I felt outside myself, witnessing this. I heard my voice growing even louder. "Somewhere, there's a little girl in hibernation. Her body full of poison. Waiting for treatment. And she'll die if she doesn't get it. Do you understand me?" My voice broke and my eyes burned. "She'll die *forever*."

Wide eyes stared at me, Casper's included.

I came back to myself. *What have I done?*

Blinking, knees weakening, I sat down.

Stunned silence. Casper's gaze stayed locked on mine, his expression unreadable.

Heart thudding, I glanced at the circle of interns exchanging shocked glances. I'd just done the polar opposite of blending into the background. The virchip implantation program was a cornerstone of Virchuous, and I'd just called it into question. *Zuggers.*

Beneath a holo-palm tree by the entrance, an enormous security guard took a step toward me. He was clad in army green and his belt held a small silver instrument I'd only seen in shows: a zapper. His glare made my insides clench. He positioned himself a couple of meters from me, close enough that I could read his nametag. *Borg.* Not scary at all.

At last, Casper said evenly, "Thank you, Liv." He'd thanked every other intern after their contributions, but tension laced his voice now.

Wolf leaned in and whispered to me, "If life was a virch game, you'd get bonus points for the most gutsy what-if."

I covered my eyes with my hand, shrinking into my chair. "Your turn."

He stood up, waved. "Greetings, I'm Wolf."

His words sparked expressions of confusion and baffled murmurs. He ignored them and tucked a loose curl behind his ear. "Most of us have spent more time in holoscapes and virch settings than in reality. What if our illusions have become so immersive we've stopped caring about the real world? And what if we all opened our eyes to reality instead?"

He looked at me. "Like the reality that a little girl might die in hibernation."

My gaze fell to the floor. As much as he annoyed me, he sounded like Delfina. Earlier this year, when I'd ask her why she was helping me, she'd said, "There's injustice in this world, *mija.* You can do something about it. By changing your sister's fate, you can change the fate of other kids, too. I'm helping you because I love you. I love your family. I *love.*"

Wolf continued, looking at Casper, then Spiro. "And what if we explore the dangers of rejecting reality?"

What exactly was Wolf up to? Did he actually want to eliminate everything virch? Starting here in the belly of the Virch Empire? And why was he staring so intently at Spiro?

The interns looked back and forth between Casper and the two boys. Tension thickened. Fake ocean waves lapped. Faux sea birds squawked. Spiro met Wolf's gaze, and something unspoken passed between them.

Stroking his panda, Spiro broke the silence. "You can change your name, but you can't change who you are, little brother."

I stared at Wolf. *Little brother?*

Spiro went on. "You disappear for a year, you drop off the edge of the virch world, and now you show up all retro, ranting about illusion and reality. Tell everyone where you were, Nelson."

Nelson? I knew this name. In the clinic ten months ago, every other news story had been about seventeen-year-old Nelson, missing and presumed dead. A body had never been found.

Nelson was… *Wolf?*

I reeled, trying to make sense of this. We'd had our socalled buddy bonding, and against my better instincts, I'd felt some connection. Yet he'd neglected to mention he was the most talked-about Progeny ever. He'd even lied about his name.

Heat prickled over my skin, the burn of betrayal.

I studied his features with fresh eyes, comparing him to the images I'd seen. Over the past year, his face had grown more angular, his body more muscular, his hair much longer. The curls had been smooth, sculpted, and dyed the technicolor shade of the moment. The blinding colors and tattoos and eye glitter and other body mods were gone. His sparkle now was subtle and natural—sunshine highlights on brown waves of hair and those rain-gray irises.

He glared at his brother, his entire body shaking, his fists and jaw clenched. "Why are you here?"

Spiro scratched the panda's ears. "To save Sugarpie." He put the animal back into the bag, then opened his arms to Wolf.

In turn, Wolf stepped toward his brother. "Why are you really here?" he demanded through gritted teeth.

Under his breath, Spiro murmured something so low that only Wolf could hear.

And Wolf punched his brother's beautiful face.

CHAPTER FIVE
Sugarpie

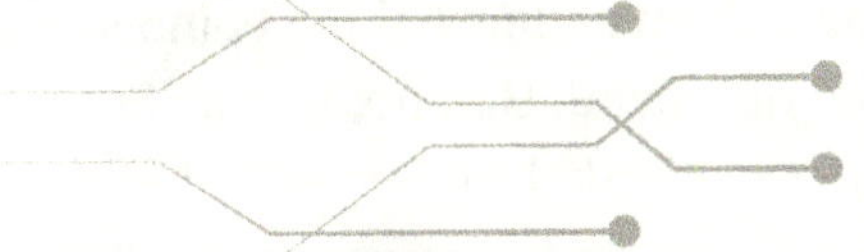

Blood spurted from Spiro's nose, spotting his jellyfish shirt with red blossoms.

Interns gasped. A wave of adrenalin swept through me. Adrenalin and… *confusion.*

For a long moment, he stayed doubled over, clutching his face. When he straightened up, he cocked back his fist.

Before he could let it fly, the security guard was standing between the two boys. "Take it easy, fellas," said Borg, clamping beefy hands onto Wolf's upper arms and pulling him away.

Wolf struggled until the man reached for the zapper at his waist. "Don't make me use this, Nelson."

Slowly, Wolf lowered his arms.

Borg kept his hand on the zapper as Wolf's shoulders slumped and his gaze dropped, sea-sticky clumps of hair curtaining his face. The guard escorted him back to his seat beside me, then approached Spiro, resting his hand on the boy's back.

"Hey, you okay?" He spoke as if they knew each other well.

Spiro gave a shrug, but his eyes were fierce and locked onto Wolf.

Within seconds, a nurse was at Spiro's side, cleaning the blood, handing him a cold-pack and pain-relief patches, then guiding him out the door.

Onstage, Casper's lips tightened into thin, white lines. His bony hands gripped his armrests.

Interns were still reeling, pressing their hands over their mouths.

I refused to look at Wolf, sitting next to me. My mind spun, head hot and prickly. *That's it.* I'd request a new buddy. There would be no further emotional bonding with him. No way could I stay under the radar with this ticking bomb as a partner. Maybe they'd kick him off-island. But, no, he was Progeny.

Stay away from Wolf, I told myself. *And Spiro.*

Snatches of shocked conversations broke through my thoughts. The phrases "Team Nelson" and "Team Spiro" echoed among the interns. This was enough to jog my memory—Spiro and Nelson were the half brothers who'd been in the sensationalized fight. I'd wanted to scream at the newscasters analyzing their every public word to each other. Fans had chosen sides—Team Spiro or Team Nelson. And even more handwringing ensued when Nelson had vanished days later.

Despite myself, I wished for my virchlens to look up details. I wasn't the only one. Around the room, interns were flicking their eyes in jagged patterns, trying to access nonexistent virchlenses, no doubt overcome by the urge to research or record the drama.

Conversations hushed when the lights dimmed to a twilight blue in the audience. In a spotlight of moonbeam, Soraya walked onstage, looking frazzled, in damage-control mode. She treaded carefully to avoid getting that enormous horse tail caught between her legs. Tossing her hair-mane over her shoulder, she forced her eyes into a bright expression. Then she gave Casper a nervous nod, almost a bow.

His ancient, patchwork face winched into a smile. After a tense wave, he left the stage and exited the room, accompanied by his Progeny and a round of uncertain applause.

Soraya cleared her throat. "Let me make it clear that the Progeny will receive no special treatment by the staff, mentors, or interns. Understood?"

The others gave anxious nods and shifted in their seats.

"Anyone in violation of the rules will be promptly kicked off the island, no questions asked." Her smug smile suggested she'd enjoy kicking someone off the island, no questions asked. Despite the bravado, I couldn't imagine she'd dare to give Wolf the boot—but if she did, all the better for me.

Soraya brought up an airscreen with scarily long-nailed fingers. "Now on to schedules."

She explained that we'd spend mornings in the labs and afternoons with free time. I'd expected more time in the lab, but I'd just plan to spend afternoons there, too.

"Directions to the labs," Soraya announced, flicking to the next screen with her finger. A 3D model of the building appeared. "You can access all of this on the public airscreens throughout the facility."

Next, with dramatic flair, she gave us each old-fashioned slips of paper with our mentor's name inked by hand.

I cradled mine in my palm and read *Dr. Kiri Hsu-Ramos*. A thrill rippled through me. The genius herself would be *my mentor*. Once Delfina had told me about her, I'd read every study she'd conducted, heard every talk she'd given. She'd graduated from high school at age twelve, college at age fourteen, and become a doctor of pathology at age sixteen. And now, at age twenty-one, she'd already done ground-breaking research in bio-tech.

One of Dr. Hsu-Ramos's current projects was a single-dose treatment to remove toxic heavy metals from the body, even in severe cases. It had proven safe and effective in clinical trials but wasn't available to the public yet. The only option the doctors at the clinic had given us involved frequent injections over the course of several months and an astronomical cost up front.

I closed my hand around the slip of paper. Dr. Hsu-Ramos had exactly what I needed to save Shell. A single vial of the treatment. For the first time since hatching this plan with Delfina, my goal in coming here felt within reach.

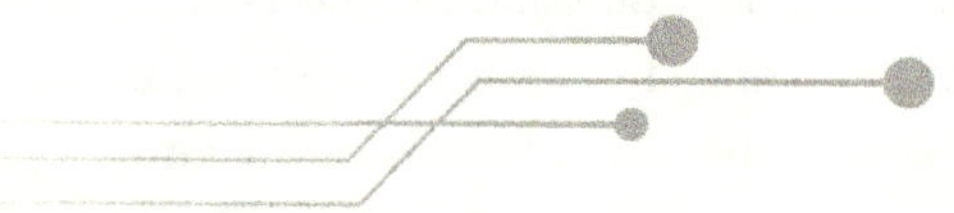

I found myself back on the virch beach, raw and
To finish the orientation, Soraya sent us off to our labs, where we we'd meet our research partner and our mentor. I grabbed my duffel and escaped the room as soon as possible to avoid talking to Wolf. I headed down a dimly lit hallway with the theme of 1900s Paris streets on a drizzly day—a common setting for my art and literature classes but jarring since I'd grown used to the beach scenes. And since I was present in my actual body.

Instead of a computer program tapping into my nervous system to produce sensations as it did with the virchlens experience, in this holoscape, hidden pumps spewed out scent particles and speakers played a soundtrack.

I breathed in the freshness, taking in the red-and-white awnings of flower markets, the widening circles of raindrops on the Seine, the Eiffel Tower in the distance. It felt so real I had to stop myself from tilting back my head and opening my mouth to the sky.

At the next public airscreen, I pulled up an interactive model of the building and figured out my route to the lab. Holding my breath, I rode up my first real-life elevator to the seventh floor and stepped into a desert-themed hallway, complete with a trail of camels on distant dunes. Berber Kasbahs and fringed carpets lined the path. The scents of mint and cumin and wool filled the air.

I found the door marked Virology-Toxicology and stood before the retinal scanner, pulse pounding in anticipation. The door slid open, and I walked into a standard lab room—no fancy holoscape, just white tile floors and a white counter around the perimeter lined with white cabinets, vials, test tubes, and petri dishes. I'd only encountered this equipment in my virch lab classes, and now I savored the real odors of chemical disinfectants.

Thick, wavy glass formed the back wall. Printed orange letters spelled BIOHAZARD on the sliding doors leading to the room beyond the glass. To the right was another interior wall made of thinner, transparent glass revealing what looked like an office, with a desk and three chairs.

In the far left corner, a young woman was speaking to a guy with his back to me—his broad, muscled back. His shirt rippled and shimmered, as if it had a life of its own. A large bag leaned against his leg. On hearing my footsteps, he turned and revealed his chiseled face, nose slightly swollen.

Spiro. He must have changed clothes—these were free of blood stains. What was he doing here?

I turned my focus to the woman. Her hair sparkled turquoise, swept into an enormous sculpted wave, brazenly impractical in the lab. Her eyes almost blinded me with that a la moda diamond effect. She wore a tight silver fish scale skirt in a mermaid style that seemed more practical for water than land.

Without her nametag, I wouldn't have recognized Dr. Kiri Hsu-Ramos. I managed to keep a polite expression on my face even as my stomach sank. She looked worlds different from the videos I'd seen of her.

And Spiro must be my lab partner. My stomach sank farther.

My mentor tore her gaze from Spiro and her bright eyes settled on me. "Liv! Welcome!"

I took a long breath, offering my hand. "Nice to meet you, Dr. Hsu-Ramos."

She threw her arms around me, gave me a squeeze before holding me at arm's length, hands on my shoulders. She smelled like synthetic lilies. "You would not believe how hard I worked to get you here, Liv. Your application just jumped out at me."

I had Delfina to thank for that. As a Virchuous employee, she'd known about Dr. Hsu-Ramos's work and had given me a radiant recommendation. My teacher had deflected my gratitude, insisting I was brilliant and hard-working and had been accepted in the program on my own merits.

As Dr. Hsu-Ramos kept gushing, I tried not to cringe at her compliments. "This girl has smarts and heart, I said to myself. And you totally get my vision of making the treatment available to anyone who needs it. You're perfect, even though it's unusual for us to take on an intern with… your background."

My fake minnow background. Delfina had convinced her parents to let me use the address of one of their rental properties in my application. I didn't want to think how Dr. Hsu-Ramos would react if she knew I came from a Null Zone. Even though Virchuous patted their own backs for sending teachers and health workers there, the organization couldn't legally employ a

Null, even a teen intern. In the eyes of society, we were criminals.

My mentor patted my shoulder with affection. "I fought for you, Liv."

Tears sprung to my eyes. Ever since Shell got sick, the path to my reservoir of tears had become worn. They didn't come so much during sad times, but mostly at moments like this, when someone showed me undeserved generosity. And here I'd been judging her outfit.

"Thanks," I said, my voice cracking.

"And how lucky are we to be working with Spiro?" Her voice sounded young and sweet compared to its starkness in the professional talks. Her accent was delicate, nearly imperceptible. She'd split her time between her parents' native homes in China and Spain growing up.

She smiled at Spiro, almost shyly, and leaned over to scratch his panda's neck.

The creature had poked its huge head out of the mesh bag, two black spots surrounding sorrowful eyes, its black nose sniffing at her arm. It felt surreal to have this live, warm, musky, creature in the sterile lab.

"I fought for Spiro too," Kiri said, stroking its ears. "The competition was fierce, as you'd imagine. But it helped that he requested my lab."

She gave him a sideways glance through jewel-dusted eyelashes. There was something awkward about how she moved, her head off-balance from the lopsided hairstyle, her eyelids straining beneath the weight of the lash décor. She looked like a kid playing dress-up.

I wondered if she'd gone on fantasy virch dates with Spiro. She was just a little older than us, and it seemed anyone who could afford it had virchdated his sim. How weird it would feel to encounter strangers who believed they knew you so intimately. But he seemed used to it.

Cupping the panda's face in her hands, Kiri murmured, "Why, hello, little miss Sugarpie. Are you a cutie? Yes, you are! Oh, yes, you are!"

The panda let out a series of squeaks that sounded oddly like a toddler whining, which prompted Kiri to squeak in response. "Together we'll form a great team," she said. "Working on behalf of vulnerable humans *and* vulnerable animals." She beamed at both of us.

"Amen to that." Spiro gave me a firm handshake. "Howdy, partner."

With his swollen nose, he seemed less intimidating. I actually felt sorry for this Progeny, a victim of his own brother's crazy outburst. "You okay?"

"Been better." He offered an embarrassed grin. "But glad to be here with you two."

Talking to him here, just the three of us, made me realize he was just a human like me. A human who bled and bruised and got embarrassed. Maybe I shouldn't have held his Progeny status against him. He hadn't chosen it, just like I hadn't chosen to be a Null.

I offered a polite smile, then turned back to our mentor. "So I'm a huge fan of your research, Dr. Hsu-Ramos—"

"Oh, call me Kiri."

A shiver shot through me. I was on a first-name basis with my most-admired scientist. "Okay, Kiri. I'm fascinated by your treatment in cases of heavy metal poisoning. I'd love to see what you're working on and—"

"Whoa!" Kiri laughed, giving Sugarpie a kiss on the nose. "What's the hurry?"

Zuggers. I couldn't appear too eager—that could arouse suspicion. "Sorry, Dr. Hsu—I mean, Kiri. I'm just excited."

"I get it," she said with warmth. "We can talk research for a bit. Most of it's done by interacting with enlarged holographic cellular material." She pulled up an airscreen, swiped and tapped in some codes, until voilà, a three-meter-by-three-meter virus hologram enveloped us.

"Cool." Spiro stroked Sugarpie, looking impressed at the RNA floating in spirals by our heads.

"Yup." Kiri flicked her finger over another icon and exited the hologram, which vanished. "But we still need assistants to do the grunt work of experiments on the real, messy stuff. Culturing the actual tissue." She wrinkled her nose in an apologetic grimace. "That's you two." Quickly, she added, "Of course, the micro-organisms you'll work with have been genetically modified to be harmless for research purposes. And you'll be doing practice assignments first, to ease you in."

Eeeee! The eerie song of whales, some kind of notification. She pulled up an airscreen that showed a man in a translucent biohaz suit. Apparently even the scientists here couldn't wear virchlenses and had to make do with retro communication technology.

"Sorry to bug you, Kiri," said the man onscreen, "but I have a question for you."

"Go on," she said.

"Project Dragon, Ki."

She nodded, then gave us an apologetic smile. "Excuse me, guys. Classified stuff. You two can get started with the first practice assignment. Basically dropping red dye into substrates in petri dishes. Simple stuff. Just follow the airscreen instructions."

Using her pinkie, she closed the screen with the scientist and brought up another one with detailed instructions. Then she disappeared into her office.

Ignoring Spiro and Sugarpie, I turned my attention to the task at hand. I needed to earn Kiri's trust so that two months from now, I could abscond with a vial of the treatment—but I was also deeply curious. Even this so-called grunt work was fascinating.

Spiro came to my side, close enough our arms brushed, and said, "Got a feeling we're gonna be besties."

My heart sank. *Please, no.*

Ignoring Spiro as much as possible without being outright rude, I read the directions and began gathering droppers and petri dishes. From the corner of my eye, I saw him struggle to tuck the panda inside the bag. The mesh allowed fresh air—still, the creature seemed too big for the bag.

He sighed. "Sugarpie keeps growing."

"That's why they call them giant pandas."

With a grin, he sat on a stool beside me and asked, "So, Liv, what'd you think about my half bro?"

I cringed. The last thing I needed was to be pitted between two of the most powerful guys on this island. Gaze fixed on the petri dish, I shrugged a shoulder.

"Really," he pushed, "what about his rant about reality and illusion?"

Without looking up, I murmured, "I'm actually more curious about what you said that made him punch you."

He squeezed his eyes shut and pressed his palms into the sockets before muttering something too soft to hear.

"What?" I was already regretting I'd even asked. I'd touched a nerve.

"I told him I love him. That no matter what—what happened with us, he's my brother."

"Oh." I looked down, taken by surprise. "Well, you're lucky you have a brother. You two should try to work things out."

He arched an eyebrow. "Wish we could."

Awkward silence ensued. The silence of diving to a deep, tender place.

Finally, he grazed a hand over his buzz cut and let out a long breath. "Watch out for him. I mean, you seem nice. The thing about my half bro is… he's crazy." He rubbed his face. "Know what kind of weirdness goes on in his brain? Know his real what-if question?"

I said nothing because yes, I was intrigued—but I really couldn't get involved in this high-profile conflict.

"Nelson has this idea that we all exist in his own virch game. Like, a super-realistic one, down to the sub-atomic level, with ultra-amnesia mode—like not even zigzagging his eyes could make him exit. He thinks there's a real Nelson kicking it back on a red sofa, while a virch Nelson is here in this fake world. He thinks he's just imagining all of us."

My insides twisted. Was Spiro telling the truth? The explanation would fit with Wolf's philosophical questions… not to mention why he'd run into the ocean as if he were invincible. As if he could restart.

"What say you, Liv?"

I breathed out. *Don't get involved.* In a 'bot's voice, I said, "As a mere element of a virch game, I lack consciousness and therefore have no opinion."

He laughed. "You're refreshing. Most people, even the scary-smart ones"—he motioned with his chin toward Kiri's office—"they get goofy around the Progeny." He lowered his voice. "Makes me wish I'd never signed away rights to those virch dates."

I breathed out, thankful I'd never been on a virch date with him but wondering now what that would be like. *Don't get involved.* Voice flat, I said, "Your brother gets the credit. The über-Wolf on the red couch must've programmed me this way."

Again, Spiro laughed, a genuine belly laugh. "I like you, Liv."

To that, I said nothing. We worked in silence, and I grew absorbed in the smells of chemicals and the smoothness of beakers and the hum of autoclaves and the bright white lights. Sugarpie had settled down in her bag and was breathing in a soft rhythm.

Every once in a while, scientists exited through the sliding doors of the Biohaz Lab and passed us on their way out of the main lab. Spiro was friendly, chatting with each one, opening the mesh bag to give peeks of a snoring Sugarpie.

Spiro seemed like a decent guy—I felt bad for keeping him at a distance. Still, I stayed laser-focused on my work, glancing occasionally at the airscreen to double-check instructions.

After a while, Spiro reached for his pocket. "Mood pill?"

I shook my head. These drugs were costly and hard to come by in the Cove, smuggled in on the junk ships. I'd tried them a couple of times for pain and hated how they made my mind feel. "Too much brain fuzz."

"Yeah. Wish I didn't need them." He put a purple pill under his tongue.

I glanced at him, wondering why someone as perfect as Spiro would need mood pills. I felt a little sorry for him.

Any sympathy I felt for my research partner did not extend to my emotional buddy. A sickening sense of betrayal and anger filled me whenever I thought of Wolf. He'd *deceived* me. And I'd actually started to like him, to think we might be kindred spirits. And all along, he'd thought I was a soul-less character in his virch game. I tried to let it go, but my annoyance at him fueled my curiosity.

"Spiro," I said, "this virch game of life that Wolf's playing. Theoretically, how would he win it?"

Spiro hunched over his petri dish, positioning the dropper. "That's the question, isn't it? At first he thought it was all about having fun, breaking the rules."

I thought back to the airscreen gossip I'd heard. I wasn't sure which brother did which stunt—but at least one involved naked skydiving.

Spiro raised a brow. "Then about a year ago, just before he disappeared, he said he figured out how to win."

"How?"

Spiro looked at me, gaze intent. "Think about it. What would make the game really exciting?"

Love was what first came to mind. The image of a kiss. Embarrassing. The absolute last thing on my agenda. *Love* was the kind of answer Shell would give. She was always urging me to have my first kiss, find a boyfriend—no matter how many times I told her I was too busy with responsibilities. She'd just give me a wry grin and say, "It's all about love, sis."

Anyway, I didn't deserve love. Or a kiss.

Not when Shell was in a coffin.

Not when it was my fault she was there.

Collecting myself and shoving the thought back to its dark, off-limits place, I sat up straight, stretched my neck, and pressed a palm against my strand of shells, feeling the broken edges jab my skin.

When I didn't answer, Spiro said, "Changing the world as we know it. That's how he thinks he'll win the game."

So that's what Wolf meant about changing the world.

"Well, that's noble," I said, swirling the red liquid in the test tube. I tried to keep my mouth shut, but I couldn't help asking, "But then why did Wolf punch you? I mean, if you were just reaching out?"

Spiro brushed his swollen nose. "Who knows."

I nodded, unwilling to push him, but then he whispered, "We've both been to hell. He thinks he found his way out." Spiro's voice trembled, just the tiniest bit. "But we're both still here."

I set the test tube in its holder. There was something real and tender just beneath his words. For a split second, I wanted to hug him. *Don't get involved, Liv.*

"Spiro," I said softly, "what happened to you guys?"

He rubbed his face. "Did he tell you anything?"

I shook my head.

He pulled Sugarpie from the bag, and like a child hugging a teddy bear, pressed its face to his. Feebly, the animal swiped its black paws in the air—a clumsy, faint-hearted effort at play. Then it hung its head and closed its droopy eyes in a kind of surrender. Its smile looked even sadder than before.

And Spiro's face, too, looked suddenly heavy. "Ever since the big fight, people are choosing Team Spiro or Team Nelson. You know?"

Refraining from rolling my eyes, I nodded.

"If you choose sides, Liv, I hope you'll choose mine."

The only side I'm on, I thought, *is my sister's.*

CHAPTER SIX
Peaches

The holoscape of the dining hall was sunset-picnic-in-a-meadow, complete with fake rabbits hopping between tables. The interns tried to score a seat near Spiro as first choice, Wolf as second, and surprisingly, me as third. The other three interns at my table begged me for details about the brothers.

A girl with undulating, purple medusa-hair fixed her glittered gaze on me. Strawberry was her name… or no, this was Melon. An a la moda fruit name, just like the other two. Must have been some trend among the shark moms in 2137. "So retro girl, are they as heart-quakey in real life as they are on a virch date?"

"Who knows."

Plum twirled his hair, which shared the same indigo color as his name. "Too bad Nelson's sim hasn't been updated since he disappeared."

"I know!" Melon sighed. "But Spiro's is up to date. You know the virchrelax Riviera cruise? That's where he took me last week! He has this way of whispering your name… He looks into your eyes like you're the only one in the universe." She shivered. "It's so weird to see the real Spiro. I mean, I feel like I know him really well already."

"Really well?" said Strawberry, wagging her eyebrows.

Melon blushed. "Really, really, *really* well."

I looked away, past their heads to the patch of real indoor garden, where sparrows flitted among tree branches. At least I *thought* they were real.

Once my companions realized I had no juicy scoop on my Progeny partners, they moved to other topics. I focused on my pear-gorgonzola ravioli. The fruit crew had popped their effi-food pills—short for efficient food—but I'd slid mine under the plate. The idea of taking a pill to make food flow through you, mostly unabsorbed—well, it made me want to cry.

Food was so scarce in the Cove during the winter, we had to ration it, our bellies never full. Even during the summers, when we were harvesting vegetables and fruit from our gardens daily, we limited ourselves, preserving most of it for later.

As the others gorged on three-course desserts of rosemary flan and chocolate-rose cake and violet meringue, I worked through a small bowl of sliced peaches, thinking of Shell with every bite.

The peaches had been at the pinnacle of ripeness the evening my sister had collapsed.

We were heading home from the junk heaps and she was chattering with excitement about the peaches, when we'd run into our favorite teacher.

Shell threw her arms around her. "Delfina!"

"Why, hello, *corazón*!" She pressed her hands to my sister's face, gazed at her with fondness.

Warmth for this woman swept over me. None of the other shark teachers showed my sister affection with words like *corazón*—heart—or Shell's favorite, *mijita*—my little daughter.

"What are you two *chicas* up to?" Delfina asked.

"Peaches!" Shell announced. "Want to have dinner with us?"

On reflex, my stomach tightened. Did we have enough to share? No matter. I nodded to Delfina. "You should come."

"All right then, *mija*." Everything about her glowed—her bright smile, soft brown skin, sparkly eyes. "I'll bring a roasted chicken."

Of course she would. Gratitude filled me.

After a quick chat, Shell watched her go, black braid swinging. "Wouldn't it be great if she was our mom?"

I grinned. "So that's your plan, huh? Get her together with Dad?"

She laughed impishly.

If only, I thought. Sharks never married people from the Cove. Still, Delfina might break the mold as she had in so many other ways.

"You're quite the matchmaker." I ruffled Shell's hair.

She gave me a piercing, old-soul look. "It's all about love, sis."

Her eyes rolled back and she dropped to the ground like a limp ragdoll.

I fell to my knees in a panic, moved my cheek to her mouth, felt her faint breath. "Shell. Can you hear me?"

Silence.

"Please, Shell. Wake up."

She drew in a deep breath and blinked. "What happened?"

I pressed her thin body to my chest, pushing back tears. "You fainted."

I kept my arm around her all the way home, then had her lie down in our hammock. "Rest here, Shell."

A weak smile. "I'm okay, Liv. Exquisite, really."

I ran to our grove and picked the biggest, rosiest peach. Together, my sister and I swung in the hammock beneath the pines as juice dripped down her chin.

"Look at the sky, Livvy! Doesn't it look like the inside of a giant peach?"

Pink and orange and gold clouds streaked the sky, shimmering, unearthly. How could she notice this stuff after she'd just *collapsed*?

"Exactly," I said, my voice breaking.

A week later, Shell fainted again. And again two days after that.

A month later, she couldn't keep down any food, not even peaches.

The Cove felt like a different world from this dining hall, filled with shimmery interns and a bounty of food. Just as I finished the last slice of peach, Wolf approached my table, the sound of his flip-flops preceding him. I'd managed to avoid him all afternoon, staying in the lab during my free time. At a glance, I saw that the redness in his calf had subsided. I let my gaze lift to his eyes—which looked raw.

"Hey, Liv, can we talk?" He motioned with his chin toward the indoor garden.

The fruit crew scrutinized us. Reluctantly, I wiped my mouth, picked up my bag, and followed him behind a banana tree, hearing whispers left in our wake.

"What?" I demanded.

"About what happened, Liv—"

"You lied to me. You really thought you could hide the fact that you're Progeny?"

His face fell. "I didn't want that to be your first impression of me."

I hugged my arms. "Want to know my first impression of you? A liar. And an assaulter."

"Assaulter?" His brow wrinkled.

"Already forget about punching your brother?"

He ran his fingers over a banana leaf. "Right, listen, I can explain."

"No, you can't." His virch game delusions just added insult to injury. How could he think people's suffering was unreal? Glaring, I added, "I'm not here to play games."

And with that, I turned on my heel and scanned the room for Soraya. There she was, roaming the room, flipping her horse tail with her hand, surveying the interns. She was thoroughly unlikable, but at least seemed unsympathetic to the Progeny. She might serve as an ally.

Heart racing, I strode up to her. "Uh, excuse me."

When she turned to me, I said, "My Progeny partners aren't working out." I steadied my voice, holding her gaze. "I'd rather just work with my mentor."

She raised her eyebrows. "We picked well, then."

"Excuse me?"

"Wasn't easy to find interns who wouldn't be seduced or in-timidated by the Progeny. It was you and Sam over there." She motioned with her chin toward a flustered boy surrounded by interns. Spiro must be his bonding partner and Wolf his lab partner.

"We knew you'd be perfect." Soraya patted my shoulder.

"But the Progeny's dramas…" I searched for inoffensive words. "They're too disruptive. It's not—"

"You're smart enough to deal with it." She smiled with her eyes—brown, but unnaturally large, like actual horse eyes. "Give it another week and let me know how it's going." She turned and left, tail swishing.

Feeling awkward, I glanced around. Through the crowd, Wolf caught my eyes. He looked hurt, must have guessed I'd asked for a new partner.

My jaw clenched. *Stay out of this, Liv.*

Both brothers were hiding something. Both brothers were aching. And both brothers, for some reason, wanted me on their side.

I would give them nothing.

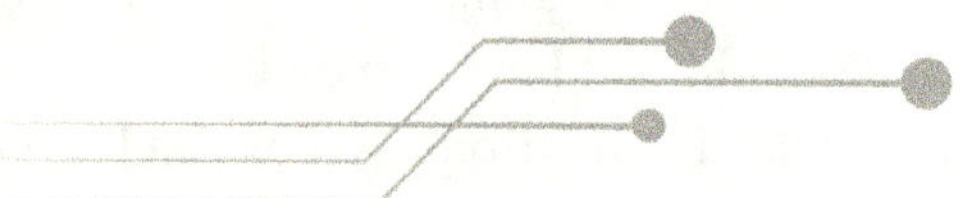

Leaving the dining hall with my duffel, I checked a public airscreen for directions to my room, then headed down the corridor, bathed in a fake sunset, all pinks and oranges, with a humming soundtrack of crickets. The elevator was a holo-waterfall. What an odd feeling to be engulfed in rushing water while staying perfectly dry.

The elevator doors slid open, revealing a hallway lined with doors that I assumed led to interns' quarters. It was also a fake sunset, although now the pink and orange had melted into dusky purple.

My door opened after a retinal scan, and just inside I dropped my bag. The room was stylish and simply furnished with chairs, a desk, and a bed. A sliding door to the right led to a sleek bathroom. Near the bed hung an airscreen, designed to look like gauzy tropical netting.

I took off my shorts and top, which now smelled like seaweed, and draped them over an armchair. The outfit was sticky-stiff, still dusted with sand. Fratch that goblock Wolf for making me mess up my new clothes.

Unpacking, I shook wrinkles from a tan pair of shorts, courtesy of Delfina. Something fell from the pocket—a scrap of worn, lavender cotton the size of my palm.

Puzzled, I picked it up. Stitched in red thread were letters: LOVE.

I smiled. Delfina's work, no doubt.

With my fingertips, I traced the stitching. She must have slipped it into the pocket when she'd bought my clothes. Or maybe she'd asked Dad to sneak it into my bag along with his gift.

LOVE. Was it a statement? As in an almost motherly "I love you, *mija*"? Or an instruction? As in "Liv, go love someone." Or maybe she meant it not as a verb, but a noun. As in, "Here is a bit of love for you." Or "There's a love out there for you."

I was overthinking it. Shell always pointed out my tendency to lead with my head, not my heart. Maybe I should just let the LOVE sink into me. I tucked the message back into the pocket so that I could carry love around with me tomorrow.

From my duffel bag, I took out Dad's driftwood message and set it on the bedside table. He was counting on me. Delfina was too. And so were our other friends and neighbors in the Cove. There were over a thousand people in our community, and everyone knew the name of the girl with the perpetual smile. Shell.

It wasn't until now, worlds away from the Cove, that I understood how deeply I loved my home. Life there wasn't easy. We collected our water from the river with buckets, boiled it over a wood fire to kill germs. We relieved ourselves in outhouses over deep holes, bathed in cold water with harsh lye soap. We lived in shacks of scavenged metal and tarps and wood, vulnerable to hurricanes and floods.

Yet it was *home*.

I put on my ragged pajamas, stitched together from scraps of our worn-out, too-small clothing. Delfina had offered to buy me a nightgown, but I'd declined. This was one expense I was happy to spare her—I'd have something familiar with me where no one could see it.

Exhausted, I flopped onto the enormous mattress, opened the airscreen, and shuffled through the menu. Free virch dates, I noted. They wouldn't be as immersive on an airscreen as with a virchlens, but they piqued my curiosity.

I flipped through dozens of options until I reached Spiro with a baby bunny perched on his shoulder, and beneath, a warning that the dating scenario contained over-17 content. Toward the bottom was Wolf—or Nelson, or whatever. His sim looked years younger, maybe from age fourteen, with a rating of over-13 due to mild sensuality.

I wondered what mild sensuality meant. Handholding? A fingertip grazing a cheek? Hands running through hair? Lips brushing? Or maybe an actual kiss? Against my better judgment, I tapped the icon.

A life-size image of young Wolf appeared before me. He looked less solid somehow, and not just because he was on an airscreen. He felt un-formed, a work-in-progress. This was the slighter and more dazzled-up Wolf I remembered from the news.

His sim said, "Hey, Liv, I'd love to go on a date with you, even though I'm on the young side." A shy laugh. "But if you want an older version of me, there may be hope! My fans made a waitlist in case I come back. Just sign up and you'll be notified the second I'm available."

I tapped the sign-up form. Over a billion people had already signed up.

A billion.

The number made my head spin. Embarrassed, I exited the program.

I switched to the bed icon and played around with the settings. Cloud Puff, Ocean Current, Mossy Forest Floor, Swaying Hammock—each deliciously lulling. Just when I was wishing I had a bed like this back home, I realized the cost of this bed alone could probably pay for my sister's treatment.

So I set it to Classic Futon, most similar to my own rag-filled mattress. On the bedside table sat a bottle of yellow pills labeled EFFI-SLEEP, short for "efficient sleep." I didn't touch them.

Instead, I picked up Dad's driftwood message, pressed it against my forehead, then closed my eyes, floating through the events of the day, reminding myself why I was here. *Liv, my hero, do your best, that's enough.*

The heavy, natural tug of sleep overtook me like the tide.

And here, on this strange bed, on this strange island, the world as I knew it imploded.

CHAPTER SEVEN
Nightmare

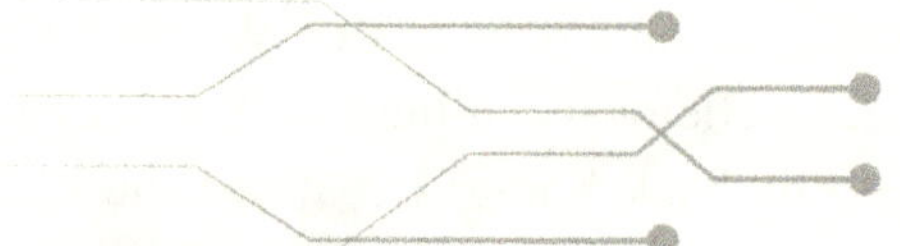

Every once in a while, over the course of my life, I'd had lucid dreams—dreams in which I realized I was dreaming and could do anything. Then, when I'd taken a virch elective on the topic, I learned how to induce them, control them. Sometimes I even managed to bring Shell into my dreams, fully alive and exuberant and huggable.

The first step to lucid dreaming was to develop a habit in real life of asking yourself, "How do I know I'm not dreaming?" You noticed how things felt with all your senses and tested for discrepancies. Once you had that real-life habit, it transferred to your dream life. Then you'd notice contradictions—for example, how could you be in the snow in shorts and a T-shirt and not be cold? The inconsistencies would help you realize you were dreaming.

There was a chance you were in a holoscape, but the mini-projectors and the insubstantial imagery made that fairly easy to recognize. If you could wave your hand through a solid object, then it was a hologram. There was also a chance you were super-immersed in a virch world, in which case you'd zigzag your eyes to exit. If you remained in the world after checking for solidity and zigzagging, *ta-dah!*—you must be in a lucid dream.

And in lucid dreams, you could do whatever you wanted.

Once I'd kissed a boy in my dreams. It was quick and sweet, but more than I'd done in real life. When I woke up, I wondered if my only kisses would be imaginary. Would I fall in love one day? What would it feel like? And did I even deserve that joy?

That first night of my internship, my dream turned lucid.

And it was the most bizarre dream ever.

I was standing on the sunny beach where I'd been earlier that day with Wolf. The surf tickled my toes, and it all felt so real—the salt, the sand, the stickiness, the smell of fish and seaweed.

A girl appeared in front of me. She was… *me*. But me *covered in blood*.

Fresh scarlet stained her clothes and matted her hair. Blotches covered her damp face, as if she'd been crying. Pink welts—burns?—spotted her exposed flesh, which was splattered with more blood. Shadows ringed her bloodshot eyes, the pupils huge. There was something haunting and gaping about them… almost zombie-like. She stared at me with a chilling intensity.

My heart pounded and a sick feeling came over me. I wanted to close my eyes, run away.

"Liv," she gasped. "Liv. Listen carefully."

Background crashes and muffled shouts competed with her words. Resisting the urge to flee, I strained to listen.

"Everything depends—depends on you. Listen… remember… do w-w-what I tell you." She wiped away tears, sniffed, took a quivery breath. "You and Wolf."

Her next words were drowned out by thuds. I held my dream-body still, concentrating on the movements of her lips, trying to decipher her words.

"W-w-work together. Trust Wolf." She doubled over, clutching her belly.

What was happening to her? She looked like the survivor of an explosion, her organs and bones and tissue damaged from shrapnel and who knew what else. I tried to determine where all the blood was coming from. Her abdomen seemed the main source of pain.

Should I help her? Hold her? Run for help?

She gasped for breath. "Liv, you both—you both—" She stopped and let out an animal groan. "Help…" Her voice broke. Even her breathing seemed tortured.

Part of me felt drawn to hold her. Still, terror rooted my feet to the beach. My entire body shook so badly that I might not be much of a comfort.

More bashing sounds thundered in the background. She let out a cry. "He'll k-kill everyone. On-on earth." She crumpled again, clutching her stomach as her face wrenched and twisted.

Tears ran down my cheeks, and my hand flew to my mouth. I ached just witnessing her pain.

She forced out more words. "Stop him." Another wince, eyes squeezed shut. "It starts here. He—he'll destroy…" Again, she doubled over in agony.

I couldn't bear to watch her suffer. I stepped toward her, arms open, ready to draw her weak body against mine.

But my fingers swept right through her body. Reflexively, my eyes zigzagged. No change. Couldn't be a virch world. Or an airscreen. A hologram? But no mini-projectors. This was clearly inconsistent with reality. It must be a dream, but it felt different than anything I'd experienced before.

Trembling, I pulled in my arms, hugged myself. "Is this—are you… *real*?"

She kept talking, apparently unaware of my questions. And as she spoke, I realized she wasn't so much looking at me but *through* me.

"I-in the morning. Go to-to the beach, first thing." She gasped as her body convulsed. "W-w-wolf will be there. T-together, you… fi-find a way." More crashes wiped out her words. "Two days… no, even less… Stop this—stop this before—" Again, she cried out an animal sound. Her entire face quivered. "A-and save soul… please… please. And the p-panda."

Again, she contracted in pain.

I let out a helpless cry, wiping at my tears. What had *happened* to her?

Something fell from her fist, something like feathers or leaves, in pale, dusky colors, floating toward the ground and vanishing.

With enormous effort, she straightened up, continued speaking. The last part streamed out so fast I almost didn't catch it, as if it were her final breath, her final words. "I just—I—I love you and I love life and I love Wolf, and that's why—why—why I'm doing this, and oh, Liv, I hope it's the right thing. Liv, please… please just live your life… live your life… live your life…"

She buried her face in her hands and cried out again in a whimper of surrender.

I winced, feeling echoes of her pain. Again, instinctively, I reached out to hug her, help her somehow.

She collapsed through my arms and vanished.

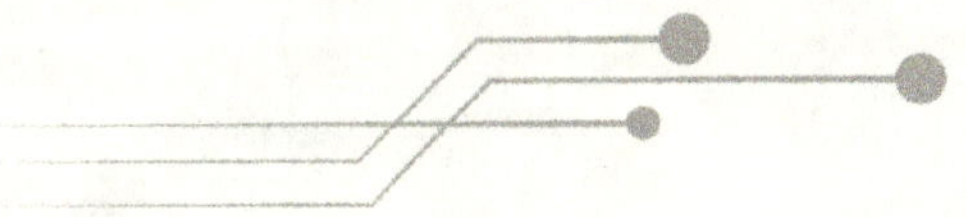

I woke with my heart racing, sweat dampening the sheets. I sat up in bed and turned on the light, shaking. What was that? I rubbed my eyes, got up, drank from the bathroom faucet, splashed water on my face.

In this luxurious bathroom, I glanced in the mirror and saw myself terrified but healthy. Skin smooth, free of blood, normal eyes. I held myself, tried to calm the shivering. How chilling to see myself so tortured and strange and despairing—with a body so *wrecked.* What weapons had inflicted that damage?

I reached out to steady myself against the cold, glassy sink, going over everything the dream me had said. But it only led to frustration and questions. Stop what? Stop who? Why did this guy want to kill everyone? And what was this about *two days*? And what had she said about a soul and the panda? What had happened to her—*to me*?

And the bizarre stuff she'd said about Wolf. Loving him, trusting him. What did he have to do with this? How was I supposed to trust him?

My insides felt on the verge of exploding. Nothing made sense. Maybe all this was just the stress of being in a new situation—a messed up version of a nightmare.

By the bed, I brought up the airscreen, switched the mattress setting to Cloud Puff, took the effi-sleep pills, and forced myself to sleep.

My last thought: *What will tomorrow bring?*

A Bubble

Day Two on the Island
Year 2154

CHAPTER EIGHT
Live Your Life

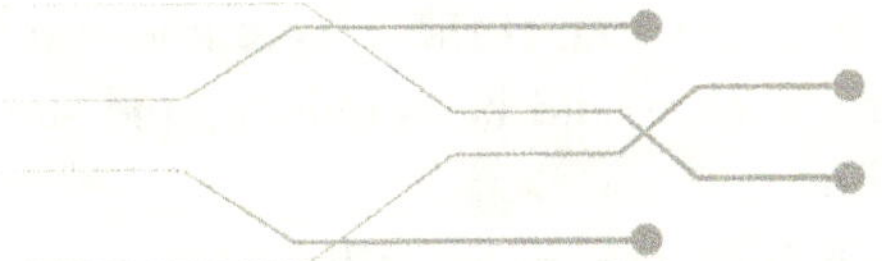

It felt like a blink later when the tinkling bell alarm sounded. Now, with the holo-sunrise filling my room, things seemed less urgent and creepy. Already, the dream me's instructions were fading into morning mist.

Feeling the need to wash the nightmare away, I stepped into the shower, taking a minute to figure out the settings before landing on Relaxing Rain Forest, complete with hot steam and cool downpour and holo-foliage. With a deep sigh, I lathered up the ginger-orange soap. My fingers ran over old scars, slips from oyster knives and machete blades and metal scraps.

I lifted the strand of shells to wash my neck. I always wore the necklace, even though the tiny fragments left indentations and tiny cuts in my flesh. Taking it off felt like a betrayal to Shell. A sign I might be forgetting my promise to save her.

Rinsing off, I wondered if I should show up at the beach. Was there any remote possibility Wolf would be there?

After some debate, I decided I'd go, and if he wasn't there, then I could be sure it was only a dream.

I switched the shower to auto-dry and moisturize, and felt the droplets evaporate. Back in the bedroom, I checked the time. If I downed a coffee and vita-bar now, I could make it there and back before lab time started. Then I could put the dream distraction behind me and get on with what I'd come here to do.

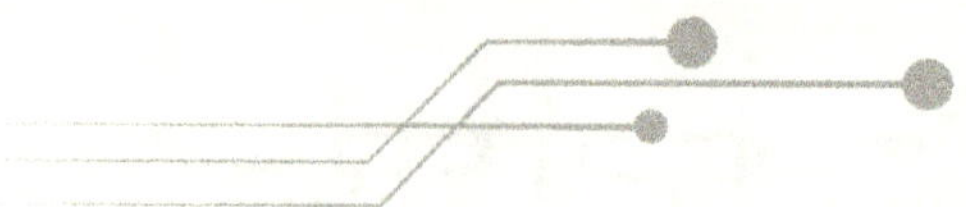

The real sun rose over the horizon, shining a path of light toward me on the shore. Funny how sunlight on water always seems to blaze a line straight to you. If there were a whole line of people along the shore, each would be convinced the sun was beckoning to them alone.

I glanced behind me, pulse still racing from my jog here. The beach was deserted. I pulled off my tank and shorts, down to my polka-dot swimsuit. If Wolf didn't show, I could tell myself I'd just come for a swim. That way, I wouldn't feel ridiculous.

An enormous water bird swooped in front of me, close enough I could have touched it. My breath caught. A heron?

My last heron sighting had been shortly after we hibernated Shell, before Delfina and I had come up with a plan to save her. I'd been sifting through the recycling mound, trying to work despite tears, wondering where my sister's spirit was. She wasn't fully alive or fully dead—just existing somewhere in a strange limbo. At that moment, a rare great blue heron had alighted on the junk pile. There it perched, like an angel or a flag or a call to action.

Now, I watched the water bird before me on the beach, balanced on tall twig legs, its neck a graceful S. Some kind of heron, I was sure of it. After a long moment, it stretched its wings wide, and flew away. I watched it shrink to a speck and vanish over the forest.

I dropped my clothes onto the dry sand. Arms folded, I waded into the water, cool in the brisk morning air. Not a fin or tentacle in sight, just smooth ripples of sea. With abandon, I dove into the waves, just as Wolf had done yesterday.

Beneath the surface, my body stretched and undulated with the currents. I felt comfortable in my skin, alone in the quiet blue. My hair brushed against my shoulders like kelp.

I savored the feeling. Seeing my dream self on the verge of death made me want to revel in the real, live, thrumming health of my body—something I'd felt guilty about since Shell's illness. I never spoke about my role in it. I tried not to think about it.

This deep, hidden shame was why I had to bring her back to life. If I didn't, the consequence would be even worse than having a forever-dead sister. It would be knowing that, for the rest of my life, I'd have to live with the knowledge that I killed her.

I shoved the thought away, let it settle back into the dark, watery depths of my mind.

Live your life… live your life… live your life . . .

For a while, I swam and flipped and dove. Then, with my eyes closed, I floated on my back. Yes, reality could be blissful, if I could let go of shame and anger and vague fears of venomous tentacles and that creepy dream.

At some point, I opened my eyes. And there he was, just meters away.

Wolf, dripping in the sunshiny sea.

My heart pounded. Wolf, here, just as my dream had predicted. I gathered a shaky breath. *Calm down, Liv. This could be a coincidence.*

He pushed wet hair from his eyes and looked at me. Without greeting, he said, "You know that story of Zhuangzi? The one who dreamed he was a butterfly? And when he woke up, he wondered if he was a man dreaming he was a butterfly or a butterfly dreaming he was a man. Remember?"

I nodded.

"Well, what do you think of dreams and reality, Angel?"

I stared at him, at the water lacing his lashes, glistening on his chest. I closed my eyes. Somehow, my dream self had been right about him being here this morning. Here he was, asking me about—of all things—dreams. Coincidence? Or something more? What else could the dream me be right about? Loving Wolf? Impending doom?

Panic rushed in. I channeled scientist Liv, reminded myself of my one and only purpose here—*Shell*. I breathed in, then out. Rationally, I had no reason to confide in him. According to Spiro, Wolf was insane. Not to mention he'd already proven himself a violent, lying Progeny. I felt his betrayal from yesterday, a still-raw wound.

"Well? What do you think, Liv?"

I opened my eyes, regarded him coolly. "Dreams have a scientific explanation. Most are random, the by-product of our brains cleaning up and getting ready for a new day."

"That's it?" he asked, looking almost… *stricken.*

"Once in a while, maybe there's something meaningful." I chose my words carefully. "Maybe some unconscious part of our brain knows something that hasn't entered our awareness yet."

Wolf licked seawater from his lip. "I'm glad you're at least *open* to taking dreams seriously." His voice lowered. "Liv, I had a really weird dream last night."

Goosebumps sprouted over my skin. "What was it?"

"Promise you won't think—"

"I promise."

He rubbed his face. "In my dream, I saw myself on this beach. I was a mess, all bloody and beat up and hurt—like *dying hurt*—and… sad and scared."

My knees grew weak.

"I gave myself instructions," he continued. "To stop some plot to destroy…" He paused. "I sound crazy. You're looking at me like I'm crazy."

I finished his sentence. "A plot to kill. On a massive scale. And we have to work together to stop it. And you were told to meet me here, on this beach."

His jaw dropped. "How—?"

I hugged my elbows, shivering. "I had the same dream. I got instructions from my dream self, too."

His eyes locked onto mine. "What else did you—or she—say?"

I looked away. Just remembering her made me wince. "She was hurt badly, too. Her eyes looked kind of creepy. And she was upset, and crying, and she could barely talk, she was so— she told me she loved life and—" *Don't mention the loving Wolf thing, Liv.* "She said she hoped she was doing the right thing."

He rubbed his chin. "It's all the same. And the me in my dream—he was *emotional,* too."

I wondered if his self had said he loved me.

"You're shaking," he said.

"It's a lot to process."

He extended his hand. "Let's warm up on the sand."

I considered his open palm, waiting and empty. His Progeny palm.

He was squinting at me in the dazzling light. His expression was vulnerable, frightened, hopeful.

My sole reason to trust this Progeny boy was the dream.

Trust Wolf.

But that wasn't enough.

After a stretched-out moment, I folded my arms over my chest and waded out of the ocean alone.

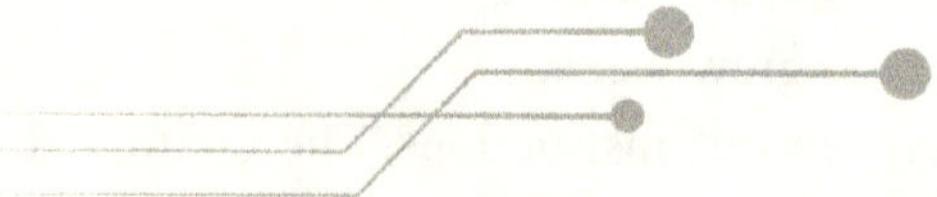

I made it to shore first and sat down, facing the sea, letting the sun and sand calm my shivering. I stared at wave after hypnotic wave, trying to figure out what all of this meant.

After a couple minutes, Wolf splashed out of the surf and sat down beside me, a few arm lengths away. Like it or not, we were in this together. We had to at least discuss the next move.

I steeled myself. "First, I have to know—do you really think we're in a virch game?"

"Where'd you get that idea?" he asked, visibly startled.

"Do you?"

He hesitated. "I have no solid reason to believe this isn't real." With a sigh, he asked, "Did my brother tell you otherwise?"

So either Spiro was lying or Wolf was. "Do you believe our dream selves?"

He picked up a spiraled shell, turning it over in his hands. "I have to. The stakes are too high."

I wrung water from my hair, squeezing harder than necessary. I was supposed to focus on Shell. But he was right about the stakes. If everyone on earth died, that would include my sister.

"Agreed." It pained me to admit that either way, if I failed, Shell would die.

Wolf sucked in a breath. "Who's behind it? Any ideas?"

"That part was blocked out by the noise." I shut my eyes, scanning the dream for a clue. Nothing. "It could be anyone. We need to tell the security team, let them handle it."

"They wouldn't believe us." He studied the waves. "And what if they're in on it?"

Talk about paranoid. But maybe paranoid was a good thing to be in this situation. Or at least cautious. "There has to be someone we can trust," I said. "How about your dad?"

Wolf made a face, shook his head. "What exactly is this guy's plan anyway?"

My gaze landed on a pile of beach debris—old coconut husks, seed pods, insect-laden kelp. Dread churned in my gut, wordless and insistent. I thought of the blood, the welts, the pain. "A bomb, maybe? Or a lot of bombs, if the scale really is planet-level."

He took this in. "Anything else you remember?"

I closed my eyes, dredged through the nightmare. "Something about saving soul. And the panda. Sugarpie, I assume. Guess I'll talk to Spiro about that."

"Careful around my brother. Don't believe—"

"I'll work with you on this dream thing, but don't pull me into any fights with your brother."

Clenching his jaw, Wolf watched a crab skitter across the sand. "Okay."

"Remember anything else?"

He twisted the tiny knob on his watch, held it to his ear. "That we have to act now. But I couldn't tell if we're talking weeks or months or what."

Urgency stabbed me. "Wolf, she said something about two days or even less."

His eyes widened. "That's it?"

"We have to go straight to the top." I stood up, brushing off sand. For once, I had a connection to the über-powerful. Why not use it? "Let's talk to your dad. Now."

"I don't think so." Wolf remained seated.

I slipped on my shirt and shorts. "Why not?"

"He'll think we're nuts. And you have the most to lose here." He tossed a handful of sand into the sea.

Why was he putting up this wall? "I don't want this thing dragging out. Either talk to Casper yourself, or I will." Impatient, I shifted feet.

"He already thinks I'm crazy."

I considered revealing everything Spiro had told me. Instead, I said, "You're Casper's son. He'll have to listen. Unconditional love and all that."

"Love?" Wolf let out a bitter laugh. "He nearly killed me, Liv. And my brother too."

Spiro had mentioned he and his brother were in hell, but what did their dad have to do with it? "What? How?"

Wolf shook his head. "Experiments. I can't—I can't talk about it." He rubbed his face so hard his fingertips dug into his flesh.

I didn't push. Who knew if this was another lie—or part of his virch game delusion—but there was no time to figure it out now. "If you have a better plan to stop a planet-wide crisis in two days, I'm all ears. But your dad's one of the most powerful people in the world. And we have access to him. We'd be crazy not to go to him."

I walked up the beach toward the path while he struggled to keep up, still limping. When we reached the fringes of the forest, I turned to him. "So you're in?"

"I hate my dad." He looked as if a battle was raging inside. "But fact is, the old man has power. A galaxy of it." A long exhalation. "Okay, I'm in."

CHAPTER NINE
Marshmallows

Casper's residence and office took up the entire ninth floor. A hallway lined with private rooms led from the elevator to his waiting room, where Wolf and I now sat on vintage red glass chairs.

Behind a rounded desk, the receptionist was preparing tea. According to him, Casper was in a meeting, which meant we'd have to wait. Indefinitely.

I tried to calm my bouncing knee as the young man handed us clay cups of jasmine tea.

"Thank you." I attempted politeness, but frustration filled me—I was supposed to be in the lab now. How long would we be wasting time here? "Excuse me, sir, but this is an urgent matter—"

"You'll just have to wait, dears." His voice was saccharine. "And call me Wind. There's only one sir around here," he added, with a wry nod to Casper's office.

Exasperated, I sipped the tea, running my finger over a chip at the base of the cup—a tiny imperfection.

I surveyed the holoscape—a peaceful forest clearing, the opposite of how I felt. Flute melodies and sparrow songs drifted from hidden speakers. The room smelled sweet, of pine and wildflowers, almost indistinguishable from the scent of real plants, but somehow cleaned up. These manufactured olfactory delights left out the decaying part of the forest—rotting logs and fungus-laced soil.

Meanwhile, Wind worked at his airscreen, posture perfect as his hands swiped and tapped in the half sphere of space around him. I shifted in my seat, feeling sand stuck between my toes and trapped in my swimsuit. I combed my fingers through my tazzled hair and pulled out some kelp. Not exactly presentable.

Wolf had barely spoken to me on the way back from the beach. Now he fiddled with his watch. Kelp was stuck in his hair, too, but I resisted the urge to pull it out. What was going on inside his mind? Was he reliving the alleged experiments? Or was he just plotting the next move in his supposed virch game?

Over the next twenty minutes, I kept glancing at the airscreen's clock, registering how late I'd be for lab time. Zuggers. I was supposed to be gaining Kiri's trust, getting Shell's treatment.

Finally, the door slid open. Out stepped a man in a turquoise-striped bowtie that matched his tropical-sea-themed hair. He turned back toward the open door and said with a distinctive drawl, "See you bright and early tomorrow!"

"The long-awaited day," said Casper, appearing at the threshold of his office. His clothing today was something from an ancient 2D photo—a red-and-green plaid button-up, collared, and made of a natural fabric. And old-fashioned jeans, complete with zipper, as if he were playing dress-up as a retro. But given his age, these might have been the clothes of his childhood.

"You're the best, Mo." Casper patted his shoulder. "Like a son to me. Even more loyal than any of my own."

"That's my mentor," Wolf murmured with an eye roll. "Mo Boudreaux. Director of the virch research lab."

Mo gave us a quick wave as he breezed out of the waiting room, leaving a cloud of clove cologne in his wake.

Casper's gaze skimmed over us. Then he turned and vanished back into his office.

After the door closed, Wolf said, "Such a loving dad."

I turned to the receptionist, my voice strained yet courteous. "Can we see Casper now?"

He held up a manicured finger. "Patience, my friends."

Wolf shook his head. "My dad's messing with me. He can't stop playing god. Even with his own kid."

After fifteen minutes that felt like fifteen years, a notification sounded on Wind's airscreen. "Casper will see you now," he said.

When he stood up, I noticed a zapper strapped onto his belt. Unsettling. Maybe he did double duty as receptionist and bodyguard. He paused at the entrance as his retina was scanned, then ushered us through the door once it slid open. We entered a vestibule with a second door before us. "Good luck," he said, and returned to his desk.

The door closed behind us. For a moment, I stood beside Wolf in the small, dark space, the only light coming from a glowing blue icon by the door ahead of us. When my eyes adjusted to the dimness, I registered the misery on his face. "You can do this, Wolf."

Breathing deeply, I touched the icon, and the second door slid open.

We stepped into a moonlit forest.

I paused, disoriented, taking in this high-luxe holoscape. I couldn't even make out the walls—there were simply woods all around. The floor beneath was soft, like damp earth, with leaves crunching underfoot. An owl hooo-ed in the corner, its eyes glowing yellow circles. Bats flitted far above our heads. Clouds passed and stars hung in the firmament. In the distance, a wolf howled. Through the trees, orange flames flickered, and smoke rose to the sky.

It made me feel off-balance and on alert. Was it easier for others to sink into these illusions? Was it my lucid-dreaming-testing habit that made me so aware of the impossibility of a nighttime forest inside a room at nine a.m.? Or was it just that these holoscapes were all brand new to me?

Unsure what to do, I moved toward the light.

And promptly walked into a tree. "Ow!" I yelped, rubbing my shoulder. "These are real!"

Wolf stretched out his arms, testing the solidity of the trunks. His hand waved through one and hit another. "Some are holograms, but better to treat them all as real."

Now I was thoroughly bewildered. Squinting in the darkness, hoping no branches would poke an eye out, I stayed close to Wolf. We walked toward the flickering light, weaving around trees, and soon found ourselves at a blazing campfire.

Casper sat on a tree stump, holding three sharp sticks. It felt surreal to see this bigwig in such modest surroundings. He passed one stick to me and one to Wolf. Motioning for us to sit by the fire, Casper handed us each a marshmallow. Then he jammed his onto the end of his stick and held it over the flames.

Wolf and I followed suit. I stared at the fire, uncertain about the etiquette.

"The woods at night," Casper mused. "An infinity of stars above. A fire warming you. It makes a life feel small and insignificant on one hand. And on the other, so close and big. Know what I mean?"

I didn't—after all, it was mostly fake—but I nodded. I did some mental calculations. For the price of this extravagant holoscape, you could clean up the polluted waters of the Cove. You could get comfortable protective gear for workers in the junk heaps. And decent filtration systems. The fortune spent on this could have prevented Shell's illness.

I held my tongue and ate the gooey, warm marshmallow, the first I'd ever had. Too sweet for me, but Shell would have been enamored.

Casper finished chewing his, then looked at me. "Ah, the intern with a social conscience."

"I'm Liv. You have a good memory, sir." Some kind of buttering up felt necessary.

His gaze sharpened, and I wondered if I'd said something wrong, but then he offered a small grin. "Well, my memory's not what it used to be. I remember that I'd go camping with my grandfather and roast marshmallows… but I'm having trouble *feeling* it now. In my bones."

"You've lived such a long life," I said diplomatically. "You have more to remember than most of us."

He tapped his chin, staring at the fire. "I do remember most events of the past century. It's details of the earlier ones, the first fifty years, that have just begun to elude me." He gave an uncomfortable chuckle before turning to Wolf. "Now what's the reason for this emergency appointment, son? Did enlightenment finally strike?" His tone was mocking.

Wolf didn't laugh. "Dad," he began. The word sounded forced. "Liv and I think someone's plotting something violent. With the goal of mass death. On a planetary level."

My stomach sank as I realized how absurd this sounded. On the way here, Wolf and I had strategized how to best communicate our concerns—without coming across as insane. He'd felt that direct was best, but now I had doubts.

Casper smiled. "Oh really. And why would anyone do that?"

"Who knows," Wolf said flatly. "The joy of destroying humanity?"

After a beat, Casper wheezed in laughter, slapped his knee. Once he caught his breath, he looked at me. "You let him pull you into these shenanigans?"

Heat rushed to my face. I was glad for the dim light.

Casper pierced another marshmallow with his stick and held it over the fire, watching it expand and darken. "You should be focusing on this once-in-a-lifetime opportunity, not getting distracted by Nelson's delusions. You're a gem in the rubble. A scientist minnow."

The last thing I wanted was to talk about my background. I tried to get back on track. "Wolf and I have good reason to believe this threat. We just need you to—"

Casper waved my words away with his stick. "Oh my dear. You do realize my son is not sound of mind. He's only here as a kindness. A charity case."

I glanced at Wolf. He was sunk low, caving in on himself.

Casper's marshmallow caught fire, and he blew it out. "Really, I thought you were smart enough to understand his pathology."

The insult-compliment felt like a kick to the stomach. *Was Wolf mentally ill?* That's what his brother claimed—his brother, who Wolf had *assaulted.* And he had hurled himself into the ocean in a possibly suicidal fit.

Then again, I was in an unfamiliar world that operated by the strange rules of the rich and famous. Maybe I was more naïve than I'd thought.

Wolf was rubbing his temple, slouched in his seat, a curtain of hair over his eyes. He'd shut down—more fodder for his father's accusations.

Meanwhile, Casper slid the blackened, burnt skin from the marshmallow and popped it into his mouth, leaving behind an oozing blob.

Again, I glanced at Wolf. The dream me was so certain about trusting him. *Loving* him.

"Please, sir," I said, "even if you don't believe Wolf, you have to believe me. I have a strong feeling we're in danger. And it starts here, on this island."

"Oh, a *feeling*." He gave me a patronizing grin. "Tell me then, who's behind this dastardly plot? And how will this mastermind go about killing off humanity?"

I said nothing.

"No evidence? My son's just convinced you of his conspiracy theory?" He slurped his remaining marshmallow goo. "You're a scientist, my dear. You should know the importance of evidence."

"But with so much at stake, it can't hurt to look into it."

He reached down and stuck a new marshmallow onto the stick, held it above the flame. "You want to talk about motives? Nelson went off the deep end last year, ran off to a Tibetan monastery. Lost a grip on reality. Started coming up with his own fantastical theories."

Tibet? That was the last place I'd guessed he'd been hiding.

Casper chuckled. "And now he's back. You're worried about someone plotting revenge and destruction? Well, look no farther than the boy beside you." He flashed unnaturally glowing-white teeth.

I felt the need to come to Wolf's defense. "I-I trust him." At least more than I trusted this man who treated his own son like dirt on his shoe.

Casper rubbed his jowls and gave me look of pity. "You don't have much experience in our world, do you, dear?"

I rose, face burning with humiliation. Wolf was useless at the moment, a husk of a person. I took a brazen step toward Casper. "Sir, I'm just asking you to look into this matter. Put the security guards on high alert. Run through safety drills. Make sure no weapons get into the wrong hands."

He studied me, face impassive.

Shaking, I turned on my heel. Weaving through the trees, I pushed aside real branches, then felt off-balance as my hand passed through others. I wondered if I was the first person ever to walk away from Casper, mid-conversation, in disgust. Probably. I just wished I could find my way through this ridiculous forest to the door. And I hoped I hadn't ruined my mission.

"Wait," Casper barked. "Come back."

I braced myself, breathed in the wood smoke and burnt-sugared air. I turned. Past the trees, his face was obscured by branches and shadows and smoke. Gathering my strength, stretching tall, I walked back to the edge of the clearing and stopped, arms crossed.

He slid a new marshmallow onto his stick. "The last thing I want is more fodder for gossip, especially something as absurd as this. The paparazzi would have a field day with more of Nelson's dramas."

Holding his marshmallow over the flames, he added, "I can't have the masses thinking we let psychologically unfit interns in our program. They need to have confidence in Virchuous." He frowned. "You will not breathe a word of your suspicions to anyone. Neither of you. As you well know, I could easily ship you both off the island."

Casper's marshmallow swelled and deepened brown, melting and sagging on the end of the stick. He rotated it, letting the other side bubble and blister. "Now, Nelson," he continued, as if he were speaking to a young child, "you're clearly fond of this girl. You don't want to see her dreams destroyed. See *her* destroyed." He paused, letting this sink in, then leaned in toward Wolf. "Am I understood?"

Wolf made a grunt—of assent or defiance, it was impossible to tell.

Casper turned to me, held up his marshmallow stick like a scolding finger. "Understood?"

I ground my teeth. Crickets chirped. An owl called. A bat flitted by my head. My moon shadow stretched over the mossy ground, so much taller than my real self. I felt… small. Powerless. Worst of all, I'd jeopardized my chance at saving Shell.

The old man gave a smug smile, brushing a finger over his caramelized marshmallow, testing the consistency.

Wolf shifted on the tree stump, tucked a curl behind his ear. Even in the dim light, I could see the veins in his forehead popping out.

As sudden as lightning, he lunged toward his father, grabbed the man's marshmallow stick.

Casper wobbled as Wolf held the stick over the blue center of the flames. Within seconds, the tip caught fire and he swung it close to his father's face. Casper flinched, drew back his head, scooted to the back of his tree stump seat.

Standing over him, Wolf spoke in a growl. "If you hurt her, I'll kill you."

I held my breath, waiting to see what Wolf would do to his father. And what his father would do to him. Casper could probably have Wind in here zapping us in ten seconds flat, followed by that giant security guy, Borg.

Wolf turned to me and tossed the stick into the fire. The blackened marshmallow dissolved in the flames. He grabbed my hand and led me into the forest, walking fast. The farther we got from his dad, the calmer Wolf grew. I pulled my hand from his as I navigated the tree trunks and branches.

With the exit in sight, he moved a pine bough aside for me and whispered, "Thanks, Angel."

I tried to catch my breath. "For what?"

"You must be the first person in—in *forever* who's stood up to my dad." He paused. "You made me realize I could do it, too." His mouth turned up at the corner. "But I probably shouldn't have threatened an old man."

My blood was pounding, but I tried to keep my cool. "Marshmallows should be a weapon of last resort."

"Seriously, Liv, thank you."

I stared at him. "So *are* you deluded, Wolf?"

"Aren't we all?"

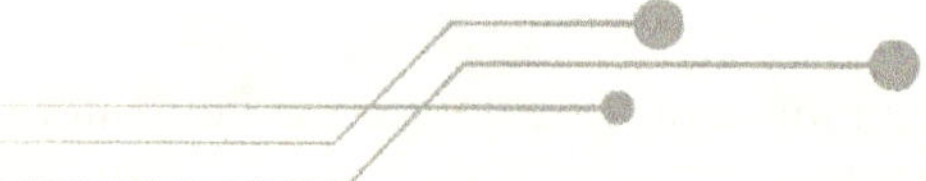

We reached the first door and entered the vestibule. In the darkness, I paused, trying to sort my own thoughts. Did I think Wolf was sane? No, not really. Did I trust him? No, not really.

But my dream self's voice was so certain, so firm, so desperate.

Forget the state of Wolf's mind. There's no time to waste. Find a plan B to prevent the disaster. Then focus on Shell.

"I'll see Kiri soon," I whispered. "I'll confide in her. Maybe she has some pull with the security department."

"Why do you think you can trust these people?" asked Wolf. "You assume they're responsible adults or decent human beings. How do you know she won't call you crazy and get security to lock you up?"

Talk about paranoid. "Kiri's just a few years older than us, but she's got power. And a good heart. And she's brilliant. I trust her, okay?"

The contours of Wolf's face shone in the light of the door-open icon. He looked torn. "Fine."

Trust Wolf. I would only trust him at arm's length. I wouldn't reveal that I was from a Null Zone or why I was really here. The stakes were too high. If I somehow ended up on his bad side and he reported me, I'd be sent to a refugee camp far from everyone and everything I loved. And Shell would die.

"What'll you do now?" I asked.

"Guess I'll go to the virch lab, test the waters with my mentor. I doubt he'll take us seriously, though. Seems like Mo and dear ol' dad are buds, practically father and son." Wolf paused. "I have another idea, too."

"What?"

He glanced at his watch. The dial glowed firefly yellow. "Too dangerous to tell you in the building. Hidden cameras. During free time, let's meet at our place. I'll explain then."

Hidden cameras? Classic paranoid delusion of the "they're watching us" variety.

I thought of Casper's threat to send me home. To destroy me, whatever that meant. How far was I willing to go? Would I be endangering my mission to save Shell?

As if sensing my quandary, Wolf said, "If you don't want to take the risk—well, I'd understand."

I studied his glowing face, asked myself if *I* was deluded. At the heart and soul of it, I didn't want to die. And I didn't want Shell to die. And I didn't want humankind to die.

The image of my dream self, tortured and desperate, flashed in my mind. Real or illusion, I had to believe her.

"Well, what do you say, Liv?"

Everything depends on you. On you and Wolf.

"Okay. Let's do this."

CHAPTER TEN
Project Dragon

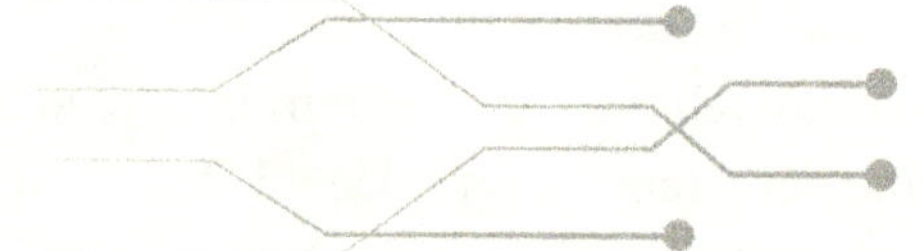

I stopped by my room to rinse off and change into clean clothes. Via the airscreen, I messaged Kiri a quick apology for being late. Late for my second day of the internship. *Way to make an impression, Liv.* But the threat of mass destruction made my priorities clear. I had to believe that Kiri would feel the same way, and that she would know what to do next.

Heart still hammering, I tore off my shirt and shorts and hung them on hooks. I peeled off my swimsuit and shook out the sand, hoping a 'bot would deal with the mess. Remembering the possibility of hidden cameras, I glanced around the room, but there were only the tiny projectors for the airscreen. As I headed into the bathroom, I rubbed the tension from my neck and tried to make sense of things.

One thing was certain: I'd just made a bad impression on the most powerful person on the island—maybe in the world. A burnt-marshmallow feeling settled in my gut.

I set the shower to Peaceful Sprinkle and stepped inside, rinsing away sand. I clung to the hope that Kiri could help us. She struck me as familiar enough with the facility to figure out what was going on. And to stop it.

After my two-minute, not-so-Peaceful Sprinkle, I put on a white tank and the tan shorts. The entire time, my dream tumbled around in my mind, the terrifying parts tangled up with the weirdly romantic parts. The loving Wolf thing…

Love.

I stuck my hand in the shorts' pocket to check for any more hand-stitched love messages. I pulled out a fabric scrap, a muted twilight-blue color, which read FLY in silver stitches.

I smiled and resisted checking my other shorts, wanting to spread out Delfina's gifts, savor each one. FLY. What did she mean by that? I'd told her about the heron on the junk heaps after Shell's hibernation. Was it a reference to the bird? The messages were like the Buddhist koans I'd encountered in my philosophy elective—riddles meant to somehow enlighten you.

I tucked the FLY message back into my right pocket and retrieved the LOVE message from the other pair of shorts. Slipping the scrap of LOVE into my left pocket, I hurried toward the lab. The gifts in my pockets made me feel stronger— charms from a fairy godmother, secret powers to battle whatever was to come.

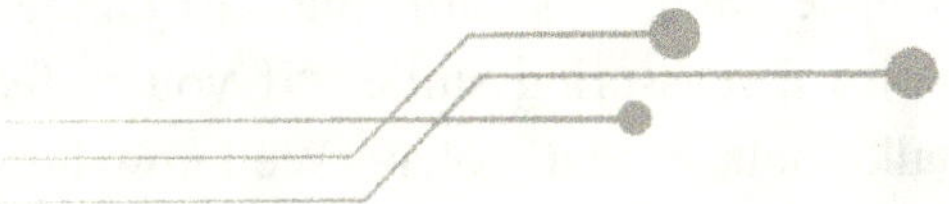

Zipping past busts of ancient gods, I half jogged down the Greek-holoscaped hallway, around marble columns. Through the interior window, I saw Spiro in the lab. From the bag, his panda's fuzzy face poked out, its droopy eyelids heart-wrenching.

Save the panda. The creature was already terminally ill with a rare virus—how could I save it? Develop a cure? And what, if anything, did that have to do with preventing the destruction of humanity?

Spiro and Kiri were talking, heads close over steaming mugs. When I entered, they looked up and smiled. "Morning, Liv," Kiri said, bright-eyed.

"Hi. Sorry I'm late. Something came up."

"Oh, no problem. Coffee?"

"I'm good."

Eyeing Sugarpie, I drew in a breath. How much to divulge? *Save the panda.* I could start with that. Wolf had warned me to be careful around Spiro. I suspected it had more to do with sibling rivalry than reason—still, I measured my words. "Hey, Spiro. I'd like to help you save Sugarpie."

He did a double take. "Really?"

I leaned against the counter beside him. "Could you tell me the name of her illness? I can research it, and once I'm up to speed, we can brainstorm ideas."

Kiri beamed. "That is so sweet, Liv!"

"Yeah, thanks." Spiro stroked his cheek, considering. "I'll message you about it."

Two days. That's what my dream self had said. Time was of the essence. "Could you just tell me now?"

The silence hung, awkward, and Kiri jumped to the rescue, offering Spiro a reassuring smile. "If you're feeling too emotional to talk about it, that's okay. We know how close you are to Sugarpie."

"Oh, right, sorry." I glanced at Spiro, whose face was now buried in the panda's fur.

When he didn't respond, I leaned toward Kiri and asked softly, "Hey, can I talk to you?"

"Sure." She looked at me expectantly.

"I mean, just the two of us?"

Spiro kept stroking Sugarpie, his jaw tensing at my question. Great, the last thing I wanted was to make him feel excluded or give him a reason to dislike me.

Kiri glanced at him. "Liv, the three of us, we're partners. Friends. A family, even. Complete with a pet," she added, motioning toward the panda.

I nodded. She was tough to figure out. When she was talking science, her brilliance shone through. Other times, the *child* part of the former child prodigy took the wheel—trying so hard to be liked.

"Well, okay." I opened my mouth to share my concerns. Then I remembered the hidden cameras. Just in case, Kiri's office might offer more privacy. "Could we all talk in your office?"

She gave me a strange look, then a shrug, and led both Spiro and me inside a small room with blinds over the interior glass walls. A single, neat desk and three chairs. A few hovering images of family and vacations.

I tried to arrange my thoughts, figure out what to say. Then it hit me. Spiro was Casper's son. The old man had threatened Wolf and me, and if word got back to him that we weren't letting this go, he might send us off the island. I scrambled to find an approach that wouldn't get us in trouble. "I'm wondering if— if there are any weapons of mass destruction on this island."

Kiri widened her eyes.

"Planning to blow something up?" Spiro asked.

I rubbed my temple. "Just wondering about safety protocols."

Spiro let out a long sigh. "Been talking with my brother, huh?"

I kept my eyes on Kiri, who smiled kindly.

"Well," she said, "weapons are prohibited here, just like on the mainland. The security staff just carries zappers. A little smuggling goes on by cargo pilots on the airstrip across the island, but that's mostly illegal food additives and mood pills and whatnot."

"Anything else?" I pressed.

Measuring her words, she said, "We do have classified research going on in the Biohaz Lab." She nodded to the sealed-off lab behind us. "I'm limited in how much I can say about it."

I glanced at the interior wall, where BIOHAZARD was stamped in large orange letters. Through the thick glass, I glimpsed a series of decontamination chambers that must lead into the actual lab, hidden behind an opaque barrier. Squinting, I could just make out a row of biohaz suits on hangers in the vestibule. "Like… bioweapon research?"

She spoke carefully. "Project Dragon, we call it. A genetically engineered virus that has the potential to be a deadly epidemic. The ultimate bioweapon. We've developed it to stay ahead of the game, come up with treatments and vaccines before we need them. Of course, as interns, you won't be involved in that project."

Even in the Cove we'd heard of the bio-attacks of 2139 and 2142. I was a little kid then, but I remembered they'd been nipped in the bud, just a few hundred deaths. Now people seemed more worried about space weapons like targeted asteroid bits and burgeoning easy-fusion bomb technology.

And the Virch Empire had calmed most bigger global conflicts in the past decade. In my current events elective, we'd learned that the corporation was more effective than our faltering government at keeping world order—the empire had too much business to lose if sanctions were placed or war broke out.

Still, a leaked bioweapon could spell deaths for millions, even billions.

"Sounds dangerous," I said finally, my thoughts racing.

Kiri waved a hand. "Don't worry, we have a strict policy for decontam. If the virus escaped, the island would go into lockdown. We'd give the anti-viral serum to everyone at risk of exposure in the immediate area, and then, in a wider circle, we'd give the vaccine serum. The serums are still in experimental phases, but effective according to virch models. For now, we have plenty on hand in case of emergency. And of course, we'd quarantine everyone for several weeks."

My face must have shown fear—she paused, offering a sympathetic look. "Liv, you seem irrationally anxious. There's nothing to be concerned about, okay?"

I gave a dazed nod. I'd been focused on bombs because of my dream self's physical traumas. But what if . . .?

Looking curious, Spiro joined in the conversation. "What are the symptoms, Kiri?"

Her eyes flicked uncertainly around the room.

When Spiro leaned in with a smile, she brightened. She was an insecure girl, trying to fit in with the cool kids. "I'm not supposed to go into too much detail with you. Just keep it in this room so that the other interns don't freak out, okay?"

"Of course." I gave an emphatic nod.

"Fever, chills, rash, severe abdominal pain…"

As her list progressed, I saw my dream self clutching her stomach and spotted with what I'd assumed were burn welts and abrasions—but could have been rashes.

I forced down rising panic as Kiri continued. "Delirium, dilated pupils…"

My dream self's eyes had been black gaping holes. Zombie eyes.

"Organ failure, and death," she finished.

I reached out to steady myself against the desk. *Don't faint, Liv.* My mouth was dry and my head on fire and my throat closing. *Breathe.*

"Hey, you okay?" Kiri put her hand on my shoulder.

"Mhm." What if my dream self hadn't been the victim of an explosion? What if she'd been *infected?* Any last hope that Wolf's and my dreams were random coincidences fled. Our unconscious minds couldn't have come up with this precise set of symptoms independently. This was proof that our dreams had meaning.

"What about bleeding?" I heard myself ask.

"Internally, yes. And possible bleeding out through nose, mouth, and eyes."

Was my dream self actually my future self, returning to warn my present self? Or were Wolf and I psychic, glimpsing the future? I couldn't shake the feeling that there was a *me* out there somewhere, a *me* with the virus, a *me* that was desperate and suffering.

"Liv," Kiri said, concern in her voice. "We've got so many safety measures in place. There's no way you could get infected. And even if you somehow did, we'd treat you right away. Okay?"

I nodded.

She patted my shoulder. "Is this why you wanted to talk in private? You were scared and embarrassed? Well, don't worry, Spiro understands, too."

"Sure," he murmured.

I wanted to say more, warn her about the dreams—but I'd have to catch her alone for that. Spiro would only turn her against his brother, and for now, Wolf and I were a team. "I feel better, Kiri." I forced a grateful smile. "I'll just get to work."

"Great, Liv. Now why don't you continue with the practice assignment? I'm gonna steal Spiro for a bit. My colleagues wanted to meet him."

Of course the other scientists would jump at a chance to meet a Progeny. And Kiri was right to assume I needed time to compose myself alone. The mindless task of dropping dye into petri dishes would give me a chance to calm down.

But when I watched the red liquid drip, all I could think of was blood.

CHAPTER ELEVEN
The Panda

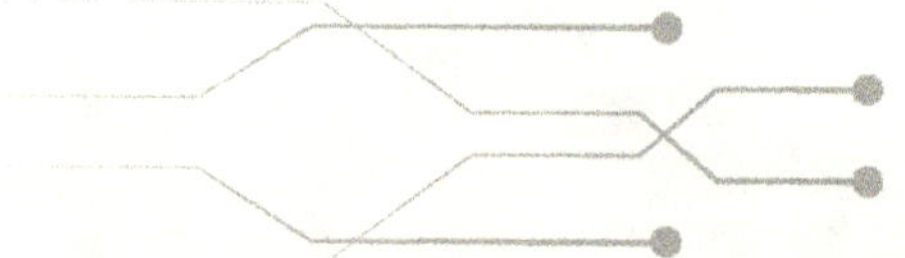

ave the panda. That was relatively straightforward. The idea that my dream self somehow had a deadly virus—a virus that could destroy humanity—was too much to process. Pausing my lab work, I pulled up an airscreen and consulted articles on pathologies affecting giant pandas. None of the diseases were incurable.

Every few minutes, I checked on the bear, stroking its giant head and soothing my own nerves. Its fur was surprisingly coarse and it smelled like sour milk. Did all baby pandas smell that way or just the sick ones?

After a half hour of fruitless searching, I heard the creature gurgle and rasp. I jumped up, knocking over a bottle of red dye. The liquid formed a puddle on the counter and began to drip onto the white floor. The test tube rolled off the edge and shattered.

As I examined Sugarpie, the creature's eyes rolled back and it collapsed.

With alarm, I picked it up—a heavy, limp ball of fur in my arms. Cradling the animal, I jogged down the hallway, panting as I stumbled down the emergency stairs, too impatient for the elevator. Remembering the infirmary that I'd passed on the ground level, I headed straight there. Maybe Delfina's aunt could help me—the doctor with the big heart.

In the infirmary's reception area, two women sat at a desk. The one in nurse's scrubs didn't greet me, absorbed in the air-screen before her. The other woman looked a little older than my father, with gray-white hair in dozens of braids like snowy willow branches falling against dark skin. She didn't notice me either, too focused on something on her lap—a yellow ball of yarn. Was she *knitting*?

"Excuse me," I said, struggling to catch my breath. My arms ached beneath the weight of the panda.

She looked up from her half-finished scarf and brightened. "Good morning!" Then her eyes traveled to the giant, motion-less fuzz ball in my arms. "Oh my stars!"

She took the flaccid bundle from my arms, whisked us into a private room. "I'm Doctor Nguyen-Obi. Call me Zinnia."

"Thanks," I managed to eke out.

She didn't look like Delfina, but I remembered she was an aunt by marriage. Her eyes, though, brimmed with the same compassion as my teacher's.

I followed the doctor inside, then watched her examine the creature with tender, expert hands. "By any chance, are you Delfina Estrada's aunt?" I asked.

She lit up. "Yes! You know her?"

"She's—" I choked up just thinking about her. I *missed* her. "She's like a mother to me. She's the reason I'm here. She sends you love."

Zinnia's eyes teared up. "I wish I could keep in closer touch with her. My favorite niece." She lowered her voice. "They're strict about off-island communication here. Paranoid about classified information getting out." With a sigh, she added, "We're pretty much limited to holiday and birthday cards, and even those are monitored."

She grabbed a scanner and pressed it to the cub's temple, where presumably its virchip had been implanted. "You'll have to tell me all about Delfina after we help this panda."

"Definitely," I said.

Zinnia studied the medical jargon on the airscreen, furrowing her eyebrows. "Hmm. No sign of illness or injury."

"You mean except for the rare virus?"

"Virus?" She looked at me, forehead creased. "No indication of any virus. White blood count is completely normal."

I took this in. "So, what's wrong with the panda?"

"She appears dehydrated and malnourished. Neglected. And her heartbeat and breathing rate are dangerously slow. She has very low oxygen levels. When did she lose consciousness?"

"Just a few minutes ago."

"Good, there's time." She hooked the cub up to a machine, programmed in the instructions. Within moments, Sugarpie's eyes fluttered open.

I breathed out in relief. "Will she be okay?"

Zinnia shut the door. "She's been overdosed with mild tranquilizers. Long-term and chronic use." She shook her head. "An endangered giant panda. She can't be more than a few months old. Drugged since birth." Her gaze fell. "This is Spiro's latest pet, isn't it? A so-called rescue animal?"

"He thought she had a rare virus. I guess she was misdiagnosed…" My voice trailed off. "Maybe the tranquilizer was part of her treatment plan. To keep her comfortable until—"

"Well, it certainly makes her docile." Zinnia smoothed the animal's fur. "She's only been half-conscious all her life. Easy to tote around and cute people out."

I gaped at her. She thought Spiro had done this on purpose?

She lifted a shoulder when she saw my look. "The Progeny live by their own rules." Her jaw tensed. "Animals are trendy accessories in their world. It's Spiro's brand, right?"

I took this in. "But he cares about her."

Zinnia's gentle eyes hardened. "My guess? He's drugging the creature for his own benefit. The whole rare disease thing is a lie. A way for Spiro to manipulate his fans' emotions. In my experience, that's how the Progeny operate."

It seemed too terrible to believe. Hand trembling, I reached out to touch Sugarpie's fur. She whimpered. *Save the panda,* my dream self had said. She'd predicted this. She'd warned me. And she'd warned me, too, of something with much bigger consequences.

Overwhelmed, I felt tears burn my eyes. Zinnia reached out, pulled me toward her. She had a generous, substantial build. She was a *presence*. A warm and comforting presence. You could imagine lots of children and puppies scooped up in those arms over the years. "What's your name, sweetie?"

"Liv."

"Liv, you just saved this panda's life. We'll keep her here another few hours, maybe a day or two, hydrate and nourish her, get the drugs out of her system. Nano-tech and slow-release pills will help with the withdrawal."

"So she'll live?"

"Yes. Thanks to you." She paused. "Come back to chat soon, okay? I'll give you a knit scarf for Delfina. I want to hear all about her life now. And yours."

"Of course. Thank you." I stood up. "I should tell Spiro about his panda."

Zinnia gripped my shoulder and gave me a long look. "Obviously, my niece trusts you. Cares about you. So I feel responsible for you. I trust you, too." Her voice lowered, urgent. *"Liv, be careful."*

Shaken, I waited for her to say more, but she just gave my shoulder a squeeze and walked me out.

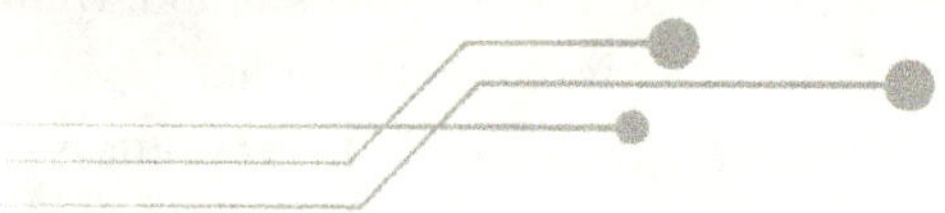

I headed down the corridor toward the lab, my nerves frazzled. The panda's near-death experience made memories of Shell's last day alive flood back to me.

When my sister's health had spiraled downward, Dad and I had scrounged together money—with help from Delfina. We'd snuck Shell onto a junk ship to Northern Maryland and brought her to a health clinic.

After her virchip scan, the doctor had explained that the treatment was a kind of "orphan drug," which made its cost exorbitant. The only people who needed the drug were Nulls like us, exposed to toxic heavy metals through our work in the junk heaps. And we didn't have money to pay. The sharks had no motivation to make the treatments cheaper or more accessible.

The doctor said we could place Shell in a state of suspended animation to buy us time to find funds. Delfina was generous enough to pay for hibernation, but she didn't even have a fraction of the cost for the treatment Shell needed. It was a staggering sum, even for sharks.

In the clinic, when we were saying our goodbyes to Shell before her hibernation, my heart froze. Were we doing the right thing?

Her eyes were closed and she made no movements besides her chest rising and falling with weak breath.

Holding her limp hand, Delfina whispered, "It'll feel like a long, peaceful sleep, *mijita.*"

I hoped Shell heard "my little daughter," but she stayed motionless.

"And when you wake up," I added, "you'll have your treatment. I promise." I lowered my head to hers. Her shiny acorn hair intermingled with my brown frizz. My nose touched her cheek.

Dad kissed her forehead. "We'll see you again soon, sweetie."

The nurse changed Shell into a whisper-thin, tight garment. Next, the doctor began putting her to sleep, monitoring her descent via airscreen.

I held my sister's hand, bowed my head, and pressed my damp face against our interlaced fingers. "I'm so sorry, Shell."

And to my surprise, she spoke. "It's okay." Her voice was a raspy whisper, so soft I could barely make out her words. "Let me go."

I shook my head, tears spilling. Beside me, Dad was red-eyed, his face crumbling. He held her other hand to his lips.

"Please, Livvy," she said, "remember to…"

Somehow I found my voice from the ocean floor. "Remember to *what,* Shelly?"

"Remember to…" She let out a breath.

A long silence.

"She's under," said the doctor, moving quickly to the next step: replacing her fluids with a protectant to avoid cell damage.

Dad and Delfina and I held each other, watching the nurse move my sister into a coffin-like box that slid from the wall like a drawer. It looked like pictures of ancient crypts or mortuaries.

Shell is not dead yet, I reminded myself as more tears slid out.

The doctor spoke mechanically as he programmed instructions into the airscreen. "The patient's body temperature will be lowered and her metabolic activities will shut down. Preservatives will fill the container. We'll monitor her via virchip."

"I know she's still alive," Dad said, wiping his eyes. "But it feels like she's—she's gone."

The doctor tilted his head. "Well, actually, she'll be in biostasis, which is technically dead, with potential for revival. And as we discussed, the upper limit for hibernation is one year."

Technically dead? My head spun.

"Just rest, Shell," I whispered. Inside my head, the words "in peace" followed. *Rest in peace.*

No, no, no. This wasn't her death. This was a step to bringing her fully back to life. It had to be.

And now, ten months later—with only two months left—I held onto the hope of bringing Shell to life again. I imagined her spirit out there, face upturned to the ocean sky like she was drinking up every last drop. Here on the island, her treatment was within my reach.

I'd managed to save the panda, with Zinnia's help. Now I just had to figure out how to save soul—whatever that meant— and prevent the crisis. Then, most importantly, bring the cure to my sister.

Minutes later, I walked into the lab. Kiri's office blinds were drawn. Maybe she was in there, or maybe she and Spiro were still with the other scientists. I paced the lab, unable to bring myself to drop red dye into a petri dish. My mess had been cleaned up, maybe by a 'bot.

The office door opened and out stepped Spiro, saying good-bye to Kiri. They must have gone into the office before I'd returned. And closed the blinds.

"Oh, hey, Liv." He glanced around the room, under counters and tables. His brow wrinkled. "Thought Sugarpie was with you."

"She doesn't have a virus, Spiro." I steadied my voice. "She's just been drugged."

I expected him to be shocked, or *act* shocked, or at least offer an explanation. Instead, exhaustion weighed down his face. "You don't understand, Liv. Nothing's what you think."

"Then tell me."

He shook his head. "This is a waste of my time," he mumbled, his face flushing with emotions I couldn't comprehend. "There are easier ways to do this."

"What are you talking about?"

Ignoring me, he opened the door to the hallway, glanced right then left, and vanished through the doorway.

Moments later, Kiri came out of her office. "Liv, you okay? You left a mess in the lab."

"Sugarpie's been drugged and—"

"Liv." Kiri held up her palm. "Listen, I'll be honest. I just got a message from Casper. He said you and Nelson were causing trouble, making false claims. Paranoid stuff." She gave an exasperated sigh. "I care about you and Spiro. You're my mentees." Another sigh. "But his brother's violent and delusional. Stay away from Nelson, okay?"

"But Kiri, there's something going on—"

"Liv," she warned, pressing her fingers to her temple. Each nail featured a whale in indigo waters. "I don't have time for intern scandals or mental health issues. That's Soraya's job. But here's the bottom line. I put myself on the line to bring you here. So please, prove me right."

I wanted to defend myself. I wanted to explain everything. But without evidence to counter Casper's message, she wouldn't believe me.

Then there was the heartbreak of my mentor thinking I'd let her down. I needed her to show me the treatment for Shell. So far, I'd only made her suspicious and wary of me. Now I just hoped she wouldn't have me sent off the island.

Sighing, she shook her head and disappeared into her office.

Part of me wanted to break more test tubes. Part of me wanted to curl up in the corner and cry. And part of me knew I had to make a decision.

Things were happening on this island, things hidden beneath the shiny silver surface. And I had to reveal them. Saving Shell and the panda and soul and humanity were somehow all tied together. I'd do whatever it took.

I sped out the door just in time to see Spiro at the far end of the hallway, stepping into the elevator. I ran after him.

CHAPTER TWELVE
Carnival

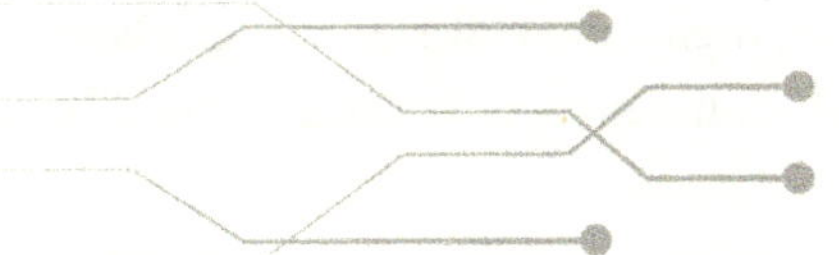

I raced down the corridor, beneath the Parthenon, past a statue of Artemis with her bow and arrow. In my path, sheep grazed among olive trees. Bracing myself, I ran straight through them, hoping they were holograms. They were.

Ahead, the elevator doors closed, Spiro oblivious to my approach. Where was he going? Why wasn't he looking for Sugarpie? Was the panda really just an accessory?

Moments later, I skidded to a stop in front of the just-closed doors. The floor numbers were flashing higher, so I touched the UP icon, catching my breath. The numbers stopped on nine.

Casper's floor.

I sucked in a breath and watched the numbers lower again. The last thing I needed was another confrontation with Casper. His words haunted me: *See her dreams destroyed. See* her *destroyed.*

The elevator doors opened and I darted inside. My belly lurched as I rose to the ninth floor. This elevator was a medieval castle turret holoscape, with velvet-framed windows overlooking peasants tilling fields, knights fencing, princesses riding white horses. I longed to stay in here wrapped in flute melodies, riding up and down all day in this protected tower, away from the crushing pressure of the real world.

But I had to find out what was going on.

When the doors opened again, I stepped into jarring African grasslands, complete with hippos, lions, giraffes. No humans.

Spiro must have already made it down the hallway and entered his dad's waiting room. I ran across the savannah, keeping clear of a yawning lion. Along the way, I passed closed doors that Wolf had mentioned were his dad's private quarters— bedrooms and lounges and bathroom-spas, each with distinct mini-worlds.

I paused outside the waiting room and peered through the door's window. Inside, Spiro was arguing with the receptionist, who was blocking Casper's office entrance. Spiro yelled until Wind lost his composure and pulled out his zapper.

Undeterred, Spiro banged on his father's door. His shouts carried through the walls. "Dad, it's Spiro! Open up!"

Wind stood there with his zapper, pleading with Spiro, who was now hurling his body against the door. When it finally slid open, he stumbled inside.

A frazzled Wind followed on his heels.

Heart hammering, I took the opportunity to slip inside the waiting room, which required no retinal scan. Meanwhile, the door to Casper's office was whispering shut.

It was on the far end of the room, past a row of chairs and a table, still holding the teacups from Wolf's and my visit earlier today.

In a gamble, I grabbed a teacup. With an underhand toss, I flung it toward the shrinking gap. The cup skidded between frame and door, wedging it just centimeters open. Somehow the cup hadn't broken, only spilled a puddle of jasmine tea at the threshold.

After a stunned moment, I ran over and jammed in my hand, pushing the door open and kicking the cup out of the way. The interior vestibule doors had already closed, leaving me alone in the small, dark space, pulse thundering in my ears. My thoughts caught up with my actions. *What the fratch are you doing, Liv?*

If there was a fast track to getting the boot, this was it. Sneaking into the office of Casper himself? Spying on him and his son? He'd welcome the excuse to make me disappear.

I imagined what was happening on the other side of the door. By now, Spiro had probably made his way to the campfire with Wind on his tail. There was probably a confrontation with raised voices, which meant I might be able to sneak inside.

Two days left to stop the mass destruction. I had to take the risk, follow the lead. I'd hide in the tree shadows and listen in on their conversation. I just wished I had my virchlens to record the evidence.

I touched the blue open icon. The door slid open, and I stepped through.

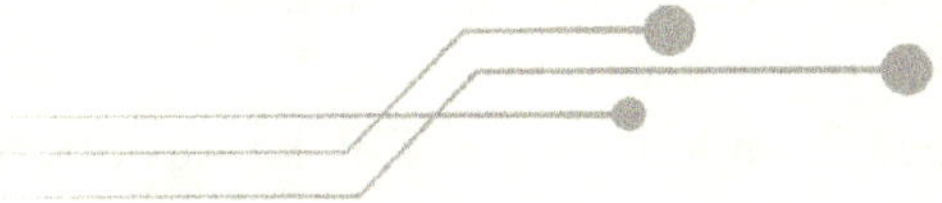

Blinking, I shielded my eyes, blinded by sunshine on a blazing hot day. I was standing in an expansive field, blue skies overhead. All around me, people milled and music blared and lights flashed and rides zipped. A Ferris wheel towered above, rotating slowly. Legs dangled and faces beamed. To my left, a roller coaster swept its cars up and down and around as people shrieked, arms flailing.

Each ride had its own soundtrack, creating a cacophony of rhythms and melodies, along with children's laughter and squeals. Sweet, greasy scents mixed on the breeze—cotton candy and fried dough and caramel corn.

I reeled, my senses overwhelmed—I'd been expecting a dark forest. My breath quickened as my brain caught up with the holoscape before me. This was some kind of fairground, maybe circa the early 2000s, judging by the crowd. People were staring at old-fashioned phones, either holding them up to take 2D photos or cradling them, heads and shoulders hunched. That technology was a short-lived phenomenon, I'd learned in history class, because of the chronic pain and skeletal deformities resulting from the posture.

Casper would have been a child during this era, just after the turn of the millennium. Was this another sentimental walk down memory lane for him?

I scanned the crowd for him and Spiro and Wind. The holograms looked so real, it felt like searching for three people among hundreds. When I stubbed my toe walking into a real arcade game, I realized that this landscape, too, was a mix of reality and illusion.

I almost walked into a cotton candy stand next, but skidded to a halt when I heard Casper's voice.

"Cotton candy rocks my world."

I zeroed in on him. Mouth full, he was offering bags of turquoise fluff to Spiro and Wind.

I backed away, then ducked behind a real, rusted fortune-telling machine. Behind thick glass was a mechanized puppet—a wizened, scarf-clad woman, nodding her head and haltingly moving her arms. She only existed from the waist up, like a doll cut in half. Her eerie, garbled voice came from a speaker. "What does your future hold? Wealth? Work? Luck? Love? Hear the Mysterious Esmeralda tell your fortune from the beyond."

Maybe I could catch Casper's conversation over the fortune-teller's recorded loop. Crouching down, I peered around the corner just as Spiro grabbed a bag cotton candy from his father and threw it to the ground. He stomped it once, hard. No pop, just a slow hiss of air.

Casper chuckled as though his child were having a temper tantrum, then proffered a bag to Wind.

"Oh, why thank you, sir." Wind took the bag, plucking a small piece. "Excellent."

"Leave us now, Wind," Casper said with a dismissive nod.

The receptionist shot a worried glance at Spiro. "But sir, is that a wise idea considering—"

"Leave us."

Like an obedient dog, Wind walked toward the door, taking a path right past me. I held my breath, hoped he wouldn't notice me. But he was clearly preoccupied, his expression distraught, his cotton candy forgotten at his side. When the door closed behind him, I released my breath.

Casper shoved the last bit of candy into his mouth, licked his fingers, and tossed the empty bag on the ground. He brought up an airscreen, then swept and tapped sticky fingers—issuing instructions? In one swift movement, he reached out and pulled his son backward by the arm.

"What the—?" Spiro shrugged away but stopped as something enormous emerged from the floor. It rose straight through the hologram of a juggling busker.

I gasped in disbelief.

It was a merry-go-round.

And it was real.

I knew because Casper stepped onto it and motioned for Spiro, who reluctantly hopped on after him. The ride began revolving, horses moving up and down. With effort, Casper climbed onto a black stallion then nodded to the chestnut horse beside him.

With a defiant eye roll, Spiro climbed onto a different horse—a white mare several meters away. Both men clutched the gold poles before them. Casper said something I couldn't quite catch as his horse moved in time to a violin and trumpet melody. *What a Wonderful World.*

Some evenings, instead of classical music, Delfina would play scratchy twentieth-century songs while I studied and she prepped for classes. For a moment, I was back in the Cove, in her cozy shack full of music and warmth.

Casper's next words were clearer as he circled closer to me. It helped that he had to yell over the music to reach Spiro, several horses away. "Now what's this all about, son?"

Spiro scowled, although the carousel seemed to have dampened his fury. "Give me universal retinal access . . ."

My chest constricted—what was his plan? They rotated out of earshot, but Casper looked amused. He asked something, and Spiro shouted, "You owe me, Dad."

Casper gave him a measured look. Then I caught the old man say, "I owe you nothing, son. You owe me. I designed you. I *made* you."

Spiro's response was garbled. A holographic family passed between me and the carousel, kids tugging their parents' hands as the adults hunched over phones.

Spiro rotated back into view, letting his head fall back and releasing a cry of frustration. "Give me retinal access, Dad."

"No way." Casper grinned.

"One. Whole. Year. That's how long I've been your lab rat, Dad . . ."

My leg cramped and I shifted my squat, struggling to hear over the din. The Mysterious Esmeralda's fortune looped in the background. *Wealth, work, luck, looooooove.*

Casper sat up straighter and launched into a soliloquy, drifting in and out of earshot. "The experiments have been a gift to you, son… You've had the rare chance to develop your mental and physical powers to an über-human level. You're no longer bound to the limitations of mere mortals and… You're like me now, son. You can do anything."

What the fratch was he talking about? *Über-human?*

"Don't squander this opportunity," Casper continued. "Whatever your goal is, son, be resourceful."

Even though I had no idea what he was talking about, a chill shot through me.

"Be resourceful," Spiro echoed through gritted teeth. From his pants pockets, he pulled out something with a metallic gleam, held it up, flicked it open. A switchblade. It reflected lights from the carousel. "How about I gouge out your eyeball and use that for retinal access?"

I winced but Casper chuckled, and music drowned out his response.

"Your experiments made me a *wee bit ruthless*, Dad." Spiro's voice fell, as if deflating. "We both know this is another one of your games. Just let me out of it. *Please.* I'm done."

"If this is a game, then you'd better figure a way out yourself."

A metaphorical game? Or a *virch game*? Was it Spiro, not Wolf, who was deluded? Had Spiro been dumping his own paranoia onto his brother?

Casper spoke with odd delight. "I have my hands full at the moment. Mo and I are working on something huge. It will bear fruit tomorrow at dawn."

This must have been what they'd referred to in Casper's office this morning. *Something huge.*

"What?" Grudgingly, Spiro slid the knife back into his pocket.

"Classified, son. But if it's a success, you'll know about it soon enough."

"So you're giving me nothing. And you're hiding stuff. Stuff that experiments *on me* probably helped create."

"Correct, son." His voice was cold through his smile. "But why not use the experiments to guide you? Surely you've learned something from them."

Spiro sunk into himself. And in that moment, I almost felt sorry for him. At the heart of it, he wanted some sign his dad cared. Which he hadn't gotten and wouldn't get. I'd seen how Casper operated with his sons. If the century-and-a-half-year-old man had ever experienced love, he must have outlived it.

Spiro made a last-ditch effort. "Will you ever give me... *anything?*"

Casper tilted his head. "Limitless cotton candy. A sugar high always improves one's mood."

Spiro's shoulders caved.

My own father's hugs were few, his words rough and practical, yet love infused his every action toward Shell and me. Love was the undercurrent in every word he'd spoken to us, every gift he'd slipped us, every sunset we'd watched. His love was unselfish, deeper than genes or legacy. He'd give up his life for mine in a heartbeat.

Spiro hadn't experienced anything like that. Apparently, Casper would offer his son only terror and sugar. And maybe the occasional private jet. Spiro climbed off the merry-go-round, stumbling, wincing, rubbing his leg. "I'm done with you, Dad. Done."

He was heading straight toward me.

Zuggers. I scooted to the other side of the fortune machine, breath held, nervous sweat trickling down my torso. Hopefully he wouldn't be able to *smell* me.

When Spiro didn't pass me after a count of ten, I peeked around the machine. Esmeralda was crooning, *"Wealth, work, luck, looooove."*

"Shut up." Spiro was standing in front of it.

I ducked back behind it. A moment later, his kick rocked the machine.

Cringing, I scooted farther away.

"What does your future hold?" Esmeralda asked, mindlessly insistent.

"There is no future." He sniffled, crying now. He trudged to the door.

Once Spiro had left, Casper continued spinning on the merry-go-round, smiling and stroking his horse's mane. When he revolved to the far side, I stood up, ready to run to the door, but tripped on my fallen-asleep legs. Desperate, I stretched them out, shaking my feet to get the blood flowing.

As the merry-go-round circled back, Casper looked directly at me.

My blood froze. A group of holo-teens moved between us, laughing, heads bent over phones. Frantic, I joined their group, pasting a smile on my face and holding my empty, cupped hand near my chest. I leaned forward, let my hair fall over my eyes, feigning interest in an invisible phone. I peeked through my hair and saw Casper craning his head and looking confused.

Had I fooled him?

The carousel was slowing now, and he shifted, as if preparing to get off.

Panic gripped my throat.

When he reached the far side, I darted to the exit, touched the open icon, and dashed into the vestibule. Was he coming after me?

I'd figured out how to get inside his office unseen, but not how to get out. How to sneak past Wind? He'd have no qualms zapping me and turning me over to Casper.

Bracing myself, I tapped the next door-open icon and took a cautious step out.

The waiting room was empty.

Miraculously, beautifully empty.

I didn't waste a second wondering how I got so lucky, just ran out the door, into the African safari corridor. Remembering the hidden cameras, I kept my head down and slowed to a walk.

My brain felt dizzy with questions and revelations. Was Spiro the insane brother? Why was he so desperate to access off-limits parts of the facility? What was he up to?

I needed something to hang on to, someone to trust.

CHAPTER THIRTEEN
Rebel

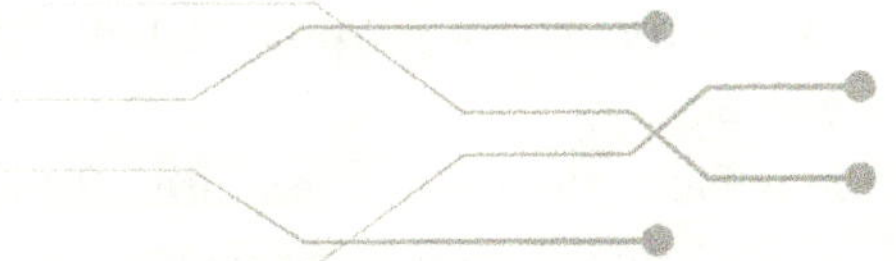

burst into the infirmary and headed straight into the exam room. Zinnia was perched on the bed, knitting a yellow scarf beside a sleeping Sugarpie.

Save the panda. My dream-self's instructions weren't yet completed. To save Sugarpie, I had to protect her from Spiro.

Zinnia dropped her ball of yarn. "Liv! You okay?"

"You're right," I said, breathless. "We can't trust Spiro. We can't give Sugarpie back to him."

She gave me a long look, as if measuring me up and finding me worthy. "For all Spiro knows, his cub escaped and died. We'll find her a new home."

I commanded my lip to stop quivering. "We can't trust Casper either." As soon as the words left my lips, I wanted to snatch them back. Of course his employees would be loyal to him.

Zinnia picked up the yarn, weaving the yellow strands around her fingers. "I know."

Before I could follow up, her voice dropped to a near-whisper. "Talk to the cargo pilots. They oversee the small heli-planes that drop off food and supplies. They can discreetly get the panda off-island." She paused. "Tell you what—I'll ask a nurse to contact a wildlife refuge. Hopefully we can hand the panda over within a day or two."

"Thanks." I breathed out in relief.

She continued. "You'll just bring the panda to the cargo strip, out past the tropical gardens."

"Tropical gardens? Real ones?"

She nodded. "A maze of paths inside a rain forest."

"Wow. I saw the tree canopy from the heliplane but didn't realize it was a garden."

Zinnia made a face. "Sweetie, there are all kinds of things going on here that you interns don't know about."

I took a long breath, trying to process everything.

As if sensing my overwhelm, Zinnia stroked my hair the way Delfina often did. They were cut from the same cloth—both had a fierceness hidden beneath the gentleness. A sense of *rightness* that cut through the crap.

"You okay, sweetie?"

I nodded. "It's not just the panda. It's also… other stuff." Sitting beside the sick panda was bringing up more memories. And in Zinnia's warmth, I felt safe to confide in her. "My sister, Shell, got sick last year."

"What kind of sickness?"

"Heavy metal poisoning."

She rubbed her face, looking pained. "What caused it?"

Me.

When I didn't answer, she said, "You're from a Null Zone, aren't you." A statement, not a question.

I'd assumed I'd panic if a shark discovered where I came from. Instead, with some relief, I let out a breath. Then, shame and anger at my role in Shell's death flooded in. Before I ruined everything, I tamped the feelings back down into the hidden place inside me.

My eyes met Zinnia's. She looked genuinely concerned.

"For a while," I said, "we didn't know what was wrong with Shell. None of our healers could afford a virchip scanner. Delfina and our neighbors pitched in to get her a scan, but the results recommended a treatment we couldn't come close to affording, especially not in the weeks she had left. She's in hibernation now… until—"

"Until you find a way to treat her," Zinnia finished, eyes welling up.

"She only has two months left," I said as my voice broke.

"I'm so sorry." Zinnia squeezed my hands. "You're here to get her the new treatment from Kiri's lab, aren't you?"

I said nothing, just eyed our joined hands, swallowing the lump in my throat.

"Well, I think what you're doing is brave. Noble. No wonder my niece took you under her wing." She exhaled. "If I had access to the treatment, I'd pass it along to you now. But for now, it's only available in Kiri's lab."

"That's okay. Just talking to you helps."

"Listen, Liv, there are other reasons why I'm not in a position to help your sister." After a pause, she opened her mouth to say something, and then—as if reconsidering—closed it again. There were things she wasn't telling tell me. *Couldn't* tell me? She forced a smile. "But Kiri's got the resources. She's a smart, caring person. And she's on Casper's good side."

So Zinnia was on Casper's bad side? Slowly, I said, "I'm on his bad side. I tried standing up to him. About—something else. No luck. I doubt he'd help with my sister, either."

In a voice so quiet I had to lean in to hear, Zinnia said, "The problem is motivation. Casper—and Virchuous—have no motivation to help your sister, or anyone like her. I realized this while volunteering as a health worker in another Null Zone. I doubt Kiri's new treatment will ever reach the people who need it most."

I wrinkled my brow. "But the whole point of a charity is to help people in need."

"Keep your voice down," Zinnia whispered. "The security cams should be off in here, but just in case."

So there *were* hidden cameras.

Her hands tightened around mine. Her entire body was filled with such intensity it seemed her braids might rise up with a life of their own. "Liv, when Casper invited me here, I came to figure out what was going on. But it turns out he just wanted to keep me close. He's stopped my efforts every step of the way, even threatened me. It gives me hope that someone like you has come along. Someone driven. Honest. Determined."

I bit the inside of my cheek. My guilt over Shell's sickness blocked me from absorbing the compliments.

She didn't seem to notice my unease. "Things are only getting worse," she whispered. "Casper's planning something big."

I processed this. Could he be involved in the bioweapon release? But what would his motive be? If you killed everyone on earth, there would be no one left to profit from, right? Finally, I asked, "What's his plan?"

Zinnia studied my face. "If I tell you more, it could put you in danger. Is that a risk you'll take?"

I didn't feel worthy of trust, but maybe preventing the impending disaster could somehow redeem my failure to keep Shell safe. Casper had already made veiled threats toward me—I was probably already in danger. And if Zinnia's information might relate to the crisis, I needed to know it.

I met her gaze. "Yes."

The doctor gave a firm nod. "First, tell me what you know about the virchip implant program."

I blinked. And then I dove back a decade, to one of my earliest memories of Shell.

I'd been five years old and Shell, just a baby. Our mom had died days after giving birth, and I was still trying to grasp how to live a motherless existence—and trying to mother this needy little creature myself.

That morning, two sharks in hazmat suits came to our door and introduced themselves as health workers from Virchuous. Their faces were hidden behind cloudy plastic as they bent down to talk to me.

"Why, hello, there!" one of them said. Glancing at Shell in Dad's arms, the man added, "We heard you have a new baby sister. We're here to put a free virchip in her. To keep her safe!"

This was no surprise—I'd been implanted as a baby, and so had my parents and grandparents. As far as I knew, everyone in the world had, even in the Null Zones. The Virchuous workers came to the Cove yearly to put chips into new babies.

Dad kissed the silky wisps on Shell's head, so smooth and fragile against his black stubble. With a weary sigh, he said, "No one here can afford a scanner. Much less the treatments. So what's the point?"

A beat of silence. "This is a free service. It would be irresponsible not to do this for your daughter."

Dad let out a strangled laugh. "Her mother died three months ago. She had a virchip, but that didn't help her postpartum infection. What we needed was *medicine*." His voice trembled and again, he pressed his lips to Shell's head, breathed in her sweet baby smell.

The health workers assured him they'd pass his comments along. One reached for Shell and the other pulled an injector from his bag. "Now, this won't hurt a bit."

Looking defeated, Dad handed her over, and the health worker inserted the virchip into Shell's temple. Her little face screwed up and she let out a wail. It *hurt* her.

"Liars!" I kicked the man in his shin. *Hard.*

I grabbed my baby sister and held her tight.

Already, I loved her fiercely.

"Oh, Liv." Zinnia exhaled. "I'm so sorry your family went through that." She patted my shoulder and added softly, "But you actually kicked the guy?"

I gave a modest shrug.

"I approve." She smiled sadly. "So, you already know that Virchuous is rife with contradictions. The charity arm of the Virch Empire implanted chips for free, which opened the door to charging a fortune for the scanners and treatments. A medical monopoly under the guise of do-gooding."

I furrowed my brow. "Why would Virchuous—"

"Sh, voice down, Liv."

Right. Hidden mics and cameras. Not to mention, I didn't want to wake up Sugarpie, who was stirring in her sleep beside us. "Why would Virchuous bother with places like the Cove?" I kept my voice low. "Or other Null Zones? Why would they spend a century implanting virchips in people they'd never profit from?"

She twisted her yellow yarn around her fingers. "That, my dear, is exactly what I wonder every day."

I scrambled to collect my thoughts. "Why are you trusting me with this?"

"Liv, in the three decades I've been a doctor, you're only the third person I've known who's stood up to Casper. You're being brave. A rebel."

I cringed at the praise, feeling undeserving. Then I forced myself to look at her. Her expression was torn and complicated, as if she understood that nothing was simple and pure in life. As if, maybe, regret and courage were tangled together.

"Zinnia," I whispered, "why haven't you just left this place? It must be so hard, so frustrating, for you to be here."

"I was the physician to one of Casper's wives, oh, nearly two decades ago." She gave my hand another squeeze. "Let's just say he has reason for wanting to keep a close eye on me."

"Is that why you haven't visited Delfina?"

She nodded, her expression full of distress. "I haven't been able to leave this island."

A knock on the door made me jump. The door slid open and the nurse walked inside. At the sight of the sleeping panda, her face dissolved into mush.

In a low, authoritative voice, Zinnia said, "Tell no one about its presence here. Is that understood?"

Blinking in confusion, the nurse nodded.

Zinnia smiled. "Good. Now why don't you get this critter some milk?"

"Regular milk?"

"Unless you happen to know a nursing mama panda. Just find some in the cafeteria, please."

The nurse left, still looking baffled.

Once the woman was out of earshot, Zinnia turned to me. "And Liv, dear, please keep our conversations confidential. Trust no one here."

I considered asking if I could tell Wolf but decided to keep my mouth shut. If she knew my closest thing to a friend here was Casper's son, she might regret having told me anything. "Of course."

After our goodbyes, I realized that lab time had ended, even though I'd missed most of it. According to the internship schedule, afternoon free time had begun. Wolf had suggested meeting at "our place." I could only assume he'd meant the beach, so that's where I headed.

As I walked toward the ocean, Zinnia's words echoed in my head.

Trust no one.

CHAPTER FOURTEEN
Retro Watch

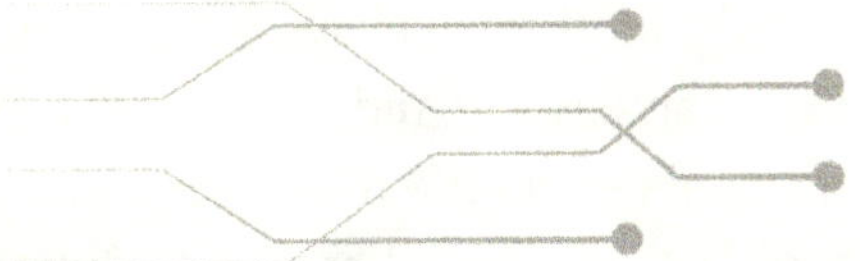

When I reached our place on the beach, Wolf was waiting for me, surf lapping his ankles.

"Hey, Angel."

"Hey." I shielded my eyes from the dazzle of sand and sky and sea. "Can I ask you something? And you promise to tell me the whole truth?"

He shrugged. "Our world might fall to pieces in the next couple days. I have nothing to lose. Nothing to hide, at least not from you. My dream self was very convincing about that."

As was mine. "Do you think we're in a virch game right now?"

A pause, and then, "No." Another pause. "But my brother does."

So the game Spiro and his dad were talking about—it wasn't just a figure of speech. "He told me you're the delusional one."

"Spiro's charming." Wolf squinted at the horizon. "And manipulative."

Frustration welled inside me. "Why would he lie?"

"My guess?" He tucked flying curls behind his ear. "Psychological projection. Narcissism."

I'd learned about these conditions in Twenty-First Century US Presidential History. When afflicted people can't face their own negative feelings, they accuse others of those very emotions. They feel such a deep sense of shame, they deny it all and project their darkness on people around them. Their inflated sense of self-importance and lack of empathy for others leads to destructive relationships… and general *destruction*.

"So you think it's an unconscious defense mechanism?"

He nodded. "My brother's always been narcissistic, like my dad." Wolf's face darkened. "And after all the trauma Spiro's been through, his ego's so fragile it's barely holding together."

I studied Wolf's face, framed by wind-whipped curls. Spiro wasn't the only one who'd accused him of being delusional—Casper and Kiri had, too. "But Wolf, what if you're the one projecting?"

He closed his eyes. "You'll have to decide for yourself."

I listened to terns calling, water whispering, palms rustling. The quiet before a storm. And I heard my dream voice: *Trust Wolf.*

"Okay," I said. "I believe you."

I held my sandals as my feet sunk deeper into the wet sand. I could have told him about the carnival or virus symptoms or our possible new ally—but first, I slipped into a pocket of peace. And Wolf didn't interrupt me.

Eventually, I asked, "How'd your conversation with your lab director go?"

"Mo Boudreaux is my dad's lap dog, like I expected. Classic narcissist enabler. Acts like my dad's a god. The guy's too scared to even hear me out. Apparently, my dad warned him about my so-called paranoia."

"Same with Kiri. So I took a less direct approach. I just snuck into Casper's office."

He grinned. "I know."

I stared at him. "How could you possibly know?"

He held up his watch, silhouetted against the bright sky. "This baby. I tweaked it in the lab this morning."

"What?"

He flipped open the watch face, moved his wrist toward me.

"Go ahead, put it on. And these too." He pulled a pair of ancient virchgoggles from his pocket and unfolded them. They were an early model, from a century ago, the kind you wore on your face and secured behind your ears. From time to time, I'd come across a beat-up pair in the junk heaps.

Tentatively, I slid them on, rested the center on my nose and adjusted the earbud.

Footage from inside the facility surrounded me in a dome. The time and date in the lower corner showed it was live. A rudimentary version of a virchlens, only seen by me. Dazed, I focused on one area, then another, then another, as I revolved. Some rooms and corridors were empty, while some contained scientists and interns, working, talking, eating.

I zeroed in on the waiting room of Casper's office. Wind sat at his desk, and at a nearby table sat the tea tray, holding neatly arranged cups and pot. The floor was dry—a 'bot must have cleaned up the mess.

I circled around and stopped at Kiri's lab, where she leaned against a counter, talking with Spiro. "Is there audio on this thing?" I asked Wolf.

"Hold on." I was vaguely aware of him making adjustments to the watch. Soon, muffled voices became audible through the earbud.

"Nice whales," Spiro said, taking Kiri's hand in his, admiring the sea creature décor on her nails.

He must have headed there straight after leaving Casper's office. *Be resourceful,* his dad had said.

"Security feed," I said, impressed. "How'd you get it?"

"Hacked into it." I heard Wolf's voice through one ear but couldn't see him outside the virchgoggles. It was disorienting. "When I got it working," he said, "first thing I see is you following Spiro and Wind into Casper's office. Nice move with the teacup, by the way."

I sighed, unsure how I felt about Wolf kind of spying on me too. "Well, I was lucky to escape. The waiting room was magically empty." I pulled out the earbud, lowered the goggles, blinked, and gave him a pointed look. "As you saw."

He raised his eyebrows with an innocent expression. "Right, it's almost as if a fake maintenance worker made an emergency call to Wind—had him running to the opposite end of the building." He gave a half smile.

My mind spun. "You?"

"If I didn't step in, you'd either get kicked off the island, no questions asked, or get trapped in the nighttime forest."

"Actually, it's a carnival now. At least I would've been entertained. Maybe even won a giant stuffed bear. But thanks," I conceded, "that was a fairly angelic move." Before he could respond with any angel-themed repartee, I said, "So tell me about this retro-watch-goggle-thing."

He pushed hair from his face. "I rigged it up so we can keep an eye on suspicious activity, even collect information and evidence. Mostly from public areas. Some areas don't have cams—the Biohaz Lab, private offices, infirmary rooms, a few others." Looking puzzled, he added, "And I've noticed that some cameras only show a pre-recorded loop. Like in the stairwell."

"Weird."

"I know. But we can at least monitor most of the comings and goings."

"Any video of the door to the Biohaz Lab?"

"Nope. I think there's a camera, but it's been disabled. Just a blank screen now. But cameras do show other areas of the main lab."

I pushed the goggles back over my eyes, inserted the earbud, and focused on the video feed of the lab. "Kiri and Spiro are getting pretty cozy," I observed.

He was holding her hand, trailing a finger down her cheek.

I pulled down the goggles, uncomfortable with spying on their intimate moments. I turned back to Wolf. "Spiro asked Casper for universal retinal access. He said no."

"So my dad's not a complete goblock."

"And Spiro lied about the panda virus." I was about to give details when I remembered my promise to Zinnia to keep our chats confidential. "Sugarpie's fine now, but Spiro had her drugged to stay docile." I thought of how Zinnia had put it. "To cute people out."

"Glad she's okay." Wolf's voice held no surprise at this revelation either. "I figured Spiro would do something like this. He's manipulative, like my dad, with a monster-sized ego. That's how he responded to—to the experiments."

"So the experiments messed with his mind?"

Wolf gave a terse nod, his face pained, vulnerable.

I studied his reaction. "Casper was talking about the experiments as a gift, a way to develop powers, to become über-human or something."

Wolf snorted, but he looked shaken.

This was clearly hitting a nerve. I didn't want to push him more, so I swallowed my questions and repositioned the goggles to survey the other video screens. It was all so old-fashioned, pixilated with rough seams at the edges, nowhere near as realistic as the virchlens experience. And it made me dizzy and queasy. Still, it was impressive that all this came from a retro-fitted watch and tweaked-out goggles.

Out of the blue, Wolf said, "You saved the panda. Just like your dream self told you to."

This was ultimately not a good sign. The panda's near-death encounter only validated my dream self's predictions. And if that prediction had played out, then the end-of-humanity scenario could too.

Which reminded me I hadn't told Wolf my most important discovery. I removed the earbud and lowered my goggles, finding his eyes. "Wolf, there's something else."

"What?" he said cautiously, as if sensing my dread.

"Kiri said they're researching a virus, a deadly bioweapon. Project Dragon. The symptoms are dilated pupils, internal bleeding, abdominal pain, rash…"

With each symptom, he winced more. At the end, he puffed out his cheeks and let out a long sigh. "Our dream selves had the virus."

"Right. I'm thinking either we're psychic or we somehow sent ourselves holograms from the future." I paused, thinking of Spiro's words to the Mysterious Esmeralda. *There is no future.* It made me shiver, even in the warm sunshine. Lightly, I added, "Or we're crazy."

"Hm."

I shifted as a hermit crab crawled past my toe, on its own mission. "Speaking of crazy," I said, "I think your brother's manipulating Kiri to get to the bioweapon. If he believes life is a game—and if he believes the way to win it is by changing the world—what bigger change is there than killing everyone?"

Wolf frowned, then nodded slowly. "I think you're right."

"You do?"

He hesitated. "I suspected my brother all along."

"Why do you keep hiding things?" I said, bristling.

"I couldn't be the first to say it, Liv. Just like I couldn't warn anyone about the panda. If I brought it up, you'd think I just had a grudge against Spiro."

I had to admit he was right. "Promise you won't hold anything else back, okay?" As I spoke, I realized I was holding back too. Not lying exactly, more like honoring my promise to Zinnia to keep our conversation confidential—but still. Anyway, nothing she'd said would help us decide what to do next.

"I promise." He gave me a meaningful look. Could he tell I wasn't being entirely truthful? "So, next step," he said. "We need evidence. We can't lock up my brother based on a dream and a hunch."

"Right. I think the doctor who treated Sugarpie could help us," I said, careful not to reveal too much, "but she'll probably need evidence, too."

I pushed the goggles back into position on my nose and refocused on the security footage in my lab. Spiro was drawing Kiri close, then leaning in and kissing her. The kiss looked gentle yet full of longing. She wrapped her arms around him, meeting him with equal passion.

Something welled up inside me. Not jealousy exactly—more like wistfulness or yearning.

Wolf's voice broke in. "Evidence?"

I took off the goggles, handed them back, rubbed my eyes. "A scientist mentor hooking up with a Progeny? Definitely breaking some rules. If Spiro gets booted from the island, problem solved, right?"

Wolf nodded. "And even if he doesn't get booted, he'll be watched. Maybe assigned to a different lab. He won't be able to access Project Dragon, at least not through Kiri."

"Think we should tell Soraya about them?"

He considered this. "She does seem pretty determined not to coddle the Progeny. Treat us like everyone else. Let's give it a shot."

He folded up the goggles, stuck them into his pocket. The lab feed was still visible, now only on the solid little 2D screen on the watch face. He made some adjustments and said, "Okay. Now we're recording the lab footage. Let's keep an eye on my brother on the way back."

We headed up the beach. Hope filled me for the first time since my awful dream. Maybe we could actually do this—stop the virus outbreak together, and then I could still save my sister. I felt a rush of warmth toward the boy beside me.

"Tech genius," I said, taking his wrist in my hands, brushing my fingertip over the frayed leather watchband. "Up till now, I thought the genius thing was just Progeny hype."

He laughed. "Probably is," he said, watching my hands on his wrist. "But over the past year, in between Himalayan hikes and meditation, I've been geeking out and polishing my hacking skills. Laying the foundation for my plan to change things."

"So, what's your plan, genius?"

When he wavered, I said, "You promised to hold nothing back. Spill it. And please don't tell me it involves ending the world as we know it."

Beneath the palm trees, Wolf handed back the goggles and tapped the miniscreen on his watch. Bracing for another queasy experience, I focused on the world in the goggles. White-tipped mountains, green meadows flecked with wildflowers, sheep grazing. Alpine Meadow—one of the most popular virchrelax settings. My virch Physics and Human Anatomy classes had used this setting. Of course, it felt less immersive now without the sensory nerve hookups of the virchlens experience.

"So why am I in Alpine Meadow, exactly?" I said.

"Just hold on."

He changed the setting to a lakeshore, surrounded by golden-canopied trees and smooth boulders. Water lapped at the pebbles by my feet, and chipmunks scurried along logs. The virch setting of my Differential Equations lectures. "Autumn Pond," I said.

How long he was going to keep this up? There were hundreds of virchrelax settings, from Sedona Sunset to Antarctic Peace. The sharks used them not only for school, but for work and relaxation. Back home, I'd always had to return to the real world after my virch classes. But my classmates would hang out in a virchrelax setting. Yellowstone Beauty was the most a la moda at the moment.

"Okay, Wolf," I said, impatient, "what's your plan with virchrelax?"

"I'm going to hack into every single setting." He made a dramatic pause. "And replace them all."

What a ridiculously brazen idea. A fake orange leaf fell from a branch above, settled on the carpet of leaves. I took off the goggles to look at Wolf, backlit by light from the ocean. "Is that even possible?"

"As Progeny, and being here in the heart of the Virch Empire, I think so. I hope so."

I tried to connect the dots. "And how will that change the world?"

"It'll take people out of their own self-serving illusion, give them a dose of reality."

I tilted my head. "A dose of reality via virch? How does that work?"

"They'll see how the rest of the world lives." He grinned, unable to hide his excitement. "The setting will be a Null Zone."

I didn't know whether to laugh or cry.

"You know," he said, "one of those contaminated areas?"

"Uh, yeah. I know."

"The real reason I'm on the island? The practical one? To get the rest of the passwords and bio-codes. I think I can do it over the next two months, here in command central. Then I'll go into a Null Zone, work as a Virchuous volunteer, and do multi-sensory filming for the setting. Help people tell their stories. I'll hack in my replacement virch setting. Then, when sharks go into virchrelax, they'll actually enter a Null Zone. They'll experience what's happening outside of their own illusions. They'll *feel* it, Liv."

He brushed an ant from his calf. "Why're you looking at me like that?"

I burst out laughing. I laughed until my belly ached, until I was gasping, until I was crying.

"What?" He looked hurt. "It's not a joke."

I wiped my eyes. "It's just that—Wolf, oh, Wolf. My home is a Null Zone."

A hummingbird darted between us, hovered and whirred by our heads, then shot off into the forest. Wolf's eyes stayed locked onto mine. "Really?"

It felt good to let the truth out. "And if we manage not to get killed in the next two days, I'll be your personal Null Zone tour guide. You can stay in our house in the Cove. You want heart-breaking stories? I'll give you stories."

"I knew you weren't a shark, but I never imagined…" A long pause. A rearranging of assumptions. "Tell me everything."

I bit my lip. "Not now." I handed him back the goggles and glanced at the security footage on his watch screen. Kiri and

Spiro were still kissing. It looked so genuine. No wonder she was falling for him.

"We have to get back to the facility." I headed toward the path.

Wolf rushed to my side. "Tell me on the way. And no holding back for you, either."

No holding back.

But there were things I held back from myself. Things I kept hidden deep underwater. Things I couldn't bear to bring to the light of the surface. If I couldn't even look at them, how could I tell him? How could I tell him the truth of why my sister was in the coffin?

CHAPTER FIFTEEN
Poison

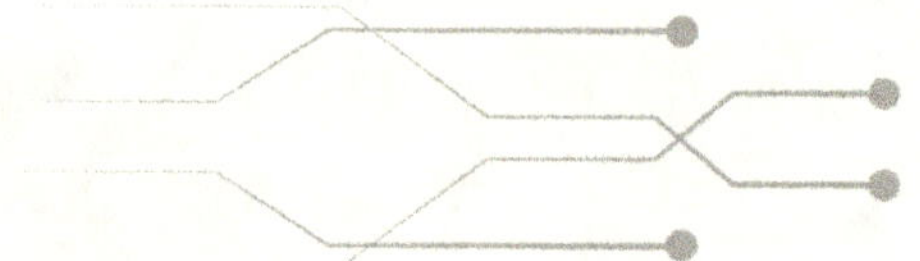

"History lesson first," I said as Wolf and I walked toward the silver palace. I'd start with the easy stuff, the stuff I could hold up at a distance. "Stop me if you already know this."

He looked at me intently, as if ready to memorize every word.

"The Cove used to be a legal place to live," I explained, "complete with solid houses and farms, until the Great Crisis a century ago. That's when hurricanes and nor'easters raged through the Chesapeake watershed, destroyed barrier islands, took down all the trees and structures."

"Right," Wolf said. "I researched this. Insurance companies went under. The government was too overwhelmed with an economic crisis and other disasters to do anything. The land became wild marsh, a dumping ground for e-waste along the coast. The government just made it off-limits. Declared it a Null Zone."

I nodded. "Back then, most people who lost their homes left for North Maryland as refugees. They still do, sometimes. They always come back home."

"Why?"

I thought about how to explain this. After all, it wasn't exactly rational to choose to live in a contaminated zone. But at the heart of it, it wasn't a choice—it was home.

Dad hated talking about the humiliation and hopelessness he and Mom had felt during their brief stint at the refugee camp before I was born. They'd essentially been prisoners there, fed inadequate rations, surrounded by concrete and wire, doing soulless forced labor—there had been no trees or wood, no work for a carpenter. No bay or deer or gardens or herons. No meaning. My parents had escaped and returned to the Cove, never looking back, even when Mom was dying.

"It's worse for us in the refugee camps," I said. "In the Cove, we have our dignity. We have everything we love."

"Weren't your ancestors worried about the pollution?"

"I don't know," I admitted. "Maybe they thought our homes were far enough from the junk heaps. Maybe they thought the contamination risk was the least of the other evils. Maybe the authorities didn't communicate the risks. Maybe there was nowhere else to go that felt like home."

He nodded, expression thoughtful.

I took a long breath. "Anyway, after the Great Crisis, our ancestors salvaged what was left of the old houses and rebuilt them as one-room shacks. They scavenged wood wreckage for heat and cooking. They supplemented traditional fishing and oystering and crabbing with foraging through the heaps of e-waste. When the ships delivered junk, our ancestors extracted minerals to sell on the black market."

I paused to steady the tremble in my voice. I pictured Shell's tiny, delicate fingers picking apart ancient phones and motherboards.

"By the time my parents were born, the bay's watershed was too polluted to sustain much marine life. They burned their boats for heat, spent their days sorting through e-waste. Our community is a couple kilometers from the junk heaps. We plant trees and gardens and try to make things better. But we're light years away from the sharks. From virch worlds and holoscapes. I've spent almost every day of my life sorting through waste."

I avoided Wolf's eyes, but in my peripheral vision, I saw him nodding and listening with an open expression. Still, I felt like I'd just given a school report in my underwear, exposing everything. Nearly everything.

How to broach the subject of Shell's sickness? Giving a history lesson was one thing, but talking about my sister pressed on the raw place inside me. I touched the strand of chipped shells around my neck. If Shell were here now, she'd be skirting the forest's edge on skinny heron legs, collecting flowers and tree nuts. She'd be grabbing my hand, pulling me along with her.

She should be here. She should be alive.

I wound the string of shells around my fingers till they pierced the skin.

"You okay?" Wolf slowed his pace to match mine.

I forced myself to meet his gaze. "My sister. I raised her with my dad. Our mom died when she was a baby. Last year, Shell got sick. She's in hibernation now."

His face fell. "I'm sorry."

I nodded, taking in his empathy, which felt genuine. "I'm getting the treatment she needs from Kiri's lab. It's newly developed, fast and effective. That's why I'm here. I made Shell a promise. To let her live again."

"She will." Wolf plucked a hibiscus, handed it to me. "You're strong and smart and determined. You'll make it happen." He paused. "Maybe there's a reason our dream selves chose each other."

I held the flower in my palm, unsure what to make of the gesture but moved by his undeserved confidence in me.

"I can't say I know what you're going through, Liv, but I know what it's like to have your mom die."

"Really?" I tilted my head in sympathy… and confusion. Sharks didn't die young. Anything was curable with enough money and influence. "I'm so sorry."

"It's okay. My godmother's like a mother to me. Amala. She raised me."

"How did your mom die?"

"Accident," he said. "In Kauai, where she was from. I was a toddler, too young to remember, and I wasn't there when it happened. She was picking mangos, fell off the ladder. Her head hit a rock. She died instantly."

I stared at him. What a freak occurrence.

"My mom always wanted to keep me out of the Progeny limelight," he said. "And Amala tried to honor that wish. She was the one who arranged for me to disappear for the past year. She risked a lot for me."

"They both sound like good people."

"They stood their ground. My mom wouldn't even let Casper design my genes. Amala says that's why he calls me weak. He couldn't control my mom and he can't control me."

Wolf looked different now that I knew he hadn't been designed. I'd just assumed that as Progeny, his features were predetermined and carefully selected. I had a new appreciation for his mop of copper curls, his fish-scale irises, his earnest voice. They all came from a random collision of genes.

Underneath it all, he was a mishmash like me.

I studied his features, curious about his mother—what had she looked like? *Been* like? Of course, he wouldn't remember the answer to that second question, and it might pain him for me to ask it. I could relate. I rarely volunteered what I knew about my own mother. And I could barely talk about Shell without breaking into pieces.

A warmth was flooding me, something… undammed. I shook myself, forced myself to stop staring at him. "I didn't realize you lost someone too."

He brushed his palm over grass tips alongside the path. "I was so little when it happened. Can't really remember her. Anyway, it was an accident." He focused on me. "What happened to your sister?"

I breathed in, out, in, out. I had to tell him about Shell. The whole terrible truth.

"At first," I began, "we didn't know why Shell was sick. When things got bad, we snuck on a junk ship and took her to a clinic." I paused, gauging Wolf's reaction so far.

His face looked open, as if he could accept whatever I threw his way.

So I let myself fall into the memory that had stayed clamped inside an oyster shell in the dark bay of my mind. I let myself fall and trusted that Wolf would pull me back up to the light.

I fell back into that day in the clinic, where the doctor was frowning at the results of Shell's scanned virchip on the airscreen.

I fell into every excruciating detail… and recounted it to Wolf.

Uncensored.

I told Wolf how terrified I'd felt, sitting next to Dad and a sound-asleep Shell as the doctor studied her diagnosis on the airscreen. Finally, the man spoke. "The girl has been poisoned by mercury, lead, cadmium, beryllium, barium, hydrocarbons, and more." With biting accusation, he asked, "Has she been exposed to these contaminants?"

Dad covered his mouth with his hand. His lids closed like a stubborn dam. His whole body shook.

Darkness formed at the edges of my vision and spiraled toward a black hole in the center.

"I'm guessing she's been exposed to e-waste," the doctor added, studying the screen. "Through play? Or work? And you didn't let her eat crops grown in contaminated soil, did you?"

Dad's tears were spilling off his chin, dripping into his lap. He sat there, helpless and speechless. But it wasn't his fault. I was the one responsible for getting our food—by growing or trading or foraging it. And I was the one who took care of Shell all day and slept beside her all night. I was the one who mothered her.

And I'd failed.

When neither of us answered, the doctor concluded, "So you *did* feed her contaminated food then."

I gritted my teeth. "Are there pills to fix this?"

"Oh, she needs more than pills. You waited too long to bring her here. She needs long-term, intensive, intravenous treatments to remove the toxins."

He went on and on, and when he told us the unthinkable cost—required *up front*—my body and brained numbed.

"You shouldn't have exposed the child to these toxins." He spoke to us as if we were dull-witted or spoke a different language. "*These. Substances. Are. Deadly.*" He studied the screen again, shook his head. "A main vehicle for the worst of these poisons is shellfish." He shot us a look of rebuke. "I hope you weren't feeding the girl black market oysters. Those are nothing more than little pockets of poison."

Oysters. Her favorite food, the one I brought her as often as possible. Our love language.

Slammed by a wave of nausea, I reached out for Dad's shoulder. I barely heard him say, "Lots of people eat oysters and work in the junk heaps and eat food grown in our soil... and they don't get sick." He put an arm around me. "My other daughter never did."

The faces of others from our community who'd gotten sick and died too early flashed through my mind. I knew that my neighbors and friends and grandparents rarely lived past their fifties, half the life expectancy of the sharks. I'd always thought it was because our lives were all-around harder, working from sunup to sundown no matter the weather, with never quite enough food. But what if the culprit was toxins?

With a condescending shake of the head, the doctor brought up a new screen. "It can take decades of chronic exposure for the symptoms to worsen to the point of death. The severity depends on the degree of exposure as well as each individual's metabolic pathway. This patient is more vulnerable for some reason."

He looked at me, blame darkening his eyes. "Maybe this patient was regularly exposed to an especially large amount of toxins."

A hurricane crashed into me, or so it felt.

Thanks to me, my sister had eaten ten times the number of oysters other kids ate.

Pockets of poison.

I'd been poisoning my sister all these years.

My soul weighed heavier and heavier with the knowledge: *I could have prevented this.*

And worse, the heaviest of it all: *I caused this.*
It's my fault.
I killed my sister.
And how many other people had I killed?

CHAPTER SIXTEEN
Tibet

Wolf and I reached the facility just as I finished speaking. He stayed quiet for a moment, maybe waiting to see if I had more to say. We stepped before the retinal scanner and walked through the main entrance. My guts were spilled, my heart raw. I couldn't bear to look at his face to see his reaction.

Instead, I surveyed the lobby's current holoscape—an Italian villa balcony. Around the perimeter, waves pounded against cliffs below us. Ancient, pastel houses nestled into the hillsides.

I was in a fake Mediterranean paradise.

And Shell was in a coffin.

Beside me, Wolf sniffled, and I forced myself to look at him. He was crying, full-fledged crying. Tears and snot and the works. Wiping his eyes, he said, "Thank you."

I reeled. "For what?"

"For telling me. And for what you're doing for your sister."

A heavy silence. I clenched my hand over the sharp-edged necklace. "Don't you get it? I fed her *oysters*. Even after she got so sick she could barely chew, I cut them into tiny pieces and fed them to her. *I poisoned my sister.*"

"Angel—" he said, looking pained.

"I brought her to the junk heaps with me for *years.* I exposed her to the toxins. Shell's dead because of me."

"But it wasn't—"

"If I don't save her, I'll never be able to live with myself."

As I spoke, I realized how much poison I'd been holding inside for the past ten months. Because that's what those feelings were. Poison. For months, I'd been poisoning myself. Feeling ashamed to be alive.

Wolf took my hand from the necklace, held it in his. "You didn't know. And you're doing everything you can to save her. You're not a murderer, Liv. The murderers—they're everyone who lives in their own illusions. Everyone who ignores the reality of a girl being poisoned, of an entire community at risk. Everyone who has the power to do something but does nothing."

His voice dropped. "People like me."

Strange how it's easier to find goodness in other people rather than in yourself. "No, Wolf, you're doing something. Your plan to raise awareness about Null Zones—that's huge."

"Angel, whatever happens, I promise we'll get your sister the treatment. No matter what. If we can't get the new one from Kiri's lab, I'll pay for the old one."

I tried to wrap my head around a seventeen-year-old having such a staggering amount of money that he could pay for the treatment. I had no idea how money flowed in shark families, much less in Casper's family. What if his father cut him off?

"But you're on your dad's bad side now—"

"I can round up the funds. At the very least, updating my sim for virch dates will bring in more than enough revenue. It'll go to treat your sister. And other kids like her."

A load lifted from my shoulders—I'd been carrying around this staggering weight for nearly a year. And now I felt so light I was nearly floating. "Thank you, Wolf."

"Getting Shell treatment is our first priority." He looked at me, full of hope. "And once she's cured, want to work with me? We can go to the Cove, do the filming, make the virch setting, and spread the word. I think we can spark some real changes."

"Of course. Yes." Knowing that Shell would live again let me widen my circle of compassion. And there was more. Telling Wolf about Shell—and seeing him *care*—was somehow releasing the poison. I could practically feel it flowing from my pores, floating away, dissipating. "We'll do this together, Wolf."

He stepped toward me, pulling my hand toward his chest. Shell's last words came back to me: *Remember to . . .*

Remember to what?

His forehead bent to touch mine. Everything was breath and light and heartbeat and nearness of skin. A river moving between us, through us, clear and fresh. After a moment, I lifted my chin to look up at him.

And then, giddy voices came from the corridor, intruding into our moment. The fruit crew appeared across the Italian-holoscaped lobby, and when they spotted Wolf, they rushed past the marble statues and swarmed us.

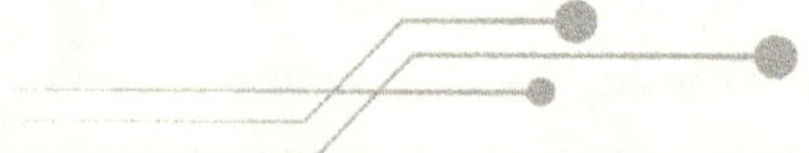

Bewildered, I looked around at the interns—Melon, Strawberry, and Plum—waving and sparkling and talking in animated voices.

"Hi, Lil!" said Melon, moving in for a hug.

I withdrew my hand from Wolf's, suddenly self-conscious. "It's Liv."

"Right, *Liv*! How *are* you? Want to come have gelato with us? And bring your partner?"

All eyes were on Wolf—expressions curious, even jealous.

"Oh, no thanks," I mumbled.

They ignored me. "So Nelson, when are you going to update your virch date sim?" Melon asked.

Wolf caught my gaze. "Sorry," he told them, "but Liv and I, we're in the middle of—"

"But we've been on the waitlist forever!" Strawberry said.

"You have to update it!" Plum begged.

"I will," Wolf said, rubbing his neck, shifting his feet.

I thought of the other billion people who were waiting for a virch date with him. I thought of that money going to my sister, and kids like her. And a rush of something warm and happy came over me, the feeling of a sweet peach sunset.

"Enjoy your gelato," I told them. I grabbed his hand and pulled him across the lobby, hoping the fruit crew would take the hint. Just in case, I tugged him behind a cluster of potted lemon trees—real ones. We sat down on a carved stone bench.

"Thanks," he breathed.

I peered through the leaves and relaxed. No sign of the other interns. We were alone. The scent of lemon blossoms filled the air. He moved his head close to mine. "The thing driving you, Angel—I don't think it's guilt. Or shame. Or anger."

"Then what is it?"

He blushed. "Love."

My breath caught. I slipped my hand into my left pocket, felt the outline of LOVE. My other hand went to the string of shells around my neck. For months I'd been angry. Angry at myself and the world.

But swimming in the ocean this morning, I had loved myself. My body and my mind and whatever else I was. *I love you,*

I love life, I love Wolf. The dream words repeated themselves like a mantra. Like some kind of absolution.

"Maybe you're right," I said. Fake gulls called back and forth. I closed my eyes, feeling the sunshine and the Mediterranean breeze. Even after all I'd been through, I did love life. I'd never thought about it before, the idea of loving… *all of this*, but I did.

I closed the fabric scrap into my fist. We had things to do, urgent, life-or-death things. Shell's future was safe, but first we had to make sure there'd be a world for her to return to. I motioned to his watch. "What are Kiri and Spiro up to?"

He opened the little screen. It showed Kiri and Spiro locked in an embrace in the lab.

"Groan," said Wolf.

"I think he really likes her." Despite everything, I felt the need to stick up for Spiro. I'd witnessed his unguarded flashes of emotion. I couldn't un-see them, un-hear them, un-feel them. "But we have to alert Soraya. Make sure he doesn't have access to the virus. Where is she?"

Wolf swiped through the videos on his watch screen, pausing at one with us. There we were, tucked behind the lemon tree—with the fruit crew sidling toward us, relentless, and just meters away. Great.

Soon he reached a video feed with Soraya in a hallway, scolding a group of interns.

"Typical Soraya." Wolf flipped down the watch face. "Fourth floor, near the dorms."

"Let's go." Again, I took his hand, and we broke into a run for the elevators. We skidded and slipped and laughed, the interns on our trail. I felt *brighter*, as if, with the poisonous shame gone, there was new space for light to rush in.

On the fourth floor, Wolf and I stepped from the elevator into a rugged mountain landscape. Ornate temples were tucked into the hillsides. Giant, shaggy cows grazed nearby—bison, maybe? Their saddles were adorned with embroidered fabrics and bright pom-poms.

Above, colorful prayer flags flapped in the breeze. With each gust of wind, brass bells clinked, making mysterious music. There was something special about this holoscape—it had more *soul* than the others.

A strange look came over Wolf's face—a mix of wonder and nostalgia. "We're in Tibet."

"What's that smell?"

He smiled, looking almost homesick. "Yak butter tea."

"Yum?" I grinned, trying to imagine the taste.

"I was hiding out in a monastery like that one." He gestured to a snow-white building in the distance. Monks in burgundy robes clustered nearby. "Helping monks with the chores, doing some hacking, plotting my mission, hiking, meditating." With a grin, he added, "And drinking lots of yak butter tea."

Breathing in the fresh mountain air, I watched fabric squares fly like little kites. "The holoscape's a weird coincidence."

"My dad's doing, no doubt. Playing mind games with me." He made a face. "Knowing him, those yaks are probably programmed to attack me."

"Really?" The yaks looked so peaceful.

Again, I wondered what big project Casper and his virch lab director, Mo, were bringing to fruition tomorrow morning. For the moment, though, Spiro was the immediate threat. We had to convince Soraya to kick him off the island—or at least keep a close eye on him. It might be an easy task—she seemed to relish her role as rule-enforcer, and she'd made it clear that she wouldn't give the Progeny special treatment. If anyone here could restrain Spiro, it was her.

And there she was, just beyond the second row of prayer flags, striding toward us, tail in hand, sun shining off her mostly bald head. Behind her, the interns she'd scolded scurried away.

"Hi, Soraya." I figured I'd do the talking since she thought I was a neutral party.

"Well, Liv." Her eyes flicked from me to Wolf and back again. "Looks like you've found a way to make your partnership work."

"Yes. Thanks for your encouragement." I took a deep breath. "Listen, Soraya, I know the rules about the Progeny not getting special treatment. Well, Spiro has been—" My face flushed.

I cleared my throat, feeling a stab of guilt, realizing Kiri would get in trouble, too. Not to mention, they seemed to really like each other.

"What?" Soraya demanded.

"You should see the video yourself. Just ask the security team for recent footage of the Virology-Toxicology Lab. You'll see Kiri and Spiro. Together."

She fell silent, flipping her horse tail. There was only the ringing of brass bells and the chanting of monks. Her giant eyes moved back and forth between Wolf and me, unreadable. Finally, she said, "So you two were spying on them?"

"I noticed them flirting and—"

She turned to Wolf. "You tampered with the security footage, I'm guessing. Trying to frame your brother, poor boy. Your father warned me you were tech savvy. And that you and Liv were up to something."

She walked to the nearest airscreen, swiped and tapped. "Borg," she said to the security guard onscreen, "I need you here on the fourth floor."

My stomach sank. I'd gone to the people who I'd thought would act responsibly, the ones who had power here—Casper, Kiri, and now Soraya. But none of them dared to take us seriously, just treated us like high-strung interns. These adults were worse than useless.

"Listen," I pleaded. "Spiro's trying to access the Biohaz Lab. That's what Borg needs to be worried about."

"You have no place telling us how to do our jobs. And I'll have you know, Casper alerted the whole security team about you. If you continue to make yourselves a nuisance, Borg is instructed to kick you off the island, no questions asked. Even you, Nelson, Progeny or not."

With Shell safe, the threat of expulsion hit differently this time. I only had to stay on the island as long as it took to stop the virus outbreak. According to my dream self, that meant another day or two.

I tried to anticipate the next steps. When Borg came, he'd search Wolf and find out his watch wasn't so retro after all. And his virchgoggles—though ancient—were sure to be confiscated. It was a matter of time before the security team discovered he'd hacked into their system, and then they'd definitely ship him off the island. Or worse. And I'd be guilty by association. Then neither of us would be here to prevent the outbreak.

I looked at Wolf and flicked my eyes from him to the hallway behind me, where three well-dressed yaks roamed beneath frosted peaks. From the opposite end of the corridor, the hulking shape of Borg was heading toward us.

I sucked in a breath, then grabbed Wolf's hand. "Gotta run."

"See ya," Wolf said with a wave to Soraya.

And together, we ran through the faux Tibetan countryside.

CHAPTER SEVENTEEN
Puppy Paradise

As Wolf and I ran, a thump and a shriek came from behind us. *Yak attack?*

I couldn't resist looking back.

Soraya was sprawled on the ground beside a yak. But the hologram was still calmly munching grasses. Soraya must have tried to follow us and tripped over her horsetail. Borg was helping her up.

Wolf and I didn't stop running till the emergency stairwell.

"You said the cam footage here is on a recorded loop," I said, gasping for breath. "Right?"

"Right. It's safe."

We slipped through the doorway and paused, panting, on the landing.

"Any ideas on who might've done that?" I asked. "And why?"

He shrugged. "Right now, it's working in our favor. Maybe we have a secret ally. Or maybe someone else is hiding something." He motioned to the staircase. "Up or down?"

"Anywhere without real camera feeds."

He flipped open his watch, tapped his fingertip till a layout of the facility appeared on the tiny screen. Squinting, he zoomed in to our location.

Voices rose from the hallway, one of them Soraya's, growing louder, closer.

"This way," Wolf whispered.

We raced up the stairs, three at a time, up to the sixth floor, and skidded to a stop in front of an unmarked door. I touched the door-open icon.

Nothing. Zuggers, there was a retinal scanner.

But Wolf positioned his eyeball in front of it and the door slid open. After a split-second of confusion, I slipped inside after him. It was dark, but ambient light glowed from the ceiling. The door hushed closed behind us.

I gaped at him. "How'd you do that?"

"Already hacked into some maintenance and security worker accounts," he said with a grin. "We can get in anywhere they can."

"Well played." Once my eyes adjusted, I could make out control panels and airscreens around us. A few broken cleaning 'bots stood in the corner, in various states of disrepair. We were in a maintenance closet, about two by two meters.

Wolf surveyed the equipment. "Jackpot."

"What is this stuff?"

"Backup control system for temperature, lighting, holoscaping."

My eyes widened. "Can you adjust it?"

He was already opening his watch, tapping his finger. "Should be able to. I spent months getting passwords and exploring all the systems in the facility." After a few minutes, he said, "Well, we're mostly in. Enough to make temporary changes. Now what to do with it?"

I considered the possibilities. "We could try dealing directly with Spiro. Somehow prevent him from doing the deed."

"Like trapping him? Restraining him?"

"I don't see that going well, not with Casper and Soraya and security on his side. And anyway, we couldn't keep him locked up indefinitely. What if we could convince him it's a bad idea? I think he's got a good heart, underneath it all."

"He's a psychopath," Wolf said, shaking his head. "Casper turned him into one."

I hesitated. "What exactly were these experiments?"

"They—" He closed his mouth again, struggling for words. Maybe he'd never talked about this before. Maybe he'd hidden it deep, just as I'd done with my guilt over Shell's death. Finally, he said, "They—they messed with our sense of reality."

"Then let's remind Spiro of life before the experiments. What he cared about."

He shook his head again. "Too late, Liv. It won't work."

But I'd seen tenderness in Spiro. Tiny flashes of hope. "We have to try, Wolf. I think there's still a piece of him we can reach."

Wolf didn't look convinced.

"Hey," I said, inspired. "Remember what Spiro said before you punched him?" But as the words left my mouth, I realized that was probably a lie, too.

"He said—he said he'd kill me, Liv." His voice wavered, maybe from fear, maybe from anger, or maybe even from sorrow. Maybe a mix of all three. "And everyone I care about."

"Oh." I tucked my arms under each other, wishing I could hug him. "He said he told you… he loved you."

Wolf blinked, looking too shaken to speak.

How many times had Shell told me she loved me? Had Wolf ever heard those words from his brother? *It's all about love, sis.*

"Maybe that was another kind of projection," I ventured. "I mean, maybe on some level, that's what he *wanted* to tell you. What he wants to hear from you." I paused. "Can you remember a time Spiro showed love—real love?"

Wolf rubbed his forehead. "He used to love animals." A pause. "I mean, really love them. Not drug them."

He perched on a stool in the corner as I sat cross-legged on a table beside him. Colorful lights from the equipment shone on his face as he thought. Something sparked in his eyes. "Pomeranian pups."

I couldn't help smiling. "Details?"

"When we were little, we made joint visits to my dad. Spiro was the closest half brother in age, so Casper thought we'd entertain each other. But we mostly competed for his attention. He liked egging us on. A divide-and-conquer strategy."

"What?" I'd never heard that term applied to a *family*.

"That's how he operates. A consequence of extreme narcissism. He didn't want Spiro and me loyal to each other, just to him. The only time I remember having fun together was when Spiro's Pomeranian had puppies. They looked like tiny, wild bears."

He grinned. "Hold on, Liv. I might have a recording. It was special to me—the first time I felt a bond with my brother."

It took Wolf a few minutes to sift through his video album on the virchgoggles. Then he laughed and set the goggles on my face. And there they were, an adorable heap of puppies, playing at my feet—fuzzy little brown balls, each small enough to fit in my hand, so hyper and happy I couldn't help laughing too. I adjusted the earbud, heard their squeaks and yaps.

"Perfect!" Excited, I pulled off the goggles. "Let's make a Pomeranian Puppy Paradise holoscape."

Wolf didn't look convinced. "That would be a ton of work. I can hack, but I can't work magic."

"Can't you just stick some puppies into the holoscape outside the lab?"

"It's a pretty long shot." He did some tapping and swiping, brows creased. "Okay, looks like it's Summer Garden now. I could probably add dogs." He sighed, looking doubtful. "So when Spiro comes out of the lab, he'll be greeted with flowers and pups?"

"Yes!" I overcompensated for his lack of enthusiasm. I liked the idea of approaching Spiro with kindness. A scared, love-starved little boy hid under his façade, I was sure of it. "And then we'll talk to him. Connect with him. Find his compassion."

Wolf gave a skeptical shrug. "Guess it's worth a try."

While he worked, I monitored the security feed, watching Kiri and Spiro, who were engaged in close conversation in the lab—it had been hours now. Whenever another scientist came in, they'd step away from each other. Whenever they were alone, they'd come back together, all whispers and kisses.

During their more private moments, I kept flicking to Casper's waiting room. Mo came by his office again, but no one else came or went.

My belly rumbled. I hadn't eaten since breakfast. It had to be near dinner time—Spiro and Kiri would have to come out to eat.

"There, I think I did it." Wolf shook out his hands and pulled a couple vita-bars from his pocket. "Hungry?"

"Thank you!" I tore off the wrapper. I forced myself to take small bites—who knew when we'd be able to snag more food?

It would be risky to eat with the other interns if Soraya and Borg were hunting us.

By the time I finished my bar, Kiri and Spiro had extricated themselves from their embrace. She re-applied sparkle to her lips and headed out the lab door, glowing beside her secret new boyfriend.

Wolf and I checked the security feed to make sure no guards were between us and the Summer Garden. Then we crept out of the maintenance closet and headed to the seventh floor.

In the corridor, scientists and interns were streaming toward the elevators en route to the dining hall. We kept our heads down, blending into the crowd.

No one seemed to notice us, thanks to the holo-puppies frolicking among buttercups. People were giggling at the sight, even crouching down to try to scratch the puppy bellies. Since most holoscapes were just background scenes—glorified wallpaper—these puppies were a novelty. I imagined the delight Spiro would feel, remembering these pets, how they'd bonded him with his brother.

Soon, the rush-hour foot traffic was gone, and Wolf and I stood alone in the corridor. We'd positioned ourselves about ten meters away from the lab door, pressed against the wall.

Wolf stared at the mini-screen on his watch. In the footage, Kiri and Spiro were walking toward the exit, about to enter the corridor. "This is it," Wolf said, his voice nervous.

The door slid open and they stepped outside, into the garden of playful puppies.

Kiri squealed with joy and bent down to pet them.

Spiro screamed.

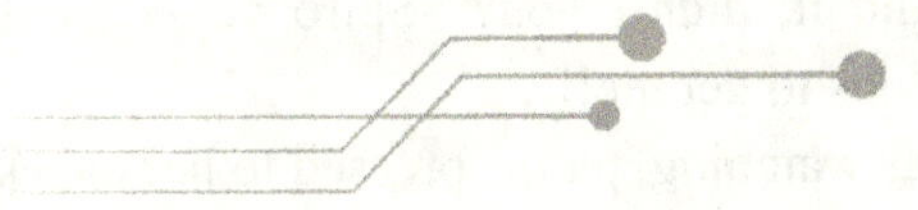

Time slowed.

Spiro was yelling, kicking at the dogs, shielding his face with his hands, as if these were deadly monsters instead of tiny, cuddly pups.

A bewildered Kiri tried to wrap her arms around him.

He only screamed louder.

Beside me, Wolf looked panic-stricken. He fumbled with his watch, his fingers shaking as they swiped and tapped.

Spiro pressed himself against the wall, protecting his head. "It's not real, it's not real, it's not real!" On and on, he wailed and sobbed this mantra. "It's not real!"

I stood paralyzed in shock.

All at once, the puppies vanished, leaving only the Summer Garden. The scent of roses and grass filled the air. Butterflies floated from bloom to bloom. Sparrow chirps replaced puppy yaps.

Spiro lowered his hands, revealing a pale, sweaty face, and pushed Kiri away. Warily, he looked around, blinking as though he'd just woken up. His eyes rested on Wolf, who was flipping down the watch face.

Spiro's expression turned murderous. In three steps, he'd grabbed his brother by the arm and flung him away from me, into the middle of the hallway.

Wolf grunted as his head slammed into the floor.

With a shot of adrenalin, I ran toward the brothers.

Spiro dove on top of his brother and began pummeling his face.

"No!" I clawed at Spiro's back, trying to pull him away, but he shook me off.

"You did it, didn't you?" Spiro yelled, spit flying. "You sent those dogs to get me!"

Kiri was watching, palms pressed to her cheeks in horror.

"Spiro!" I yelled, struggling to pin his arms to his body.

When he threw me off, I tried putting him in a chokehold. "Stop! We thought you'd like the puppies!"

My efforts were in vain—he ignored me and redoubled his efforts. His fighting seemed strategic, yet reflexive, almost second nature. With each punch, he released a sharp exhale. He punched from his elbow, not his fist. He feinted blows to Wolf's head, then struck his abdomen. He focused precise punches on Wolf's jaw and temples, which must have sent shockwaves through his skull.

Whenever Wolf managed to hit back, Spiro leaned into him, taking the power away from his blows. No doubt about it, Spiro was a skilled fighter. Expert, even—as if he'd been professionally trained.

Soon Wolf could only lay there, protecting his face. Blood trickled from his mouth, puddling on the floor. A couple of times he managed to eke out a "sorry," only to have his brother let loose another savage blow.

Panting, Spiro paused. "Dad turned them to monsters! They tore me apart! Ate me alive!"

"I didn't know," Wolf gasped. "I didn't—"

Spiro resumed his punching. "You left me in hell, Nelson!" More blows to Wolf's head, gut, neck.

I yanked Spiro's shirt, but the thin fabric just tore. "Stop, you're killing him!"

And it seemed clear—he was an expert not just at fighting, but killing. Part of the experiments?

He kept screaming at Wolf, his voice raspy with exertion. "And now you've come back to torture me! You've tried to kill me, over and over. But know how many times I've killed you? A hundred, you fratching loser."

Terrified for Wolf, I tried tackling his brother.

As soon as my arms latched around Spiro's chest, he swiveled and flung me off.

With a sob, I slid along the tile floor.

Looking desperate, Kiri brought up an airscreen and called for security in a shrill voice.

Spiro paused in his punches and pulled out the knife—the one he'd threatened Casper with on the carousel. He fumbled to open it with one hand while the other choked his brother.

Wolf looked on the verge of passing out, eyes rolling beneath swollen lids. By the time help arrived, he could be dead.

Channeling my fury, I launched myself at Spiro, whacking the knife from his hand. It skidded across the floor, out of his reach.

He pushed me away, but I rebounded in a flash, grabbing his sparkle-sculpted hair, looping my arm around his throat. With all my might, I squeezed as his hands raked at my arm.

At the end of the hallway, Borg appeared. He barreled through the daisies, wielding a zapper.

Registering the guard, Spiro dropped his arms.

When I released my grip, he stood up, rubbing his neck. Kiri ran to him and wrapped an arm around his waist.

On the ground, Wolf didn't move.

I knelt at his side, scared to touch him.

"What happened here?" Borg placed one hand on Spiro's shoulder, and with the other, pointed the zapper at Wolf and me.

"Borg." Spiro coughed, his voice hoarse. "My brother attacked me. Again."

"That's not true!" I shouted. "Spiro attacked Wolf!"

Borg spoke in a gruff voice. "All I saw on camera was a scuffle." He shot a look at Wolf, who stirred weakly, smearing his own blood. There was no sympathy in the guard's eyes.

He turned to Kiri. "Thanks for your call, Dr. Hsu-Ramos. What happened?"

She let out a breath, pressed her sparkled lips together. "Nelson hacked into the system. He replaced the holoscape with something he knew would terrify his brother. Psychological torture."

"Kiri, that's not true!" I turned to Borg. "Wolf was trying to do something kind, then Spiro attacked him."

Borg sighed. "You're Liv, right?"

I nodded.

"You were strangling Spiro when I got here." Borg snorted and glanced at Wolf. "Got a crush on the Long Lost Progeny, huh? Ready to defend him to death?" Condescension edged his laughter.

I was about to point out Spiro's switchblade on the floor, but it was gone. I eyed him and Kiri, wondering which of them had retrieved it.

With two conflicting stories of the fight, Borg didn't hesitate to believe the wrong one. He looked past my head to another security guard jogging toward us. This man was younger, slimmer, not much older than Wolf and me. *Socrates*, his nametag read.

"Socrates," I said. "Wolf's being falsely accused."

The man just looked obediently at Borg, who shook his head.

"Take Nelson to the infirmary," he instructed the younger guard. "I'll help Spiro." Borg put an arm around Spiro and led him to the elevator.

Kiri's arm stayed wrapped around his other side as he groaned in supposed pain.

Wolf, on the other hand, needed help to sit up. I looped my arm under his armpit and gently pulled him upright. Flinching, he made it to his feet but stayed hunched, his hair falling over his face. I leaned over and whispered, "What just happened?"

Wolf spoke under his breath, voice slurred. "In the experiments—my dad must've tweaked the puppy scene, made it nightmare material. I had no idea."

I felt terrible. I'd insisted, even though Wolf had warned me this was a bad idea. Just as he'd warned me that going to his dad would fail.

"I'm sorry, Wolf." Before I could ask more, Socrates put his arm on the other side of Wolf to support him. At least this guard was treating him with basic decency.

Straggling along, we followed the others through an arch of giant sunflowers. The six of us waited awkwardly for the elevator beneath a rose-studded arbor. I kept my arm around Wolf's torso, aware of the pattern of muscle and bone just beneath the skin. A mix of solid and fragile. His breathing was labored, his eyes closed, hands on his knees.

Kiri was busy fussing over Spiro. The one glance she gave me weighed heavy with disappointment.

Maybe I could get through to Socrates. "If you check the security footage," I told him, "you'll see what happened."

Like a 'bot, the young guard stared straight ahead.

Kiri turned to Borg, chin raised with indignation. "They've been using Nelson's watch to tamper with the cams and holoscapes. The security footage can't be trusted."

Her betrayal felt like a kick in the gut. And it hurt even worse when Borg grabbed Wolf's wrist, tore off the watch, and turned it over in his meaty hands. "We'll keep this."

"Just check the footage, Borg," I pleaded. "It's all valid."

He leveled his gaze at me. "Listen up, little lady. Just hours ago, I got a call from Casper himself, warning me about you and Nelson here. Next thing I know, the cams show Wolf beating up his brother again. With your help. Casper already instructed Soraya to kick you both off the island. She's doing the documentation as we speak."

I swallowed a scream. Wolf seemed in too much pain to register the conversation. I kept my grip on him firm as his blood dampened my hand.

Lips at his ear, I breathed in his smell of sweat and sea mixed with harsh iron. "Hang in there," I whispered.

And to my astonishment, Socrates gave Wolf a soft pat on the shoulder.

CHAPTER EIGHTEEN
Secret Murder

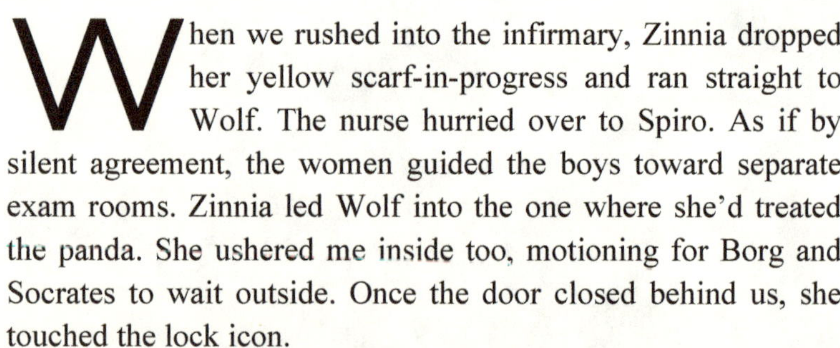

When we rushed into the infirmary, Zinnia dropped her yellow scarf-in-progress and ran straight to Wolf. The nurse hurried over to Spiro. As if by silent agreement, the women guided the boys toward separate exam rooms. Zinnia led Wolf into the one where she'd treated the panda. She ushered me inside too, motioning for Borg and Socrates to wait outside. Once the door closed behind us, she touched the lock icon.

As she arranged Wolf's head on the pillow and moved the virchip scanner over his temple, I told her about Spiro's attack. When she shook her head in sympathy, a wave of relief came over me—she believed me. The only adult to do so.

Something rustled in the corner where a white sheet was draped over a large cage. Whiny squeaks escaped.

While Zinnia tended to Wolf, I lifted the sheet and saw the panda playing with sticks and pillows, as lively as I'd seen her. Eyes alert, she rolled onto her back, cradling the toys.

Since she'd been half-hidden in the mesh bag before she'd fainted, I hadn't been able to appreciate her fur pattern up close and unobstructed. Her black rear legs looked like dapper pants, and her front legs had a strip of black stretching around her torso like a cropped jacket. The rest of her was creamy fuzz, punctuated by black ears, eyes, and nose.

"In a few minutes, we'll get the virchip analysis of your injuries," Zinnia told a half-conscious Wolf as her fingers moved over his torso, checking the ribs and organs.

She glanced at me. "You see that Sugarpie's recovering well?"

I scratched the nape of the panda's neck where she leaned against the side of the wire cage. "Can I take her to the airstrip soon?"

"She's all ready." Zinnia motioned to a small cooler in the corner. "I packed milk for her journey. The nurses know you'll be taking her. They won't say anything."

"Thanks, Zinnia." I wanted to hug her.

"A wildlife sanctuary in California is expecting her. You'll just need to arrange transport with a pilot. Too risky for me to do, since I'm so closely watched," she added. "And Liv, you'll need to pay the pilot a few mil. Can you—"

"I'll cover it," Wolf said under his breath.

Zinnia gazed at him… *fondly.*

As if she knew him well. It was the kind of look Delfina would give to Shell and me. Almost maternal.

I pet Sugarpie's ear and asked Zinnia, "How do I find the pilots?"

"The cargo airstrip's in back of the facility. Be warned. It's a no-man's land out there—the pilots are more or less outlaws, running their own black market dealings."

"Casper allows that?" I asked, surprised.

"They're contractors, not beholden to him, not like his employees here at the facility. He accepts it since he doesn't have to offer them benefits like sick leave or health care." She gave a cynical eye roll. "But this way, the pilots can ignore his rules. It works for everyone."

"Interesting arrangement."

She barked a laugh. "Okay, so to get to the cargo strip, just exit on this side of the building and head west. The paths can get confusing." She furrowed her brow in concern. "If you see a gardener, ask for directions—or better yet, pay one to go with you."

I nodded along, even though I could look out for myself. "Thanks, Zinnia."

From the bed, Wolf mumbled, "I'll go with her."

Zinnia gave him a motherly smile. "Sweetie, you're not going anywhere. Let your body heal."

I'd wanted to give Wolf privacy during the exam, but now I let myself look at him. Around his jawline, spiraling strands of copper were matted with blood, and his T-shirt had torn at the collar. His face was red and swelling in places, bruises in the midst of formation, but his eyes themselves were clear. Two rainy scoops of sea.

Flushing, I moved my gaze to the air screen, where the virchip scan now revealed a series of letters and numbers I couldn't interpret. "How is he?" I asked Zinnia.

"No breaks or internal bleeding, thank goodness. Just expect some soreness." She pressed a small patch onto his upper arm.

I was all too familiar with the painkiller patches, how they worked through micro-needles. Ten months ago, in the week before Shell's hibernation, I'd begged the nurses for free sample patches for her. I'd rationed them out, terrified there wouldn't be any left if her suffering grew worse.

"The patches should start working in a few seconds," Zinnia assured Wolf.

"Thanks," Wolf whispered, his face relaxing as they took effect.

She applied thicker patches to areas of broken skin. "Nano-generators to speed up wound-healing." She tilted her head, taking in the screen's data. "The virchip indicates that blood flow to the brain and neural activity is close to normal. Just a mild concussion. We'll keep you under observation for today. You'll probably be feeling dizzy."

I was impressed, seeing effective virchip technology in action twice in one day. Shell's nurses and doctors had never taken the time to explain it. "Can you tell me more about the virchip?"

"It gives an instant map of the brain's activity, down to the last neuron. We can correlate types of activity with different health problems." She swiped through the airscreen data, pointing out examples and answering my questions, as Wolf half dozed. She concluded with, "Pretty abracadabrant stuff." She patted my hand. "Stuff that should be accessible to everyone."

She handed Wolf a cold pack.

"Thanks," he murmured, pressing it to his head.

Resting a hand on his shoulder, she offered him water and had him swallow some anti-inflams. "Glad you're okay, Nelson." She paused. "You know, I delivered you."

He furrowed his brow. "Delivered me from what?"

She laughed. "Delivered you at your birth. I was your mother's doctor. I'm Zinnia." She reached out her hand.

Wolf blinked and shook it slowly. "Call me Wolf."

"Sure thing, Wolf." She smiled. "May I ask, why the name change?"

He closed his eyes. "Last year, something happened that made me want a fresh start. There'd been so much fakeness in my life. All the Progeny hype, the virch worlds—I needed to let go of the old me. I needed something… *untamed.*"

"I like it." Zinnia nodded in approval. "You know, Wolf, your mother and I were friends, in the same circle of women."

His eyes shot open and he stared at her.

"When I heard you were a new intern, I was hoping we'd get a chance to talk." She chuckled. "Not under these circumstances, of course."

I stood up, realizing they might want privacy for a heart-to-heart. "I'll leave you to talk alone."

Wolf reached out a hand. "Please, stay."

I hovered by the door.

"Yes," Zinnia said, "stay, Liv." Perched on the edge of the bed, she patted Wolf's knee. "Your mother would be proud."

His voice creaked with emotion. "Why?"

"For your decision to step out of the Progeny limelight. And be true to yourself." Zinnia waved away the virchip air screen and pulled up a fresh one. She opened a file labeled AMIGAS and tapped on one labeled SPRING-2137.

Four life-size women showed up on the translucent screen in 4D, arm in arm, wrapped in light floral-citrus scents, faces aglow. The one on the far left was a younger, slighter version of Zinnia, her braids fully black, a contrast with her white-and-yellow polka-dotted sundress.

And on the far right stood a pregnant woman—she looked like Wolf, with her cascade of deep-brown curls and bronze skin just a shade richer than his. Tucked behind her ear was a plumeria bloom, white-tipped petals with a sunshiney center. She seemed carefree, giddy to be with best friends.

I had nothing to do with any of this—still, a lump lodged in my throat.

Wolf's jaw quivered. He leaned forward and reached out his hand, moving his fingertips through his mother's hair. He brought the screen closer, and then, in a tender gesture, put his head to her shoulder in a kind of air-hug. Breathing in the scent, he murmured, "I think I remember this smell."

I felt his ache, wanted to hold him.

Zinnia wrapped an arm around him. "Lilikoi shampoo. Passion fruit, her favorite. Your mother was magnificent. Kalea got involved in virch research because she wanted to make the world a better place. She had determination." The doctor winked at me. "You remind me of her, Liv."

Blood rose to my face. "Was she one of the other… rebels you mentioned?"

A heaviness came over Zinnia as she nodded. "Kalea stood up to Casper, too."

Tilting his head, Wolf asked, "How—how did she even end up with my dad?"

"Oh, she was a bright light. Her energy was infectious. Your father fell in love with her, Wolf. And although Casper was much older, she was drawn to his philosophical nature, his visionary brilliance, his out-of-the-box thinking. He came from humble beginnings—his empire was self-made—and this appealed to your mom. She brought out the best in him, and she believed that together, they could improve things. For everyone."

Zinnia rested her gaze on Wolf, her eyes shining. "Your mother was determined that her son would live a normal life. She asked Amala to be your godmother." Zinnia pointed to a petite woman with a warm complexion and smile.

Wolf's brow wrinkled. "But Amala was always so honest with me. So... *real*. Why didn't she tell me more about my mom? About their friendship?"

A shadow passed over Zinnia's face. "Your father instructed her not to." Her voice dropped to a grave whisper. "Listen, we don't have much time before a guard checks on us. But there's something you need to know."

"What?" Trepidation filled his voice.

"The day before your mother died, she changed her will. My wife, Milu, was her lawyer." Zinnia gestured toward a woman with long, black hair in a thick braid. The day of the photo must have been breezy—her scarf was blown in mid-flight toward us.

For a moment, Zinnia's hand lingered there, the backs of her fingers brushing Milu's cheeks. "The will said that in the event of Kalea's death, your godmother would care for you until adulthood. And she left all her money to support Amala and you. Your mother called her up in a panic that night. She asked her to love you like a son. The next morning, your mother died."

My hand flew to my mouth. I remembered what Wolf had told me about his mother falling off a ladder. "You think it wasn't an accident?"

Zinnia raised an eyebrow. "Each of us—her three best friends—we've had our doubts. However, each of us was... *coerced* into keeping our suspicions to ourselves. Still, not long after your mom's death, my wife told me she was going to report Casper to the police. The next day, her autocar malfunctioned. Drove her off a bridge. Killed her."

Wolf said nothing, as if rendered speechless.

My throat tightened. "I'm so sorry."

Zinnia sniffled, her eyes brimming. "I assumed I'd be next. But your father—he must've decided it would be too suspicious. Instead, he kept me close."

She squeezed Wolf's hand. "I just wish I'd been able to tell you sooner. It's impossible for me to communicate anything meaningful off-island. My every message is watched and censored. And you were under such close tabs in the virch world—at least, until you disappeared."

She paused. "There's more. Your father monitored your mother's interactions, unbeknownst to her." She pressed her lips together and pulled up another file on the air screen.

There, hovering before us, was a paragraph of garbled, nonsensical words. "An encoded message from your mother to me," she explained, entering instructions.

Soon the decoded words appeared. It was a message, dated August 31, 2138.

```
Zin! Found out something CHILLING about
the virchip campaign. Scary stuff. Will
go public with it tomorrow. Making a new
will with Milu tonight. She'll fill you
in. If anything happens to me, protect
my baby. Help him understand. Love you.
— Kalea
```

Wolf's face fell into his hands. "My dad found the message."

The horror sunk in. I tried wrapping my head around the fact that Casper had killed the mother of his own child over this secret about the virchip campaign.

Footsteps sounded outside the door. There was knocking, then banging. A man's voice growled, "Open up!"

Zinnia waved away the air screen as I dashed to the now-sleeping panda and threw the sheet over her cage. Wolf lay back on the pillow, shielding his tear-swollen eyes with the crook of his elbow.

Zinnia planted a professional smile on her face and opened the door.

Borg stood before her, a vein in his neck popping out. "Why's this door locked?"

"Oh, hello, there." Zinnia remained shockingly unruffled. "We locked the door for the boys' safety. In case one of them decided to renew the battle." She clucked. "Boys will be boys, right? And brothers are the worst!"

He frowned at her, then gestured for her to move aside.

She complied, but positioned herself between him and the panda cage, blocking his view.

When Sugarpie rustled, I let loose a flurry of coughs to cover it up.

Borg's attention moved to me, beside Wolf's bed, instead of the panda cage. He sneered at me, then at Wolf on the bed. "Nelson, you're officially being removed from this internship. Soraya will come here with documents to be signed—in person, with her as a witness."

He turned back to me, still sneering. "You're also being removed. Soraya will bring the documents to your room. You'll be confined there until the heliplane comes for you both tomorrow morning."

Wolf and I exchanged glances. If we were forced to leave the island, how could we stop the bioweapon release?

Borg continued, "If you leave the infirmary, Nelson—or if you leave your room, Liv—then we'll lock you in a holding cell and escort you to the passenger airstrip at dawn."

My hands clenched into fists. Frustration and fury mounted inside me. Casper was a cold-blooded murderer. He deserved to be held accountable, not cozy in his illusion-filled office with his henchman doing his dirty work.

"Sir," Zinnia said, face serious, "as this boy's doctor, I can't allow him to be transported anywhere in his injured state."

Borg scoffed. "I don't care what state he's in, he's leaving this island tomorrow morning." He snapped his fingers as if just remembering something. "Oh, and Nelson, your father said to tell you that you've been a huge disappointment to him."

Wolf didn't react, but Borg's words set me ablaze. I glared at the guard. "Tell *Casper* he's a huge disappointment to *us*."

"How dare you insult him." Borg curled his lip. "We did some digging, found out where you're from. And you should be grateful to him. You're trash."

My blood boiled.

"So, of course, you'll be delivered straight to a refugee camp." He let this sink in, as if enjoying my torment.

Zinnia took him by the arm. "Borg, that's enough. Leave her alone, and let my patient rest."

When he hesitated, she gave him a gentle push toward the door. Her motherly touch was so powerful, it even worked on this thug. Softening ever so slightly, he turned to go.

As soon as he left, I kicked the door after him.

Instead of scaring me, he infuriated me.

A fire lit inside me.

CHAPTER NINETEEN
Tropical Gardens

"Sweetie, enough door-kicking." Zinnia touched my shoulder. "Wolf needs quiet now."

"Don't let Borg take him," I rasped.

"Of course not. Listen, go change out of those clothes. Clear your mind."

I looked down at my shirt and shorts, spotted with Wolf's blood. "Okay, I'll be back soon. Then we'll make a plan."

Before leaving, I leaned toward Wolf, tugged on my favorite curl, right in the middle of his forehead. His lids were fluttering shut, the pain meds working in full force, giving him some relief.

Not me. Rage pulsed with each footstep, all the way to my room.

Inside, I closed the door behind me and sat on the bed, freshly made by a 'bot in my absence. I punched the pillow, over and over, then let my face fall into it. I wanted to scream or run or maybe just take a long nap.

I picked up Dad's engraved driftwood. *Do your best.*

Wolf and I were in this together. It was deep and real, and I couldn't abandon him or our mission. Our *missions*. Together, we would stop the virus from escaping. Together, we would save Shell. And together, we would make the world care.

Two days or even less. That's what my dream self had said. Which meant I'd have to avoid Soraya and Borg and Casper. I wouldn't sign anything. And I definitely wouldn't be packing my bags.

One thing I knew: I had to leave my room. I couldn't be here when Soraya came with the documents.

Anyway, I'd need nourishment for whatever was coming. Venturing into the dining hall might be dangerous, but I had to eat. Soraya and Borg couldn't expect me to starve in my room.

I stripped off the blood-stained clothes and let them soak in cool water in the sink. Then I put on the only clean outfit left, a silvery tank and pale blue shorts.

I stuck a tentative hand inside the right pocket, hoping for another message. When I felt the soft cotton, I smiled. This one was a faded indigo with moon-white stitches forming the word BREATHE.

I could hear Delfina's voice saying the word like the pluck of a low guitar string, the tone she used when I'd get frustrated over a math problem.

Breathe. A simple, easy-to-follow instruction. I sipped air like an elixir, letting it fill me, and then exhaled a breath, slowly. More clear-minded now, I tucked the fabric into my right pocket along with the other ones. My secret amulets. *Breathe, fly, love.*

As I walked to the dining hall, there was no sign of Soraya or Borg, just scientists and interns chatting over their meals.

In a moment of paranoia, I wondered if Casper and his cronies might track me through my virchip. But I had no reason to think they could—virchips were just diagnostic health tools, only able to connect with nearby scanners, not with spyware. At least, I hoped that was all they could do. Zinnia's revelation of a secret about the virchip campaign was making me question my assumptions.

The scents of sautéed garlic and tomato let me forget my worries and focus on how ravenous I was. From the buffet, I chose a plate of sweet-n-sour spaghetti, then headed into the dining area—Shady Treehouse holoscape, complete with fake squirrels scampering over leafy branches. Dappled light and foliage obscured faces, giving each table a pocket of privacy. Head down, I searched for an open spot.

"Hey, Lil!" Strawberry called, pointing to a chair beside her.

"It's Liv, actually." Joining the fruit crew could help me avoid attention. I sat down and dove into the noodles.

After twenty-four hours straight in reality, my fellow interns had embraced their lack of virchlenses as a kind of trippy altered state. They'd set their sights on more attainable love interests—real ones at the table next to ours. Even über-geek Sammy was getting some attention.

"That guy with the titanium dust hair," Strawberry said, gesturing with her eyes. "He's been hanging around Melon all day."

"It's so weird to smell their actual smells," said Melon, popping an effi-food pill. She pushed her undulating snake-hair aside and bit into a curry burrito. "You know, instead of just virch cologne."

"I know!" Strawberry waved her spoonful of rose crème brûlée in the air. "It does something to me."

"Pheromones," Plum said with a smug grin, eyeing a guy through leaves at the next table.

I thought of Wolf. He tapped into something inside me, something oceanic. A whole underground sea of churning, foaming, crashing *something*. And even if I tried to ignore it, it rose to the surface—flashes of his skin dripping saltwater in sunshine.

Sneaky pheromones. I shoveled my pasta in faster—I had to get back to the infirmary before Borg or Soraya crossed my path.

I tried to focus on making a plan. Wolf wouldn't be much help until he recovered. In the meantime, I could work on getting Sugarpie to the airstrip. And I'd keep an eye on Spiro until Wolf and I figured out how to handle him. I'd have to somehow keep tabs on Casper and Mo, too. Their mysterious project bearing fruit tomorrow disconcerted me. Without Wolf's retro watch, we were at a big disadvantage.

But Zinnia was our ally, and she knew this island inside and out—she could keep helping us.

I scanned the room and spotted Kiri dining with Spiro a few tables over, half-hidden behind a magnolia tree. And just beyond them was someone barreling through the holo-branches, heading my way. Soraya's brown equine eyes latched onto me. Zuggers.

I stood and sped through the forest canopy to the far end of the dining hall. Glancing back, I saw Soraya behind me, wielding her tail like a whip, presumably so that she wouldn't trip this time.

I raced full-speed down the corridor, squinting into the pink-golden dazzle of the holo-sunset.

Galloping footsteps sounded behind me.

I darted around the corner and touched the door-open icon at the infirmary, hoping she wouldn't see me before the doors swooshed shut behind me. Inside, the nurse—a different one this time, with pointy elbows and chin—glanced up from his airscreen.

"Visiting Wolf," I mumbled. "Zinnia knows I'm coming."

"She had to step out, but go on in," he said, then went back his screen.

When I slipped inside Wolf's room, his eyes fluttered open. "Angel."

A sheet was tucked around his neck, his head propped on a pillow. Unruly, dark curls spread over the white fabric. The dried blood had been cleaned up, the patches removed, and now he just lay there looking *angelic*—in a retro surfer-dude way. His lips were curved and tender, his brows raised in delight. And those eyes were the hue of a mist on my bay—all freshness and hope.

He spoke in a whisper. "Hey, you."

Warmth filled me. I was worse than the fruit crew. If I believed my dream, I was on the verge of falling in love with the most famous Progeny boy ever. From the look of it, he was on the verge of falling in love with me too.

Voices in the reception area broke the moment. The nurse's voice, confused, and Soraya's voice, sharp. Zuggers. What had I been thinking, coming here?

I blamed the pheromones.

Frantic, I dashed inside the nearby closet, closed the door, and held my breath. The space was larger than expected and filled with biohaz suits, hundreds of them. Enough for everyone on the island?

I pushed my way past the slippery fabric, toward the back.

Moments later, I heard the exam room's door slide open, and footsteps enter.

Soraya's shrill voice rang out. "Where is she, Nelson?"

No audible response from Wolf.

The nurse's deep voice: "Soraya, please, he's supposed to be resting."

"He's *supposed* to be leaving the island."

"Zinnia says he's not in any shape to go on a heliplane."

"Where's the girl?" Soraya demanded. "I saw her come in."

The nurse sighed. "She must've left already."

"Impossible," said Soraya. "What's beneath that sheet in the corner?"

The panda. If Soraya found her, she'd bring her right back to Spiro.

The nurse's voice grew as sharp as his elbows. "Soraya, I have to put my foot down here. You need to leave."

Soraya cursed. "If you see her, call security. And tell her she's going straight to the holding cell."

Footsteps, then the swish of the door opening and closing.

I waited a minute just to be safe.

Wolf watched me come out, still shaky. "Hey, Angel. I thought I imagined you."

I pressed a hand to his forehead. "You okay?"

"Now that you're here."

"How're you handling all this?"

His voice emerged, soft. "I already knew Casper was capable of hurting his own family. And what he did to my mom and Milu—it just makes me that much more determined. I'll make people see the truth about him. And the entire Virch Empire."

"I'm with you, Wolf." I rested my hand against his cheek. "And I'm not leaving the island tomorrow. Not until we stop the outbreak."

He gave a fragile smile. "Me neither."

"Good. Listen, I'm taking the panda now."

"I'm coming, too." He tossed off the sheet. He was fully dressed underneath, from his ripped T-shirt to his worn-down flip flops. This shirt was a blood-free sunny yellow—someone must have brought him a change of clothes.

"Stay here, Wolf. If you just—"

"It's too dangerous. You can't go alone."

"I'll be fine. But you're hurt."

He stood up, looking unsteady. "We might have only a day, Angel."

Gently, I pushed him back onto the bed. It was easy—he was floppy. "Rest."

I peeked under the sheet and observed the panda in her cage. She was on her back, rocking and sucking on a bottle of milk, looking content. I couldn't help smiling at how her giant paws clutched the bottle and her rear legs splayed out, revealing her white belly. She was such a roly-poly ball of fluff. And now she was healthy.

"I want to meet the pilots too," Wolf said. "In case we need to escape on a cargo heliplane."

"Escape?"

"My dad's ruthless. If he forces us onto one of his passenger heliplanes, it could conveniently crash."

I swallowed hard. I wouldn't put it past Casper.

Wolf took a deep breath. "And there's more—something my dream self said about you."

Suddenly nervous, I looked away, reaching my hand through the cage and letting it sink into Sugarpie's coarse fur.

"What was it?" I asked with trepidation.

After a beat, he said, "Just something that makes me want to protect you."

I didn't push it. I wouldn't know what to do with the answer.

"I can take care of myself, Wolf." I walked back over to the bed, pressed my hand firmly on his shoulder. There was the sharp line of his clavicle, the layers of muscles. Invisible pheromones wending their way around my body. "Stay here and rest."

"I'm coming with you." He put his hand over mine.

For a moment, our gazes connected, filling me with heat.

"Fine." I removed my hand and headed to Sugarpie's cage, which had been placed on a cart with a small cooler of milk bottles attached. I booped her nose, then rearranged the sheet around the cage.

"Wait!" Wolf said when I reached for the door-open icon. "The nurse—he won't let me leave."

I breathed out, exasperated. "Then stay."

He climbed onto the cart and slipped under the sheet beside the panda's cage.

Really? With a resigned sigh, I tucked the sheet around him and with all my weight, rolled the cart out the door. The nurse gave me a conspiratorial wink, clearly unaware that Wolf was hitching a ride with the panda.

Straining, I maneuvered the cart down the hallway and turned the corner, hoping Soraya or Borg weren't waiting there. With most people at dinner, the sunset-lit hallway was deserted as we walked toward the west door. Sweet relief.

And if Borg spotted us on hidden cameras, at least we'd have a lead on him.

I pushed the Exit icon, the door slid open, and Wolf and I headed into the unknown.

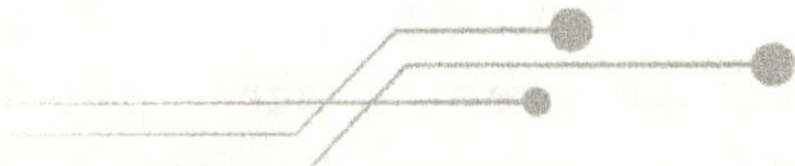

How strange to be outside in the humid evening air. The actual sunset wasn't as dramatic as the holoscape inside. Mist wrapped around us and the sky hung low, a heavy gray.

Voice muffled, Wolf asked, "Coast clear?"

"Yeah."

He staggered out from under the sheet and swayed beside me. I peeked at the panda, relieved she was content—rolling on her back and sniffing at her paw, her eyes drowsy. Maybe the motion of the cart would ease her into sleep.

Next step: Take cover in the forest.

I let Wolf help me push, suspecting he was using the cart to steady himself. There were only our rasps of breath and hurried footsteps and the squeak of a wheel. Every so often, the path branched off and we headed in a general western direction, though it was hard to tell with the thick, tall foliage.

Shiny green engulfed us—tropical, giant-leafed trees laced with orchids and looped with vines. Lianas wound up a ceiba with buttressed roots as tall as me. Feathered ferns poked out from logs blanketed in fungi and moss. Heliconia blooms hung like orange bells.

And all of it was real.

I'd been in virch rain forests for field research. But that had felt different, a layer of *pretend* superimposed over my own reality. I'd always had a vague awareness of Delfina's shack in the background.

Here, in the real thing, in my real body, I noticed what the virch rain forest hadn't included: sweat beading on my flesh, carpenter ants marching by my toes, gnats buzzing at my ear, the air weighing heavy with smells of rot and nectar.

All of my self was here, now.

Sugarpie let out a relaxed sigh. Apart from her rustling, there were only plant and animal sounds, no signs of other humans. Still, I kept my voice low. "Think we'll find a gardener?"

"They're probably instructed to stay out of sight so that they don't break the illusion. That's how it always was at my dad's homes." Wolf's voice was a murmur. "He wanted you to think the bushes naturally stayed pruned, that the dead leaves magically disappeared, you know?"

"I know how it feels to be invisible." I paused, gathering courage to open up to him. "It's like people in the Null Zones are cogs in a machine that preserves illusions for the sharks."

Wolf nodded. "The rich and powerful don't want to know what happens to their e-waste after they throw it out. They don't want to know about toxic chemicals poisoning kids in the junk heaps. They don't want to know that while they're agonizing over which five-mil jellyfish shirt to buy, or which shade of sparkling jade to color their irises, people are dying from something as simple as contaminated food."

Wonder swept through me. "You get it."

He lowered his eyes. "For most of my life, I was one of them."

"Well, you're not now."

We pushed Sugarpie through a tunnel of green, birds flitting from branch to branch like feathered rainbows—quetzals, parrots, toucans.

"No one even uses these gardens," Wolf said. "Everyone just goes to the ones inside. Humidity and temperature controlled, everything in bloom all the time. Why does my dad even have these?"

I considered this. "Kings throughout time have had their gardens. Mini-worlds that exist to amuse them. Your dad—he's like a modern king playing god."

Wolf lifted a shoulder. "Everyone's a god now, controlling their own virch worlds."

"Everyone who's a shark," I corrected him.

"True." His hand grazed my arm, fingertips trailing down my elbow to the sensitive part of my wrist. His hand stayed there lightly, fingers tapping like a little pulse. "I'm going to do everything in my power to change things with you."

I swallowed. "I know."

"Listen," he whispered. "Now that we're away from cameras, I can tell you about the experiments." He hesitated. "But it could put you in danger if you know about them."

A blue macaw swooped past us, exposing its brilliant gold belly, trailing a fan of sunshine feathers. My breath caught and my nerves lit up. I was very aware of Wolf's skin against mine. "If you risk telling me, then I'll risk hearing it."

His voice dropped even lower. "Last year, Spiro and me—we were Casper's guinea pigs. It was über-classified stuff. With brand new tech. At first, we wanted to do it—I mean, when you have a hundred siblings, it's pretty incredible when your dad shows you special attention." His words crackled, low and raspy. "But then things got bad, Angel."

I thought of the monster puppies, the terror in Spiro's eyes. I remembered Spiro's words about his brother. *We've both been to hell. Only he thinks he found his way out. But we're both still here.* That fear I'd seen in Spiro's face was now spilling over Wolf's.

His voice broke as he said, "Really bad."

I wanted to hug him. And I wanted to smack his father for whatever hell he'd put his sons through. "What happened?" I asked, moving closer so that our sides touched as we walked.

"I don't know where to start." An evening sunbeam broke through the clouds, casting rippled shadows over his face, patches of light and dark.

"Anywhere."

He drew in a breath. "It was the end of the world—"

Something moved in the bushes to my right.

A flash of silver.

A sharpened blade.

CHAPTER TWENTY
Invisible

I zeroed in on the rustling foliage. "Stay with the panda," I whispered, pulling away from Wolf.

He nodded, stunned, still half lost in whatever he'd been about to tell me.

I scrambled off the path and stumbled through the underbrush. Part of me wondered if running *toward* a blade was a good idea. But there was something even scarier about the idea of cowering while someone stalked us.

When the person ran in the other direction, I chased him—better to face the threat head on. He was fast and agile, keeping far enough ahead that I couldn't see any more than the vegetation shaking in his wake.

But picking through unstable junk piles had made me agile too.

When he slowed, I hurled myself forward for the tackle. I managed to grab his leg, and we both thudded into the soft earth.

But wait, no, not a he, but a *she*. And a little one.

I kept hold of her thin ankle and scrambled forward, finding myself face to face with an elfin girl. She held up a huge, old-fashioned machete, the blade as long as her arm. Freshly sharpened.

I let go, raised my palms, then scooched backward. "I'm sorry." Slowly, I stood up. "Did I hurt you?"

Clutching the machete with both hands, she regarded me, wary. She stood up, too, then backed away, still facing me. She couldn't have been more than seven or eight, the age of my sister when she started working in the junk heaps. This girl's adult teeth had just come in, looking too big for her little heart-shaped face.

Her dark hair had tiny pink shells woven into haphazard braids. Her shorts and T-shirt were smeared with dirt, threadbare in spots. She looked sturdy and tough, with a streak of soil on her cheek. She reminded me of Shell—pretty, with a spark in her eyes. Her complexion was the same woodsy shade, and around her neck, she wore a necklace of tree nuts, deep brown and red. Exactly the kind of thing Shell might make.

"Why'd you chase me?" she demanded.

"I—I thought you were going to hurt us."

"What're you doing here?"

"I'm Liv. I'm looking for the pilots."

"They're dangerous." Her body shifted, her feet poised to run at any second.

I softened my expression, willing her to stay. "What's your name?"

She glanced away, at a blue-winged macaw perched atop a giant palm.

I tried another approach. "Where are your parents?"

She stared at me for a moment, considering, and then let out three loud, bird-like trills. A warning? A summons?

"You live here?" I asked.

She rammed the tip of her machete into the earth and leaned on it, letting out three more bird trills. "My daddy's a gardener. I help him."

So she was a child laborer, just like the kids in the Cove. Just like my sister had been. A lump formed in my throat.

"Bet you know a lot about plants—" I cut myself short. The leaves were moving at our side, just a meter away. Someone was coming. My muscles tensed.

A man stepped out. He was stocky and wearing a dark green jumpsuit. Swiftly, he wrapped an arm around the girl, lowered his head, and started apologizing.

"Oh," I said quickly, "I'm the one who's sorry, sir. I don't mean to bother you." I reached out my hand. "I'm Liv. An intern at the facility."

Keeping the girl—his daughter?—close with one arm, he stuck out his other elbow to shake, since his hands were covered in soil. He studied me. "You okay, miss? You lost?"

I gave a weak smile. "Any chance you can bring me and my friend to the airstrip?"

"Oh, I don't know." His forehead creased. "We're not supposed to—"

"We can pay you well."

He and his daughter exchanged looks. Finally, he gave a reluctant shrug. "Okay."

A muffled voice rose over the trees. "Liv?"

Wolf. He must be worried.

"Yeah," I called out. "Be right there."

The girl and her father led me back to the path, where Wolf was waiting by the cart.

She stared at him in that unabashed way little kids have.

For a moment I let myself stare at him, too, taking in the landscape of his body: his strong calf ridges, his forearms with their rivers of muscles and veins, the broad plane of his shoulders—all well-defined from his year trekking around the Himalayas. Even in his weakened, bruised state, he was solid. Whatever he'd been through had somehow given him a foundation of stone. I'd glimpsed his layers, like striations of earth— his sincerity, his earnest way of listening, his determination to do good in the world.

"Hey!" he said with relief. "You all right?"

"Yeah."

He waved at my companions. "Hi, I'm Wolf."

The gardener nodded and said in a low voice, "This way."

As his daughter darted around like a squirrel, the man led us along curving paths, a labyrinth branching left, then right, then left, until I stopped trying to keep track. Instead, I used the flowers as landmarks—pink orchid, purple orchid, golden orchid. I paused to check out a bromeliad with thick red and green leaves.

The girl noticed my interest. "Look, they catch rainwater and make tiny ponds inside. See?" She pulled back a leaf and out jumped a little frog.

I jumped, too, my nerves jangled.

She laughed. "Come on, I'll show you other stuff."

She proved an eager nature guide, pointing out a carnivorous pitcher plant that devoured insects and lizards, then giant red blooms that looked like dandelions gone to seed. "Blood lilies," she announced, explaining that this variety was particularly poisonous.

I kept zigzagging my eyes, trying to bring up my field journal, but of course, my virchlens wasn't there. I had to use my old-fashioned memory.

"Hey," I said, "maybe I could come out here sometime and help you garden." I paused, wondering if I'd even be on this island in the near future—and if it would be safe for her to meet me. But we'd be protected in the thick forest, and it seemed fairly isolated. "You can teach me about these plants. And maybe there are science things I could teach you."

She beamed at her dad.

"Thanks," he said, nodding. "We hardly ever run into people from the facility out here. And when we do, they barely say three words to us."

"I get it," I said. "I'm from a Null Zone by the Chesapeake Bay." For the first time ever, I said this with pride.

His face softened. And just like that, a bond formed between us.

As we walked, he spoke more freely. "You have teachers where you're from?"

At my nod, he sighed. "We don't have any here. Not enough kids for one. No access to virch schools either. Everything my daughter knows she learned from the plants and me." He chuckled. "And I don't know much."

He was being humble, of course. I had the feeling he knew plenty.

"I didn't think anyone besides the pilots lived outside the facility," Wolf told the gardener. "Where do you two live?"

He gestured with his chin. "North side of the gardens. Underground dwellings with trap doors. We stay out of sight. Not supposed to ruin the landscape."

Staying invisible. "You have neighbors here?" I asked.

"A few other families. Outdoor maintenance workers."

"Where are you from?" Wolf asked.

"Our ancestors were the original inhabitants of the island. Years ago, when Casper built the facility here, he let us stay and work if we wanted. Without the benefits the scientists get. No vacation or education or medical care." He shrugged. "But we love these forests and our island."

I understood this in my core. "It's home."

"For generations," he continued, "my family oversaw the wind and solar energy functions. But now Virch has mostly switched to easy-fusion reactors."

"Easy fusion?" I echoed. I'd taken a class on renewable energy. "That technology's still at the experimental stages. You mean it's actually in use here?"

He nodded. "I don't know much more—just that we have it. Think it's powered by the ocean or something. The 'bots run it themselves."

An easy-fusion operation would be enormous, but as far as I could tell, the only big structure here was the facility with the labs and dorms. "Where?" I asked, confused.

"Oh, it's all deep underground." He frowned. "Lots of reactors down there. All self-sufficient. The mechanic 'bots can repair anything—even each other. No need for humans really." He laughed. "Except for gardening. They tried it with 'bots, but they messed it up pretty bad!"

The girl gave a triumphant grin. "That's why we're gardeners!" She darted off the path, picking hibiscus blooms as she went.

Wolf looked disturbed. "That's a staggering amount of power. Millions of times more power than wind and solar. What's it all for?"

I said nothing. *Massive bombs* was what I was thinking, but I didn't want to scare the gardener. Easy fusion could power a weapon of mass destruction. Were we following the wrong lead?

Glancing at Wolf, I could practically see his neurons sparking. Maybe he had his own theory. Either way, thanks to this gardener, we were getting closer to some hidden truth.

I ducked under a banana leaf, eyeing his daughter through the foliage, her hands now full of blooms. "What's your name, sir?"

"Call me Sodo." His voice was gruff but infused with gentleness. "And if the pilots ask, don't tell them it was us who brought you there."

"Why?" asked Wolf, wiping sweat from his forehead.

"We're just gardeners. If we lay low, do our job, Virch pays us and gives us food. But the cargo pilots play by their own rules. Better to stay out of their way."

The closer we grew to the airstrip, the more skittish Sodo looked.

"You okay?" I asked.

"Just—watch yourselves. Don't disappear out there."

CHAPTER TWENTY-ONE
Grizzlies

Twilight had fallen by the time we reached a swath of pavement cutting through wild grasses and forest. Jupiter and Venus glowed against an indigo sky. I rubbed my arms in the cool, moist air.

Heliplanes waited on the tarmac—six-bladers, the kind I'd flown during a virch piloting elective. They were easy to maneuver on autopilot, but the tricky part was landing manually—knowing when to engage the rotors, interpreting the sensors, gauging wind and pressure, lowering it steadily to the ground. The only time I'd crashed had been in manual mode, during a simulated storm that cut system communication and rendered autopilot useless. Sim or no sim, that had been scary.

Sodo pointed to a simple hangar—a raw-cement, one-story building. Through the propped-open doorway, light spilled and music blared—the screechy, growly kind made from animal noise mixes, loud even from twenty meters away.

He and his daughter stayed at the forest's edge, as though there were an invisible electric fence. "This is as far as we go," he said, tightening his arm around her.

I crouched down to her height. "Can't wait to see you again for a nature tour. Where should we meet?"

She looked at her dad hopefully, as if asking permission.

"How about at the entrance to the gardens?" he suggested.

"Day after tomorrow?" I asked. "Around three o'clock?"

Wolf gave me a strange look.

I guessed his thoughts: why make a date when we were busy saving the world? But in two day's time, we would have either succeeded in stopping the disaster or not. And I felt a connection with this girl, wanting to form a friendship with her.

Maybe the day after tomorrow would come, and it would be a normal day. Or at least, as normal as things got on this island. I reached out my hand and she took it. I savored the feel of her sticky, grimy little-girl hand in mine—it felt like Shell's hand.

My chest ached and I wanted to hug her, or at least give her something. I wanted to bring her to the dining hall, feed her sweet-n-sour spaghetti and rose crème brûlée, introduce her to the other interns. Let this extraordinary child be *visible* to them.

Meanwhile, Wolf was shaking Sodo's hand. "Thanks for everything." He dropped some gold coins into the man's palm.

Strange that he carried actual coins with him. I'd assumed that as a shark, he just transferred funds via compubank. Maybe the coins were a retro thing?

He gave one to the girl. "And thank you, too."

Her face lit up. A gold coin would have been an enormous sum for me and Shell back in the Cove, where we still used the currency. It apparently was for this child, too.

I couldn't resist—I had to offer her something. I'd noticed her eyeing Sugarpie's sheet-covered cage with curiosity. "Want to see what's under here?"

When she nodded, I lifted the blanket. Wonder flashed over her face and she glanced at me eagerly.

"Meet Sugarpie," I said. "Go ahead and pet her."

She reached her hand through the wires and ran her fingers through the thick fur on the cub's neck. With a wet black nose, the panda nuzzled her hand.

Fresh determination washed over me. Here in the darkness, this girl's silhouette was just like Shell's, and so was her delight.

Sodo pulled her gently away. "Time to go, love."

She plucked a pink orchid and handed it to me. A talisman of sorts, to keep us safe. Or maybe just a thing of beauty to share.

"Thank you." I tucked it behind my ear.

Looking pleased, she took her father's hand and headed with him down the path.

Over his shoulder, Sodo said, "Good luck."

They vanished into the shadows, footsteps melting into rain forest sounds.

And just like that, my world expanded. My *worlds*. Not just the small world of my family, or the world in the Cove, or the world of other Null Zones, but this girl's world, right here on this island. I understood Delfina's courage to change things, and Wolf's courage, and I felt it myself now, down to my bones.

I took a deep breath, touched the petals in my hair, and prepared to face the pilots.

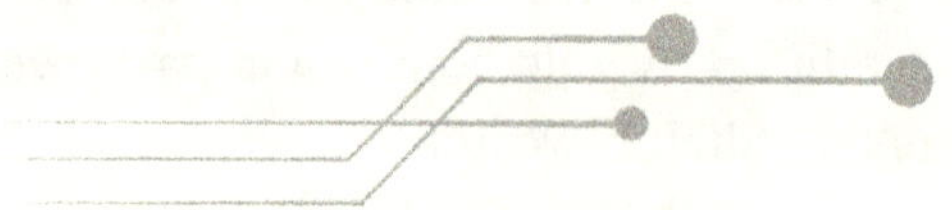

Harsh light illuminated Wolf's face as he stared across the tarmac at the hangar. I checked on the panda—she breathed in a steady rhythm, hopefully about to doze again.

"Think we'll find our way back after this?" I asked, rubbing the orchid petals between my fingers.

Wolf shrugged. "Maybe a kindly pilot can guide us."

"Right… *kindly*."

"I bet they're just big, soft teddy bears." Wolf's hand brushed my elbow. "Come on."

We walked across the airstrip toward the squat building.

"Wolf." I stopped in my tracks. "We don't even know the girl's name." It seemed vital that I know her name. To make her real.

"You'll see her again soon." His voice wasn't convincing.

My chest clenched. "What if I don't?"

It came in waves, this acceptance that if our dreams were to be believed, we might be dead in two days. Maybe everyone else would be, too.

There was nothing to do but forge onward. I resumed pushing the cart, Wolf beside me. The music grew loud as we approached, further rattling my nerves. "So, you have enough money to pay a pilot, too?" I asked, wondering how much they'd demand.

He nodded. "I brought plenty. More than enough for bribes to get passwords and biocodes to hack into virchrelax." He looked almost apologetic, or maybe embarrassed at his wealth. "Couldn't leave a digital money trail."

It flustered me, this talk of bribes and money—such a foreign world. "Well, your coins will help get Sugarpie to her new home." I peeked at the sleeping furball. "Let's leave her outside. The noise might scare her."

"Agreed." Wolf adjusted the sheet over her and we stepped inside.

The place vibrated with screeching music. It lacked any holoscape—just bare gray walls with ancient ads made from paper, edges curled and yellowed. No faux scents, only a close, damp smell of sweat and the reek of homemade liquor and sizzling grease. Against the back wall, on an old-fashioned counter, sat glass displays of nachos and cheese sauce, empanadas, samosas, and wontons.

Substitute deep-fried catfish nuggets and it could have been a pub from the Cove. Weirdly enough, it made me homesick.

A single bulb hung from the ceiling, shedding dull light on three men and two women sprawled on beat-up couches, playing a game with worn paper cards. The men's faces were unshaven, wild hairs poking out from eyebrows and noses and ears, and carpets of beards over their cheeks and chins. The women looked just as raw, everyone sporting scars, presumably from real blades.

I guessed these were grizzlies—a prickly and unpredictable bunch, from what I'd heard. I'd never met any in person, but glimpsed airscreen news about violent outbreaks in places like this.

"Who're you?" The question came from a thickset guy in a baseball cap, barely audible over the shriek of howler monkey music.

I offered a friendly wave. "Interns. I'm Liv and this is Wolf."

No one volunteered their names. They stuffed onion rings into their mouths and wiped grease from their faces with their sleeves.

"We're wondering if you could transport some live cargo to California for us," I shouted. "We can pay you well."

They conferred with each other, washing down their onion rings with beer. Unable to hear them over the music, I stood awkwardly with Wolf, still steps from the doorway. One of the men—an older one whose face was half covered in a peppered beard—began to cough, a rattle deep in his lungs.

The sound set off a visceral reaction in my body. This was an echo of the deadly coughs that some of my friends in the Cove had suffered. The only meds we could afford were old-school antibiotics that didn't work against resistant pneumonia strains. Our sweet neighbor had struggled with a cough like this in the weeks before she died. Years earlier, she'd taught me to dive for oysters, shown me how to hold my breath for minutes underwater. Ironically, her own lungs had led to her death.

A lady with tazzled gray hair whacked the man on the back. It didn't help.

She folded her arms over her camo jumpsuit and trained her eyes on Wolf. "You're Progeny, right?" Her voice was growly and slurred, her tone flat. Grizzly speak. "That Nelson kid? The one who disappeared?"

Reluctantly, he nodded. "Call me Wolf."

They conferred again, shaking their heads. The old man fell into another coughing fit, gasping for breath between explosions of phlegm. I shuddered as the woman whacked him again on the back.

The others looked away, as if to give him privacy in his efforts to breathe.

Another woman whistled and the guy behind the counter brought out a plate of nachos dripping in orange sauce. It and looked—and smelled—like black market food, some crapulous chemical combination simulating fat and salt that put your taste buds in heaven but wreaked havoc on your innards.

I was just wondering how to politely refrain if they offered us nachos, when the youngest man—not much older than Wolf—pulled out a handgun from his waistband.

A grizzly crowd I could handle, but a gun was a different story. They'd been illegal for generations—I'd never seen one in real life, never even heard of someone owning one. I'd used them in a violent virch game that my classmates liked, but I couldn't get into it. I felt too icky *killing*, even for pretend.

This man's gun was black and small, the size of a zapper. He pointed it at us, thin lips twisted into a smirk. "You got a hit out on you, boy."

In a show of courage, Wolf raised his chin, but his eyes betrayed fear.

Chest tight with dread, I glanced behind us, saw that two large men had blocked the doorway. Their hairy hands held switchblades, sharper and shinier and cleaner than anything else in the place.

The man with the gun stepped toward us. This close, I could see the sunburnt skin of his face, free of wrinkles but marked by blade scars and acne spots.

"We thought we'd have to go looking for you. But you came right to us instead. Introduced yourself and everything. Thanks for that."

He winked. "Ready to kiss this world goodbye, shark-boy?"

CHAPTER TWENTY-TWO
No Man's Land

A coil of fury sprang inside me.

A jolt of courage.

I stepped between Wolf and the gunman. "No one's stupid enough to kill a Progeny."

His eyes narrowed. "Oh, we'll arrange a tragic accident. Something simple like getting sucked into the propeller. Accidents are easy out here."

Wolf's mother had been murdered in an "accident." I couldn't let that happen to her son, too. And since I was here, a witness, I'd probably be part of the accident. Which meant that neither of us would be around to act on our dream's warnings. Or save Shell.

At the heart of it, I really didn't want to die. Not before making a difference in the world. Or falling in love. Maybe I was on the cusp of so much joy—if I could just make it through tomorrow alive.

I glanced at Wolf. His defiant expression was gone—now he was holding his head, off balance. His concussion. He was barely able to stay conscious, much less bargain for his life.

I leveled my gaze at the gunman. "Whatever they paid for the hit, we'll double it if you let him live."

The grizzly turned the gun over in his hand. "Fifty mil."

The number knocked the wind out of me.

"Done," Wolf said with a grimace. "Let's up it. A hundred mil to not shoot me. Paid up front. Another hundred mil to deliver this cargo. And another hundred mil for a couple of guns."

Guns? My skin crawled, but I could probably make myself use one for self-defense.

The man kept his gun trained on us while he and the other grizzlies conferred, crunching nachos. That bone-chilling cough competed with the screech-song soundtrack for ear-drum-shattering agony.

"No deal," said the gunman. "Just the hundred mil to not kill you."

"But why?" I asked, wondering what on earth we'd do with Sugarpie.

A well-muscled woman with hair in a bandana answered. "Already got enough secret deliveries and weapon sales going on lately." Her smile revealed a collection of crooked, half-rotten teeth. "Getting risky. Just give him the money not to kill you. He'll divvy it up for us later."

Wolf stepped forward, still wobbly, and handed the guy five emerald-studded platinum discs. The sight of so much money made my knees weak. I'd never seen anything like it. Probably very few people in the world had.

The gunman tucked the discs into his pocket, looking smug. What was stopping him from swiping the rest of Wolf's money?

As if reading my mind, Wolf turned his pockets inside-out. "That's all I've got with me."

This staggering amount of money could mean the difference between life and death for Shell and kids like her. And seeing it go to this ruthless man made me furious. So furious that lava burst inside me and wiped out any fear.

"Who ordered the hit?" I demanded.

The guy scowled. "Why'd I tell you that?"

"Was it my dad?" Wolf's words were soft, nearly drowned out by the music.

Even this crowd seemed shocked at the idea of a father ordering his own son's death. And it *was* shocking, but Casper had ordered his wife's death, and now his son was a threat, too. If Wolf went public about the experiments, it would cause a scandal and interfere with his dad's secret plans.

"My brother, Spiro?" Wolf guessed next.

The grizzlies' shifting eyes made me think he'd guessed right this time.

My voice came out, urgent. "Don't trust Spiro. He's plotting something dangerous. Don't transport anything off-island for him. It could be a lethal virus from the Biohaz Lab. A bioweapon. He could be putting your lives in danger. Your families' lives."

A flurry of talking, and then the bandanna woman said, "Spiro's having us ship cargo here *to* the island. Not *off* the island. And it's not weapons. It's for a party."

I tilted my head. "Then why couldn't it get shipped here through regular channels?"

"It's fireworks. Black market since no explosives are allowed here. Spiro's throwing a surprise party for Casper. Isn't the geezer turning three hundred or something?"

As they snickered, Wolf and I exchanged glances. What did Spiro really have planned?

I took a step toward the gunman. "You think that someone terrible enough to put a hit out on his own brother would be nice enough to plan a surprise party for his dad?"

"Who the fratch knows how the Progeny's cushy little minds work?" He walked toward me, waving the pistol in my face. "Get out of here. If Spiro sees we let you go, he'll kill us himself."

My every muscle was wound tight, but I managed not to flinch at the gun. I headed to the door with Wolf, hoping we wouldn't be shot in the back. A new round of coughing started behind us.

I took a deep breath and turned around. Then I walked straight to the man with the cough. He looked like a dried-up corn husk. Up close, I saw his eyes were bloodshot and shiny with fever. "Sir, that sounds like pneumonia to me."

"Re-resistant strain," he gasped. "Can't get meds for it."

"They must have some in the infirmary."

"That's for scientists only," said the bandana woman. She glared at us. "And interns and Progeny."

I shook my head. "But that hundred mil we gave you should be enough for meds, right?"

No one answered.

I glanced at the sick man, then at the others. "He's your buddy, isn't he? Can't you each give him your share of the money to save his life?"

"We would," said the woman next to him, the one with tazzled gray hair. "Doesn't matter how much money we scrounge up. The meds just aren't there. Not unless you're a shark."

It was the same story as my neighbor's. The same story as my sister's. The same story as my mother's. Treatments existed, but only for the sharks. It wasn't just money that mattered, but power and connections.

Zinnia would have meds for resistant strains. And she'd give them to me, I felt sure of it.

"I'll get you the meds," I told him. "I'll ask the gardener to bring them to you."

Hope brightened his face. "How much will it cost me?"

"Nothing," I said, with a pointed look at the gunman. "You can't put a price on human life. I'm sure you have someone who feels that way about your life, too."

And I walked outside, blood thundering in my ears.

At the cage, I peeked under the sheet, saw that Sugarpie was playing with her sticks, swiping at them in clumsy, toddler movements. With trembling hands, I removed her emptied milk bottle, opened a fresh one, and stuck it through the wires. She took it in her thick paws and suckled it, rolling on her back in bliss.

"Let's go." I pushed it toward the garden entrance.

At my side, Wolf whispered, "Not bad, Angel."

"You okay?" I hoped he couldn't notice me shaking.

"Yeah. You?"

I nodded, aware of nervous sweat trickling down my torso. "We're alive. But still stuck with Sugarpie."

"At least we got some intel on Spiro. And warned the pilots."

"True," I agreed. "The question is, what's he going to blow up?"

"And what, if anything, does that have to do with releasing the virus?"

"And do the easy-fusion reactors play some role?"

A sliver of moon sliced through the darkness. How would we navigate our way through the gardens? I ran my hands through my hair, dejected. Spiro was out there, up to no good, and here we were, pushing around a panda cub. About to get seriously lost. And we had just over a day left.

I wondered if we should return to the facility or just hide out in the forest. But then how would we stop Spiro? I turned to Wolf. "How will we find our way back?"

"No idea."

A woman's voice called out behind us. "Hey, Progeny boy."

We spun around to see the gray-haired woman approaching. "I'm his wife. The sick guy. Tor."

Behind her, the other pilots came out, carrying their drinks, encircling us. I sucked in a breath.

"What you got in there anyway?" she asked.

I pulled off the sheet and revealed the panda. She was clutching her bottle between her paws, white belly exposed, and wriggling her fluffy torso to scratch her back.

In the dusky light, every face melted. There was *awww*-ing that I'd have thought impossible coming from this crowd.

"Her name's Sugarpie," I said. "Spiro nearly drugged her to death. We're rescuing her."

"Spiro hurt this cutie?" the gunman asked, looking indignant.

"Yup."

As if on cue, Sugarpie squeaked and rolled up to sitting, tilting her huge head at the grizzlies. *I love you,* those droopy eyes said. *I hope you love me, too.*

"We'll transport her," said Tor's wife.

"But—" said another.

"We'll do it," she said, eyes fierce.

"Thanks." Wolf gave her a grateful look. "We'll come back the day after tomorrow with payment."

She held up her hand. "No need. Just get those meds for Tor."

I nodded. "Of course."

I said goodbye to Sugarpie, touched my cheek to her nose, laced my arms through the cage to give her a hug. With a lump in my throat, I inhaled her smell of sour milk and animal fur.

Wolf said his goodbyes to Sugarpie as I gave the woman feeding instructions and contact details for the wildlife center.

"Here's to a new life," Wolf said, rubbing the panda's black button ears.

We shook hands with Tor and his wife. I let my hand linger in hers, squeezed it. "Listen, we really need weapons—"

Her brows creased. "For what?"

"Self-defense. Against Spiro. And to protect other people on this island."

Tor let loose another round of coughing. Once he caught his breath, he said, "F-fireworks aren't the only thing your brother got from us." He doubled over in chest spasms.

Rubbing his back, his wife finished his thought. "We sold him our stash of guns. Except the ones for our personal use."

"Got any smartlasers or minis?" Wolf ventured.

"That high-tech stuff's too hard to smuggle on-island." Her expression softened. "You just better watch your backs." She looked at Wolf. "And Progeny Boy, you got yourself a quanking tough girlfriend. Don't mess it up."

"I won't," he said. "I promise."

She pulled something from her bosom—a knife in an old-fashioned leather sheath. "Better than nothing, boy."

"Thanks," he said, tucking the knife in his waistband, then taking my hand.

I imagined Shell's spirit watching this whole scene and laughing triumphantly. She'd especially love the boyfriend part.

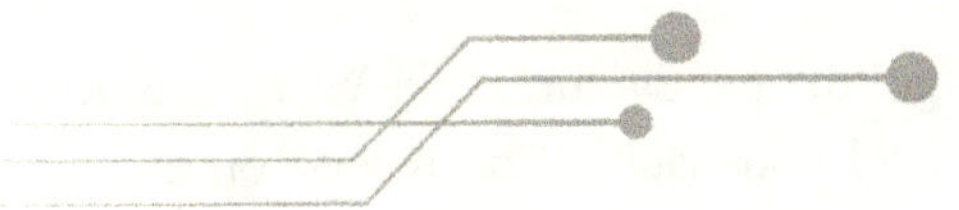

Wolf and I walked in silence, moving deeper into the forest, until the first fork in the path. The lights from the airstrip were behind, and now we were cloaked in darkness.

"Which way?" he asked.

I sighed. "We'll be lost in here all night."

He nudged me with an elbow. "I can think of worse things than getting lost with you, Angel."

I let my hand relax in his. "We do have a gun-wielding, panda-drugging evil-doer to follow. And a day to foil him."

"Hey," he said, "you really were quanking tough back there."

"I just—I couldn't stand hearing that poor guy, and I knew he'd die without…"

Wolf squeezed my hand. I leaned into him as we took the path to the right.

And there was a rustle, a crunch of footsteps in the foliage.

Zuggers. Was it Spiro? He was probably done with dinner by now. He was clearly familiar with these gardens, since he'd been to see the pilots. And he had guns.

The footsteps grew closer. Metal glinted in moonlight.

Wolf's hand tightened around mine.

Heart racing, I said, "Who's there?"

A girl's voice answered. "Just me."

A wave of relief swept over me. "Come here, sweetie." She came close enough that I could just make out her silhouette.

"I wanted to make sure you're okay," she said.

Tears sprung to my eyes. This little girl—concerned about *us*.

I rested a hand on her shoulder. "You're a life-saver, actually."

"We got the panda out," said Wolf, "but now we're lost."

"I'll lead you back." She turned on a flashlight, forming a pool of light.

"We never caught your name," I said.

"Soul."

Cricket songs rose and fell. "What's that?"

"My name's Soul." She spelled it out. "S-O-U-L."

Save Soul. That was the urgent instruction from my dream self. But this child looked fine. Save Soul from what?

My insides clenched.

Wolf's eyes met mine, full of questions.

I slipped my hand into the girl's small one. "Soul, listen. If you ever need help, come to the facility and ask for Zinnia the doctor."

"But we're not allowed."

"I'm saying you are," said Wolf. "And I'm Progeny."

"You are?" Eyes wide, she directed the flashlight beam at him.

"He is." I squeezed her hand. "But he's also one of us."

My other hand tightened around Wolf's, and together, the three of us walked deeper into the darkness.

CHAPTER TWENTY-THREE
An Ancient Tale

As lights of the facility came into view, our hands were still interlocked.

I made a mental list of priorities. First, get meds to the pilot. Second, locate Spiro and stop him. Third, find out about the experiments on Wolf, which could be useful for understanding what made Spiro and Casper tick. Fourth, find someone from the security team who might take us seriously.

It scared me, knowing that Spiro was insane and armed. We had nothing, unless you counted the knife from the grizzly lady's cleavage.

While we hovered at the edge of the gardens, I turned to Soul. "Listen, can you call for your dad again? We need him to deliver medicine to the pilots."

She bit her lip. "I don't think he'll go there at night."

Wolf turned to me. "Liv, why don't you get the meds? I'll explain to Soul."

I nodded and walked toward the building, trying to appear nonchalant. Behind me, three distinct bird calls rang out—her signal to her dad. *Thank you, Soul.*

Once inside, I headed down the corridor, in mild shock at the difference between the tropical gardens versus this manufactured interior with fake cricket hum, temp-controlled air, faux starlight. I tried walking calmly to avoid attention, but I was so pumped with adrenalin, I couldn't help jogging. When I burst into the infirmary, Zinnia was pacing with the ball of yellow yarn, lacing the strands between her fingers.

"Liv!" She disentangled herself from the yarn and wrapped me in a hug. "Is Wolf okay?" she whispered, soft enough that the nurse wouldn't hear. But he didn't glance up, too absorbed in his airscreen.

"Fine," I breathed.

She took my arm, led me into the exam room, and shut the door. "Liv! Honey! I nearly fainted when I found the bed empty! I thought someone took Wolf. My nurse said that Soraya had been harassing him. I was frantic that Casper had transported him off-island in secret."

"Sorry." I gave her the short version of events, ending with the sick pilot. "Please," I said, "please, can you give me some meds for Tor?"

"Of course, sweet girl, of course." She breezed over to the far wall where the medicine cabinet towered. "Now under normal circumstances, I'd use his virch chip and personalized medical data, but since that's not an option, we'll go old school."

"Thank you."

"Contractors or not, it's wrong that the pilots can't get medical care here." Her voice lowered. "Casper's paranoid about letting them inside. Worried about spies. Only lets 'bots do the cooking and cleaning. Drives him crazy he doesn't have the pilots under his thumb. Such a control freak."

As she stood before the retinal scanner to unlock the cabinet doors, I whispered, "Zinnia. There's something else we need to tell you. You might think we're crazy, but it's life or death."

She looked at me in alarm.

"We have reason to believe that Spiro is plotting something big, something deadly. Maybe with explosives. Maybe with an easy-fusion reactor. Maybe with the Project Dragon bioweapon."

"The virus they're working on in the Biohaz Lab?" Her voice shook.

I nodded. "We tried warning Casper. He didn't take us seriously. And he's busy planning something with Mo. But Spiro's the one we have to focus on. He thinks—he thinks this world is just a virch game. That he can only escape it by doing something drastic."

She pressed her lips together. "There are serums on hand, right? Anti-viral and vaccines?"

"Only here on the island, in a warehouse."

"I wish they'd trust me to keep some in the infirmary." Zinnia tapped on the cabinet and drew in a long breath. "Listen, Liv, I don't have much clearance. I'll try my best, but unless you have proof, I'm limited in what I can do."

"Security footage proves that Kiri and Spiro are having a fling. He's manipulating her to get access to the virus."

"A relationship between an intern and scientist is against the rules," Zinnia said, "but it doesn't prove any criminal activity." She paused, thinking. "If you were able to record Kiri or Spiro plotting something illegal, that would force the security team to take action."

"We're already on Borg's bad side."

"Just get me the proof, and I'll make sure the rest of the team acts on it."

I hugged my arms around myself. "Could they circumvent Casper?"

She raised her brows. "If they had evidence someone was planning to let loose the virus? Or blow something up? You bet." From her desk drawer, Zinnia pulled out a rhinestone-studded brooch in the shape of an elephant. She handed it to me.

"Um… thanks?"

"An old-fashioned spy camera," she whispered with a wry grin. "From the days before virchlenses." She clipped it to my shirt.

"Goes with my retro look."

Another grin. "The elephant's eye is the lens. Just squeeze this stone on its trunk to stop and start recording. The stone turns green when it's on, red when it's off."

"Pretty abracadabrant." I ran my fingers over the rough jewels, practicing turning the recording on and off.

"The batteries are old-fashioned," she said. "You'll have to preserve their charge."

"Why do you have this?"

She rubbed her neck, wavering over something. "There's a resistance group," she murmured. "We're working together, gaining Casper's trust, while secretly making plans to oppose him. We have the people in place to stop this. If you record the evidence."

"Thank you!" On impulse, I hugged her.

She held me for a moment. "Thank *you*, Liv."

Warmth flowed through me. I savored the feeling, then pulled away. There was no time to lose. "Okay, Wolf and I will get this medicine to Tor. Then we'll stay on Spiro's tail. We'll record anything suspicious."

She handed me a red plastic container of pills and shut the cabinet. "Good luck."

"We'll need it. We might have only a day left."

"A *day*?"

I nodded, wishing my dream self had been clearer with the timeline. Then again, she'd been in so much pain, I was grateful she'd made any sense at all, especially with that background racket.

"Careful, sweet girl. And look after Wolf. Tell the patient to take three a day for one week."

"Thanks, Zinnia." I tucked the bottle in my pocket. "Oh, and if a little gardener girl named Soul ever comes to you, will you help her? S-O-U-L."

"Of course. How could anyone turn away a little girl named Soul?"

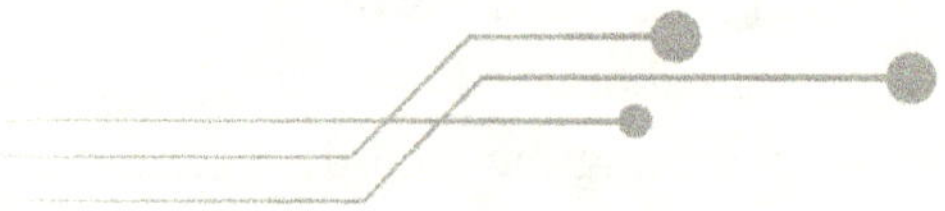

Outside, I found Wolf with Soul and her dad, waiting in the night mist.

I gave Sodo a look of thanks. "I know you're not a fan of the pilots, but they'll be grateful to get the meds. We really appreciate you delivering them."

He took a deep breath and nodded.

I handed him the pills and instructions.

Wolf pulled two gold coins from his back pocket—he'd conveniently not revealed this pocket to the pilots. He handed the money to Sodo and his daughter, who nodded in gratitude.

I bent down to eye level with Soul. "And thank you for guiding us back." I opened my arms and she reached hers toward me. Her hair smelled like earth and bark.

"Wolf and I care about you," I said, "and your dad, and your neighbors. And we'll work together to make things better. I promise."

"Bye, Liv. Bye, Wolf." She waved as she vanished into the shadows with her dad.

I turned to Wolf. "She reminds me of Shell."

"Wish I knew her."

"Me too."

"I'll be there when she wakes up, Liv. I'll meet her soon."

If Shell were here now, she'd be whispering, *Kiss him!*

But there was no time for kissing. I was just turning back toward the facility when Wolf said, "Interesting elephant."

Laughing, I explained the workings of my secret spy camera.

"I like it." He pushed his hair from his eyes. "Time to find Spiro. Where do you think he is?"

"Wherever Kiri is. Maybe still in the dining area? On their third dessert?" They could be lingering over a long, romantic dinner. At least it was a place to start.

Making sure the coast was clear, we entered the building and, with heads down, walked to the dining hall. If we could avoid notice, maybe Borg and Soraya would assume we were where we were supposed to be—me in my room and Wolf in the infirmary.

At the indoor garden, we ducked under the cover of real foliage. Leaves and blooms enveloped us—hibiscus and bougainvillea and heliconia. Dangling from fruit tree branches were limes, oranges, and pomegranates.

This garden stretched the entire west side of the dining hall, and we peered through leaves as we walked its length, scanning for Spiro in the Shady Treehouse holoscape. There were still some tables of couples and groups, but most people had left.

Spiro could be anywhere. He could be in the Biohaz Lab. He could be releasing the virus right now.

"Look," said Wolf, pointing past banana leaves, at a table nestled in the boughs of a holo-tree. "Still chowing."

Spiro was eating strawberry mousse, leaning across the table, head tilted toward Kiri's swooping blue hair. They gazed at each other, absorbed in their date, as if no one else existed.

Wolf and I found a spot inside a cluster of banana trees, not quite close enough to hear Spiro's and Kiri's conversation. They seemed in no rush to leave.

Spiro pulled something from his pocket and held it in his palm, showing it to Kiri. Pills, tiny purple ones. The mood pills he'd offered me earlier? As she smiled, he slipped two between her lips. Their heads were close, faces earnest, as though they were spilling secrets to each other.

If it weren't for the drugs, I could almost believe they were falling in love.

Wolf grabbed a bunch of bananas. "Hors d'oeuvre?"

I laughed and accepted. "Hey, how're you feeling?"

He touched the knot at his temple. "Better. Not so dizzy."

I munched on a banana, eyes trained on Kiri and Spiro through the leaves. "There aren't any hidden cameras or mics in this garden, are there?"

He looked around, studying the trunks and branches. "Nope. And there was no video feed of this area."

Tentatively, I asked, "Think it's safe to tell me about the experiments now?"

He drew in a breath, all humor leaving his expression. "First, a story."

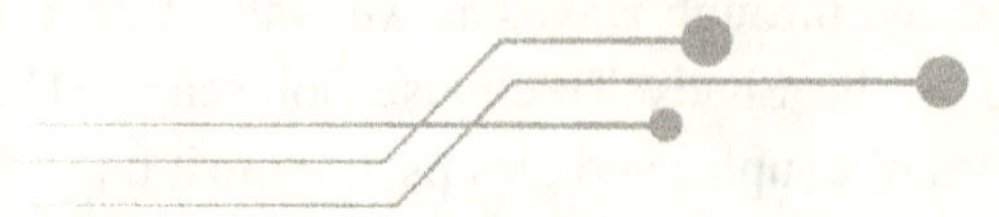

"Many years ago," he began, "there was a boy who sought enlightenment. So he went high up a mountain, to a wise master, and said, 'Please, can you tell me the nature of reality and illusion?'"

I dropped my banana peel. "Wait, is this some kind of parable? Like the guy who wonders if he's a butterfly dreaming he's a man?"

"Hear me out, Angel." He closed his eyes while I kept mine trained on Kiri and Spiro. "The wise man said, 'First, take this cup and fetch me some seawater.' He handed the boy a blue clay cup."

From my peripheral vision, I saw Wolf mime the gesture.

"So the boy went off with his cup. He was just approaching the water when a storm struck, and the ocean grew wild. He noticed something in the distance—a girl swept out to sea. He dropped the cup, ran into the waves, and saved her."

Wolf spoke slowly, almost rhythmically, the way the grandparents from the Cove did. "They fell in love and got married and had children. He lived a long life with her, full of joys and sorrows and fears and laughter."

He paused for so long that I said, "So, what about the cup of sea water?"

He gave a mysterious grin. "One day, as an old man, he was walking along the beach when he came across that blue clay cup, half buried in the sand. He picked it up and smiled at the questions he'd had as a boy. He bent over and filled the cup with seawater."

Wolf mimed the labored movements of an old man, leaning over with shaking hands, turning his lips under as if toothless.

"All at once, he found himself on the mountain before the wise master. The old man looked down at his own hands, still holding the cup of seawater. He gasped. His skin was smooth, his body free of aches and stiffness. He was a boy."

Wolf paused for dramatic effect. "The wise man took the cup from him. With a smile, he said, 'And that, my son, is the nature of reality and illusion.'"

There was a stretched-out moment of silence. Still processing his words, I asked, "So his whole life—the wife, the children, everything—it was an illusion?"

Wolf lifted a brow. "Does it matter?"

"Of course. What he thought was his life was a meaningless *dream*."

He looked at me, crinkling his eyes. "I used to feel that way too. That it was a meaningless dream. That was before the experiment." He waited a beat. "And after the experiment, I felt like the confused guy holding a cup of seawater." Another beat. "And now, I believe the illusion matters. Whether it's real or not, you act the same. You live, you love, you do good."

I furrowed my brow. "I don't know. If life was a meaningless dream, it would crush me. I mean, how could you live through the hard stuff, knowing it wasn't real?"

"You might know with your head it's not real. But your heart goes on believing it is. Living, loving, doing good."

Sounded like something Shell would say. But I'd had enough of cryptic hints and folktales. I wanted the straightforward, scientific details laid out for me. "What was the experiment, Wolf?"

He let his curls fall over his eyes, a kind of self-protecting gesture. "On the morning when Casper's jet came to get Spiro and me, I said goodbye to my godmother. She was scared. She didn't want my dad to take me."

Now I was just using my peripheral vision to observe Spiro and Kiri at their table. My main focus had shifted to Wolf.

His expression was distant. "Inside the jet, he gave us some pills, supposedly to relax us on the journey. The next thing I remember, I found myself in a small room with a big red sofa.

Spiro was next to me. My dad was there with a scientist. He gave us more pills to take, different ones this time. I dozed off and then…"

"Then, what?"

He worked his jaw. "I woke up back in my bed at home. I figured the experiment was over, that it happened while we were unconscious. Amala was so glad to see me, hugging me and asking me where my dad had taken me. I told her I didn't know. I figured Spiro was back in his home, too. Everything seemed totally normal. Until after breakfast. That's when a news alert said that a giant asteroid was hurtling toward Earth. It was predicted to hit the planet by nightfall. Cause mass extinction. Wipe out humankind."

"What?" I blinked, trying to follow. A giant asteroid? That was something we would have heard about even in the Cove.

"Amala and I hugged each other and cried. We took out our virchlenses. We wanted to spend our last hours in full reality. We packed a warm casserole and walked through our neighborhood, carrying our last meal with oven mitts, which was weird, but no one noticed. People were yelling and sobbing in the streets. Amala and I walked to a forest grove by our house, a nature preserve with a little stream.

"And we spent our last day on earth together in nature. Late in the afternoon, the sun disappeared—blocked by the asteroid. Everything was dark and we held each other and closed our eyes and the air smelled like our dinner, cinnamon and coriander and cardamom."

A long silence. "And then, I opened my eyes and I was back on the red couch next to my brother."

"Wait." My thoughts were scrambled, struggling to make sense of this… and what it meant for our current situation. "So your last day on earth— it was some kind of virch thing?"

"An illusion. Indistinguishable from reality. Down to the sub-atomic level. There was no way of knowing." He paused. "Back on the red couch, my brother and I were freaking out. The scientist injected us with tranquilizers to calm us down. Then my dad explained. They'd put our consciousnesses into a simulated reality."

"Amala, too?"

"She was just an AI."

He'd clung to Amala with so much love at the end... yet he'd been alone.

"My dad told us that the next morning, we'd go into a different scenario in a sim reality. He had a whole week of this planned."

"But why?" Part my mind was still racing at what this might mean for us now. Part of my mind went back to Casper's comment about the experiments creating an über-human. "What was his goal? Entertainment? Psychological research?"

Wolf shrugged. "It was a phase of some bigger project. He didn't tell me much. At least not much I can remember. I think ultimately, he wanted to make replicas—like downloads— of people's consciousnesses."

"But why?" I pushed, struggling to wrap my mind around this. "Talking to dead relatives? I mean, what were the practical applications? How would he make money from it?"

"No idea."

I furrowed my brow, thinking of what I'd learned about the barriers to downloading human consciousness. "But the whole thing's impossible, anyway. Consciousness is fluid, not static. It's a process of neurons firing and electrical impulses moving. A download would only give you a fleeting snapshot."

"Exactly," said Wolf.

My mind scanned relevant information, settling on a memorable fact from one of my classes. "And even if he'd somehow recorded every neural connection from birth, it would take too much power to run an exact replica of a human brain. I mean, it would take all the electrical and solar and wind energy on earth to just run one brain for a minute."

But as the words came out of my mouth, I remembered the easy-fusion reactors, hidden beneath the forest, right here on this island. "Those reactors…"

Wolf sighed. "Might be for this purpose."

I looked away, to a lemon hanging from a tree branch, its own tiny world that could fit in your hand.

How had my world become so *complicated* in just one day? So much hidden, things stranger than I'd ever imagined. I took a quivery breath. "What did you do after that experiment?"

"I told Casper I wanted nothing more to do with his research. I demanded he send me home. At first, he tried to force me to stay. I went ballistic, screaming, bashing things. He sedated me, and next thing I know I'm on the jet, heading home. But after that, he kept trying to convince me to try again. He said Spiro was tough enough to handle it, so why wasn't I?"

Poor Spiro. He'd truly been through hell. No wonder he thought he was still there.

"My dad promised he'd let me choose an easy scenario next time, something fun. I said no way, but I got really depressed. I felt paranoid that Amala could be an AI, wondered if anything mattered. All the meaning was sucked out of existence. I didn't want to be alive anymore."

"Oh, Wolf." My chest ached for his younger self. "What a nightmare."

"Amala was worried about me. She suggested we go to Tibet to live with her great-uncle—a monk. I could get away from my dad and his experiments and try to heal. And I did. My soul was broken, Angel. The monks helped me fix it."

His past was starting to make sense, all the pieces coming together.

"After a few months, I felt strong again, stronger than ever. Ready to make people think about what was real in their lives, in the world. My dad's Virch Empire has the sharks convinced they have to live in illusions to have a good life. Meanwhile, they ignore everyone who's struggling and suffering in reality. When I was living at the monastery, I drank yak butter tea with locals in their homes, got peeks into their lives. It wasn't as rough as a Null Zone, but I got a sense of the real world. And I want to do something about the inequality."

"I'm glad." And yes, I was glad he'd saved his soul and found his purpose—but I couldn't stop thinking about the teacup tale and the reality experiment. Or, more precisely, I couldn't stop *feeling the sensation* they gave me. The idea that everything was a dream made me feel lost and suffocated. It was as though I'd fallen through a crack in the ice with nothing to grab onto, flailing in the depths, drowning in the dark.

The question on the tip of my tongue was so absurd I could barely ask it. I mean, I was looking at his face, so close I could see a tiny, barely-there zit, and no way would a sim reality show miniscule flaws like this. But he had said *indistinguishable from reality*.

"Wolf, do you think we're in a simulated reality now?"

CHAPTER TWENTY-FOUR
Potato Peels and Bread Crust and Soil

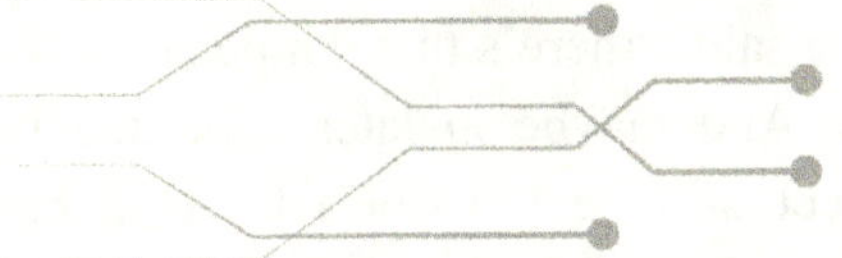

The question hung there like something you could pluck from the air.

I was sinking deep—water in my ears, blood rushing, darkness enveloping me, outlines blurred, light refracting, angles altered, distance drowned, everything drifting like kelp in secret currents.

"I think all of this is real." Wolf's voice pulled me to the surface.

"Why?" My voice shook.

"Like I said before, there's no solid evidence to suggest otherwise."

I ran my tongue over my teeth, felt the ridge of my upper right wisdom tooth just breaking the gum's surface. A replica consciousness wouldn't have these hidden details, would it?

He continued. "The experiment—it changed me. I want you to understand me, all of me." He paused. "It might help you understand my dad and brother too." Softly, he added, "But there is a remote possibility that this is a simulation."

Remote possibility. I looked around at the scientists and interns through the leaves. There were Spiro and Kiri, heads close over faux candlelight, wrapped in their burgeoning pseudo-romance. Was it possible these people weren't real consciousnesses? I stared at the scars on my hand. Was it possible this body wasn't made of organic matter?

I forced myself to stop my questions there. Who knew what particular form of hell they could lead me to. "But Wolf, you'd never consent to another experiment. And neither would I."

"Right. Of course not."

My mind turned over possibilities. "You think this might relate to our dreams?"

"Well," he said, "there's that whole end-of-the-world theme my dad likes. And maybe in later experiments, he wanted to somehow direct us to act. I don't know if he could actually watch me in the virch scenario, but maybe he felt bored with me eating a casserole in the woods with Amala. No action or adventure."

"Like monster pups," I said bitterly.

"Right. This could be more subtle, though. Maybe he introduced our dream sims into the equation to propel us to act."

How could Wolf talk about this so *coolly*? Inside, I was reeling. "So what do we do?"

"We have to assume our world's real, Angel." His voice was surprisingly calm. "If we think it's fake, we might get depressed or destructive or lose a grip on our sanity."

"Like Spiro?" I glanced at him leaning close to Kiri.

Wolf nodded. "My relationship with him was always charged. Full of jealousy and stupid sibling rivalry. Before I disappeared, I went to his house to convince him to refuse the experiments. He got mad, said I was abandoning him. As I was leaving, he jumped me from behind, beat me up pretty bad. Casper said I deserved it. That I betrayed my family."

"That's horrible." My chest ached for him. "And a lie."

He nodded, eyes raw. "But it still hurt. When I came back from Tibet last week, I got in touch with my dad, asked him if I could do this internship. He was suspicious but agreed. He said Spiro had kept doing the experiments, that he'd undergone more than a hundred over the past year, and he was totally fine. Casper said each scenario was more intense than the last—but that Spiro was tough enough to handle it. That they'd made him an über-human. Unlike me. Dear old dad wanted me to feel like a wimp, pit me and my brother against each other."

Wolf's voice dropped to a rasp. "Angel, I can't imagine how messed up a person's mind would be after a hundred times."

Darkness surged through me. A gathering dread. "Wolf, if we're in some experiment, I want out."

"Of course. Me too. But whether it's reality or illusion, we need to act in the same way."

I echoed his words. "Live, love, do good?"

"So are you in?"

I drew in a long breath, hugged myself. "Okay, Wolf, I'll assume there's some other explanation for our dreams." My voice faltered. "I'll believe this world is real because if it's not, I couldn't handle it. I'd just want to make it end."

I searched Wolf's eyes, trying to absorb his confidence. It wasn't easy. He'd spent months coming to terms with the uncertain nature of this reality. But for me, this felt like a bomb dropped onto my world.

He closed his eyes, ran a hand over his face. "Angel, I'm sorry I told you. It's too much to put on you. But for what it's worth, I think you *are* strong enough to handle it. To handle anything."

That's what my dad would have said. *Do your best, Liv.* I missed him. He felt a world away… and what if he was?

"Listen," said Wolf. "I don't want this to interfere with our plans. If we're alive after tomorrow, we'll change things together. For the better. We'll get your sister treated. We'll get people in the Null Zones scanners and meds, whatever they need. I promise." His eyes locked onto mine. "We'll help Soul and other minnow kids."

I thought of his mantra. *Live, love, do good.* But the words rang hollow—I couldn't believe them, couldn't *feel* them. It would be too devastating to think that Shell's suffering wasn't real, that the suffering of so many people around the world wasn't real.

That the feeling of falling in love wasn't real.

I tried to think like him, to assume this existence was real—in theory, an easy task because down to the tiniest dust mote in the air, it *felt* real. But questions kept popping up, and my curiosity got the better of me.

"Hey," I said. "How do you know my consciousness isn't an AI?"

He grinned. Again, I noticed his front left tooth, how it was the tiniest bit crooked, overlapping the right one just a sliver.

"You're like no one I've ever met before," he said. "Like no one else on earth. There can't be some AI computer program behind you. You're too unique."

"If by unique, you mean the one-of-a-kind pattern of oyster knife scars on my hands, then you have a point."

As I waved my hand, he took it in his, examined the tiny white lines crisscrossing the flesh.

"Wabi-sabi," he said.

"Wabi *what*?"

"An ancient Eastern concept. Finding beauty in imperfection. In simple things, rough things, flawed things, close things."

He kept one hand around mine, drawing it to his chest. With the other hand, he reached for my necklace.

"The broken shells, the jagged edges. The missing shells that have fallen off. Nothing lasts, nothing is finished, nothing is perfect. More beautiful than a necklace without flaws."

"Shell made it. She was—*is* a wabi-sabi master. You have to be if you're a budding artist in the Cove."

But I didn't want to think about this string of broken shells around my neck, didn't want feel its weight or its edges. "Take a rest," I said. "I'll watch for a while."

"Thanks." Wolf reclined onto the ground. On impulse, I picked up his head and laid it in my lap. I stroked his spiraling hair, avoiding the bruised lump on his temple.

Within minutes, he was asleep. He dozed for a few hours, and the whole time I kept one eye on him and one eye on Kiri and Spiro. I didn't feel bored or restless watching Wolf sleep, only captivated by the micromovements of his eyelids, the occasional twitch of his lips.

When he woke up, I smiled. He gave me a sleepy smile back, then glanced at his bare wrist, the watch gone.

"You slept a while. It must be two in the morning by now."

"They're still here?" he asked, gaze flickering toward the tables.

I nodded. "On their fifth dessert." Lightly, I boinged the curl in the middle of his forehead. "This one's my favorite."

He let out a soft laugh. Then he reached a finger to my cheeks, ran it over my freckles, twirled a strand of my hair. "Your hair's abracadabrant too."

"Über-wabi-sabi?"

"Yeah," he said drowsily. "It's so… non-glittery."

I rolled my eyes. "Thanks."

"Makes me think of real things. Potato peels, bread crust, soil."

"So my hair looks like compost. Charming."

"In the best way. It's just *real*." He slipped his other hand behind my neck, pulling my face closer.

I moved my face toward his.

The scraping of chairs broke through the quiet. I pulled away and peeked through the leaves. My heart sunk. "They're leaving."

Once Spiro and Kiri passed, Wolf stood up and held out his hand. I took it, stretching out my legs.

As we waited for a safe distance to follow, he took a strand of my hair in his fingertips again. "More than anything, I want something real. Someone real." Heartbeats passed. Five, ten. And then, "I want you."

Every nerve cell in my body lit up, ablaze and alive. He'd flicked some switch that flooded my skin with a buzzing, humming heat.

Before I could find words, he said, "I just wish—I wish I deserved you."

"What?"

He spoke slowly. "When I try to make a difference in the world, I end up almost drowning or punching my brother or getting beat up or stung by a jellyfish or something stupid. Meanwhile, you—you weren't born into privilege, but you've taken these solid steps toward doing something good. And big. And world changing."

I tightened my hand around his, felt the warmth passing back and forth between us. "Maybe we're not the best judges of what we deserve."

I took in his grateful smile, then noticed that Kiri and Spiro were disappearing around a corner down the hallway. I tugged his hand and together, we followed their rainbow shimmer through manufactured starlight, riding our tiny boat of reality in a sea of illusion.

CHAPTER TWENTY-FIVE
Moonlit Snowdrifts

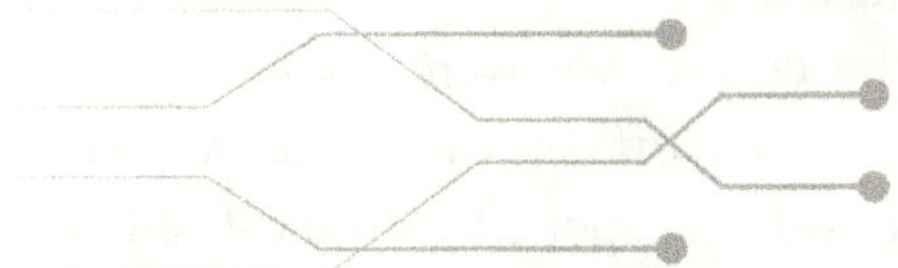

Wolf and I stayed a good twenty paces behind Spiro and Kiri, even though they seemed oblivious. Spiro walked more or less in a straight line, but Kiri meandered along in a spacey way, probably due to the mood drugs. She wore an auto-swirling iridescent dress with a peacock pattern and a slit revealing a tree-bark tattooed leg. Any attempt at sexiness was backfiring since each stumble tore the delicate fabric.

I winced each time the dress ripped a little more. More painful than the damaged dress was the knowledge that her brilliant brain was dulled by the drugs. I wanted to grab her hand and lead her away.

The facility had an eerie, empty feeling at night, with most people in their rooms. A few little 'bots floated here and there, just centimeters off the ground, doing cleaning and maintenance. I watched them zip past, impressed they anticipated our path and gave us sufficient berth.

Kiri and Spiro shuffled past the mopping 'bots and the airdome lobby, now deserted. And then they paused—of all places—at a door by an airscreen labeled Moonlit Snowdrifts.

Awkward. My face flushed.

This must be the holoscaped version of the virchrelax setting—a romantic scenario I'd heard my classmates mention but never tried myself.

Kiri yanked Spiro inside, already kissing his neck.

I glanced at Wolf. Eyeing me as if we shared a secret, he took my hand. I sucked in a breath, and we followed. A darkened foyer led to a short hallway. I took tentative steps forward as my eyes adjusted.

Turning the corner, we were bathed in opal-blue light—moonbeams reflected off snow. It was a pine-forested park, frosted with snowdrifts, spotted with old-fashioned streetlamps, and above it all, a giant, full moon. The room felt as large as Casper's office, the boundaries uncertain, disguised by the mixture of real and holo-trees.

Couples embraced behind bushes and tree trunks, on benches and logs, and some on the moss below pines. All shadows and murmurs.

"Shall we act the part?" I asked, suddenly shy. "To avoid suspicion?"

Wolf put an arm around my hip and pulled me close. I felt myself sink into him. Our hips and waists and torsos pressed together like puzzle pieces. Thankful for the darkness, I let my head fall onto his shoulder, my hair tumble over my face. There was no way a body made of zeros and ones could feel this hot river of blood rushing through it.

I wondered what an actual kiss would feel like. I heard Shell's impish voice: *Kiss him, Livvy!*

We settled on the ground near the door, hidden by a real juniper bush, waiting. The room was a comfortable seventy degrees. The snow beneath us, although the right powdery texture, wasn't cold and didn't melt on my skin. Every blossom of snow kept its crystalline perfection.

Couples came in and out, arm in arm—both interns and scientists.

An hour passed, maybe two, maybe more. Time moved differently in this magical, snowy realm. Our conversation wandered in and out of comfortable silences as our bodies nestled into one another.

My thoughts meandered but kept returning to Wolf's plan to hack into all the virchrelax settings and replace them with the Cove. It occurred to me how angry people would get if they'd planned a rendezvous in a place like Moonlit Snowdrifts but found themselves instead in a Null Zone. They'd figure it was a glitch and zigzag themselves right out.

No one would stay long enough to meet cute kids or watch a ripe peach sunset or start to care. Wolf's plan had a major flaw. I glanced at him, looking so peaceful as the snow fell softly around us. I couldn't burst his bubble, not right now. I'd just have to think of a better strategy.

Flurries drifted and settled on my eyelashes. It felt like a movie set, with us as the actors. I held some flakes in my palm, looked at them closely. I squinted at these heat-proof holoflakes—each had the same pattern of spokes from the center.

Wolf was stroking my hair now, as if savoring the potato-peel-colored tazzle.

I leaned into him. "It's weird how something so fake can make me feel so… *so much.*"

In the faux-cold air, his breath puffed like smoke. "Stars, darkness, a lantern, a phantom, dew, a bubble, a dream, a flash of lightning, and a cloud. Thus we should look upon all that was made."

His words settled inside me like snowflakes, unique ones that melted into me. "Learn that in Tibet?"

He nodded. "What do you think it means?"

"They're beautiful things. And mysterious. And fleeting. And, maybe, in a way, illusory."

"A wise man came up with it millennia ago. He was thinking about illusion and reality way back then. Wonder what he'd say about this place?"

"Probably the same thing. Dreams existed back then, too. This holo-stuff—it's like artificially manufactured dreams. Nothing completely new."

Wolf was staring at me with an expression I couldn't quite grasp. Amazement? Anticipation? Surrender? His fingertip brushed some snowflakes from my brow. "Angel, there's something I didn't tell you about my dream. Something my dream self said."

My heartbeat quickened. "What?"

"I love you." Then he added, "I mean, that's what *he* said, or what *I* said—well you, know."

Blood stampeded through my body.

He tucked a strand of hair behind his ear. "My dream self said the only way we can be together… is if we stop the virus outbreak."

"My other self said I loved you, too," I whispered.

His eyes filled with hope and moonlight and wonder. Our faces were close, growing closer, our lips a breath apart. His lids drifted shut.

And then, shoes crunching over snow. Spiro and Kiri crossed the clearing, heading toward the exit.

Not fair! I took a breath, tried to get my body under control. Wolf seemed to be doing the same, mentally dousing himself with cold water.

Once Spiro and Kiri turned the corner of the hallway, we stood up. I stretched, stamped my feet, adjusted my clothes. He did the same.

We'd come *so close* to a real kiss. To something that might be—or become—love. And then had it snatched away.

"I wish we could stay," he said.

"Me too. But there'll be time for… *this*… later," I added, my face warming.

He pressed his palm to my cheek. "There will be. I promise."

Hand in hand, we walked out of Moonlit Snowdrifts and peered into the faux-starlit vestibule. Finding the coast clear—just a 'bot polishing the floor—we forged ahead. The doors slid open to reveal Kiri and Spiro heading toward the elevators.

After the elevator doors closed, Wolf and I ran closer and watched the floor numbers rise to seven. The lab floor.

Unexpected. I'd assumed the next step would be the living quarters.

Then I realized with a sickening feeling, this was Spiro's goal—getting his hands on Project Dragon.

Wolf shook his head. "Their whole date—it's his ploy to get into the Biohaz Lab."

"But Kiri's brilliant." I tried to wrap my head around it. "I can't believe she'd do something so stupid."

"Spiro's spent the evening over-dosing her on mood pills. Making her pliable, easy to manipulate. Tapping into her insecurities. He's despicable."

"Come on." I pulled Wolf toward the emergency stairwell, wanting to avoid the cameras.. "Feeling okay for stairs?"

He nodded. "The dizziness is gone."

He looked much steadier, but I kept a hold on his elbow as we climbed the steps. On the seventh floor, I cautiously opened the door. The Sunny Garden holoscape was gone, and this hallway, like the others, was set to Starry Night—a silvery haze above and hushed cricket hums.

A light glared through the window of the lab door. Kiri and Spiro must have gone inside. Now for the tricky part—filming them entering the Biohaz Lab off-hours, in secret. After that, we'd have to rush the footage to Zinnia before Spiro did any damage.

"Wait out here, Wolf," I whispered.

"What? Why?"

"Putting you together with Spiro can only result in disaster. Let me and my elephant handle this." I unpinned the ugly brooch from my shirt. "If I'm not out in a half hour, call security, okay?"

Wolf grasped the knife at his waist. "I'm coming too."

"Wolf, he put a hit out on you. I'll be fine. I'll just go in, record the evidence, and get out."

He touched my arm. "Liv, just—be careful. I mean, maybe in some world, in some time…"

Inside my head, I finished the sentence:… *we already love each other*.

"I'll be okay." And before I could change my mind, I positioned myself before the retinal scanner. It worked—Soraya must not have removed my access privileges yet. With conjured confidence, I strode through the open door.

Spiro and a wobbly Kiri were already in the first chamber of the Biohaz Lab, suiting up. It was a disturbing mix of comical and heart-breaking to watch her try to fit her auto-swirl dress into the biohaz suit.

My eyes flicked to the walls of the lab, knowing there was a hidden camera—the one responsible for the footage Wolf and I had seen via his retro watch. Well, if security came, all the better for us—as long as it wasn't Borg. They would catch Spiro in the act.

Wolf had said the other camera in the room had been disabled—the one that pointed toward the Biohaz Lab door. By Spiro? Supposedly, there were no cameras inside the Biohaz Lab itself. It would be up to me and my elephant.

Peering through the window, I wondered how to get through the retinal scanner. I activated the brooch, hoping it might focus on Kiri and Spiro, despite the thick glass. But their faces were obscured as they put on the suits.

Throwing caution to the wind, I rapped on the window.

Kiri jumped. Panic flooded her emerald-crusted eyes.

Spiro's face shot up and he glared.

Would this footage be proof enough? But they were only in the decontam chamber. I needed to record them in the Biohaz Lab itself for any real proof. And, I now realized, I wouldn't be able to leave Spiro in there with access to the virus, even for just minutes. I doubted he'd release the virus without vaccinating himself first and stashing away his own supply of anti-viral serum, just in case. Still, who knew how his twisted mind worked? Or what, exactly, his plan was?

I'd have to take the risk. As they whispered an argument, I banged on the glass again. "Kiri! Can we talk?"

Clearly against Spiro's wishes, she opened the door.

I stepped inside and smiled big. "Thank you."

"Liv!" she cried. "Weren't you kicked out?"

I tugged her by the elbow, out of Spiro's earshot. "Kiri," I whispered, "Can you please take me inside with you?"

"Why on earth—?" Her autoswirl dress started working its way out of her half-closed suit. She pushed it back down.

"It would mean the world to me."

"Liv, I'm kinda on a date." She fumbled to seal her suit, but her fingers lacked coordination.

I started fastening the torso part of her suit as she struggled with the hood. "Listen, Kiri, you can't trust Spiro."

"I totally trust him. Gut feeling." She teetered and held my shoulder to steady herself. "His dad put him through hell and I'm helping him get over it."

"He told you about the experiments?"

"Yeah. He was traumatized." Her eyes welled up and her voice strained. "But your Nelson buddy—he's beyond saving. A lunatic."

"Spiro's the lunatic." I glanced at him across the decontam chamber, sealing up his suit and eyeing me suspiciously. "He's got weapons. He's planning to release the bioweapon, kill everyone, win his so-called game."

She barked an exaggerated laugh. "And what is your theory based on?"

"A dream," I admitted. "It was like my future self warned me. Wolf had the same dream."

Another over-the-top laugh. "Okay, Liv, so even if your dream is valid—which is absurd, but let's say for the sake of argument it is—did it ever occur to you that Nelson's the bad guy? I mean, he's a tech genius, right? He could've hacked into your room and rigged up some virch thing to give you a freaky dream. Just to convince you to help him with whatever treachery he's up to. Liv, you're trusting the wrong brother."

Even on mood-drugs, with a slurred voice and slowed-down speech, she made a good point. The main reason I trusted Wolf was because my dream self told me to. And, well, honestly—because maybe, just *maybe*, I was starting to fall in love with him. Just as Kiri was with Spiro.

"I mean, come on, Liv. Nelson holoscaped his brother's worst nightmare today. He attacked him at the orientation. He's always been jealous. And the experiment made him crazy-evil-jealous. He wants to frame Spiro."

I struggled to compose my thoughts, clinging to the bits of evidence I'd accumulated today. "But Spiro's panda—she wasn't sick, just drugged up on tranquilizers."

"I already know about it," she said. "Spiro told me. Nelson was secretly drugging Sugarpie to set him up. I mean, how low can you get? Nearly killing an innocent creature?" She paused, blinking as her eyes struggled to focus. "You think you're smarter than me?"

Kiri was a *genius*—it was well-established. "Of course not."

"Well, we're in the same position, you and me. We've both got our Progeny boyfriends. You think yours is the good one, and I think mine is. Both are charming and brilliant. So really, it comes down to which of us, you or me, is smarter."

Spiro, now sealed in his suit, called across the chamber, voice muffled behind the face mask: "What's going on?"

I answered. "Kiri's agreed to let me come on the tour."

Behind the transparent fabric, his forehead wrinkled. "Seriously, Ki?"

She leaned against a wall, looking woozy. Her mood-drugged brain was still sharper than most normal brains—it was her judgment that appeared most damaged.

"Liv got kicked out, remember?" Spiro said, his face reddening. "Don't let her come. I wanted this to be just… *us*."

"We're still a family, though, right?" I searched Kiri's eyes, trying to connect.

Her gaze flickered, as if she had vertigo. "Well…"

Taking that as a yes, I grabbed a suit for myself.

Spiro cursed under his breath, then started helping Kiri with her hood. Before sealing it, he kissed her, then slipped a mood pill between her lips and gave her another kiss, long and passionate.

Nausea welled inside me. Not only were his actions disgusting, but another mood pill could make her pass out altogether. I wondered if they might be more than mood pills, some drug to override rational thought with impulsive emotions. I wouldn't put it past him.

Disturbed, I sealed up my own biohaz suit. The few available in the Cove were decades old, worn thin, with duct-taped holes. These were state-of-the-art, the material so thin it allowed sound to move through. The entire suit was transparent and as lightweight as a sundress.

Maybe we could make this style available to the workers in the Cove when all this was done. When Wolf and I were making real changes in the world.

Because we would.

Because he was *good*. And he was *sane*.

He had to be.

Once we were all suited up, Kiri swayed before the retinal scanner. The next door opened, and we walked through two more enclosed chambers involving directional airflow and disinfectant lights. Then we stepped straight into the biohazard heart.

I held the elephant camera in my gloved hand, since I couldn't very well pin it to my suit. I kept it off for now to preserve battery life. As soon as something incriminating happened, I'd try to discreetly record it.

Hand clenched around the brooch, I kept one eye ahead, on the home of the world's scariest bioweapon, and one on the bulge beneath the back of Spiro's waistband.

The bulge in the shape of a pistol.

CHAPTER TWENTY-SIX
Late Night Tour

Inside, the Biohaz Lab was windowless, large, and purely functional. A 'bot floated over the counters, scrubbing surfaces with a pungent disinfectant.

Ignoring the mechanized creature, Kiri pointed out features of the lab, falling into tour guide mode. Although her speech was fuzzy and her balance questionable, she was coherent. This was her job—she could probably recite this stuff in her sleep.

I positioned myself behind Spiro and pressed the stone on the elephant, watching it change to green. Holding it in my palm, I aimed the lens at Kiri, whose attention was focused on Spiro. He was ignoring me, which meant he wouldn't notice the elephant.

Kiri brought up an airscreen showing a translucent image of a virus stretching from floor to ceiling. The exterior was a sphere with spikes protruding, as menacing as a medieval flail. She led us inside the cell, where RNA strands floated like spiraling seed pods.

Kiri ticked off the unique characteristics that made the genetic material particularly deadly. "Extraordinarily fast reproduction, ability to take over reproduction of other cells, extremely high level of contagion."

Spiro interrupted her in that warm, intimate voice of his. "Where do you store the virus, Ki?"

She pointed to a row of refrigerated cabinets. "We have dozens of specimens, variations of the basic Project Dragon virus." She opened a cabinet, revealing row after row of vials.

Hoping Spiro wouldn't notice, I angled the camera in my palm to get the shot, then moved closer to make sure the camera picked up their voices.

But he was busy caressing Kiri's hand through biohaz fabric. "No retinal scan necessary to get into the cabinets, huh?"

"Well, no. Only people with highest level clearance can even get in here." Looking confused, she added, "Present company excluded."

He pointed to a closed door. "That where you keep the cure?"

Kiri blinked, as if trying to keep up with his questions.

"Yup," she said. "We just developed it—an anti-viral serum for all the strains of the Project Dragon virus. We've done virch human subject tests, and it works beautifully. And we've developed a highly effective vaccine serum in tandem. We're working on getting the patents for both now."

She paused, put her hand to her head, looking dizzy. Now I felt even more certain he'd given her something stronger than mood pills—maybe something like the tranquilizers he'd fed Sugarpie. Concern gripped me and I reached out to take her arm.

But Spiro pulled her against his chest, steadying her. "You were saying?"

"We've, uh… We've got about a million vials of anti-viral serum on hand. And even more vaccines. Epidemiological models indicate this would be enough to contain an outbreak, assuming immediate quarantine and burial protocols are followed."

Anger welled up inside me over the fact that this bioweapon even existed—that these scientists had created something so destructive. "What's the point of this research, Kiri?"

Spiro sneered at me, as if remembering I was here. He seemed to view me as an annoyance more than a threat. I closed my gloved fingers around the elephant, clenching it by my side.

"We need to be one step ahead of potential enemies in case of a bioweapon attack." She spoke with obvious pride, though her ability to form words was sloppy, as if her tongue were two sizes too big for her mouth.

"Shouldn't the government be doing this work?" I asked.

She laughed. "They contracted it out to us. We've got tons more tech resources than they do. And they owe the Virch Empire sandillions of favors. Come on, it's pretty obvious the government can't even clean up its own messes, much less prevent future ones."

True, they'd abandoned the Null Zones. "But why would Casper be sponsoring this work in secret?"

"To protect our country. And to help all of humanity—the main value of Virchuous."

Spiro rolled his eyes. This had clearly hit a nerve. "More likely to profit. How much do you think my dad will sell those serums for? Ten mil a vial? And what if he accidentally let some virus slip out? No one would have time to develop a cure, so they'd have to pay up. And he'd still come away looking like the good guy. The savior."

Goosebumps sprung up on my arms. Could Casper do something so horrifying, so selfish?

Of course he could.

But if he had his own motivation to unleash Project Dragon, was I wrong about Spiro? And was Kiri right?

She waved her blue-manicured hands around in protest. "Oh, Casper's motives are noble. Look at all the good he's done with virchips."

Spiro stroked the fabric over her cheek. "You see the good in everyone, don't you?" He kissed her through the biohaz suit.

I took the opportunity to resume recording with my elephant.

Gazing into Kiri's eyes, Spiro asked softly, "So, from the point of contact, what's the incubation period?"

Kiri flushed and brought up an airscreen full of diagrams and statistics. I cringed as she laid out detail after detail—all of which must have been classified. She was drugged, of course, but her willingness to share seemed to stem from something deeper. Wolf had mentioned his brother tapping into her insecurities. Maybe she still felt like a child prodigy, in over her head, trying to please her peers, seeking approval, wanting to be loved.

Deep-seated insecurities could make people do monumentally stupid things. Especially in the hands of a psychopath like Spiro.

"Look," she said, gesturing to the airscreen, "it's transmitted through breath and lingers in the air for hours. Within thirty minutes of exposure, symptoms occur."

"Thirty minutes?" I gaped. "That's impossible."

"For a naturally evolved virus, sure. But for a human-designed virus, trust me, it's very possible."

She enlarged a two-hour-long circular timeline, made it stretch across the room and from ceiling to floor. It began with exposure and ended with death.

"Once death occurs, the virus morphs to spore form and is released on the breeze. Then, when it finds a new human host— even up to a week later—it morphs back to virus form and rapidly kills the next person."

As horrified as I felt, Kiri was obviously proud of this research. And she wanted to show it off to the guy she loved, blind to his true intentions. It had probably been hard for her to keep her research secret all this time, I realized. And now, uninhibited thanks to the drugs, she was spilling it out.

"It's a perfect bioweapon," she continued. "High contagion level, quick onset of symptoms, extreme hardiness, and one hundred percent death rate. Better we design them and create serums before potential enemies do."

I tried to steady the camera. Inside my gloves, my palms were sweating, making the fabric slide on my flesh. All Spiro would have to do right now was grab a vial, run out into the hallway, and release it. Then give himself the serum and make sure only he had access to the rest.

But how could he manage to stop others from getting treatment after the virus release? Security was armed and could overpower him, even with his gun.

With a start, I remembered the fireworks that the pilots had brought him.

Explosives.

What if he was planning to blow up the warehouse of serums?

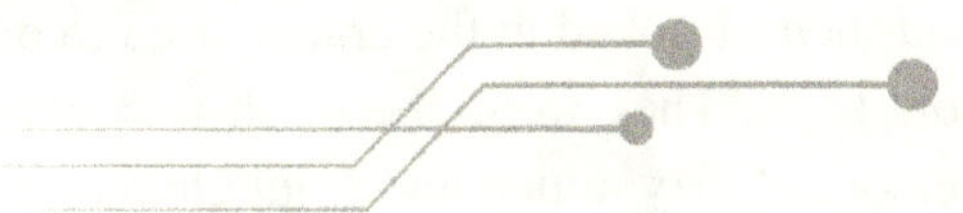

As if confirming my worst suspicions, Spiro turned to Kiri. "Can we see the warehouse?"

"Oh, I don't think so." She gave him a loopy grin. "I'm already risking enough."

He leaned into her. "Just take me in there," he murmured. "Real quick."

"Weeeell… real quick." With a sigh, she stood before the retinal scanner and led him inside.

I slipped in behind them. Maybe I could pocket some serums, just in case. We headed through another series of decontamination chambers. I discreetly exposed all surfaces of the elephant brooch to the disinfectant light. Soon we exited the third chamber, free of our suits. The final door slid open to reveal a vast storehouse, dim lights illuminating silvery crates piled ceiling high.

After a moment of awestruck silence, I panned the tiny camera around, then focused on the pistol in the back of Spiro's waistband. It was visible since his shirt had ridden up—and accessible now that the biohaz suit was off.

Just as I recorded the gun, he seemed to remember it. Casually, he reached to the small of his back and adjusted his shirt, covering the weapon.

When he glanced at me, I pretended to be busy examining the mountains of crates. There were alternating rows of crates labeled PROJECT DRAGON ANTI-VIRAL and PROJECT DRAGON VACCINES.

Stroking his jaw, he turned back to Kiri. "How would these get distributed?"

"Follow me," she said, her skirt twirling like a carnival ride.

Behind them, I poked at the crates, tried to open one. Hopeless without tools. They were über-high-tech plastic and too big for one person to carry, much less smuggle out undetected.

I walked toward Kiri at the far end of the warehouse—she'd stopped before another retinal scanner.

A garage-style door opened to the misty night outside, revealing a large concrete patio. Fuzzy moonlight shone off Spiro's abalone hair and Kiri's silk dress. Head back, I breathed in the moist air. Here on the roof, everything felt exposed. Hope, fear, everything.

"Come on out," she said.

A slow smile spread over Spiro's face. His eyebrows shot up, as if a surprise gift had fallen into his lap. "Yeah, come on out, Liv."

My muscles tensed. Anything could happen out there.

Wary, I hovered near the doorway, watching Kiri and Spiro move toward the building's edge.

She motioned around her. "A landing pad. In the unlikely event of an off-island emergency, we'd load up heliplanes with the serums and send them to strategic distribution points."

From the virch flying I'd done, I knew it would be a challenge to land a heliplane on such a small space, even on autopilot. A few meters too far on one side, and you'd crash into the storeroom, and on the other, you'd drop off the edge. I wondered if the pilots I'd met were skilled enough to land here, and whether any of them would do it if we offered enough money. Maybe we could move some of the serums to a secure location that Spiro couldn't access.

"You're sure a heliplane could land here?" I asked.

"Of course. The design was based on calculations by a team of engineers, security specialists, epidemiologists."

My mind raced. If the pilots could fly us here, maybe Wolf could hack into the warehouse lock. Maybe he already had access from his maintenance worker retinal data. But Borg had taken his computer-watch. The security team had probably noticed his tampering and reset the retinal scanners. Still, we could come up with something.

Spiro had reached the far side of the landing pad. There he stood, balanced at the edge, his toes in the air, leaning back on his heels. He spread his arms like a hawk about to take flight. Not the slightest fear of death. It couldn't have been clearer: life was a game for him.

"Come here, Spiro!" Kiri called in alarm.

"Why don't you two come here?" he countered.

I grabbed Kiri's arm. If we approached the edge, it would be easy for him to push me off. Then to push her off… possibly with only one eyeball intact. My stomach torqued. "Don't go over there, Kiri," I whispered. "Let's go back now."

She gave me a strange look but stayed put.

"He's got a gun," I said under my breath.

"It's for self-defense against his brother."

"Kiri," I said gently. "Maybe you feel like you know Spiro from virch dates. But that wasn't the real Spiro. It was an AI programmed to be exactly what you wanted. The real Spiro— you just met him. And he drugged you. He's using you."

Her eyes narrowed. "And what about your Nelson? You've known each other just a couple days, too. And you like him because of a weird dream? Have you ever even had a boyfriend before?"

The hurt must have shown on my face because her anger dissipated. "Sorry, Liv. It's just that my whole life I've been the prodigy scientist. I never goofed off. Never went on real dates. Never had a la moda hair. Never wore abracadabrant dresses."

Her chin trembled. "My life was studying, all day, every day. So yeah, maybe I first fell in love with Spiro on virch dates. But then it happened in real life, too. This is *real*."

"Enough with the secret girl talk," Spiro shouted across the landing pad. "Come on over, Ki!"

She put her arm around my shoulders. Maybe to be friendly, maybe to steady herself. "Let's wrap this up, Spiro," she called out. "It's nearly dawn."

I took in the faint glow on the eastern horizon.

And with a start, I remembered Wolf, waiting for me. Had it been a half hour yet? He must be panicking. Even though I hadn't snagged any serum, I'd recorded enough suspicious activity. And I knew exactly where the vials were and how to get to them. That was enough for now.

I leaned into Kiri. "Thanks."

In return, she hugged me. Sooner or later, she'd discover Spiro's real motives. And her heart would be crushed.

As he crossed the landing pad toward us, dragging his feet, I asked her, "Hey, could you do me a favor? Put a box of serums away somewhere secret—maybe in the infirmary?"

She gave me a sympathetic smile. "Nelson got you paranoid, didn't he? Just let it go, Liv."

When Spiro reached us, he helped her stumble back into the warehouse. I followed them inside, eavesdropping as he asked her more about the serums—and their vulnerabilities.

"Well," she said, her voice tired, "they need to be stored at room temperature, plus or minus twenty degrees." She paused, grabbed Spiro's elbow. "Sorry, I'm… just a little woozy."

Spiro steadied her by the waist. "I've got you."

Bile rose in my throat.

Kiri led us back into the decontamination chambers, where we sealed up new biohaz suits and re-entered the lab filled with virus samples.

As we crossed the room toward the next series of decontamination chambers, Kiri mumbled, "Groan. Decontam. Again." She staggered through the door into the vestibule.

For a moment, she swayed, then her eyes rolled back and she crumpled to the floor.

"Kiri! Are you okay?" I ran to her, checked her vitals. She still had breath and pulse. "Kiri?"

No answer.

I glanced up to see Spiro touching the door close icon. As the door began to slide shut, I realized he was on the other side, alone with vial after vial of virus.

CHAPTER TWENTY-SEVEN
Trapped

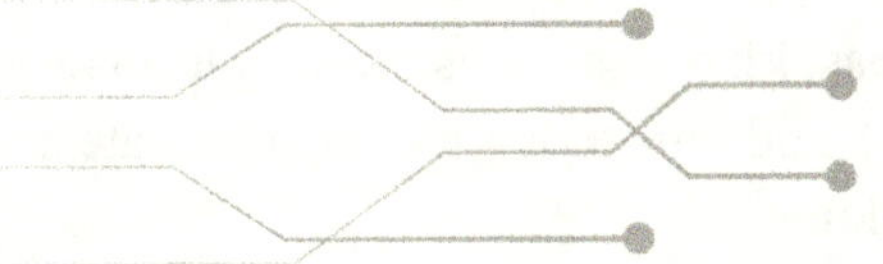

I hurled myself toward the door just in time to stick my hand between the last two centimeters of space before it shut. The hand with the elephant brooch.

The door shut on my wrist and the brooch fell from my fingers, bouncing and skidding farther into the lab. As I wrenched open the door and squeezed through, Spiro turned to me, then spotted the elephant.

Zuggers.

He picked it up, examining it as if it were something gross or dead. "What's this?"

I headed toward him, ready to snatch it away. "Family heirloom."

He made a face and tossed it toward me.

I stumbled forward and caught it just before it hit the ground. Not my most graceful move, but at least the elephant was safely in my hands. I pressed the stone to record, thankful I didn't have to hide it anymore. I felt a visceral need to run far away from the virus samples, but I couldn't leave him alone with them.

If only I'd gotten a weapon from the grizzlies. He had a gun. I had nothing.

"You don't have to do this, Spiro."

He stared at the cabinets of vials, as if weighing something. Would he try to grab some vials now? Release them near me? Tear off my biohaz suit?

Maybe the only thing left was an appeal to his humanity. It was dangerous—the puppies had completely backfired. But they were holograms, and I was real. *It's all about love, sis.* What if love—or at least kindness—was the simple answer?

"Spiro," I said, mustering a compassionate a voice, "I know what you're doing."

He eyed me warily.

I tried to project calmness, hide my fear. "You're planning to release the virus. And blow up the cures."

His face twitched.

"Spiro, listen to me. You have to assume this isn't a virch game. You have to assume it's real." I thought about what would happen to my own mind if this world wasn't real. How soul-shattering it would feel. "You have to, or else it'll wreck you."

"Already wrecked."

"Please, Spiro. I swear to you, I'm real. We're real."

"I wish you were." He gave me a sad smile. "But that's exactly what an AI consciousness would say. You have any idea how many fake worlds I've been in?"

"It must've been horrible."

"Sometimes I have memories of the other worlds, sometimes not. Depends on the experiment. At the moment, yes, I remember them. And statistically, it's highly probable that I'm in one of the sims now."

His voice lowered. "Killing everyone is my only way out. The game will end and it'll send a message to my dad. This is the last experiment."

He turned away and flung open the cabinet filled with vials.

"Stop, Spiro!"

And surprisingly, he did. Maybe there was a piece of him that wanted to be talked out of this. I felt like shaking him, gun or no gun.

"Isn't there anything—anyone—you care about?"

"Of course." He rested his hand just centimeters from the vials. "If this was real," he began, his eyes heavy, exhausted. It had to take a toll on a person to live an existence devoid of love. A life of self-imposed loneliness.

"What?" I urged.

"Maybe I'd like Kiri." His edge had fallen away. There was a trace of something genuine.

I was just trying to grab onto this and work with this fragile glimmer, when the acid returned to his voice. "But she's an AI consciousness." He turned back to the vials. "And don't try to stop me, Liv. Even though you're just an AI, I'd rather not deal with the blood and whatnot."

I yelled, "We! Are! Real!"

The door slid open and Kiri stumbled in the room, her face panicked beneath the transparent fabric.

Spiro stepped back in alarm. "Ki, what—"

"Hurry!" She slammed the virus cabinet shut, grabbed our arms, and dragged us toward the door. "Security's coming!"

Spiro and I exchanged one last look and then walked into the decontam chambers. We tore off the biohaz suits, blinking as the disinfectant light zapped us. Again, I held up the brooch to thoroughly zap it too. I peered through the glass of the final door to see if security had arrived yet.

There before us, brandishing the knife, was Wolf.

I tossed an anxious glance back at Spiro. It was too late. He'd caught sight of his brother. He was already reaching for his gun.

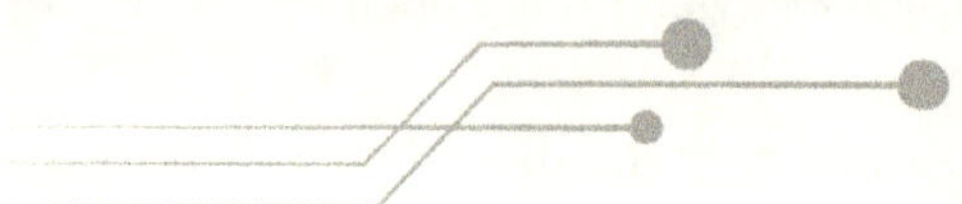

"What the—?" Spiro sputtered, hand on the pistol. "Ki, I thought you said it was security."

She nodded, looking bewildered. "I came to and saw someone coming into the main lab. I thought it was a guard. Look, the alarm light's going off out there."

In a quick movement, I touched the door-open icon and stepped through.

"Liv!" Wolf stopped just short of hugging me. "What took you so long? You okay?"

"I'm fine," I murmured. "Put the knife away." It would just give Spiro an excuse to use his own weapon in so-called self-defense.

"I called security," Wolf said under his breath. "Maybe it was stupid, but it's been an hour and I got worried."

"Hopefully Borg's not on duty."

If other guards came, they might delay Spiro from going back into the lab, which would be useful. But they'd put Wolf and me in a holding cell and ship us off-island in the morning. They'd have no reason to believe my elephant camera held valid evidence, no reason to take it seriously—in fact, they might just take it from me as they'd taken Wolf's watch.

Wolf lowered the knife and with his other hand, tugged mine. "Let's get out of here."

We backed toward the door as Kiri entered the lab with Spiro, clutching him for support.

"He's got a gun," I told Wolf under my breath.

"No surprise."

I tried to imagine seeing life as a meaningless game. Spiro's consciousness might have spent whole lifetimes in worlds devoid of other people with real consciousnesses. I tried to really feel it—his sense of isolation, the depths of his sorrow, so deep it had dissolved into a vast pool of nothing. Insanity.

Which meant he had nothing to lose by going on a killing rampage, starting now. The one thing he felt invested in was ending this game, *winning* this game. And in his deluded mind, this meant killing not just a few people on the island, but all of humankind.

Maybe that was a good enough reason—albeit a deeply disturbing one—not to shoot us before he completed his plan.

That said, if he wanted to get rid of Wolf now, he'd have a valid excuse to shoot him in self-defense. Plenty of people had witnessed Wolf punch him, and the fight that later ensued. Security footage would show that Wolf had been brandishing a knife just minutes ago.

Spiro's allies would leap to his defense. Borg believed I was a Progeny-stalking fan girl. Casper and Soraya had officially given us the boot. And Kiri would protect Spiro at all costs.

"Wolf," I whispered, "we have to go straight to Zinnia. Show her the evidence."

He turned around slowly to face the door to the hallway. "My brother can't shoot me in the back. No self-defense argument there."

I followed him, hoping for no gunshot.

"Hey!" Spiro called after us.

We kept walking toward the door. Behind us, Kiri was moaning about how much trouble she'd get into and begging Spiro to leave before the guards came.

Sucking in a breath, I touched the door-open icon.

In two steps, we were safely out of the lab, the door whizzing shut behind us. We turned right and hurried down the hallway. No footsteps followed. Part of me wanted to turn back to make sure Spiro didn't get near those vials again.

We'd nearly reached the elevators when Borg appeared around the far corner. Eyes locked on us, he sped toward us. Socrates trailed behind him. This younger guard seemed to have more humanity, although less power.

Another wave of adrenalin rushed through me. We had to warn them before we escaped. Maybe Socrates would listen.

"Go to the lab!" I shouted. "Spiro's trying to release a bio-weapon!"

Borg picked up his pace. Of course nothing I said would sway him. The huge guard pulled out his zapper, hurtling down the corridor.

We broke into a sprint away from him, passing the elevators and zipping down the hallway. Anticipating our speed, the floor-polishing 'bots drifted out of our way.

Breathless, I glanced back. Borg had passed the lab and was closing in on us. Socrates had disappeared.

"Here!" I yanked Wolf toward the emergency staircase, then down the stairs by twos and threes, hoping his body had healed enough for this. But he was keeping up—adrenalin was probably giving him extra strength and speed too.

Within seconds, Borg was in the stairwell, clomping around several landings above us.

Blood thumped in my ears. As we skidded around the next landing, the door opened and there was Socrates, zapper in hand. Zuggers. He must have taken an elevator here.

Wolf and I stumbled to a halt less than a meter from the guard. Clutching each other, we exchanged frantic looks.

We were trapped.

CHAPTER TWENTY-EIGHT
Secret Room

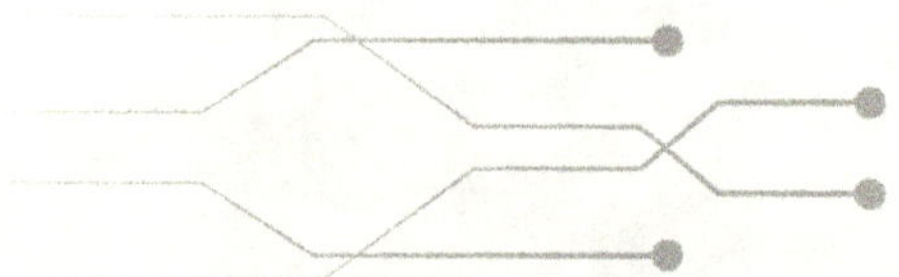

I faced Socrates, who wielded his zapper with one hand. With the other, he reached for the cuffs on his belt.

"I got them!" he called up.

A few flights above, Borg's footsteps slowed. "Zap 'em and cuff 'em," he called, panting. "We'll bring 'em to the holding cell."

Wolf gave me a look, then clenched his hands into fists at his sides. I guessed he was about to hurl himself at Socrates so that I could slip past with the camera.

Before I could bolt, Socrates whispered to us, "Where's the elephant?" He glanced at my closed fist that hid the brooch. "Give it to me. I'm with Zinnia."

Was he part of the resistance? Unsure whether to trust this man, I flicked my eyes to Wolf. He raised an uncertain eyebrow.

Borg was just a couple flights above us now.

"He's almost here," warned Socrates. "And cameras are watching."

"They're on a recorded loop," I said.

"They *were*. I rigged it up weeks ago. For secret meetings. But Borg noticed. He reset it." His words were barely audible, urgent, left no time for questions. "And don't go to the maintenance closet again. He knows you snuck in there."

I struggled to make sense of all this.

"I've been helping you, stopping Borg, erasing camera footage." He glanced up toward Borg, whose labored steps and breath grew closer. "Give me the elephant. I'll make sure it reaches our allies."

I recalled Socrates's tender gesture of patting Wolf's shoulder. His gentleness in helping me lead Wolf to the infirmary. I took a deep breath and hoped I was doing the right thing.

Stepping toward him, I slid the elephant pin into his hand.

And in return, he slid something into mine. Wolf's watch.

Under his breath, Socrates said, "Third floor. Employee lounge. Scanner's been deactivated. Far wall. Second mirror on the left. Push the rose. Hide in there."

Aware that Borg and the cameras were watching, I darted past him and raced down the stairs.

Behind me, I heard a scuffle—a pretend one, I assumed—and then, Wolf's voice, calling out, "Right behind you, Liv."

I glanced over my shoulder, saw Socrates skidding down the steps after us. "Stop!" he ordered. He sounded genuinely enraged, even though it was just an act.

Wolf and I ran down to the third floor. "Here," I said, touching the door-open icon.

I looked behind once more, heard Borg cursing from above, saw Socrates a full flight behind us yelling, "Stop!"

Wolf and I flew out the door into the hallway, through the faux star-lit hallway, to a red door labeled EMPLOYEE LOUNGE. For a split second, our eyes met.

Please let this not be a trap.

Biting my lip, I touched the door-open icon.

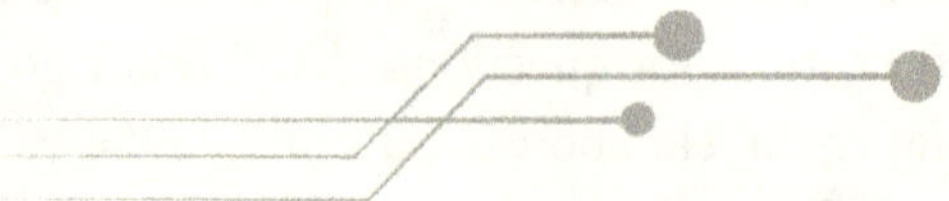

The door slid open. Wolf and I stepped into a Baroque salon holoscape, ridiculously ornate, lined with velvet curtains dripping silk tassels. Fainting sofas with embroidered pillows were scattered around the room. Beyond, a huge tapestry of a royal hunting scene covered one wall. Like the other holoscapes, this appeared a mix of reality and illusion.

The door hushed closed and music surrounded us, violins rising like storms. Beethoven. The seventh symphony, second movement, Delfina's favorite. Memories of the Cove flooded into me.

I remembered my exhaustion after a long day of work, with a long night of classes ahead. Everyone else would be asleep in their shacks, and I'd sometimes wonder who I thought I was, to be different from them, to think I could fly when they stayed earth-bound. To think I even had a right to fly when my sister's body was lifeless in a coffin. And I'd almost let sleep overtake me... but then the music would rush through me and surge and grow. And inside me, something would lift—a heron taking off into flight. Delfina would set a chipped cup of steaming mint tea before me, whispering encouragement. And my eyes and heart would clear once again.

For a moment I felt frozen, disoriented by the music and grandeur.

Wolf grabbed my arm, his breath ragged. "Angel, this is familiar. Like a dream. Déjà vu. These mirrors, there's something strange about them."

The far wall was covered in a row of gilded mirrors stretching from floor to ceiling. They looked too over the top to be real. What had Socrates said? Second from the left.

"They are weird," I murmured, moving to the mirror second from the left, running my fingers over the real carvings. My hand paused on a sculpted rose blossom.

I pushed and the entire mirror lifted, revealing a hidden doorway. The symphony was reaching its thundering climax and filling me with something terrifying and thrilling, something so much bigger than me.

"Liv," Wolf breathed. "I've been here before."

Shouts echoed in the corridor we'd come from. I pulled him forward and the panel closed behind us. We headed into a vestibule and through another door, into a small room.

The door slid shut. The Beethoven disappeared. Silence, save for the patter of rain, the crackle of fire.

In the center of the room was an enormous scarlet sofa, piled with pillows and blankets, practically a bed.

A red sofa in a secret room.

Wolf was trembling. "This is it. Where they did the experiment."

He turned on his heel, ready to run.

I rested my hand on his shoulder, feeling it shudder. "We can't go back out there, Wolf."

Panic filled his eyes.

"Listen," I said, "We'll make it through this."

Sliding my arm around him, I took in the rest of the room—the kitchenette along the left wall and an open door leading to a bathroom on the right. Computers and virch equipment lined the back wall.

Holoscaped windows featured rain drumming and dripping on the glass, water trickling down spouts, and beyond, a slick city street with Model T's splashing through puddles. A holo-fire flickered in the corner, creating a warm glow. It would have been a cozy refuge if it hadn't been the site of Wolf's trauma.

Still, despite the creepiness, it seemed like a safe place to rest. We'd been up all night—my body and mind were drained. Giving into exhaustion, I collapsed onto the sofa and oh, it was so soft. I tugged on his hand.

He resisted, looking shaken to the bone. A confused boy holding a cup of seawater.

"Come here." I drew him toward me.

He eyed the couch warily, as if it were a dangerous animal. But he let me pull him down beside me. We lay together, side by side, the lengths of our bodies touching. Little by little, his tremors calmed.

"This couch." His voice was low and vulnerable. "It's been in so many nightmares, Liv."

"I'm sorry," I said, feeling his pain. "But can you handle hiding out here for a little while?"

After a pause, he nodded.

"At least long enough for Socrates and Zinnia to watch the video," I added. "They'll keep an eye on your brother."

"Why do you think Socrates sent us here?" Wolf asked, moving his gaze over the room. His fear seemed to be dissipating. "Think he knows about the experiments?"

"No idea." But that reminded me of Wolf's watch. I held it up. "Courtesy of Socrates."

As he grinned with surprise, I strapped the watch onto his wrist.

"Thanks." He flipped open the face, examined it. "Undamaged," he said, tapping the tiny screen. After a few moments, he frowned. "Borg must've blocked me from the camera feeds." He closed the watch face, read the time. "Five-thirty a.m. now. Let's lie low until six."

He propped his head on his hand and turned to me. "Tell me about your Project Dragon tour."

"They're keeping the anti-viral and vaccine serums in a warehouse attached to the lab. There's an outside entrance. A heliplane pad. Spiro might try to blow them up, so we need to get there first. Or get Socrates and our allies there."

"Hopefully they'll stop him. But if we need to, I might be able to open the lock." From his pocket, Wolf pulled out a tiny paper notebook made from tree pulp. He opened it to a blank page and handed me the stub of an antique pencil. "How about a layout?"

"Seriously?" I held up the pencil, arched an eyebrow. "Talk about retro."

"The monks still use them," he said with a half grin.

I turned onto my stomach and sketched out a small map, with north, south, east and west.

Wolf watched me draw the Biohaz Lab, the warehouse, and the landing pad. Finally, I drew the virus itself, detailing the incubation period and mode of contagion.

"It's designed to be the ultimate weapon of mass death." I shivered. "Supposedly, the Virch Empire is helping the government stay a step ahead of national enemies. Finding treatments in advance. Self-defense. Or so they say."

Wolf's jaw was set, determined. "We can do this, Liv."

I knew we should start planning next steps, but something else weighed on my mind. "Hey," I whispered, "I'm sorry my puppy paradise backfired. I had no idea—"

"You couldn't have known."

"I'm so glad you didn't go evil-crazy, Wolf. After one experiment, you got out of there."

"Thanks to Amala," he said.

"But not just because of her. You were smart. And strong. You transformed your hell into something good."

I dared to reach over and take his hand. I wanted to do something real, something I craved with every cell in my body. With my other hand, I brushed my fingertips across his forehead, down his cheek, grazed his eyelashes, twirled my favorite curl. Electricity zipped through my fingertips. My entire body zinged alive.

He held still, trembling, only this time not from trauma. Eyes half closed, he seemed to savor every sensation. Then, as if he'd reached some limit, he put a hand on my face and moved his toward mine. His breath was warm and sweet.

My eyes drifted closed, and when his lips were just brushing mine, he whispered, "Liv, you're so *real*."

Real. I focused on the singular sensation of my lips touching his. I pressed against him, my whole body quivery-hot with anticipation.

My first kiss. My first kiss. My first kiss.

Just when our lip-touching was about to turn into a bona fide kiss, voices sounded in the vestibule.

Wolf pulled away, eyes wide, and whispering, "Under the sofa."

We rolled off and under. We barely had enough room to lie on our bellies with our heads turned toward one another. The dust bunnies made my nose itch and twitch. My face was so close to Wolf's I felt his breath. And I felt our bodies thrumming—with fear or longing or both.

Silently, I pleaded with the universe. I pleaded I wouldn't sneeze, I pleaded we'd realize that kiss, and deepest of all, I pleaded for this to be real.

The inner door whispered open. Footsteps sounded over the pitter-patter of fake rain and the crackle of holo-flames.

And then the quavering old voice of Casper. And the voice of a younger man with a slight drawl. A cloud of spicy clove cologne hung in the room.

Wolf whispered, "My dad and Mo." In the dim light beneath the sofa, he gave me a significant look. This was it—their early morning appointment.

Casper was waxing philosophical. "You know, Mo, I used to think it would be enough for my DNA to live on through my Progeny. But the closer I get to death, the less I care what happens after I die. I won't be here to see it with my own eyes. So why does it matter? Whether my Progeny are here or not when I'm gone—whether *the world* is here—truly, why would I care?"

My chest spasmed. Did Casper know about Spiro's plan?

"Interesting musings," said Mo in his lilting voice. "Shall we get down to business, sir? Everything is in place for Phase Five."

"Of course. Now for the trial run!"

"Have you decided on a start date yet?" Mo asked.

Confused, I raised my brows at Wolf.

He shook his head and mouthed, *I don't know.*

After a pause, Casper asked, "Remind me how recent it has to be?"

"Well, sir, as you know, the virchip campaign has been going on for about a century now. So it would be best to choose a date within the past couple decades." Mo spoke slowly, as if to a child.

I recalled Casper saying his memory hadn't been working well lately. I supposed a one-hundred-and-fifty-year-old brain had its limitations.

"Now, why is that, Mo?" asked Casper.

"Like I've explained, sir, we'll only get completely accurate replica consciousnesses from people whose virchips have been implanted since infancy, recording every neural connection. So it's best to start the simulated world at a time when most people have been implanted all their lives. That way, most of the fifteen billion people on the planet will have true consciousnesses, no AI necessary."

I bit my lip, tried to make sense of this. Virchips recording neural connections? Zinnia had hinted that Casper had motives besides health care for the virchip implantation program.

Oh, no, no, no . . .

"You're sure this will work?" Casper asked, sounding uncharacteristically vulnerable.

Beneath the hush of rain emerged the rumble of thunder.

"Well," said Mo in a gentle voice, "as I've told you, because of previously limited computer power, we've only done testing so far on sim worlds with a single consciousness, the rest being AI's. Results from the experiments with your Progeny give me confidence in this next phase of trials, too."

My gut twisted as I thought about the devastation those experiments had wreaked on Spiro and Wolf.

"Today," Mo continued, "this trial run will be the first time nearly all humans in the sim world have true replica consciousnesses. They perceive themselves as self-aware humans, no different from their original selves. Thanks to recent leaps and bounds in our easy-fusion tech, we finally have enough power to run fifteen billion replica human consciousnesses. And a fair number of animal consciousnesses, too, I might add."

Once, while I'd been working in the junk heaps, an avalanche of metal had come tumbling down and buried me. I'd managed to claw my way out, but for a minute, I'd been trapped in hell. Which was exactly how I felt now, in this dark, cramped space with the sofa just centimeters above me—and this new knowledge crushing me harder and sharper than a ton of steel.

As if speaking to someone with dementia, Mo asked, "You're remembering all this now, right, sir?"

"Of course." Casper cleared his throat, a phlegmy sound. "So if I start on a day sixteen years ago, the other people won't be AIs? They'll be real?"

"Well, as real as you can get in a simulated scenario." Mo sighed. "As we've discussed, if they had a virchip implanted from infancy, they'll have a replica indistinguishable from their original consciousness. They will act and think and feel exactly as in their original life, not knowing they are simply the product of a network of underground computers, maintained by 'bots and powered by the union of atoms."

My mouth went dry. My mind felt tangled and numb, struggling to weave these strands of conversation into something… something that wouldn't shatter me.

Fake rain beat against the windows, trickled and dripped and sloshed. In a low voice, Casper asked something that I didn't catch.

Mo replied, "Like I said, sir, we theorize that human reproduction will go smoothly. The mechanics of fetal development will be the same. We fully expect infants born in the sim world will possess as much consciousness as anyone else. And of course, death would simply mean the end of that human's simulation program, marking the end of that sim consciousness. In fact, all facets of life as we know it should continue in the same way."

Wait, wait, wait… is he talking about creating a whole new world? Completely self-sustaining? I wanted to press pause, make this stop, or better yet, press rewind, erase this knowledge and return to a time when things made sense.

A corner of my mind had suspected something like this all along… but I'd refused to seriously consider the possibility—to actually *feel* it.

"What about people like me, old ones implanted as adults?" Casper asked.

My nose tickled from the dust clumps. A sneeze was coming. I scrunched up my nose, rubbed it against my shoulder. And like a receding wave, the sneeze dissipated. A sliver of relief, but now I was trembling—all of me—mind, body, heart, soul.

Wolf slipped his hand into mine and I held on tight.

"Well, there aren't many of you," said Mo, "and the truth is, we don't know. Perhaps the replica consciousness will compensate for the lack of the first half century of life by piecing things together. Perhaps it will have just have gaps in memory, which happens anyway in natural aging. Or it could trigger a disintegration of memory altogether, though that's a worse-case scenario."

When Casper made no response, Mo continued, his voice upbeat. "Since this is your first trial run, sir, we'll simply observe the sim world and note how your replica handles this challenge. We can always do more tweaking."

There was another pause. More thunder rolled in. "Gaps in memory, you say?" Casper's voice shook.

It was obvious. His memory had broken down. Could this explain why he hadn't remembered details about the trial run? And what did all this mean for… *our reality?*

"Now, what's to say—" His voice broke. "What's to say we're not in a sim world now?"

Mo cleared his throat. "Well, sir, you see, the thing is, if we have this technology now and in the future, well, then it's actually possible—probable, in fact that—"

"Spit it out, son!"

"We could already be replicas living in a sim world. But if so, as you can see, it all feels entirely real."

My stomach clenched. *What's happening? WHAT... IS... REAL?* On reflex, I zigzagged my eyes, over and over, trying to exit. Yet I remained in the darkness beneath the couch. Of course, if we were replicas, the zigzagging wouldn't work.

My insides were cracking, crumbling apart in an avalanche. My entire *self* was breaking into jagged pieces. Was my mom's death real? Were our years in the junk heaps real? Was Shell's illness real? Was her hibernation real? Were our tears and anger and sorrow real? Our suffering?

Our love?

Wolf's eyes met mine in the dim light. He squeezed my hand and shifted his body closer to me.

Mo kept talking. "And of course, sir, you realize that 'original' is a relative term anyway."

"What do you mean?" Casper creaked.

"Well, what we refer to as our 'original reality' or 'original consciousness' might actually be replicas. And the so-called 'original' world relative to that replica could also be a replica. We could be living in a world within a world within a world, you see. None of them, strictly speaking, *original*." Briskly, he added, "But I find it more palatable not to worry about those semantic details."

A long beat of silence. My mind spun, churned. I was on a rope swing, spinning, spinning, dizzy, with patches of reality flying in all directions.

Mo cleared his throat again. "Now, sir, have you decided what part of recent history you'd like to simulate?" He clapped and rubbed his hands. "You mentioned something about sixteen years ago?"

Silence again. Drumming of rain. Sparking and sizzling of hearth fire. Casper's voice, soft: "I assume this is confidential?"

"Absolutely, sir."

"If you breech my confidence, you know the consequences."

"Of course, sir."

"There was a woman—the mother of one of my Progeny. She was with me for a couple years, about sixteen years ago. Her name was Kalea."

Wolf's mother. His eyes were closed, his hand clutching mine like a lifeline.

"When Nelson was barely a toddler," Casper rasped, "Kalea discovered my true motives for implanting virchips."

"What?" Mo asked in a shocked voice. "How?"

"I suspect she overheard a conversation I had with your predecessor about downloading consciousnesses via the virchip. She was planning to divulge the secret. I couldn't risk her ruining everything. What else could I do?" He paused. "Sometimes sacrifice is necessary for the greater good."

Wolf released his grip on my hand and hissed, "I'll kill him."

"What was that?" Mo's voice rose, strident with alarm.

"What?"

"Someone talking."

CHAPTER TWENTY-NINE
Replica

"Check the room!" Casper commanded.

Mo rushed around, his feet going in and out of sight as he looked behind tables and blinds. Casper stayed put, barking orders.

I held my breath. But did it matter if we were caught? Did anything matter? I let out a long, quivery sigh, just wanting this to all be over.

Mo stopped by the sofa, his shiny, pointy shoe just a meter from my face. Would he bend down to check under the sofa? Would it matter?

Beside me, Wolf was holding still. For the moment.

Finally, Mo spoke. "I must have imagined the sound. Anyway, what were you were saying, sir?"

Casper continued. "That *unfortunate event* with Kalea has always weighed on me. I want to go back and make sure she doesn't overhear the conversation. I want her to live. I want my conscience cleared, at least in a sim world. What do you think?"

"Perfect," Mo said. "And I expect that once we get this business going, our future clients will have similar requests. Paying billions to fix simple mistakes. Editing the virch record. The road not taken and all that. Really, it's philanthropy we're doing here, isn't it? Putting into motion alternate worlds where we get second chances. Someday we'll offer it to scientists to explore alternative courses of history. Once we have more easy-fusion reactors, we could have dozens, even hundreds, of sim realities happening simultaneously."

Nausea swept over me—cold sweat and dizziness and contractions inside my ribs.

Casper's voice, calculating: "How much power do we have now?"

"Enough to run one sim reality for three and a half million years. Or, about a dozen sim realities could be going on at the same time for hundreds of thousands of years. And the beauty is, with the maintenance 'bots and underground computers and easy-fusion reactors, no humans are even necessary to oversee it. Now for this trial run, we'll just set it to end in three days, then make any tweaks necessary."

All I could do was listen passively. I couldn't process this. It was… *too much.*

"What about natural disasters?" Casper asked.

"The 'bots have the tools and cognition to foresee those events and take precautions to protect the equipment. To move it or rebuild it elsewhere if necessary."

"Okay, let's do this," Casper said, drawing in a breath. "Now how will we prevent Kalea from overhearing the conversation?"

"We'll have you virchrecord your current self giving instructions to your replica. Based on our experiments, we believe the optimal way to do this is through a dream. That way, your replica can interpret it as a message from his unconscious mind, or a spiritual guide of some sort. If your replica realizes he's living in a sim world, he might react badly or appear mentally ill. So, the best catalyst is a dream."

Numb or not, my head felt on the verge of exploding. I couldn't deny it any longer. My dream self—my *original* self—had come to me. Warned me—*replica* me— to change the course of history in this sim world.

How can this not be real? Wolf's breath near my face, the dust bunnies, the fraying bits of cloth hanging from the sofa's bottom, tickling my arm.

Yet it was all coming together, these bits of knowledge colliding in my brain. My brain which was… what? A collection of zeros and ones?

My eyes shut. My hand groped in the darkness and found Wolf's. For a moment, no response, then a weak squeeze back.

I kept going back to reflexive denial.

But I'd never go along with a sim world!

Never serve as an angel-guide for a replica me!

Never!

Unless…

If I'd known that humanity would be wiped out, if I'd known that I was dying of the virus, if I'd known that other humans would have their own consciousnesses… then would I do it?

I thought of my dream self's words: *Oh, I hope I'm doing the right thing.*

I tried not to sob or sniffle. I tried to contain my shuddering. But what did it matter if we were discovered?

This isn't real.

This doesn't matter.

It wouldn't be me dying or Shell dying or the world dying… it would be an imitation of it all. An illusion.

Oh, but it feels so real.

And I didn't even get my kiss! The lip graze didn't count. I wished Wolf would kiss me, right now, here, under the sofa, and maybe I could just kiss him, because this was all an illusion and didn't matter… but now snot was running down my nose and all over my lips and I couldn't risk sniffling and making noise, and couldn't reach my hand up to wipe it, so I just lay there, shaking, salt water and mucus and sorrow pouring from me.

Where was my original self now? Alive? Dead? And what about Wolf's original self?

And were those selves even original? Or were they just replicas, too, in a long series of replicas, like Russian dolls tucked into each other?

Had we found the cure in time?

And what about the rest of humanity?

What if… what if there were no real people left anymore? What if this was it? The remnants of the human race?

My only shot at living?

Our only shot?

And I kept coming back to my embarrassing heart-question: *Did I miss my chance for a real kiss?*

Wolf clutched my hand. His hand, cold and damp, was the only thing keeping me tethered to this strange, fake world.

It was a fragile grip.

My self was disintegrating. The planet called Liv had been struck by an asteroid and burst into stardust. And the soundtrack to my world exploding wasn't Beethoven crescendoing or the ocean crashing—just Mo giving instructions in his Southern drawl with fake raindrops in the background.

"Now sir," he told Casper, "enter the exact date and time you want to give the dream instructions." A pause. "Very good, now stand here in front of the camera." Another pause. "Excellent. I'll raise my finger when I've started virchrecording. Make your message to your replica brief and clear."

A moment later, Casper's voice: "Hello, Casper. Tomorrow, during your conversation about the true purpose of the virchip program, Kalea will be listening in. Don't let her hear anything. Her life depends on it."

Chills swept up my spine. I thought of my dream self, doubled over in pain and gasping for breath, for words. Giving me instructions. Me, her replica. I was a butterfly after all, only dreaming I was a human…

At my side, Wolf was shaking too. "I'm not gonna let my dad do this."

I didn't bother to quiet him. I didn't care. The part of me that cared about anything—it had fled. I was the shed skin of a snake, the abandoned shell of a cicada.

"Now," Mo said, "after I begin the sim world, your replica will hear and see you in his dream. The following day, he will presumably act according to your instructions."

"And what happens when we end this trial run?"

"The replicas will simply cease to exist. They won't know what hit them." A finger snap. "There one moment, gone the next."

"Thank you, Mo. Nice work."

"My pleasure, sir. And of course, in longer trials in the future, we can further tweak any compromising material to protect your legacy. We can give billions of people mystical dreams that suggest you're a savior of sorts. Not only can your consciousness live forever in one new virch world after the next, but you'll go down in history as a hero, a saint—"

"A god," Casper finished.

Like a shot, Wolf slid out from beneath the sofa. And by the time I scrambled out after him, he'd already pounced on his father.

In seconds, Casper was on the floor and Wolf was on top of him, pummeling him, yelling at his father's blood-covered face.

"You killed my mother. You destroyed Spiro. You nearly destroyed me. You lied to every human on this planet. You stole our minds. You don't get redemption!" He punctuated every accusation with another blow to the old man's face.

Almost dully, I realized Wolf wasn't upset about the fact that this world was fake. No, he'd already come to terms with that possibility. What enraged him was his father's selfishness. Wolf wanted vengeance.

I considered yelling at him that it didn't matter. But I kept quiet. I didn't care.

When Mo tried to pull him off, Wolf flung him away so hard the man crashed into the wall.

In the chaos, Casper tried to crawl toward the door, but Wolf tackled him again. His father struggled and pleaded, then fell limp, silent in his surrender.

Wolf lowered his arms, shooting daggers with his eyes. His face was blotched, streaked with tears. When Casper tried to speak again, Wolf attacked him with another punch to the face.

I stood and watched, not feeling much of anything. What did it matter if he killed his father in this fake world? What did it matter if he went to jail? What did anything matter anymore?

I had to get away from this pounding and fighting and bleeding. I walked toward the door.

"Angel!"

I paused and turned.

Wolf shoved his father aside like a rag doll, stepped over him, toward me. Mo bent over Casper and grabbed some tissues to staunch the man's bloody nose.

"What?" I said flatly. I was a soul-less 'bot. A walking husk, unsubstantial and brittle.

Wolf's chest was heaving with the exertion of nearly killing his dad. "Listen, Angel, there might not be any reality left. This might be as real as we have. I need you."

A movement made me glance over Wolf's shoulder. It was Mo, staggering toward a red icon beside the kitchenette—an emergency icon.

"Security's coming," I muttered. "I'm getting out of here." And by here I meant this simulated world. I just had to leave this mess and figure out how to end my fake life. I couldn't do it under security's watch. They'd revive me. For now, I'd head for the cover of the forest gardens.

"Wait!" Wolf cried. "We have to destroy this stuff first." He raised a chair above his head and bashed the nearest computer. And then another, and another.

The rainy-cozy-day holoscape vanished, leaving naked white walls and a pocket of silence.

Next he hurled the video cam. Glass and plastic exploded and showered around us.

Mo and Casper cowered, covering their heads.

I didn't bother to shield my face. As if from a distance, I felt pain, then blood, warm and dripping from my temple. I let it trickle down my cheek, down my neck, onto my shirt.

The destruction was all pointless—of course there were backups to the program. I didn't point this out. Nothing mattered.

"You don't get another chance, Dad!" Wolf yelled.

And that's when Borg stormed through the door, right past me. Zapper in hand, he headed straight for Wolf.

I took the opportunity to slip out behind him and walk through the vestibule. Just before I reached the threshold of the secret mirror, I heard Wolf shout, "Angel! Meet you at our place!"

I picked up my pace to jog through a dramatic blast of Beethoven and gold-framed hunting scenes and silk tassels, then exited the employee lounge. I headed down the hallway, now sunrise-over-pond themed. The corridors were empty, except for a few holo-geese in the distance. Everyone else was still asleep.

I kept walking, down flight after flight of stairs, down the first-floor hallway, and out the back door into the tropical dawn air.

I headed into the gardens, lit by a faint glow from the east. A vague idea was forming in my head—finding a machete, any weapon that could end the existence of my replica consciousness. I should have taken that knife from Wolf.

Just a few meters into the forest gardens, my eyes rested on a bunch of scarlet blood lily blooms. An especially deadly variety, Soul had said.

I picked every one in sight—seven or eight. But I needed more to be sure I got enough poison. I would not die miserably of the virus. I would definitely not continue living in this illusion.

I walked deeper into the gardens, searching for blood lilies. Here and there, I found more. I plucked bloom after bloom and stuffed them into my pockets, ready to end all this.

Darkness

Day Three on the Island
Year 2154

CHAPTER THIRTY
The Ocean

As I picked deadly blooms, the sun rose, casting misty light between leaves.

A new day on the island.

A new fake day.

Over the cries of macaws, I registered a voice in the distance.

Borg's voice, growing closer. "Stop! Come out immediately. Hands on your head."

I dove off the path and into the foliage, crawling on my belly like it was a virch war game. Which it kind of was.

Once I was far enough inside the tangle of green, I curled into a ball and waited for Borg to move on. It felt like an eternity—my face pressed to the dirt, twigs poking me, insects creeping over my skin. I considered eating the flowers now. I had over a dozen in my pocket, but would they be enough?

My eyes squeezed shut. Darkness.

I licked my lips, tasted soil, pungent and earthy. A touch of metallic blood, the trickle from my gashed temple. The stickiness of it smeared across my face. *Is there another me, watching me, on the verge of death in another realm?*

I squeezed my eyes shut tighter. When had this fake reality started? The night of the dream? Before that, was everything in this sim world just a sim memory in my sim consciousness?

Borg's shouting and footsteps faded. Rousing shreds of strength, I combat-crawled back through the foliage, pausing every few seconds to listen for human noises.

And then I found myself in the mother lode of blood lilies. There had to be twenty of them right in front of my face. A laugh sputtered out.

I grabbed the plants, picked them clean. Soon there was a large red pile of poison in front of me. I'd just eat the whole plant, blooms and stems and leaves and all. Plant after plant until I lost consciousness—replica consciousness—and never woke up.

I brought the first flower to my mouth, let its petals touch my lips. It felt like the almost-kiss with Wolf.

There was a hot sea of tears inside me, and they were sliding out. Endless, bottomless, an ocean of them. My face was covered with saltwater, my nose full of it. I was drowning.

Why are you not eating the flower, Liv? Inside, I thrashed and pounded myself. *Eat the flower!* But my mouth wouldn't obey. It felt like a freezing day at the edge of the bay, one of those hollow-stomached winter mornings we desperately needed food—oysters or mussels or catfish or anything. Like I was poised on the edge with my spear and my bag, but I couldn't bring myself to jump into the ice-cold water.

With the petals still at my lips, I counted ten… nine… eight…

That was what I always did when I was stuck at the edge of the frigid bay—counted backwards from ten and told myself that was it. Period.

For a few stretched-out seconds, I rested my cheek on the soil, let my tears mix with the mud, tasted the blood and salt and earth and grit. Breathed in the smell of decay and life all mixed together.

Three, two. I was shaking, and the tears kept coming. *One.*

The petals tickled my lips.

A kiss. The first thing that had come to mind when I'd wondered how to win a virch game of life: Love. A kiss.

And the ocean of sorrow inside me churned itself into something more: rage. *I will NOT end this fake life until I get my kiss.*

I led with my heart, just what Shell would want me to do. And my heart wanted that kiss.

I stuffed the flowers into my pockets. They could wait. I was going after that kiss first.

Meet you at our place, he'd said.

The ocean.

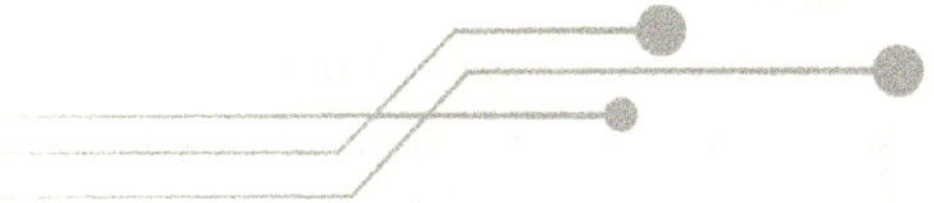

I headed toward the rising sun, stumbling right through the forest, following sunbeams that snuck through leaves. No sign of Borg or any other guards.

When I reached the grassy clearing, I ran down the path toward the beach, my legs pumping and arms swinging and chest banging and temple throbbing.

A cramp stabbed beneath my lungs, but I reminded myself it was an illusion—my whole body was an illusion. As was the blood dripping from my temple, stinging and mixing with salty sweat. I kept going, making the final sprint toward the expanse of blue, glittering and deep and infinite. *Our place.*

Once I reached the beach, I doubled over, hands on my knees, catching my breath.

"Wolf!" The waves drowned out my voice.

Was he hiding in the fringe of palms? I jogged along, calling into the foliage. "Wolf!"

Nothing. He'd probably been caught by Borg. I was alone.

I sat down in the surf, let water lap at my toes. There was something poetic about dying here and letting waves claim my body. My replica body.

The weather was cooperating, poetically speaking. Clouds were closing in on the sun. The horizon was a darkening shroud. The waves grew choppier by the second. A tumultuous end to this illusion of existence.

I slid my hands into my pockets, pulled out the flowers. But along with the flowers came the pieces of cotton—the lavender LOVE, the blue FLY, the indigo BREATHE… and another one, the one I'd been saving for later. This one was silver, stitched in deep purple. LIVE.

Tears burned my eyes. *Delfina's not real,* I told myself. *My memories of her aren't real. None of this matters.* I jammed the fabric back into my pockets, then clutched the lilies in my fist. I raised the scarlet blooms to my lips, felt the petals on my tongue.

Liv, came Delfina's voice, like a ghost haunting me.

Live, live, live.

And then a younger, higher voice—Shell's voice—chiming in.

Live, live, live.

Holding the petals at the threshold of my mouth, I took one last glance behind me.

There in the distance, a figure was running toward me, along the palms. I waited. Wolf? Or Borg? I kept the flowers poised at my lips. If it was Borg, I'd stuff the flowers in my mouth and run into the ocean, keep swimming till I lost consciousness. I doubted he could swim any better than Wolf. Definitely not well enough to rescue an unconscious girl.

But as the figure drew closer, I saw long curls flying. Wolf, racing toward me, skidding across the sand. "Angel!"

Why would my heart—made of ones and zeros—fly at this word?

"Hey," I said as he sat down beside me, chest heaving.

He ran his fingers through his hair. "Barely escaped. Even got zapped." He inspected a red welt on his upper arm. "Hey, sorry I lost it back there with my dad. I just—" He stopped short, touched my blood-matted hair, studied my eyes. "You okay, Liv?"

A raw laugh sputtered out. "Okay?" I held the flowers to my lips, like a zombie bride bouquet. The wind whipped up, blowing around the petals. I tightened my grip on the stems.

Breathe, fly, love, live. I tried to squash the insistent phantom words. "Actually, I'm just about to end this delusion."

Understanding dawned on his face. "No, Angel. You can't. We have so much left to do."

I didn't beat around the bush. "I came here for a kiss. And after that, I'm eating the flowers."

I touched his shoulder, then moved my face toward his lips. His skin was warm, damp with sweat, scented with sea. I tried to push away the knowledge that this was fake. Closer and closer I moved, till there was just a sliver of air between us.

He drew back. "Snap out of it, Angel. We kiss and you kill yourself? No way." He clasped my face in his hands, searched my eyes. "This matters. We matter."

"But it's not real."

"I think it's all we have left. It's this… or nothing."

"Then it's nothing," I said. "At least for me."

His fingers pressed into my cheeks. "I need you, Angel. I can't do this without you."

"Do what?"

"Stop Spiro. Change the world for Soul. Make good on your promise to your sister."

"My sister?" My words came out hollow. Holograms of words. "My sister was never even alive in this world." My fingers twisted the shell necklace, felt the familiar, sharp edges. I twisted so hard that a few shells cracked and fell to the sand. "She's only ever been in that coffin. In hibernation. Technically dead. And the rest of her, the part that talked and ran and laughed? Just a fake memory."

"Angel, listen." He moved his hands down my neck, over my shoulders and arms, down to my hands. Tightly, he wrapped his hands around mine, which were still clutching the poisonous flowers. "We chose this. Our original selves did, and—"

"Original being a relative term."

He squeezed my hands harder still. "Listen, we gave ourselves instructions. We had a good reason for it. We believed it mattered. *You* believed it mattered."

His words were translucent, nothing of substance, blips on an airscreen. Something you could wave your hand through.

"There are billions of people out there, Angel. Replica or not, they all believe this life matters. Some are suffering right now. Their pain is real. And if we survive this, we can do something about it. *We matter*."

I didn't bother to shrug. Didn't bother to meet his eyes. I was a robot. I looked out to the ocean, which had grown wild, the waves crashing against each other. Storm clouds had stamped out the sun. I shivered as goose bumps popped up on my cold, fake skin.

"We can cure your sister. You can be a family again. Come on, Liv, give me the flowers and we'll head back to the facility. Make a plan with Zinnia. There's not much time."

"Forget it," I said, pulling my hands from his grip. "Your kiss doesn't matter anyway." I opened my mouth and started to put the petals inside.

Before I could close my jaw, he knocked them from my hand—they fell from my mouth and fingers. The wind grabbed at them, whisking them across the sand.

I scrambled to gather them, grabbing at the crimson blooms.

Then something caught my eye. Just ahead, at the edge of the forest, stood a heron—and not just any heron, but a great blue heron. The creature I'd always thought of as Shell's spirit-bird. It was oddly peaceful, the way its smooth neck stretched high and its silver body formed an elegant curve. The blood lilies whirled around it in the breeze.

After a pause, I kept running toward the petals, thinking the bird would get spooked and fly away. But no, there it stood facing the sea, in profile, unfazed by the petals or me.

Soon I was close enough that I could see its tiny iris like a golden ring. And at the center, a black hole containing nothing... or everything. I couldn't tell if the eye was staring at me or at the ocean, or maybe, somehow, both at once.

As much as my head was telling me to end this life that was not, in fact, a real life... my heart and Shell's spirit were telling me to live it.

With a long exhalation, I let the wind carry away the escaped lilies, then turned to see what the heron was watching.

And I saw him: Wolf running into the surf. The violent, churning surf. He kept going, stumbling deeper and deeper.

I tightened my grip on the remaining flowers and kept my eyes locked on his body. His body that looked suddenly fragile in the ruthless, thundering ocean.

This is not real.

This doesn't matter.

His death won't matter. It will be a computer program ending. No meaning to it.

Still, I couldn't tear my eyes from his body growing smaller and smaller. A wave crashed over his head. I stepped forward, my heart thumping. Where was he? I saw his head for the briefest moment. And then nothing.

No more Wolf, real or fake or whatever. He would be no more.

There was only the wild, whipping sea.

He was killing himself.

Killing himself.

Rage rose inside of me. Rage at the injustice of having to live in this illusion. Rage at Casper. Rage at Spiro. Rage at the sharks. Rage at Shell's sickness. Rage at Wolf for making me care if he died.

Delfina's voice rose, tender through the turbulence. *Breathe, fly, love, live.* Shell's voice, like a birdsong, like the cascading calls of terns from sister to sister. *Breathe, fly, love, live.*

Tears poured out, hot against my face. "Wolf!" I heard myself scream. "Wolf!"

I thought of the confused boy holding a cup of ocean. I thought of this... not in my head, but in my heart. My gut, my core, my *soul*. And here I was now, holding this cup of ocean, precious ocean.

This cup of ocean.

This is my life.
This is Wolf's life.
This is our one and only life together.
And yes… I'll fight for it.
I took a last look at the great heron, dropped the flowers, and headed into the waves.

CHAPTER THIRTY-ONE
Kiss

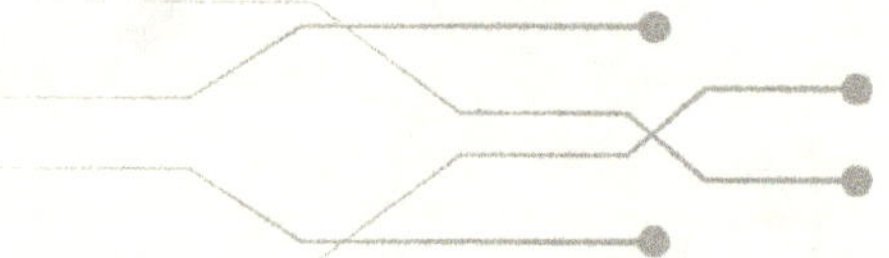

I splashed through the surf, laser-focused on the distant spot where Wolf had gone under. No sign of him. What if I was too late? Already exhausted, I redoubled my efforts.

Rage and love surged inside me, and this was fuel, and it drove me onward. Adrenalin rushed and the wild water pulled me and pushed me and soon my feet no longer touched the ocean floor.

I swam and swam, and when I reached the spot I'd last seen him, I dove, eyes wide open. The salt stung, but I refused to close them. Still, it was nearly impossible to see in the cloudy chaos of water. I dove deep, twice my body length, and raked the sea floor with my hands and legs.

Please, please, please let me not be too late.

When my lungs felt about to burst, I rose for another breath, then dove back under, searching, searching the landscape of wet sand.

And I felt something. Flesh. Cloth. Hair. All being tossed by the deepest currents. I could barely make out the form of a boy's body. I grabbed under his arms, and with all my might, tugged him up, up, up toward the surface.

His shoulders pressed against my chest, and I struggled to work against waves and gravity, upward… when something broke.

Shell's necklace.

It tore away from my body. My eyes widened, and through the turbulent water, I glimpsed broken shells falling, drifting down to the ocean floor. My impulse was to chase after them, try to gather up every last one, somehow re-string the necklace. I thought I could remember the order . . .

But Wolf was in my arms and I couldn't let him go. It took every shred of strength to move his limp body. We were heading toward the light and there was still a chance he could live, *we* could live. The shells were gone. Our old selves were gone. Our old worlds. The only thing left to do now was breathe, love, fly, live.

I exploded through the surface. I gulped air and treaded water, gasping and holding Wolf, his unconscious head tilted back in the sea foam.

Mustering my last bits of energy, I swam toward shore. I carried his lead-weight body, struggling to stay buoyant as I coughed and swallowed mouthfuls. Rain was pelting now, a full-fledged tropical storm. The sky flashed. Thunder roared. Once we reached shallow waters, I dragged him across the surf, laid him on his back, knelt by his body. With dread and hope, I moved my cheek to his mouth.

No breath.

His skin was cold and blue, from sea or death I couldn't tell. In the chaos of wind and rain and waves, I couldn't tell if his chest was rising and falling. I pressed my cheek to his chest, but my own pulse was thudding so loudly in my ears, I couldn't distinguish his heartbeat.

I turned him over, rested his chest on my lap, pounded his back, trying to force water from his lungs. No response.

Desperate, I heaved his limp body face-up again.

Please live.

"Wolf, come back!"

I held the fabric-scrap amulets in my mind, focused on the tiny stitches in dusky cotton, channeled the words to the still chest in front of me. *Breathe, breathe, breathe. Live, live, live.*

"Wolf, please!"

I tilted his head back, sucked in a breath to blow into his mouth… when he coughed. He coughed!

Oh, thank you, thank you, thank you.

He coughed again. Sea water spewed from his drowning lungs.

My hot tears mixed with the cold ocean.

After a moment, his eyes flickered open. "Angel?"

"I'm here."

He started shaking violently. Shock? Hypothermia? I had no warm blanket to offer. It was just me and Wolf in the expanse of pounding rain and wet sand and dark ocean. I lay down close, wrapped my arms around him, hoped there was heat left in me to share.

We were a little island of warmth and breath, while all around us, the waves were crashing and the wind thrashing. "You knew I'd try to save you." I pressed my face into the crook of his neck. "You risked your life."

He tried speaking, but only triggered another coughing fit.

"Sh. Don't talk." Once he was breathing normally again, I moved my face close to his. "Maybe," I began, not sure where I was going. "Maybe we're butterflies. Dreaming we're humans. Maybe that's okay. Maybe it still matters."

He struggled to say something, coughed again.

I put my fingers to his lips. "Just breathe." So much depended on his breath. I hoped my words could be a lifeline. "What if we were falling in love, Wolf? And we couldn't see it through? What if this is our second chance?"

I lowered my face to his and kissed him. He was salty and cool and waterlogged and delicious. His lips moved with mine, slowly at first, and then hungrily, and then he lifted his hand and pressed it to the sensitive part of my neck and pulled me closer. And I shivered with pleasure and wondered if this was our true first kiss or just our first kiss in this cup of ocean.

It felt like the first kiss in the history of all the worlds, all the oceans. We kissed through our tears, and even if it wasn't real, it mattered.

It mattered.

Love, fly, breathe, live. Do your best, that's enough. The words soaked into me, a part of me now.

He moved his hand over my naked neck, my neck that felt light and free without the jagged collar of shells. I imagined them on the sea floor, gradually becoming thousands of grains of sand. It had come from the sea and back to the sea it had gone. I let it go.

At some point, I opened my eyes and saw how purply-pale he looked. "Oh, Wolf, we have to get you warm."

"Yeah," he rasped. "Warm." He paused. "So you'll live?"

I gave him a secret look, a look I'd given no boy before, a look that said we were two souls in the vastness of everything and we were each other's and we were in love, or falling in love, or flying in love, or something like that, and it was as small as the tickle of an eyelash and as big as the birth of a galaxy.

"I'll live," I whispered, then moved in for another kiss.

And time and space and reality meant nothing compared to our kiss.

Despite the powerful urge to keep my lips on his, I pulled away, remembering he was probably hypothermic and needing medical help. "Can you walk?" I asked, squinting over his shoulder at the expanse of beach we'd have to cross.

And that's when I saw the truck heading for us, like a bullet through the storm, spitting up wet sand. A drenched and furious Borg was in the driver's seat.

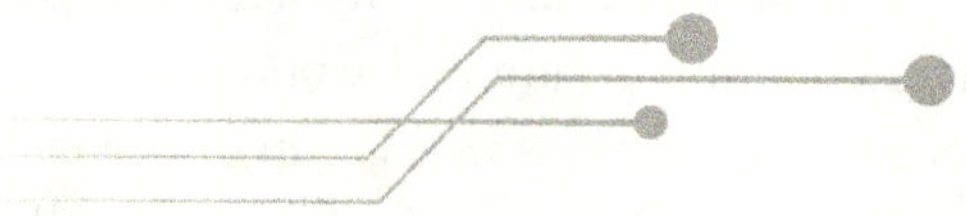

Love, fly, breathe, live.

Now that I wanted to live, what if I couldn't survive?

"Wolf," I said, trying to stay calm. "Borg's coming."

Wolf raised his head enough to see the truck. "Leave me here."

"No!"

"He'll lock me up," Wolf rasped. "I might see Socrates. Maybe he can get a message to Zinnia."

"What if they hurt you? Or worse?" My voice broke. "I can't let you go."

"Liv, go stop my brother." Wolf was still shivering but clear-headed enough to make a plan. "And warn the pilots."

My eyes burned and my mind raced. Borg was closing in.

"Okay," I said finally. "I'll have the pilots stay quarantined on the island. They can fly me to the heliplane pad by the warehouse. I'll get some anti-viral and vaccine serums, protect them from Spiro."

I squinted through the pelting rain. The truck was just a few dozen meters away now.

"Can you get in the warehouse?" He coughed again, barely getting the words out.

"I'll figure out something." Through the downpour, I saw the truck skid and lurch to a stop. Its wheels were spinning in place, spewing wet sand. Borg hopped out and began racing toward us.

Wolf tried to keep his head upright. His words slurred and quivered. "Angel—don't let him catch you."

I planted one more kiss on his lips, tenderly, like wishing on a seed. *This will* not *be our last kiss. I'll make sure of it.*

Instead of running for the trees, I splashed into the surf, deeper and deeper, and just as Borg yelled, "Stop! You are in violation—" I filled my lungs to brimming with oxygen, then dove beneath the waves.

Salt stung my already-raw eyes and storm currents thrashed me. But water was water, and it was my element, so I swam, making my breath last for minutes.

Once I was far enough away to be out of Borg's sight, I came up for air. The water seemed calmer now—maybe the storm was passing. Just in case, I submersed again, hovering beneath the surface, gathering strength and taking a long breath every so often, channeling dolphins.

And then, like a miracle, beams of sunshine shone through the surface, shimmering columns of mystical light. The water was still cloudy and rough, but now I could see shapes moving through it. A school of silver minnows glinted by, parting to swim around me, then rejoining.

I thought of the story of the cup of ocean—I thought of it more with my heart than my head. And here, inside the sea itself, I caught a glimmer of *something*, some kind of understanding.

What if our lives—our worlds—are cups of ocean? Real worlds or replicas, no matter… cup after cup of sea… all contained within the larger ocean, incomprehensibly huge… and we're all particles—organic or zeros and ones, no matter— floating inside this existence, doing the best we can… and maybe if we make a difference in our cup of sea, we make a difference in the entire ocean… maybe a kiss in our cup is the same as a kiss in the whole sea… maybe love in one piece of ocean will spread to other pieces because, either way, it's all the same ocean. And because this is it.

I dared to peek my entire head above the surface. Sweet relief. The truck was gone. The beach was devoid of people. I hoped Wolf could get a message to Zinnia in time.

I walked out of the sea, my legs wobbly. The rain had stopped and the sun was shining behind silver clouds, reflecting off wet sand. Barefoot, I jogged across the beach into the fringe of trees, and followed it until I found the exposed path. The sun dried my skin as I ran toward the forest gardens in the distance. From there, I'd have to find my way to the cargo airstrip.

With every slap of sole to earth, I repeated instructions to myself. *Get plane. Fly to warehouse. Bring serums to safe place. Find Wolf and Zinnia. Give injections.*

Please. Please. Please…

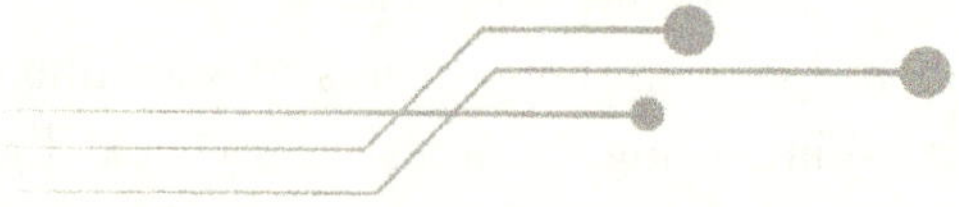

Inside the forest gardens, the tree canopy sheltered me. I started running in the direction of the cargo airstrip, but with the sun hidden again behind clouds and foliage blocking the sky, it was easy to lose my way.

Deep in the labyrinth, I needed Soul or Sodo to guide me. I simulated the bird call that they used—three trills, over and over. Mine was a shoddy imitation, but I kept going for several minutes. I was about to give up when the leaves rustled and Soul peered out, her machete glinting.

Her face lit up the way my sister's would when she'd see me emerge from the bay with a bag of oysters.

"Soul!"

The girl ran out from the trees and into my arms. Her hummingbird body felt hot in my arms. Strange—I should be the one warmed up from the run here. But maybe I held a lingering chill from the ocean.

"Am I glad to see you!" I knelt so that we were face to face.

The light brown irises of her eyes were nearly overtaken by oversized pupils. The whites were red with broken blood vessels. I pressed my cheek to her forehead. Burning hot.

"You okay?" My voice shook.

"Think I'm getting sick." She shivered despite the heat.

A faint rash covered the skin on her neck, spreading to her cheeks.

I willed my voice to stay calm. It could be normal flu symptoms. "Soul, we need to get you medicine."

Her father appeared, machete strapped to his waist. "Heard your call. Looks like my girl got here first."

With a cry, Soul convulsed and clutched her stomach. Her face clouded with pain and tears.

Oh, no. No, no, no. I pressed my fist to my mouth.

She stumbled into the arms of her father, who murmured comforting sounds.

"Sodo, have you two had any contact with Spiro recently?"

"Spiro?"

"He's Wolf's brother—Progeny. About my age, spiked blue hair?"

Sodo shook his head, looking baffled.

Through tears, Soul said, "I saw him a little while ago."

"Tell me exactly what happened," I said. "Please."

Her words spilled out, punctuated with gasps and sniffles. "He—he was coming back from the pilots and—and he was carrying a big box—and when he saw me he said—he said *come here*, so I did and then he pulled a little bottle from his pocket—and—and he said it was perfume and to smell it and I did but—but it didn't smell like anything and then—then he looked at me funny and so I ran away."

My throat constricted more with each word.

Sodo pressed her close to his torso, cocooning her.

I leaned in toward his ear, whispering so that Soul couldn't hear. "A deadly virus. Spiro exposed your daughter to it."

His face fell, stricken, and a wave of helplessness slammed into me. The feeling I'd had when Shell was suffering. When her coffin had closed.

But this was my second chance. I did some calculations in my head. Sodo and I had just been exposed to the virus via Soul. What was the incubation period? Something like thirty minutes till symptoms started?

Don't panic, Liv. But oh, I was panicking. I could practically feel the virus multiplying inside me, traveling through my air passages into my blood stream. *Stop,* I commanded myself.

I kissed Soul's forehead, took her father's hand. "There's not much they can do for her in the infirmary. And the three of us would only infect other people. She needs the cure. Listen, Sodo, can you bring us to the cargo airstrip?"

He looked bewildered. "Why?"

"I'm going to fly us to the warehouse, where the cures are."

Without wasting time, he carried Soul down the path, turning here and there, and the entire time I counted seconds, minutes, until the virus would strike me, too.

About twenty minutes had passed when we reached the airstrip. Across the tarmac, I spotted the grizzly with pneumonia. "Hey, Tor!"

He looked up from where he was fueling his heliplane. He held up a finger, finished pumping, then walked toward us, brushing his hands on his pants.

When he was about ten meters away, I yelled, "Stop! Don't come any closer!"

"Don't worry." He raised his palms. "No gun on me. And I have to thank you—the pills are working! You saved my butt, Liv!"

I didn't waste words. There was no time. "We're infected with a deadly virus. Spiro's behind it. I need your plane to get to the cure."

Tor hesitated, then shouted, "Well, I'll fly you there if you promise to give me some of that cure."

I shook my head. "Too dangerous for you. I can fly a heliplane." I didn't mention that my experience was all virch flying, mostly on autopilot. "Go warn the other pilots. Don't let anyone off the island. And stay far away from Spiro."

He ran a hand over his beard. He was too far away for me to make out his expression, but after a moment, he shouted, "All right. I'll enter my code. Then the plane's yours, Liv. And my gun's on the seat. Use it on that Progeny quanker if you have to."

Within minutes, Tor had entered his code and was giving us a wide berth as we ran to the heliplane, which sat on the airstrip like a strange, giant insect with six rotors instead of legs.

Carefully, I stashed the pistol beneath my seat. Sodo settled in the passenger seat with his daughter on his lap—the plane was a two-seater with cargo space in back. He was panting, dripping sweat.

I let out a breath and tried to recall my virch sims of heliplane flying. Last time I'd done one had been months ago. Heart hammering, I brought up the airscreen and checked the settings, made adjustments—and then caught a glimpse of myself in the mirror.

Had my pupils always been so big? The light felt bright, so shouldn't they be pinpoints? My neck started itching and a wave of heat prickled over me.

Nothing to do but grit my teeth and fly.

Next step, program the autopilot route. With trembling fingers, I brought up the 3D map, and selected the landing pad on the roof outside the warehouse. The knot in my stomach was growing bigger. *Remember Liv, you've done this before.*

I made some split-second assessments. The bee-line distance was just a few kilometers, which meant the heliplane would stay in copter mode with the rotors engaged the whole time. The auto-landing might be a bit nerve-wracking, I figured, but the laser sensors were super accurate. Even though the landing pad was small, it should all work. *You can do this, Liv.*

I tapped the airscreen icon to initiate autopilot.

A message flashed before me: AUTOPILOT DISABLED.

Excuse me? I wiped at the sweat trickling down my scalp lines, rubbed my eyes. I brought up the trouble-shooting screen, squinted at the wavery colored light, trying to decipher the letters, which were shifting in and out of focus. I made out the words: UNABLE TO ENGAGE WITH SYSTEM COMMUNICATION. INITIATE MANUAL CONTROLS.

What the . . .? After a couple of seconds of shock, my virus-addled brain put two and two together. I couldn't use the autopilot, and I was willing to bet Spiro had messed with the communication system. Without communication, he'd maximize the probability the virus would reach every last corner of earth.

But how had he managed this? Had he convinced his dad or a pilot to do this?

I shook myself. It didn't matter how Spiro had done it. What mattered was getting this thing off the ground.

And the last time—the only time—I'd used manual mode, I'd crashed. That was a sim. Now, the stakes were impossibly high.

CHAPTER THIRTY-TWO
Emergency Quarantine Situation

F*ly.* I blinked sweat from my eyes. My vision was so blurred I could barely find the icon to initiate manual mode. *There, got it.* I scratched at the bumps on my neck, then forced myself to ignore the itch and recall the protocol for manual mode.

I engaged the six rotors, heard them start whirling, saw the wind pick up stray leaves and debris. The vibration of the blades sent tremors through my body, little earthquakes in my abdomen. I winced but kept my hands by the airscreen controls.

Sodo groaned in pain. In my peripheral vision I saw him cringe, muscles tightening around his bloodshot eyes.

I issued more instructions into the airscreen, trying to ignore the memory of my sim crash. Slowly, the craft lifted. I managed to turn us around to face the facility and continued directing the heliplane high enough to fly over the forest canopy.

I steered us toward the towering silver building. The blades whipped at the tops of trees, and I kept lifting us up, up. The craft wobbled, tentatively staying on course. *So far, so good.*

As we rose above the forest gardens, it became a sea of deep green. On the far north side of the gardens, where I'd never been, a paved road led from the cargo airstrip to the facility, to what must be the loading zone for food and other necessities, lined with a tall fence. The remainder of the island was covered in more forest, spotted with towering white windmills. And somewhere underground were dwellings and rooms full of computers and reactors and 'bots.

Under other circumstances, I would have relished this bird's eye view. But now my lids begged me to shut and block out everything. My pupils were letting in way too much light. It felt like a floodlight was shining just centimeters from my eyes.

Minutes later, we approached the facility, with its painful metallic glow. I slowed and positioned the heliplane over the landing pad. But oh, it was so tiny. In my flight sim, the landing pad had been twice this size—and even then I'd crash-landed.

Even with undamaged eyes, I'd crashed. A sudden hopelessness overwhelmed me.

But giving up was not an option. I had to do this. And I had to do it right. I rubbed more sweat from my face, commanded my eyes to focus. Everything swam through my vision, as if underwater, clouded and doubled—the airscreen controls, the facility, the landing pad, the treetops. I bit my lip, centering myself on the singular sensation of teeth against flesh.

Centimeter by centimeter, I brought the craft down.

And then, a horrible scraping noise, a cracking, and out the side window, sparks were flying, bits of wall crumbling. The craft shook, fell off-balance, thrusted us to the right. A cry escaped from my throat.

With an abrupt jerk, I lifted the craft up again.

"What happened?" Sodo asked, alarmed.

"A rotor hit the building." My brain felt trapped in a feverish fog.

"You can do this," Sodo gasped. "Please. My daughter…"

In the whir of the blades, in the wind all around, I heard an echo of my own voice. My dream voice. My original voice. *Save Soul.*

Taking a quivery breath, I made adjustments, accounting for the broken rotor. And I tried again.

This time another rotor scraped the wall with an ear-splitting screech, but I kept directing the craft downward. A violent shudder, and then the heliplane hit the landing pad with a bone-thrashing thud. At the impact, my insides screamed in pain.

Close to collapse, I turned to Sodo and Soul. "You okay?"

Sodo nodded, rubbing at a rash on his arm. His irises had been replaced with gaping black holes.

Soul had nearly lost consciousness. Her face was a mass of red bumps. A thin line of blood trickled from her eye like a red tear. She was curled in a fetal position, lids drifting closed then open, zombie eyes un-seeing. She let out a whimper of misery.

Her father smoothed her hair, kissed her forehead.

"Sodo, can I have your machete?"

With effort, he pulled it from his belt and handed it to me.

"Wait here," I said. "I'll get the cures."

I grabbed the gun with my other hand and stumbled out. My muscles felt like mush. Half tripping, I made my way toward the warehouse entrance, keeping the gun barrel pointed away.

Before me, the garage-style door stretched tall and wide. I hated how the gun felt in my hand, smooth and heavy, but I needed to shoot through the lock. Then I'd use the machete to slice open a box and gather anti-viral serums for the three of us. Once we were treated, I'd distribute the other boxes.

I was just in front of the door when an explosion blew me backward.

Blackness, heat, smoke.

And pain, both sharp and roaring, throbbing in my ears, thudding in my head where it had struck the tarmac. I lay on the ground, ears ringing and cotton-balled, throat stinging, flesh blazing. Was I on fire? I scanned my body. My skin and clothes were intact.

I squinted ahead. The entire warehouse was in flames, the door exploded. Through the smoke, I glimpsed shattered glass and melted plastic—the remains of the serums. The pistol had flown from my hand, now lost in the rubble.

I was too late.

I forced myself to stand, grabbed the machete, and staggered barefoot into the vast warehouse. Fire licked the high ceiling. Black smoke enveloped the spaces between incinerating crates and walls.

One box of anti-viral serum was all I needed. Shielding my face, I raced toward the flames and searched through burning debris. But nothing was intact. Every vial—anti-viral and vaccine alike—was destroyed. Utterly and completely. My fingertips ached, scalded and blistering. The soles of my naked feet stung with every step. Still I searched, coughing and sifting through this hellish wasteland.

Just one vial, just one for Soul. Just one. Please.

Sodo appeared beside me with a fire extinguisher, barely able to hold it.

"Thanks," I rasped and took it from him. "Stay with Soul. I'm going into the lab. Maybe I can find some intact vials. And I'll get biohaz suits. And medical help."

But as I said it, I knew that if the serums were destroyed, biohaz suits and medical help would be pointless. In a matter of hours, the entire island would be infected. And in a few more hours, dead. The only hope for the rest of the world was to keep the virus on-island.

I trudged through the warehouse, dousing tongues of flame to clear a path. Through blurred eyes, I scanned the debris for an intact crate of serum. The explosives had been strategically placed to destroy every last vial of both anti-virals and vaccines.

When I got to the entrance of the first decontamination chamber, I didn't have to worry about decontamination or a retinal scan. The doors had been blown off. I walked through, right into the Biohaz Lab.

And almost stepped on a man lying face-down, riddled with bullet holes, in a pool of blood. Bracing myself, I turned his head to face me.

Casper. Eyes wide, skin gray. Dead.

My stomach lurched. I doubled over, wincing, and waited for the torment and nausea to subside. Avoiding the body, I scanned the lab for any anti-viral serum that might be stashed here. Nothing.

The cabinets were open, the glass tubes of virus samples gone.

I stumbled into the vestibule of the second decontamination chamber, which was still intact, and grabbed a biohaz suit. But when I picked it up, I saw it had been slashed to shreds. So had all the others.

Smoke alarms rang throughout the building, and an automated voice from the speakers said, "Evacuate the building. Evacuate the building."

Abruptly, the warning cut off, and a new voice boomed over the speaker. "This is Doctor Zinnia Nguyen-Obi. We have an emergency quarantine situation. Everyone must report immediately to the tropical forest gardens west of the facility."

The reality dawned on me. We'd tried our best and failed. There would be no more kisses, no changing the world, no world to change. Not for humans, at least, if the virus made it off the island.

I stumbled into the main lab and caught a glimpse of myself in the window. Even with this imperfect reflection, even through the haze of smoke, I could see the rash spotting my face. My eyes shone, zombie-like with enormous pupils. Tiny trickles of blood leaked from my nostrils.

Dizzy, I leaned against the wall, closing my eyes. Just for a minute. My knees buckled, and I slid down onto the cold floor. The machete clanked at my side. And then my cheek was on the tile, and I shivered and shook and under waves of fire and ice. My belly convulsed. It hurt too much to cry out. I could only breathe and breathe and try to make to the next breath.

Words flickered in and out of my mind: *Oh, Dad, my best wasn't enough. Dad, Delfina, Shell, I'm sorry. I failed you. I failed everyone.*

Images passed through me: Soul and Sodo in the heliplane, waiting for me. I couldn't save Soul. I couldn't save myself. I couldn't save anyone. I would die here alone and the world would die and I wouldn't see Wolf again…

And between convulsions, my fevered mind wondered if the other me, the real me was somehow still alive somewhere.

Maybe she and Wolf were dying together, and it was a reassuring thought and I tried to imagine this her-me and comfort her from across the divide of realities and zeros and ones, and I told her, *It's true, Liv. I love you and Wolf and life and oh, Liv, I tried, I tried . . .*

CHAPTER THIRTY-THREE
Save Soul

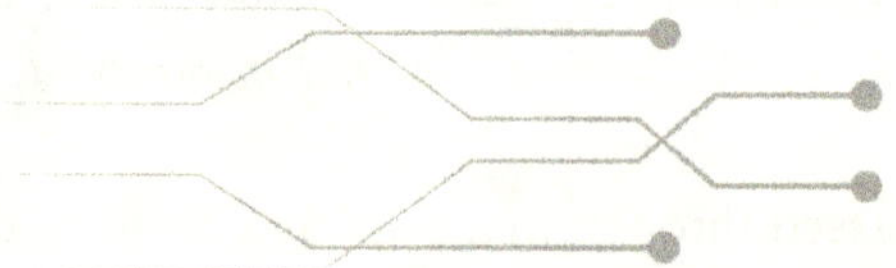

The floor was icy on my cheek and my mind felt galaxies away. I was vaguely aware of my body shaking and the smoke from the explosion and the alarms ringing and I wondered if Soul was still alive in the heliplane and how much longer I had, and if dying would get any more painful than this because I couldn't take anymore.

The next time my body spasmed I would just give in and let the misery swallow me.

Breathe. I breathed in. Out. In. I tried to make my breaths deep and long, as though I were swimming underwater, and that's how this felt, being underwater until the next freighter thrashing came, its blades ripping through me.

Live.

Liv.

Liv.

Someone calling my name.

A figure emerging before me. Wolf. My imagination? So beautiful—skin smooth and eyes perfect, irises the silver of stars… oh, how lovely…

And oh, no, no, no, no. Screaming, coming from me. My hand, clamping over my nose and mouth. The virus on my breath, moving from mine into his, and no, no, no, please, no.

Wolf, moving close and bending down to me and oh, no, no.

Wolf, I'm sick, I'm sick…

Wolf, taking my fists from my face, so gently, and holding me.

And now, Zinnia, dear, sweet Zinnia, her cool fingers on my arm. Then the tiniest prick…

And Wolf, holding me in his lap and crying droplets like rain, like the raindrops in that secret room that weren't really raindrops.

And is this real? Because I can't tell anymore…

Wolf, stroking my face, his voice faraway, asking Zinnia, will she make it? Is it too late?

And Zinnia, saying something softly, silver box beside her… the serum crate, opened.

That prick in my arm.

It was an injection.

The cure.

Slowly, my thoughts cleared like lifting fog. I took stock of my body, my poor, depleted body. Yes, the pain was subsiding, the spasms calming. But there was something important, something I was supposed to do. Something about a soul.

Save Soul.

Soul! I licked my lips with a dry tongue. "Sodo and Soul. Sick. In the heliplane. Outside the warehouse."

Zinnia leapt up and carried two vials into the blown-apart lab and *please, please live, please live, Soul.*

And now I heard Wolf saying things to me. "It's okay, you'll be okay, Angel, you got the cure, it's okay, we reached you in time, I know we did."

"How?" I creaked.

And passed out.

I woke up in the infirmary, my insides tender. My gaze settled on Soul and Sodo on the other beds. My skin was covered in wound-healing nanogenerators and pain relief patches. Tubes sprouted from my body—an IV and oxygen—but I propped myself up enough to see that Sodo and Soul were also attached to tubes and spotted with medical patches. And yes, there it was, the regular beeping of their heartbeats on the airscreen monitors. Their beautiful heartbeats.

Soul's rash was disappearing, her face clearer and smoother and nearly back to its perfect golden color. She shifted, and then, as if she could feel me staring, she opened her eyes. They looked normal, the pupils small, the irises brown and big. Pure bellitude.

She smiled at me.

I smiled back.

Wolf poked his head into the room. Seeing me awake, he ran over and pressed his hand to my cheek. "You okay?"

"I think so." My voice was scratchy. I gestured to Soul and her dad. "And looks like they're okay too."

At our voices, Sodo stirred and opened his eyes. He reached his hand over to his daughter. She took it in hers across the gap.

Wolf sat on the edge of my bed and held my hand, careful about my bandaged fingertips. "You were out for a few hours, Angel."

Zinnia bustled inside, as if swept on a breeze. "Oh, good, you're all awake now!" She checked our vitals on the virchip scanners. "Signs indicate everyone's on the road to full recovery. You'll feel sore and exhausted for a while, but there was no brain damage. And no indication of permanent damage to your internal organs. Nothing the nanotech we injected can't fix over the next few days."

"What happened?" I murmured, staring at the gauze on my fingers.

Zinnia perched on my bed beside Wolf and leaned her head on his shoulder, looking exhausted. "When Borg brought Wolf to the holding cell, Socrates alerted me. I insisted on bringing Wolf to the infirmary to treat him for mild hypothermia, water in his lungs, shock."

I gave him a relieved look.

"By then," Zinnia continued, "I'd seen the evidence you gave Socrates. We shared it with the security team. Everyone but Borg believed the threat was real. Meanwhile, the team went through the Biohaz Lab and into the warehouse. They carried out a dozen boxes of the serums to hide in the forest gardens. As many as they could carry on short notice, without time to arrange for 'bot transport. They would have brought more, but Spiro blew up the rest."

"Why the gardens?"

Zinnia sighed. "I figured Spiro might destroy the Biohaz Lab and warehouse, and maybe even the infirmary, but he wouldn't think to mess with the forest."

Gratitude overwhelmed me. Gratitude for Zinnia's wisdom and kindness and sacrifices. Gratitude for everything that had led to these people I loved being with me at this moment... and all *alive.* My gaze swept the room, resting on Sodo and Soul and Wolf and moving back to Zinnia.

I thought of our secret ally. "Is Socrates okay?"

She nodded. "Thankfully, he and the other guards were in the forest gardens when the explosion happened. He's taking the lead for the emergency response."

"Why did he send us to that hidden room in the employee lounge?" I asked.

"It had no cameras and was unoccupied." She wrinkled her brow. "We've never known exactly what it's used for. Unfortunately, he didn't know that Casper had an early morning meeting there."

My chest brimmed with warmth for Socrates and the others working behind the scenes. Hidden angels. "Anyone else get infected?"

She shook her head. "The security team and I—we all gave ourselves the serum so that we'd be ready to help others. When Wolf arrived at the infirmary, we were injecting the nurses. Right now, Socrates is in the forest gardens, injecting everyone else."

"What about the gardeners and maintenance workers?" asked Sodo with trepidation.

"Yes," said Zinnia. "And their families. And the pilots. Everyone."

Sodo and Soul looked at each other, relieved.

Relief swept through me, too. But then, with a stab of fear, I thought of my father and Delfina and everyone in the Cove. "The virus—did it get off-island?"

"We have no reason to believe it did," she assured me. "Thankfully, you notified the pilots in time. We'll have a month-long island quarantine to be safe. Even in spore form, the virus can't survive much longer than a week without human hosts. After a month, it'll be safe for people to come and go."

My muscles relaxed a bit. "Could the spores be transported off-island by the wind?"

"That's not a risk." Zinnia rested a hand on my arm. "In fact, that's one reason this island was an ideal place for the Project Dragon research. It's extremely remote, far from any shipping routes. According to the virch studies, any spores carried by the wind would die well before reaching human hosts."

My muscles relaxed further. "Thanks for everything, Zinnia." I sipped some water, and then, with some dread, said, "I saw Casper's body."

"Spiro did it," she said with a grave sigh.

Despite the horror of it all, my chest hurt for Spiro. Although he was a killer, he was, at his core, the victim of his father's experiments. A betrayed and confused boy holding a cup of sea water. I'd been trying so hard to appeal to his humanity, and yes, I'd caught glimpses of it, but maybe he'd been too far gone.

"Where is he now?" I asked.

Zinnia sighed again. "When Kiri discovered what Spiro was up to, she shot him. Then herself. They're both gone."

Sorrow filled me. Kiri had been a brilliant scientist, contributed so much to her field. She'd fought for me to be accepted as an intern. She didn't need to die too.

Looking at Wolf, I felt his ache. He was pressing his lips together, maybe trying not to cry. As terrible as their actions had been, both his father and brother were dead. Murdered.

Zinnia patted his shoulder for a moment, kissed the top of his head, then crossed the room to check on Sodo and Soul.

Now it was just Wolf and me on the bed. "Hey," I whispered. "I'm sorry."

"Me too. I just wish—I wish we'd had even a moment of connection, my brother and me." Wolf squeezed my hand. "But the important thing is that in some way, humanity survived. We survived. We did it."

He let this sink in, then leaned closer. "We have our whole, long lives ahead of us. To change the world."

He leaned closer still, letting strands of dark hair fall over me. His lip grazed my ear. "And more."

I closed my eyes and found his lips, and inside that curtain of curls, we kissed.

A Phantom

Days Four and Five
on the Island
Year 2154

CHAPTER THIRTY-FOUR
Butterflies and Dreams

The next morning, a well-intentioned nurse brought my pajamas to me in the infirmary—the tattered pair, patched together with rags from the Cove. She handed them to me, looking a bit embarrassed, and said she hoped they'd be more comfortable than a hospital gown.

With unexpected delight, I thanked her and changed into them. It felt good to wear familiar bits of my sister's and my old clothes, all sewn together.

The nurse also brought the driftwood message from Dad and propped it on my bedside table in the exam room. LIV, MY HERO, DO YOUR BEST, THATS ENUF. His words made my chest quiver. I'd done it, but there was so much work yet to do.

I slept most of the day, letting the nanotech repair my tissue. Wolf and Zinnia stayed by my side while Sodo and Soul moved to a private room next to mine.

And visitors came, including Socrates, Tor, his wife, and the fruit crew, who declared my pj's "über-retro-magnifique." Even Soraya came to thank me, wearing a humble expression— her horse tail between her legs, so to speak.

Late in the afternoon, I had an unexpected visitor—Mo, wearing a crisp white shirt and turquoise blazer. He closed the door behind him and entered the room, trailing clove cologne.

"Hi," I creaked, unsure how this visit would go. I sat up straighter in bed, sipped some nutrishake, and braced myself.

Wolf looked nervous, too. "Sorry I hurt you, Mo." He cleared his throat. "You okay?"

The man nodded, loosening his necktie. "I fared better than the equipment." He stuck out his hand and shook Wolf's, grasping it with his other hand. A gesture of forgiveness.

And then, more gently, Mo touched my shoulder. "Thank you both. You prevented a bioweapon attack. An unthinkably terrible one."

Wolf studied the man's face. "My dad—did he have anything to do with it?"

"Well, if he did, I knew nothing of it." Mo smoothed his tie, looking ruffled. "That said, I didn't always agree with his, uh, ends-justify-the-means approach."

I let that understatement go.

"Certainly," he continued, "one motivation for Casper's replica reality project was in case humanity ended by war or disease. This way, our species could continue on in some form. Noble." Smiling at us with the whitest of teeth, he added, "But thanks to you, humanity is still alive and kicking."

He sat down on the chair beside my bed and looked at Wolf. "Listen, I'm sorry about your father and brother. And your mother. And about the unfortunate way you both heard about the simulated reality research."

I set my cup down on the side table, folded my hands. "I want the truth, Mo. How can we find out what happened in the original reality?"

"Whoa! Now that's jumping the gun. I said it was *likely* we were living in a sim reality. I, for one, do not care to know the truth. Experiments have shown it could be psychologically devastating."

Wolf and I glanced at each other. This man didn't know for sure, not like we did. He knew nothing about our dreams. For all he—and anyone else alive—knew, Wolf and I had just acted on a hunch about the virus attack.

"Mo," Wolf pushed, "what if we do want to know?"

The man sighed. In a slow drawl, he said, "Well, I suppose that you have the right to know that an option does exist. A replica consciousness may choose to have a temporary virch experience of the original reality."

"Really? We can actually live through it?" I exchanged looks with Wolf. "Would this be the past or present original reality?"

"Either, actually. But like I said, I don't recommend it—as they say, ignorance is bliss in some circumstances. It's psychologically dangerous—"

"Tell us how," Wolf demanded.

Mo stood up and straightened his linen suit and tie. "I'll get you the equipment. Back in a moment." As he walked out, it was hard to miss the large bump on the back of his balding head—the aftermath of Wolf flinging him against the wall.

Soon, Mo re-entered the room, breathless. From his blazer pocket, he pulled out two tiny virchlens cases. "These are prototypes, still in development. They're programmed to allow for brief episodes of a virch experience of any other realities that may exist. Including, if applicable, the original reality. And of course, by 'original' I'm referring to the reality from which our current reality originated. A relative term."

I took a deep breath. "How does it work, exactly?"

He tilted his head. "Well, I don't know. My colleagues developed it and did some preliminary testing in virtual experiments. No actual testing on humans yet."

"What does it feel like?" Wolf asked. "A virch movie?"

Mo ran his hand over his smooth chin. "From what I gather, this is far more sophisticated. In a virch movie, you perceive sensory events from a character's point of view. Nerve stimulation reproduces input such as temperature, taste, smell, sound, and even physiologically based sensations like adrenalin release, increased pulse rate, augmented perspiration, etcetera. This experience, however, has an added layer. The replica consciousness would be embedded inside the original consciousness, able to experience the mind's *thoughts* as well."

My own mind hurt just thinking about it. "So I would still be *this* me, only inside the *original* me?"

"Yes, Liv. Assuming this you I'm speaking with is a replica, you would feel your current consciousness in the background. But you'd be unable to influence the original you's thoughts or actions. And remember, the original you would have no idea of the experiences this you has had since the sim world began. Things you've seen, people you've met—the original you will be ignorant of it all. This you would simply be an observer within."

I tried to wrap my head around it—we would be phantoms, invisible and insubstantial, inside our original minds.

Wolf piped in. "So we'd feel exactly how our original selves felt—we'd see and hear and experience everything just like they did—but we wouldn't be able to change it?"

"Exactly," Mo said. "Imagine one's original consciousness as the pilot of a heliplane on manual control. Now imagine the replica consciousness as a passenger on the ride, with only the power to observe. That's how it will feel. As a passenger, you will have your full range of memories and knowledge—but your pilot will be ignorant of what you know."

I glanced at Wolf. He looked as confused as I felt. "Well," I said, "I guess we'll just bumble along and figure it out."

Mo gave us a grave look. "This is nothing to be taken lightly, you know. It's still in the experimental phase. It could be quite disturbing to put one's consciousness in a position of such helplessness. I don't recommend it unless absolutely necessary."

I held out my bandaged hand, accepted the virchlens case. I looked at Wolf. His face was unreadable, but he reached out for the other case.

"You've been warned," Mo said, standing up. "The instructions are in the program."

"Thank you." Wolf was quiet for a beat. "Mo, how many people know about this sim reality research?"

"A handful of scientists, sworn to secrecy." He looked almost sheepish as he added, "Along with the subjects of the experiments, of course."

With a grave nod, Wolf shook Mo's hand goodbye.

I waved from my bed, holding the lens case with my other hand, like a treasure… or a bomb.

Wolf climbed onto the bed next to me and kissed me. "We can just store these away somewhere, never even open them."

"But I'm curious—I want to know what happened."

He tucked his arm around me, rubbed his thumb along the ancient cotton of my pajama's hem. "The scariest moment of my existence was when you gave up on the beach. When you were about to end your life. You looked so… *hollow*. If something like that could happen again—I can't risk it."

"But you saved me," I said, leaning into his warmth.

"Really? I thought you saved me."

"You showed me I need to live. And now I believe that, with every zero and one in my body. Whatever happened in the original reality—I can handle it."

He drew me closer. "There's more, Angel. I don't know if you were able to block out the pain you suffered with the virus—but it was torture. You might go through that all over again."

A shudder swept through me. It *had* been torture. A thousand times worse than the worst pain I'd ever suffered before. Was I willing to sign up for another round of hell?

"I got through it before. I'll do it again. Alone. You don't have to do it with me."

He traced a finger along the curve of my chin. "You really need to do this?"

I dove down to the deepest reason, the true force moving me. It wasn't found in my head, not where my curiosity lived. Not where the rational part of my self lived.

No, the deepest reason was inside my *heart*.

"Wolf—I want to feel how it felt to fall in love with you. For the first time. Without destruction looming." Softly, I added, "I want to know how our first kiss felt. Our original first kiss."

Our faces moved closer together. He kissed my cheek, a lingering kiss that slid to my earlobe. "Let's do this together."

Again, he kissed me, on the lips this time. Heat surged through me,

"But listen," he whispered, "you've been through so much. There's no rush."

"Tomorrow morning," I murmured, pulling him in and kissing him back harder. "At our place."

I found myself back on the virch beach, raw and Just after sunrise, Wolf kept his arm around me as we walked toward the sea, virchlens cases in hand. The day was sunny, just some wispy clouds at the horizon. Since I was still recovering, it took us a while to make it to the beach. When we reached it, I plopped down, my body drained. I wore my silver top and blue shorts, freshly washed. Whoever had done it had even tucked my fabric scrap amulets back into the pockets, neatly folded.

Wolf and I were positioned in the middle of the beach, a safe distance from the water's edge. We didn't want the tide to rise while we were wrapped up in another world.

Maybe it would have been safer to do this indoors—but the beach was where I'd first talked with Wolf, where we'd saved each other. Our heart place.

"Ready?" I pulled the virchlens case from my pocket.

"No," Wolf said. "Terrified."

"Me too. Let's do this."

We wiped the sand from our hands, opened our virchcases. I used my single unscalded fingertip to stick my virchlens on my eyeball, then blinked to position it. How strange to wear a virchlens after days of bare eyes.

Instantly, I felt transported to a tropical beach scene. Seriously? A virch beach? I couldn't help laughing.

I heard Wolf laugh, too. We were both within the virch world now. In the background, I could feel the actual sand on my toes, but on this virch beach, the sand was finer and whiter, like powdered sugar. And this beach had no seaweed, no dead palm leaves, no clouds. Only turquoise water and lacy surf.

"I like our beach better," I said.

"Me too. Miss the jellyfish."

I laughed again, more nervously now. Neither of us had avatars programmed on these virchlenses, so we were just disembodied voices, which was fine. Soon enough, we'd be inside our original consciousnesses. Or at least recordings of those consciousnesses.

A gray-haired woman in a flowing white dress materialized in the fake surf. "Hello." Her voice was eerily calm. "Welcome, friends. I'm so pleased to—"

"Cut to the chase, please," Wolf's voice instructed.

"Of course," she said, unruffled. "First, please choose which original consciousnesses you'd like to enter."

"Our own," I said. "Wolf goes in his, I go in mine. Oh, and we want to go to the reality that this world came from," I added, remembering Mo's relativity lecture. Who knew what kind of convoluted rabbit hole we could fall into if we weren't careful? To be completely clear, I used his phrasing. "The original reality relative to this one."

The woman smiled. "One moment, please, while we scan your virchips to establish your identities."

Two seconds passed, and the woman said, "Excellent. Now please choose which time you'd like to enter."

I heard Wolf draw in a breath. "Now," he said, hopefully. "The present."

So he wanted to see if our original selves had survived—or were still trying to survive. How strange would that be, to have two of my selves existing simultaneously?

In her honey-sweet voice, the woman said, "So sorry, but it appears neither of you have a consciousness at this point in time in your original reality."

I swallowed. So our original selves were already dead. I'd suspected as much, but it still ached. I wished I could see Wolf. I let my awareness move back to my body on the sand, touching his body along the length as we sat there, lost in this virch world. With concentration, I moved my hand to find his. He squeezed it. Then I let my awareness return to the virch world.

I thought of Shell and Dad and Delfina back home. All our friends and neighbors in the Cove. I thought of Wolf's godmother, Amala, and the monks who had helped him. "Is—is anyone from the original reality alive now?"

"There's no evidence of consciousness in any human who contains a virchip."

Wolf asked, "What about humans without virchips?"

"Unfortunately, we have no way of knowing that." The woman's voice dripped like syrup. "We only have records of the consciousness of those humans and animals with virchips. That said, given that so few humans have no virchips, the logical assumption is that they, too, are deceased."

Wolf and I said nothing.

It sunk in, this knowledge that humanity as we knew it was gone.

"Would you like to choose another time?" the woman asked patiently.

I took a deep breath, gathering courage for what was to come. I thought back to our first morning on the island, after the night of the dream. "Wolf, how about our first morning here—Tuesday morning at six?"

"Sure."

"Tuesday morning, June 23rd, 2154, six a.m.?" the woman asked sweetly.

"Yes," we confirmed.

"Please note that given your bodies' needs, three hours is the safe maximum duration. Your session will end in either three hours' time or when your original consciousness dies. You may fast forward by eye movements, as you're used to doing when you experience a movie. You'll find that the gaps in the experience will be filled in, since you'll have access to memories. Are you ready?"

"Ready," we said together.

A Lantern

Year 2154
Days Two and Three
on the Island

(In Another Cup of Ocean)

CHAPTER THIRTY-FIVE
Flying in Love

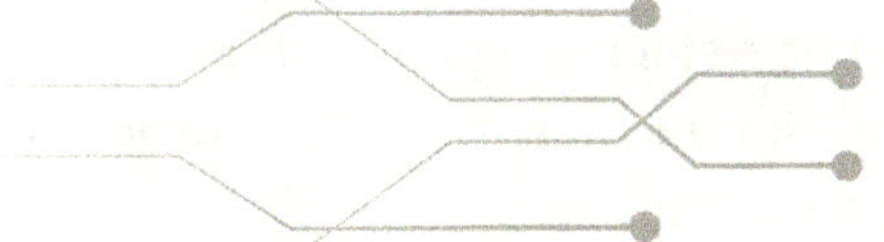

A tinkling bell sounds. My eyes open.

Hello, Tuesday morning, day two on this strange island.

I swipe at the airscreen, turn off the alarm.

Groggy, I lie in this luxurious room and replay yesterday's events. Riding the heliplane here. Meeting my buddy, Wolf, or Nelson, or whatever. Saving his goblock butt in the riptide, then rushing to the orientation where he promptly punched his brother. Meeting my other buddy, Spiro, with that baby panda.

Whoa. This immersive virch-thought thing made me feel like I'd just been dropped in the Arctic Ocean. Shock. The shock of being stuck in the back pocket of my own mind. Because yes, this was *my mind* that I was observing, I'd recognize it anywhere. But I knew so many things now that my original self didn't. I knew I loved Wolf. I knew the panda might die. I knew what Spiro was planning.

I tried passing thoughts to my original self, even tried yelling at her.

No reaction. It was like I was in a sealed, soundproof chamber back here with a one-way mirror. I wondered how Wolf was faring inside his own original mind. I attempted to feel his hand in mine back in our bodies on the beach, but now it was impossible. *Okay,* I thought, pushing down my fear. *Let's see how this plays out…*

Another chime sounds. A light flashes by the door. A doorbell? Who would come at this early hour?

And then a voice: "Hey, Angel? Hey, you awake?"

Wolf. And he's still calling me by that mawmsey nickname. I could ignore him and put the pillow over my head. Or see what he wants. Curiosity wins out.

"Uh, hold on." I climb out of bed, glance in the mirror at my sleep-tazzled hair and patched-together pajamas. Not presentable. But I'm not out to impress him. So he's Progeny. Who cares? He has nothing to do with saving Shell.

Cringing, I open the door. "Yeah?"

"Can we talk?"

"About what?"

"Can we pretend we're meeting all over again?"

I fold my arms. "Why?"

"I feel bad I didn't tell you the truth about who I was. Progeny, I mean. You were honest with me about being a minnow. I should've been honest with you. Can you please stay my partner?"

"Why?" I ask flatly.

"You're the only one here who's real."

"Real?"

He looks earnest. "I'm real, too—or I think I am—or I try to be. It's just—of all the people on this island, you're the one who matters."

My voice slides out, suspicious. "We've known each other less than a day, Wolf."

"But Angel, you have a mission, too. What you said yesterday about the girl in hibernation. You *care*." He grins at my clothes. "And you're wearing the best pjs ever."

I raise an eyebrow, ready to respond with sarcasm. But he looks so vulnerable and ridiculous with his flip flops and vintage swim trunks and sunglasses and old-fashioned watch. I feel myself laugh. It's been so long since I've laughed and it feels pretty good.

"Let's walk to the beach, Wolf. We'll talk on the way."

Argh! At this point I was practically banging my head against the walls of my original mind, trying to communicate with the replica Wolf—the Wolf I already knew so well, the Wolf who knew me better than anyone here, *my* Wolf who was somewhere in the back corner of his original's mind. But there was zero sign of my Wolf's consciousness in there—only his original, acting of his own accord. Just as Mo had warned, my Wolf and I were passengers, while our original selves piloted, oblivious to all we knew. I let go of the urge to do something and simply observed original me.

As we walk to the beach, we banter about jellyfish and riptides. He explains why he punched his brother and where he was this past year and how he hopes to make a difference in the world.

When we reach the sun-dazzled surf, he turns to me. "And you, Angel, you'll definitely make a difference."

"At least for one girl." I put my hand to Shell's necklace. "I hope." I meet his eyes, raw and honest.

"And other kids," he says.

Like Delfina, he somehow sees the hidden part of me that wants to change things on a big scale.

"I'm just one out of fifteen billion people on this planet," I say. "And the tide's against me. I'm a drop in the ocean."

His whole face lights up. "Or what if you're the entire ocean in a drop?"

I jab my elbow into his ribs.

He bumps into my hip with his.

And with this awkward, playful dance, we let ourselves fall into each other.

I didn't want to fast forward, not through this bumbling, sweet, heart-quakey flirtation—but we only had three hours. I skipped ahead to the afternoon.

After lunch, Wolf and I meander through the tropical forest gardens, making friends with Soul and Sodo, who give us an impromptu tour. Then the two of us walk back to our place on the beach, opening up more with each other—me about Shell and the Cove, and Wolf about the experiments.

Being with him is creating light together. It's the feeling I'd get at day's end in the Cove when I'd light a candle lantern and all at once, everything would feel warm and hopeful and *right*.

As the sun sets, a great blue heron lands not far from us.

I tell him about Shell's spirit animal, and we watch the bird.

He takes my hand. "We'll keep your promise to her. Together. We'll get her the treatment. And work to help other kids like her." Then, almost fiercely, he adds, "In the meantime, she'd want you to *live*, Angel."

With his words, the heron rises into flight. And just like that, I feel my own wings sprout.

This was it. What my heart craved. The magic of flying in love—without impending doom. I savored it like the first ripe, juicy peach of summer.

But our three hours were dwindling, so I reluctantly fast-forwarded to the next morning.

I wake up smiling. Day three of my internship. I wonder if it could be even better than yesterday. Yesterday was… *abracadabrant.* Sure, Spiro's panda died and he was sad about it—all of us were—but Kiri comforted him. Mostly, Wolf and I came up with plans to make life better in the Null Zones, building off each other's excitement. It's easier to overlook the hard stuff when you're flying everywhere.

Wolf and I go for our morning swim, but a sudden storm cuts it short. We huddle beneath the palms—bare, damp skin pressed close to keep each other warm. Shivers and more shivers. Beautiful ones.

Our hands stay interlaced, swinging playfully, as we head to the back entrance of the facility. Near the forest gardens, there's a commotion between Borg and Sodo, who's holding Soul in his arms. She's limp, unconscious.

"I know the rules," Sodo pleads. "But my daughter needs a doctor."

Borg shakes his head, blocking the door.

"Please," Sodo begs.

Wolf and I run over to Soul. I gasp at the sight of her, bleeding from her eyes and ears and mouth.

Ignoring the guard, Wolf takes the girl from her father's arms—Sodo looks sick, too. "Let's go to the infirmary."

Wolf and I barrel past Borg, who's holding up his zapper in protest, but apparently isn't cruel enough to use it on a sick father and daughter.

Inside the infirmary, the kind doctor, Zinnia, scans Soul's virchip. At the results, panic fills her face. "A deadly virus," she says slowly. "A bioweapon."

The next half hour passes in a blur as the nurses try to treat Soul and Sodo, as Zinnia makes an emergency announcement, as we discover that the biohaz suits have been slit, that exposed pilots have flown off-island, that the communication system is cut.

An explosion rocks the building.

Symptoms come over Wolf and me. When Soul dies, and Sodo dies soon after, the understanding sinks in—we're all going to die. Everyone on earth.

"We have to go to your dad," I tell Wolf, blinking in the bright light.

His pupils have grown enormous and a rash is spreading over his neck. "I hate him. But if anyone has a backup plan, it's Casper. Let's go."

Inside the recesses of my original self's mind, I was crying. Crying at Soul's and Sodo's deaths. Crying with dread at the pain my original self was about to suffer. I considered exiting this reality now, but no, Wolf and I hadn't had our first kiss. Our real first kiss. What my heart craved.

I fast forward fifteen minutes.

Wolf and I are standing in a secret room. Socrates told us this is where we'd find Casper. Sure enough, the old man is sitting smack in the middle of the red sofa, looking eerily calm.

Mo Boudreaux is swiping and tapping an airscreen, issuing computer commands.

Both appear symptom-free and unconcerned that we're infected—they must have been vaccinated or taken the cure.

But what are they doing? And why is Casper so composed? I want to speak, but I'm having trouble focusing, and dizziness is overtaking me. I hang on to Wolf.

He and his dad start arguing—about the experiments, his dad's plan, simulated realities. None of it is making any sense.

With unexpected strength, Wolf grabs his father's wrists, holds them like a vice. "*Dad. This is wrong.*"

The force of his words pulls me out of my stupor. I strain to listen, to keep my eyes open... to understand what's happening.

"You caused this, didn't you, Dad? This virus outbreak."

Casper says nothing.

Wolf is yelling now, shaking with rage. "Humanity is ending because of you. Because of your choices. You've hurt your children. You've destroyed our world."

The old man's gaze moves to the ceiling. "Spiro's the one who released the virus."

A beat of silence. "But he was your puppet, Dad. You made him what he is."

Casper's face grows stone-still.

"You didn't want the world to keep going after you died."

"Be quiet," Casper orders, glancing at Mo.

Although Mo appears absorbed in his airscreen task, he pauses long enough to reveal that he's heard.

Wolf persists. "The experiment—the end-of-the-world scenario you put me in—there was a reason you chose it. And with Spiro—you gave him hundreds of scenarios like that. You trained him to believe that destroying humanity was the only way out of the virch world. And you convinced him this world is virch."

"Stop talking, Nelson!"

Wolf stares at his father in horror. "But why ruin him? Why not just end it all yourself?"

Irritated, Casper turns to Mo. "Edit the past ten minutes of the virch record, okay? Along with any other compromising conversations."

Mo loosens his bowtie. "Sir, I have to ask. I've been nothing but loyal to you for years... but is there any truth to your son's accusations?"

"He's delusional. I've told you."

Mo rubs his forehead, looking torn. "Well, first let me finish these final instructions for the new world." His voice drops to a mutter. "I'm just about to add the mystical savior visions of you."

Little by little, understanding dawns over me. I move my mouth to Wolf's ear, whisper, "Casper wants to go down in history as the good guy. The guy who saved humanity. In some form, at least. And the guy who ended humanity? That would be Spiro. He's the bad guy. And Casper gets to be a hero."

Wolf reddens, wipes blood from his lip. Somehow, he musters strength to grab his father from behind, looping his arm around the old man's neck.

"Mo!" he yells. "Do what I say or I kill my father. And you next."

Mo wavers before the airscreen.

I stumble to the kitchenette, grab a ceramic teapot, and raise it over his head. I barely have the strength to hold this makeshift weapon—hopefully he won't call my bluff.

"Fine." Mo doesn't seem like the fighting type. "I'm listening, Nelson."

My eyes drift closed again as pain wracks my body. Still, I hang on to the teapot while Wolf forces Mo to explain exactly what he's doing.

His words swim in and out of my consciousness. He's talking about making a replica world, with Casper's consciousness immortal and god-like. About video-recording Casper giving instructions to himself in a dream and inserting it into the replica world. Then inserting a Casper-as-savior image into everyone's dreams, demanding their gratitude, their worship.

As Mo talks, Wolf tightens his grip around his father's neck.

Tears pour from my eyes, not just from the pain, but from the bone-deep understanding that the plan isn't about saving this world. It's about giving up on it and starting another one.

A fake one.

My teapot falls.

I fall.

Life shrinks to the space between my breaths.

Breathe.

CHAPTER THIRTY-SIX
Live

"Angel! Come back!" It's Wolf, gently slapping my cheeks and tugging me back to this world that's dying. "Liv!"

He fades out again and I try to make my mouth form words. *I love you, Wolf.* That's what I want to say. And I want to kiss him, but another tsunami of pain wracks my body.

Then staccato booms shake the room. Gunshots deafen me and I clamp my ears.

Spiro has burst inside—he's shooting the ceiling. "This is the last game, Dad. And I won." His voice sounds muffled, distant. He looks enraged but healthy. He must have injected himself.

Casper shows traces of discomfort, if not exactly fear—as if he believes himself invincible.

I press my face against Wolf's chest. I want to be alone with him in these last moments.

I want peace.

I want a kiss.

Spiro speaks again. "You taught me the only way out is to destroy everything. You destroyed me, Dad." His voice cracks.

Casper glances at Mo. "Edit these last moments for the record, too. All right, Mo? We have to protect my legacy—"

Bullets spew, riddling Casper, and Mo behind him.

Blood splatters the walls, splotches our clothes, forms puddles on the floor. The world is blurred and muted, something strange and vanishing.

Across the room, Mo and Casper lie motionless.

Spiro stares at the bodies, his voice breaking into jagged pieces. "See you in the real world, Dad." Then he glances at Wolf. "See you there, bro."

As Spiro turns to leave, Kiri stumbles into the room, makeup smeared over her face, waving a gun of her own. "I thought you loved me!"

He gapes. "I-I do." His gun hangs in his hand at his side. "I mean, if you were real, I'd love you, Ki." There's a tortured dissonance in his words and expression.

She aims the gun at his heart and sobs, "I *am* real."

His expression melts and tears brim his eyes. He looks at her with the most tender sorrow.

His face vulnerable, he glances at Wolf. Their eyes lock and something passes between them, something like regret tinged with love.

Kiri's shout breaks their moment, her voice even louder now, more desperate. "I am real!"

When Spiro turns back to look at her, his words emerge in a whisper. *"If only."*

At that, she narrows her eyes and pulls the trigger.

As the shots explode, I close my eyes, press my hands to my ears. More shots sound and I squeeze my eyes tighter.

And then, silence.

As Wolf holds me, I dare to open my eyes. By the door, Spiro and Kiri lie a meter apart, in puddles of blood that spill from their chests. She must have shot herself after him.

I let out a strangled cry. This is too much, *too much*. I drop my head into the crook of Wolf's neck. Our end is near too. If I can't speak my heart now, I'll never do it. "I just want to kiss you, Wolf."

"Me too." Wolf moves his face closer to mine, and we're in our own contained world, a candle flame flickering out. Our damaged, rash-covered faces move together, our lips parched with fever...

And this is not how our first kiss is supposed to be. It's supposed to be something pure and beautiful, on the beach, by the ocean, sparkling and full of hope.

But this is all we have.

Just before our lips meet, Wolf whispers, "Wait a second, Angel. It's all set up."

"What?" I murmur.

"The sim reality. The replicas. Look at the airscreen. It's ready. We could do this. We could be together in another world."

"But it won't be real."

"It's as real as we'll ever get," he says. "We could be butterflies dreaming of being human. Just another cupful of ocean." He winces, doubles over in pain. Once it passes, he gasps, "We only have minutes left, Angel. We have to decide." He presses a hand to my cheek. "What's your heart telling you?"

The fabric scraps in my pockets rustle like butterflies, whispering messages. *Breathe, fly, love, live.* Or so it feels in my delirium. *It's all about love, sis.*

"I want to," I say. "I want to kiss you... in that other world... I want to change things with you... save Shell... and other kids... I want to... yes."

He pulls me up, and I lean against the wall for support. I register him touching the door lock icon. I try not to look at the lifeless, bloody bodies on the floor. So does Wolf.

"When should we start the sim reality?" he asks.

My head clears enough to consider the possibilities. Before my sister got sick? Could I prevent her suffering? A glimmer of excitement. *Yes. Yes, I can!*

But then I play out the scenario in my head. We'd have to start the sim years ago, in order to stop the build-up of toxins in her body. I would be a kid, getting this weird dream with instructions to not feed my sister contaminated food, to prevent her from working in the junk heaps. I could *maybe* imagine my younger self carrying out those instructions.

But the next instructions—doing this internship and working together with Wolf—the younger me would never take them seriously. Back then, I hadn't met Delfina or taken a virch class or worn a virchlens or heard of Project Dragon or met Wolf—or any Progeny.

Most of all, if Shell hadn't gotten sick, I'd have no motivation to study so hard or to come to this island. I wouldn't have the raw determination to complete any mission. No, if I gave my young self dream instructions, she'd have no reason to follow them.

"Hey, you okay?" Wolf says.

I struggle to focus on his face, a mosaic of fear and hope. I try to straighten up, but nausea sweeps through me. I force out the words. "Let's go to—to—the middle of our first night here."

It's the only way. Any time before that, and my replica self wouldn't believe the dream. Even this was no guarantee. I squeeze my eyes shut, move my hand to the necklace. And I send a silent apology to my sister.

"Yeah," he says after a long pause. "I think that's best." He starts entering instructions. Tech genius Wolf. My Wolf.

Did he consider starting the sim world before the traumatic experiment? Did he think about preventing his replica from suffering? But as hellish as it was, the experiment must have cracked the foundations of his world, just as Shell's sickness cracked mine. The experiment sparked his mission and brought him to this island.

Truth be told, if he hadn't been shaken to the core, he might not have seen anything special about a girl like me. His young self would have ignored the dream instructions, too. Going through hell made us both stronger and more determined—and somehow, at the same time, more tender and open.

No, we can't erase the hell from our past. It's part of who we are.

I want to hug him, but it's taking all my energy to simply stand here.

Just when I'm on the verge of collapse, Wolf says, "I did it. Deleted all Mo's instructions about Casper. Entered our own."

He rubs his eyes, squints, turns on the camera. "I'm setting the dream on the beach. Our place. Okay, go ahead."

There's banging on the locked door. "Open up!" The voice is male and muffled. "Who fired those shots? Is Casper in there? Is he okay?" It must be Borg.

I ignore the noise, take the cotton scraps from my pockets, clench them in my fist as if they're magic. I squeeze them, and the force of my grip centers my last shreds of energy.

Breathe, fly, love, live. Heartbeats of words, scraps of hope.

I calm my crying enough to speak for the camera. I try to sound lucid but I'm swimming in a sea of pain. I sputter out instructions as best I can and hope they make sense.

Meanwhile, Borg is trying to kick the door in.

As I talk, it occurs to me that there's hope for Soul and even the panda, so I mumble something about them, too. A vice clamps my torso and I double over. The fabric scraps fall to the earth.

In one final burst, like the last sprint of a race, I say, "I just—I—I love you and I love life and I love Wolf, and that's why—why—why I'm doing this, and oh, Liv, I hope it's the right thing. Liv, please… please just live your life… live your life… live your life…"

Wolf stops recording and catches me just as I collapse. "Angel, can you record me?"

I nod, dazed, as he helps me up.

Behind the camera, I touch the record icon.

He gives his replica self instructions as Borg keeps banging.

It's all I can do to go from breath to breath because one more breath means one more second alive and I just have to stretch this life out the tiniest bit longer, just long enough…

There's a crash. It's me falling to the floor.

Wolf stumbles over and puts his hand to my cheek. "There's one more message I need to record. And a little programming. Just in case things don't work out. A backup plan."

He staggers to standing, moves to the screen and enters more instructions while I lie on the floor, my cheek pressed to the cold tile. There's the incessant pounding on the door and beneath it, Wolf's voice, urgent and earnest, something about the ocean and swimming and being old, a hundred years old.

Now he's beside me again. "There, I did it. I think."

He falls to my side and curls up next to me.

"Wolf, we forgot…"

"What?" he rasps.

My thoughts scatter like clouds. I grab at them before they drift away. "Our idea to help my Cove... we forgot to tell them."

"They're us, Angel. They'll—we'll figure it out... we will."

And our lips move closer, almost touching, and we draw our last breaths, together, and then I am light and free and floating above these two bodies that are curled together in the shape of a heart.

And then, a wisp of hope.

And then, nothing.

I found myself back on the virch beach, raw and aching. The lady in white appeared and said she hoped we'd enjoyed our journey. I zigzagged my eyes to exit the virch scenario and return fully to reality—or whatever I was supposed to call this world I lived in now.

Then I was inside my body once again, on the beach beside Wolf. Our hands were still clasped. My bones mourned. My blood wept. But before us was the ocean, alive and pounding.

I slipped my hand from his and stretched, as if just waking up. I shook sand from my hair, scratched a bug bite on my ankle. My cheeks felt wet and gritty. My lips tasted of salt.

Wolf was stretching, too, his eyes red and his lashes wet.

We held each other, feeling our hearts beat.

And I thanked my self, my selves, our selves, for giving us this life to live.

And most of all, for giving us our first kiss.

A Flash of Lightning

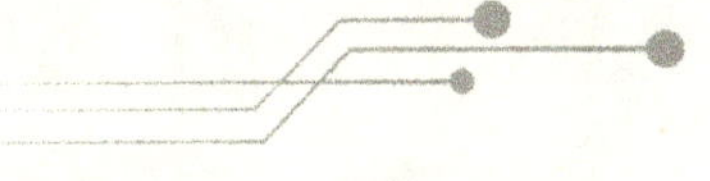

Year 2154

CHAPTER THIRTY-SEVEN
A Toast, and Another and Another

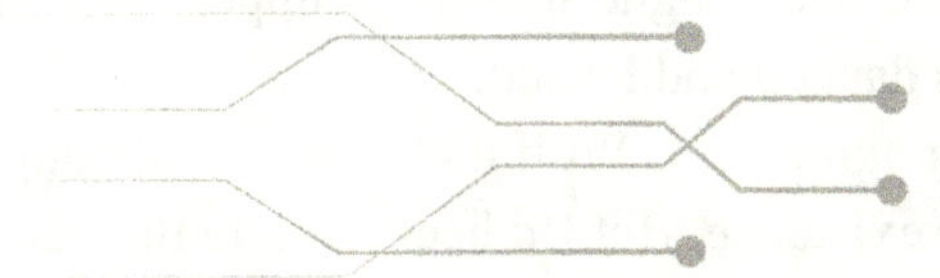

On our last day on the island, Wolf and I sat on the beach, sticky from saltwater, with sand stuck to our legs. A tropical rainstorm had passed earlier in the afternoon, leaving the air fresh and fragrant. The angled sun shone on us, but just over the line where sea met sky, a last bolt of lightning flashed. I watched the patches of light and dark shifting over the ocean, much more captivating than a perfect blue sky.

I leaned into Wolf, adjusting the hand-knit sunshine-yellow scarf around his shoulders—courtesy of Zinnia.

With a grin, he popped open a bottle of century-old champagne, an heirloom left to him in Casper's will. We'd grabbed two small clay teacups—slightly chipped—from the antique set in his lobby.

A month had passed since the virus outbreak. I'd made a complete recovery, as had Sodo and Soul. It had been a month of making plans—not just Wolf and me, but our other friends on the island, too. Baby steps toward the changes we all envisioned.

I wore a once-white sundress that Zinnia had given me, too small for her now. It was worn soft and frayed and yellowed like an ancient book. Its pockets were deep and full of messages of love, not just my fabric scraps, but tree nuts and seeds from Soul. Tucked into my braid was an orchid she'd plucked for me this morning, its petals laced with nibble marks from rain forest insects.

"Wabi sabi," Wolf said, brushing his fingertips over the bloom.

He poured champagne into my chipped cup, then into his. Tiny bubbles danced and leaped.

By silent agreement, Wolf and I hadn't told anyone the true nature of our existence. But I'd been turning the question over in my head, playing out possible scenarios. "Wolf, think we should tell anyone?"

Slowly, he shook his head. "I think we should keep it our secret."

I breathed out. "Me too. We need to let everyone… live their lives."

"We'll live in this little cup of ocean. Together."

I tugged on his scarf, pulling him closer. "Here's to us, in every cup of ocean."

He slid his arm around my waist.

We clinked cups, sipped the sparkle, and kissed.

We proceeded to toast everyone and everything else we were grateful for, in every cup of ocean. It was a long list, each item punctuated with a kiss, which motivated us to come up with more.

I stood and scooped up a cupful of seawater.

Wolf did the same.

And there we stood with our tiny cups of ocean, inside this strange world of second chances. We toasted and kissed and instead of sipping, we tossed the saltwater back into the sea, where it became part of the vastness once again.

A Cloud

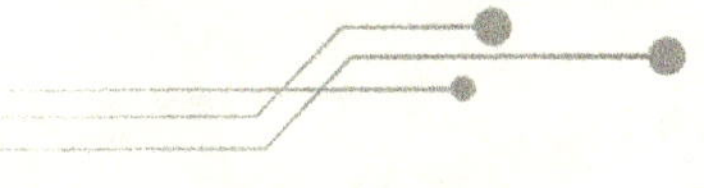

Year 2155

CHAPTER THIRTY-EIGHT
The Cove

One year later, sand-coated ankles overlapping, Wolf and I sat on the beach of the Chesapeake Bay watershed in the Cove. Our stretch of sand was gloriously free of e-waste. We were hidden in an inlet where the paparazzi couldn't find us.

And we were building sand castles. A whole sand village, in fact.

Little worlds within worlds.

I stuck an oyster shell on top of my turret.

Wolf was lining the moat with pebbles, his face glowing from light on water.

I rocked back on my heels, watching the sunset, streaks of purple and rose and gold. A cloud drifted by, curved like a smile, so different from the smoky haze that used to tinge the sky here.

Something rustled in the cattails nearby. I saw the tips of slate-gray feathers, the graceful neck, the arrow beak, the twig legs. Its wings spread wide and huge, and up it rose, silhouetted against the sky. A great blue heron.

Something else moved in the pines. Out from the shadows stepped Shell, holding hands with Delfina and Dad. Our family.

My sister smiled, her cheeks rosy, her eyes spring-green, her hair tumbling over her shoulders. "I knew you'd be here!" she declared. "A sandcastle!" She dropped beside Wolf and added mussel shells around the turrets.

Delfina settled beside Dad on a driftwood log and handed us ripe peaches.

f/I breathed in the sweetness, then bit in, letting juice run down my chin. I savored it—savored this moment—with every cell of my body.

Wolf and Shell devoured their peaches, then gathered more pebbles with sticky-sandy fingers, arranging sea treasures around the castle. They had a comfortable friendship—he was the brother she'd never had, and she was his first little sister who wasn't Progeny. He adored her.

After Wolf and I had left the island last year, with Shell's treatment in hand, we brought her back to life within days. When0 she opened her seaglass eyes, she saw me, Dad, Delfina, and Wolf, all gazing at her—our miracle.

Within a week, she was walking, and within two weeks, skipping, running, dancing.

Now, fully healed, she sat back on her heels, tilting her head, and gazed at the sunset. "Doesn't it look like the sky's smiling? And like it just ate a bunch of berries?"

Wolf studied the sky. "Raspberry cobbler?"

"Yes!"

It turned out my sister was the one who'd stitched the words on bits of cotton for me, before she'd gotten sick. Dad had found them hidden in a tree hollow in a ribbon-wrapped, cracked plastic box with my name on it. To surprise me, he'd slipped the scraps into the pockets of my new shorts.

Shell said she'd planned to give the gifts to me for my birthday. And her words had found me beyond her coffin. They had completed her sentence. *Remember to... fly, breathe, love, live.* In a way, her words had saved me.

"Best gift ever, sis!" I'd told her through tears.

On the day Wolf had released his updated virch date sim, over two billion people joined him for a date. There was no kissing, but some mild sensuality, depending on how you defined it. A hand held here, a tear wiped there.

The date was a tour of the Cove. Two billion people heard Shell's story. They saw Shell's story. They smelled and tasted and *felt* it.

And they cared.

They told others, and those others told others.

And they cared too.

It was working, this idea our original selves had imagined, this plan they'd forgotten to tell us, this vision in their minds as they died. With effort and determination, we were making it a reality.

The first step to change was opening people's eyes, making them care.

When Wolf and I had announced our mission in my Cove, we were all over the news. We welcomed it. We even welcomed the celebrity gossip newscasters. It was part of our plan—to let the sharks see what life was like here. Real life. Or as close to real as we could get.

Visiting the Cove had become almost a la moda—everyone wearing high-tech biohaz suits for safety, of course. First, we'd invited the other interns, including the fruit crew and their new boyfriends. Then Wolf's Progeny half siblings. And then more shark teens came, and more. And once they were here, you could see empathy blooming, hearts opening, souls caring.

Which is not to say it was easy.

There was push-back from some sharks who liked the status quo. There was resistance from the government. There was the worry about health risks for visitors and volunteers. There was the question of finding safe housing during the cleanup. There was the concern of the illegality of our entire community.

There was red tape, kilometers of it.

But at the heart of it, we were moving things in the right direction. We were making a difference.

Once Casper's wealth and responsibilities were divided among his Progeny, enough of them cared about the Cove that they provided funds for environmental cleanup, biohaz suits, water decontamination units, virch scanners, medical treatments, good schools, and more.

It wasn't charity. It was working together, letting the sharks take responsibility for the e-waste they created, listening to ideas, partnering in the solutions. Zinnia and I were advisors for the implementation of the new health system, finally making effective use of the virchips.

Our progress was slow and exasperating at times, full of obstacles to overcome.

But that was how real change happened, I discovered, and it took heaps of determination. Which we had.

Casper's will had appointed Wolf and several other "tech genius" Progeny to run the classified virch world simulation research. They had also suffered as victims of Casper's earlier experiments and were determined to end that practice. Together with Wolf and their lawyer half siblings, they crafted legislation about sim realities, which would make the replication of human consciousness illegal.

Casper went down in history as a psychopathic megalomaniac. Wolf and I stood firm in our decision not to reveal that our world was a simulation. And we resolved to do our best to prevent anyone from creating more cups of ocean—without a good reason.

Spiro's delusions made people concerned about the effects of too much virch and holo-experience. More and more people opted to live mostly in reality. The fruit crew—now celebrities since the virus outbreak—touted the benefits of good old-fashioned pheromones.

And my Cove was on track to becoming a safe place to live and work. I hoped our rejuvenation might serve as a model for Null Zones around the world.

From time to time, Wolf and I needed a break from the glitches and frustrations that came with changing the world. I didn't have to worry about leaving my family alone during our getaways. Delfina was living with us now, becoming the mother Shell and I had longed for. We were truly her *hijas* now.

For short trips, Wolf and I flew to the wildlife refuge in California to visit Sugarpie, who had quadrupled in size. On one of our visits, Wolf asked me why my original self had asked me to save the panda: What did that have to do with stopping the bioweapon? It didn't, I told him. It was just that of *course* the panda's life was worth saving.

And every time I buried my face in Sugarpie's coarse fur, I felt more and more grateful. If I hadn't been tasked with saving her, I wouldn't have had a reason to venture into the pilots' lair. I wouldn't have been able to befriend and help and warn them—and things might have unfolded in a less fortunate way. Every time we played with roly-poly Sugarpie, I whispered a *thank you* into one of her funny little black ears.

Sometimes, Wolf and I flew to the island. And we often took Shell. My piloting skills were improving—we landed bumpily but always safely. We visited Soul and her dad, who was now paid a fair salary, with benefits, health care, and access to the facility. And now that being virchlensless and holo-free was a la moda, scientists ventured into the forest gardens, paying Soul for nature tours. I mentored her in science, the way Delfina had done for me. Soul was like another little sister.

The best part of our trips was our place on the beach—seaweed and jellyfish and all. Every time, Wolf and I would make our saltwater toasts, then toss the cupfuls back into the sea.

Once in a long while, we'd take out the virchlenses Mo had given us and enter the consciousnesses of creatures in the present original reality. There was not a single original human consciousness left as far as we could tell, so we tried out jaguars in rain forests, birds in skies empty of heliplanes, whales in ship-less oceans. But mostly we stayed in our own reality, our own minds, our own bodies, our own souls. Because yes, these were our souls, and we loved them fiercely.

And when we returned to the Cove, we'd sneak away to build castles and watch the sunset, and here, too, we'd scoop up cupfuls of water, and whisper our mantra.

Live your life... live your life... live your life...

Stars

Year 2237
(In Another Cup of Ocean)

CHAPTER THIRTY-NINE
A World Without Humans

In darkness, the whale swims.
She moves like a ghost,
like a dream,
through quiet waters.

She remembers a time, long ago, when her sea blared with pain,
with ship motors,
with sonar waves.
She remembers the poisons, the nets, the trash, the oil slicks, the propeller blades,
the slashes and suffering.

Now her world dances with the music of whales.

Starlight filters through sea currents.
Jellyfish
pulse and glow,
flitting and fleeting.

They say there is still one island on earth
where machines hum and robots move,
where giant white trees
reach their fingers to the firmament
and gather power from the wind.

The whale stays away from that place.

And on and on she swims,
from one bit of ocean
to the next.

A Drop of Dew

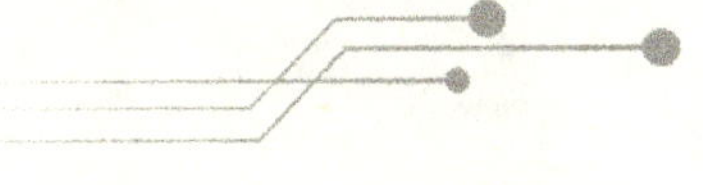

Year 2237

EPILOGUE
Tiny Worlds of Truth

ive your life. Live your life. Live your life.
That's what we do.

Before bed, Wolf and I each say something we're grateful for. Our toasts have evolved into a kind of prayer. And over the past century, we've been grateful for things as tiny as a shell found in our bay cove to the taste of uncontaminated oysters, to meeting our goals of ensuring safe food for everyone and completing pollution cleanups in one Null Zone after another.

It hasn't been easy, but our victories have outnumbered our failures. Our determination has always been stronger than our frustration. And we know our descendants will carry on our work.

Tonight, after celebrating Wolf's hundredth birthday with our children and grandchildren and great-grandchildren—along with Shell and her children and grandchildren and great-grandchildren—Wolf and I fall into bed together. Our dog,

Snowdrift, climbs up beside us, and as we scratch the animal's belly, Wolf says, "I'm grateful for your bread crust hair, Angel."

I smile. "Which is all white now."

"Okay. Your hair like bread with the crust cut off." He reaches out to touch it. "Your real hair."

"And I'm grateful for every single kiss of our life together."

With that, we kiss and curl up with our foreheads touching and our legs tucked up, making a heart shape with Snowdrift happily in the middle.

Tonight, I dream of sweet things—cake and our dog and children and dew drops—but then, all at once, I'm sitting at our place on the beach. Wolf is standing in front of me. It's my young Wolf, sick with the virus, doubled over in pain, covered in blood, pupils wide and scary. Oh, how I want to take him in my arms and soothe him, but I stay still and quiet to hear over the pounding and shouting in the background.

"Wolf is a hundred now," he says. "And Angel, you—you must be around a hundred too." He winces and clutches his belly, and I wince too, in sympathetic pain, remembering how it felt.

"Now—now that you're old and wise, Liv, you need to make a decision. If—if you want the simulated world to continue for the rest of your lives and after your deaths… if you want the billions of consciousnesses on the planet to continue… if this idea is actually working, then stand up and walk into the ocean. That gesture will signal that this reality is a good thing. But if not, stay seated, and the sim world will come to an immediate end." He wipes his tears. "I—I hope we're doing the right thing."

He vanishes.

There is only an expanse of seawater before me.

I smile to myself. This was Wolf's backup plan, the just-in-case instructions he'd recorded right before the end.

I stand up nimbly, dream legs as strong as my sixteen-year-old legs once were. I'm in that swimsuit I wore as a teen, I realize, and my skin is once again smooth and firm. I run to the ocean, splash through the surf, plunge beneath the waves, my hair spreading out and swishing against my shoulders.

I swim and swim and swim and I am one with the ocean, just another of sandillions of particles and it feels good and right and I am grateful, so grateful for this second chance.

I emerge and see a young Wolf, a healthy Wolf, swimming at my side, and our lips meet, and *yes, yes, yes*, this, too, is somehow real, even these dreams within dreams within dreams, these cups of sea, these drops of dew, these tiny worlds of truth.

My eyes open and I feel for his lips across the pillows, and by this time, Snowdrift has hopped down to his dog bed, and I scooch close and kiss Wolf in his sleep.

His eyes open, and he smiles, his own white hair spread out on the pillow, glowing in moonlight through the window. "You swam, too, Angel."

"I swam too."

And for the hundred thousandth time, we kiss.

ACKNOWLEDGEMENTS

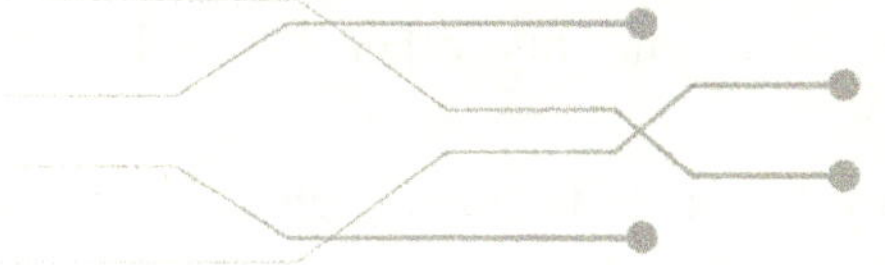

Readers, my biggest thanks goes to you. Over the years, I've discovered that the best part about being an author is connecting with you through story. Not a day goes by when I don't appreciate your magnificence!

I owe profound gratitude to the philosopher Nick Bostrom for sparking my imagination in his world-expanding article "Are You Living in a Computer Simulation?"

A thousand thanks to my longtime agent and friend, Erin Murphy, for helping this story see the light of day… and for being a genuine joy to work with all these years. I'm grateful to the incredible team at Owl Hollow Press, with special thanks to Hannah Smith and Emma Nelson for your excitement about the book, and to Olivia Swenson for bringing it to the next level with fantastic editorial guidance.

My beta readers deserve an oceanic thank you! Gratitude to my beloved writing group for giving me heaps of encouragement and valuable feedback: Karye Cattrell, Todd Mitchell, and Laura Pritchett. Sci-fi genius Parker Peevyhouse offered sharp insights on plot and theme, and crafted an enticing synopsis after reading an early draft. Brilliant writer friends Amy Kathleen Ryan, Sarah Paige Ryan, Katherine Valdez, and Carrie Visintainer each offered gems of wisdom that made this story so much stronger. Kisses to avid YA-book-reader and psychologist Ashley Harvey who made sure I didn't skimp on the romance. Emma and Joy Cailene were generous enough to read the manuscript from a teen perspective and offer fabulous advice—you both are treasures.

Thank you to all of my writer friends who surround me with such warmth and inspiration—my EMLA siblings, my Colorado writing community, and my other kindred spirits across the country.

I'm deeply fortunate to have such a supportive family. My parents, Chris and Jim Resau, read this manuscript through a scientist's lens to help make the medical and lab details ring true. (Having a book-loving mom and a cell pathologist dad comes in handy!) My sixteen-year-old son, Bran, has offered creative camaraderie and endless enthusiasm for this project (and I'm still hoping he'll compose a metal song with a *Virch* theme...)

My husband, Ian, read an early draft years ago on a plane ride—and ever since, he's declared it his favorite book and urged me to bring it into the world. This motivation has meant everything to me. And thank you, Ian, for letting me borrow your middle name. You're my very own Wolf and I'm happy to be with you in every cup of ocean.

Laura Resau is the award-winning author of nine highly ac-claimed young adult and middle grade novels, including *The Lightning Queen, Tree of Dreams, What the Moon Saw, Red Glass, Star in the Forest, The Queen of Water* (with María Virginia Farinango), and the *Notebooks* series.

Loved by kids and adults alike, Laura's novels have garnered many starred reviews and honors, including the International Reading Association's YA Fiction Award, the Américas Award, five Colorado Book Awards, spots on "best-of" book lists from Oprah, School Library Journal, the American Library Association, Bank Street, and more. Resau's writing has been called "vibrant, large-hearted" (Publishers' Weekly on *Red Glass*) and "powerful, magical" (Booklist on *What the Moon Saw*).

You might find Laura writing in a vintage trailer in her backyard in Fort Collins or in her tiny cabin in the Rocky Mountains or on her travels in Latin America and Europe. When she's not writing, she's often wandering in the forest with her husband, cuddling with her senior rescue beagle, or head-banging (very carefully) at her teenage son's rock shows.

Find Laura at LauraResau.com

Printed in the USA
CPSIA information can be obtained
at www.ICGtesting.com
LVHW050558250524
781221LV00001B/1